DUST

THE SILO TRILOGY
BY HUGH HOWEY

WOOL

SHIFT

DUST

DUST

HUGH HOWEY

A JOHN JOSEPH ADAMS BOOK

HOUGHTON MIFFLIN HARCOURT

Boston   New York

2016

For information about permission to reproduce selections from this book,
write to trade.permissions@hmhco.com or to Permissions,
Houghton Mifflin Harcourt Publishing Company, 3 Park Avenue,
19th Floor, New York, New York 10016.

www.hmhco.com

Library of Congress Cataloging-in-Publication Data is available.
ISBN 978-0-544-83962-5 (hardback)
ISBN 978-0-544-83826-0 (pbk)

Printed in the United States of America
DOC 10 9 8 7 6 5 4 3 2 1

For the survivors

PROLOGUE

"IS ANYONE THERE?"

"Hello? Yes. I'm here."

"Ah. Lukas. You weren't saying anything. I thought for a second there . . . that you were someone else."

"No, it's me. Just getting my headset adjusted. Been a busy morning."

"Oh?"

"Yeah. Boring stuff. Committee meetings. We're a bit thin up here at the moment. A lot of reassignments."

"But things have been settling down? No uprisings to report?"

"No, no. Things are getting back to normal. People get up and go to work in the morning. They collapse in their beds at night. We had a big lottery this week, which made a number of people happy."

"That's good. Very good. How's the work on server six coming?"

"Good, thanks. All of your passcodes work. So far it's just more of the same data. Not sure why any of this is important, though."

"Keep looking. Everything's important. If it's in there, there has to be a reason."

"You said that about the entries in these books. But so many of them seem like nonsense to me. Makes me wonder if any of this is real."

"Why? What're you reading?"

"I'm up to volume C. This morning it was about this . . . fungus. Wait a second. Let me find it. Here it is. Cordyceps."

"That's a fungus? Never heard of it."

"Says here it does something to an ant's brain, reprograms it like it's a machine, makes it climb to the top of a plant before it dies—"

"An invisible machine that reprograms brains? I'm fairly certain that's not a random entry."

"Yeah? So what does it mean, then?"

"It means . . . It means we aren't free. None of us are."

"How uplifting. I can see why she makes me take these calls."

"Your mayor? Is that why—? She hasn't answered in a while."

"No. She's away. Working on something."

"Working on what?"

"I'd rather not say. I don't think you'd be pleased."

"What makes you think that?"

"Because I'm not pleased. I've tried to talk her out of this. But she can be a bit . . . obstinate at times."

"If it's going to cause trouble, I should know about it. I'm here to help. I can keep heads turned away—"

"That's just it . . . she doesn't trust you. She doesn't even believe you're the same person every time."

"It is. It's me. The machines do something with my voice."

"I'm just telling you what she thinks."

"I wish she would come around. I really do want to help."

"I believe you. I think the best thing you can do right now is just keep your fingers crossed for us."

"Why is that?"

"Because I've got a feeling that nothing good will come of this."

PART I
THE DIG

Silo 18

1

Dust rained in the halls of Mechanical; it shivered free from the violence of the digging. Wires overhead swung gently in their harnesses. Pipes rattled. And from the generator room, staccato bangs filled the air, bounced off the walls, and brought to mind a time when unbalanced machines spun dangerously.

At the locus of the horrible racket, Juliette Nichols stood with her coveralls zipped down to her waist, the loose arms knotted around her hips, dust and sweat staining her undershirt with mud. She leaned her weight against the excavator, her sinewy arms shaking as the digger's heavy metal piston slammed into the concrete wall of Silo 18 over and over.

The vibrations could be felt in her teeth. Every bone and joint in her body shuddered, and old wounds ached with reminders. Off to the side, the miners who normally manned the excavator watched unhappily. Juliette turned her head from the powdered concrete and saw the way they stood with their arms crossed over their wide chests, their jaws set in rigid frowns, angry perhaps for her appropriating their machine. Or maybe over the taboo of digging where digging was forbidden.

Juliette swallowed the grit and chalk accumulating in her mouth and concentrated on the crumbling wall. There was another possibility, one she couldn't help but consider. Good mechanics and miners had died because of her. Brutal fighting had broken out when she'd refused to clean. How many of these men and women watching her dig had lost a loved one, a best friend, a family member? How many of them blamed her? She couldn't possibly be the only one.

The excavator bucked and there was the clang of metal on metal. Juliette steered the punching jaws to the side as more bones of rebar appeared in the white flesh of concrete. She had already gouged out a veritable crater in the outer silo wall. A first row of rebar hung jagged overhead, the ends smooth like melted candles where she'd taken a blowtorch to them. Two more feet of concrete and another row of the iron rods had followed, the silo walls thicker than she'd imagined. With numb limbs and frayed nerves she guided the machine forward on its tracks, the wedge-shaped piston chewing at the stone between the rods. If she hadn't seen the schematic for herself—if she didn't know there were other silos out there—she would've given up already. It felt as though she were chewing through the very earth itself. Her arms shook, her hands a blur. This was the wall of the silo she was attacking, ramming it with a mind to pierce through the damn thing, to bore clear through to the outside.

The miners shifted uncomfortably. Juliette looked from them to where she was aiming as the hammer bit rang against more steel. She concentrated on the crease of white stone between the bars. With her boot, she kicked the drive lever, leaned into the machine, and the excavator trudged forward on rusted tracks one more inch. She should've taken another break a while ago. The chalk in her mouth was choking her; she was dying for water; her arms needed a rest; rubble crowded the base of the excavator and littered her feet. She kicked a few of the larger chunks out of the way and kept digging.

Her fear was that if she stopped one more time, she wouldn't be able to convince them to let her continue. Mayor or not—a shift head or not—men she had thought fearless had already left the generator room with furrowed brows. They seemed terrified that she might puncture a sacred seal and let in a foul and murderous air. Juliette saw the way they looked at her, knowing she'd been on the outside, as though she were some kind of ghost. Many kept their distance as if she bore some disease.

Setting her teeth, foul-tasting grit crunching between them, she kicked the forward plate once more with her boot. The tracks on the excavator spun forward another inch. One more inch. Juliette cursed the machine and the pain in her wrists. Goddamn the fighting and her friends dead. Goddamn the thought of Solo and the kids all alone, a forever of rock away. And goddamn this mayor nonsense, people looking at her as though she suddenly ran all the shifts on every level, as though she knew what the hell she was doing, as though they had to obey her even as they feared her—

The excavator lurched forward more than an inch, and the pounding hammer bit screamed with a piercing whine. Juliette lost her grip with one hand, and the machine revved up as if fit to explode. The miners startled like fleas, several of them running toward her, shadows converging. Juliette hit the red kill switch, which was nearly invisible beneath a dusting of white powder. The excavator kicked and bucked as it wound down from a dangerous, runaway state.

"You're through! You're through!"

Raph pulled her back, his pale arms, strong from years of mining, wrapping around her numb limbs. Others shouted at her that she was done. Finished. The excavator had made a noise as if a connecting rod had shattered; there had been that dangerous whine of a mighty engine running without friction, without anything to resist. Juliette let go of the controls and sagged into Raph's embrace. A desperation returned, the thought of her friends buried alive in that tomb of an empty silo and her unable to reach them.

"You're through—get back!"

A hand that reeked of grease and toil clamped down over her mouth, protecting her from the air beyond. Juliette couldn't breathe. Ahead of her, a black patch of empty space appeared, the cloud of concrete dissipating.

And there, between two bars of iron, stood a dark void. A void between prison bars that ran two layers deep and all around them, from Mechanical straight to the Up Top.

She was through. *Through*. She now had a glimpse of some other, some different, *outside*.

"The torch," Juliette mumbled, prying Raph's calloused hand from her mouth and hazarding a gulp of air. "Get me the cutting torch. And a flashlight."

2

"DAMN THING'S RUSTED to hell."

"Those look like hydraulic lines."

"Must be a thousand years old."

Fitz muttered the last, the oilman's words whistling through gaps left by missing teeth. The miners and mechanics who had kept their distance during the digging now crowded against Juliette's back as she aimed her flashlight through a lingering veil of powdered rock and into the gloom beyond. Raph, as pale as the drifting dust, stood beside her, the two of them crammed into the conical crater chewed out of the five or six feet of concrete. The albino's eyes were wide, his translucent cheeks bulging, his lips pursed together and bloodless.

"You can breathe, Raph," Juliette told him. "It's just another room."

The pale miner let out his air with a relieved grunt and asked those behind to stop shoving. Juliette passed the flashlight to Fitz and turned from the hole she'd made. She wormed her way through the jostling crowd, her pulse racing from the glimpses of some machine on the other side of the wall. What she had seen was quickly confirmed by the murmuring of others: struts, bolts, hose, plate steel with chips of paint and streaks of rust—a wall of a mechanical beast that went up and to the sides as far as their feeble flashlight beams could penetrate.

A tin cup of water was pressed into her trembling hand. Juliette drank greedily. She was exhausted, but her mind raced. She couldn't wait to get back to a radio and tell Solo. She couldn't wait to tell Lukas. Here was a bit of buried hope.

"What now?" Dawson asked.

The new third-shift foreman, who had given her the water, studied her warily. Dawson was in his late thirties, but working nights had saddled him with extra years. He had the large knotted hands that came from busting knuckles and breaking fingers, some of it from working and some from fighting. Juliette returned the cup to him. Dawson glanced inside and stole the last swig.

"Now we make a bigger hole," she told him. "We get in there and see if that thing's salvageable."

Movement on top of the humming main generator caught Juliette's eye. She glanced up in time to spy Shirly frowning down at her. Shirly turned away.

Juliette squeezed Dawson's arm. "It'll take forever to expand this one hole," she said. "What we need are dozens of smaller holes that we can connect. We need to tear out entire sections at a time. Bring up the other excavator. And turn the men loose with their picks, but keep the dust to a minimum if you can help it."

The third-shift foreman nodded and rapped his fingers against the empty cup. "No blasting?" he asked.

"No blasting," she said. "I don't want to damage whatever's over there."

He nodded, and she left him to manage the dig. She approached the generator. Shirly had her coveralls stripped down to her waist as well, sleeves cinched together, her undershirt wet with the dark inverted triangle of hard work. With a rag in each hand, she worked across the top of the generator, wiping away both old grease and the new film of powder kicked up by the day's digging.

Juliette untied the sleeves of her coveralls and shrugged her arms inside, covering her scars. She climbed up the side of the generator, knowing where she could grab, which parts were hot and which were merely warm. "You need some help?" she asked, reaching the top, enjoying the heat and thrum of the machine in her sore muscles.

Shirly wiped her face with the hem of her undershirt. She shook her head. "I'm good," she said.

"Sorry about the debris." Juliette raised her voice over the hum of the massive pistons firing up and down. There was a day not too long ago when her teeth would've been knocked loose to stand on top of the machine, back when it was unbalanced six ways to hell.

Shirly turned and tossed the muddy white rags down to her shadow, Kali, who dunked them into a bucket of grimy water. It was strange to see the new head of Mechanical toiling away at something so mundane as cleaning the genset. Juliette tried to picture Knox up there doing the same. And then it hit her for the hundredth time that she was *mayor*, and look how she spent her time, hammering through walls and cutting rebar. Kali tossed the rags back up, and Shirly caught them with wet slaps and sprays of suds. Her old friend's silence as she bent back to her work said plenty.

Juliette turned and surveyed the digging party she'd assembled as they cleared debris and worked to expand the hole. Shirly hadn't been happy about the loss of manpower, much less the taboo of breaking the silo's seal. The call for workers had come at a time when their ranks were already thinned by the outbreak of violence. And whether or not Shirly blamed Juliette for her husband's death was irrelevant. Juliette blamed herself, and so the tension stood between them like a cake of grease.

It wasn't long before the hammering on the wall resumed. Juliette spotted Bobby at the excavator's controls, his great muscled arms a blur as he guided the wheeled jackhammer. The sight of some strange machine—some artifact buried beyond the walls—had thrown sparks into reluctant bodies. Fear and doubt had morphed into determination. A porter arrived with food, and Juliette watched the young man with his bare arms and legs study the work intently. The porter left his load of fruit and hot lunches behind and took with him his gossip.

Juliette stood on the humming generator and allayed her doubts. They were doing the right thing, she told herself. She had seen with her own eyes how vast the world was, had stood on a summit and surveyed the land. All she had to do now was show others what was out there. And then they would lean into this work rather than fear it.

3

A HOLE WAS MADE big enough to squeeze through, and Juliette took the honors. A flashlight in hand, she crawled over a pile of rubble and between bent fingers of iron rod. The air beyond the generator room was cool like the deep mines. She coughed into her fist, the dust from the digging tickling her throat and nose. She hopped down to the floor beyond the gaping hole.

"Careful," she told the others behind her. "The ground's not even."

Some of the unevenness was from the chunks of concrete that'd fallen inside—the rest was just how the floor stood. It appeared as though it'd been gouged out by the claws of a giant.

Shining the light from her boots to the dim ceiling high above, she surveyed the hulking wall of machinery before her. It dwarfed the main generator. It dwarfed the oil pumps. A colossus of such proportions was never meant to be built, much less repaired. Her stomach sank. Her hopes of restoring this buried machine diminished.

Raph joined her in the cool and dark, a clatter of rubble trailing him. The albino had a condition that skipped generations. His eyebrows and lashes were gossamer things, nearly invisible. His flesh was as pale as pig's milk. But when he was in the mines, the shadows that darkened the others like soot lent him a healthful complexion. Juliette could see why he had left the farms as a boy to work in the dark.

Raph whistled as he played his flashlight across the machine. A moment later, his whistle echoed back, a bird in the far shadows, mocking him.

"It's a thing of the gods," he wondered aloud.

Juliette didn't answer. She never took Raph as one to listen to the tales of priests. Still, there was no doubting the awe it inspired. She had seen Solo's books and suspected that the same ancient peoples who had built this machine had built the crumbling but soaring towers beyond the hills. The fact that they had built the silo itself made her feel small. She reached out and ran her hand across metal that hadn't been touched nor glimpsed for centuries, and she marveled at what the ancients had been capable of. Maybe the priests weren't that far off after all . . .

"Ye gods," Dawson grumbled, crowding noisily beside them. "What're we to do with this?"

"Yeah, Jules," Raph whispered, respecting the deep shadows and the deeper time. "How're we supposed to dig this thing outta here?"

"We're not," she told them. She scooted sideways between the wall of concrete and the tower of machinery. "This thing is meant to dig its own way out."

"You're assuming we can get it running," Dawson said.

Workers in the generator room crowded the hole and blocked the light spilling in. Juliette steered her flashlight around the narrow gap that stood between the outer silo wall and the tall machine, looking for some way around. She worked to one side, into the darkness, and scrambled up the gently sloping floor.

"We'll get it running," she assured Dawson. "We just gotta figure out how it's supposed to work."

"Careful," Raph warned as a rock kicked loose by her boots tumbled toward him. She was already higher up than their heads. The room, she saw, didn't have a corner or a far wall. It just curled up and all the way around.

"It's a big circle," she called out, her voice echoing between rock and metal. "I don't think this is the business end."

"There's a door over here," Dawson announced.

Juliette slid down the slope to join him and Raph. Another flashlight clicked on from the gawkers in the generator room. Its beam joined hers in illuminating a door with pins for hinges. Dawson wrestled with a handle on the back of the machine. He grunted with effort, and then metal cried out as it reluctantly gave way to muscle.

The machine yawned wide once they were through the door. Nothing prepared Juliette for this. Thinking back to the schematics she'd seen in Solo's underground hovel, she now realized that the diggers had been drawn to scale. The little worms jutting off the low floors of Mechanical were a level high and twice that in length. Massive cylinders of steel, this one sat snug in a circular cave, almost as if it had buried itself. Juliette told her people to be careful as they made their way through the interior. A dozen workers joined her, their voices mingling and echoing in the maze-like guts of the machine, taboo dispelled by curiosity and wonder, the digging forgotten for now.

"This here's for moving the tailings," someone said. Beams of light played on metal chutes of interlocking plates. There were wheels and gears beneath the plates and more plates on the other side that overlapped like the scales on a snake. Juliette saw immediately how the entire chute moved, the plates hinging at the end and wrapping around to the beginning again. The rock and debris could ride on the top as it was pushed along.

Low walls of inch-thick plate were meant to keep the rock from tumbling off. The rock chewed up by the digger would pass through here and out the back, where men would have to wrestle it with barrows.

"It's rusted all to hell," someone muttered.

"Not as bad as it should be," Juliette said. The machine had been there for hundreds of years, at least. She expected it to be a ball of rust and nothing more, but the steel was shiny in places. "I think the room was airtight," she wondered aloud, remembering a breeze on her neck and the sucking of dust as she pierced through the wall for the first time.

"This is all hydraulic," Bobby said. There was disappointment in his voice, as though he were learning that the gods cleaned their asses with water too. Juliette was more hopeful. She saw something that could be fixed, so long as the power source was intact. They could get this running. It was made to be simple, as if the gods knew that whoever discovered it would be less sophisticated, less capable. There were treads just like on the excavator but running the length of the mighty machine, axles caked in grease. More treads on the sides and ceiling that must push against the earth as well. What she didn't understand was how the digging commenced. Past the moving chutes and all the implements for pushing crushed rock and tailings out the back of the machine, they came to a wall of steel that slid up past the girders and walkways into the darkness above.

"That don't make a lick of sense," Raph said, reaching the far wall. "Look at these wheels. Which way does this thing run?"

"Those aren't wheels," Juliette said. She pointed with her light. "This whole front piece spins. Here's the pivot." She pointed to a central axle as big around as two men. "And those round discs there must protrude through to the other side and do the cutting."

Bobby blew out a disbelieving breath. "Through solid stone?"

Juliette tried to turn one of the discs. It barely moved. A barrel of grease would be needed.

"I think she's right," Raph said. He had the lid raised on a box the size of a double bunk and aimed his flashlight inside. "This here's a gearbox. Looks like a transmission."

Juliette joined him. Helical gears the size of a man's waist lay embedded in dried grease. The gears matched up with teeth that would spin the wall. The transmission box was as large and stout as that of the main generator. Larger.

"Bad news," Bobby said. "Check where that shaft leads."

Three beams of light converged and followed the driveshaft back to where it ended in empty space. The interior cavern of that hulking machine, all that emptiness in which they stood, was a void where the heart of the beast should lie.

"She ain't going nowhere," Raph muttered.

Juliette marched back to the rear of the machine. Beefy struts built for holding a power plant sat bare. She and the other mechanics had been milling about where an engine should sit. And now that she knew what to look for, she spotted the mounts. There were six of them: threaded posts eight inches across and caked in ancient, hardened grease. The matching nut for each post hung from hooks beneath the struts. The gods were communicating with her. Talking to her. The ancients had left a message, written in the language of people who knew machines. They were speaking to her across vast stretches of time, saying: *This goes here. Follow these steps.*

Fitz, the oilman, knelt beside Juliette and rested a hand on her arm. "I am sorry for your friends," he said, meaning Solo and the kids, but Juliette thought he sounded happy for everyone else. Glancing at the rear of the metal cave, she saw more miners and mechanics peering inside, hesitant to join them. Everyone would be happy for this endeavor to end right there, for her to dig no further. But Juliette was feeling more than an urge; she was beginning to feel a purpose. This machine hadn't been hidden from them. It had been safely stowed. Protected. Packed away. Slathered in grease and shielded from the air for a reason beyond her knowing.

"Do we seal it back up?" Dawson asked. Even the grizzled old mechanic seemed eager to dig no further.

"It's waiting for something," Juliette said. She pulled one of the large nuts off its hook and rested it on top of the grease-encased post. The size of the mount was familiar. She thought of the work she'd performed a lifetime ago of aligning the main generator. "She's meant to be opened," she said. "This belly of hers is meant to be opened. Check the back of the machine where we came through. It should come apart so the tailings can get out, but also to let something in. The motor isn't missing at all."

Raph stayed by her side, the beam of his flashlight on her chest so he could study her face.

"I know why they put this here," she told him, while the others left to survey the back of the machine. "I know why they put this next to the generator room."

4

SHIRLY AND KALI were still cleaning the main generator when Juliette emerged from the belly of the digger. Bobby showed the others how the back of the digger opened up, which bolts to remove and how the plates came away. Juliette had them measure the space between the posts and then the mounts of the backup generator to verify what she already knew. The machine they'd uncovered was a living schematic. It really was a message from older times. One discovery was leading to a cascade of others.

Juliette watched Kali wring mud from a cloth before dipping it into a second bucket of slightly less filthy water, and a truth occurred to her: An engine would rot if left for a thousand years. It would only hum if used, if a team of people devoted their lives to the care of it. Steam rose from a hot and soapy manifold as Shirly wiped down the humming main generator, and Juliette saw how they'd been working toward this moment for years. As much as her old friend—and now the Chief of Mechanical—hated this project of hers, Shirly had been assisting all this time. The smaller generator on the other side of the main power plant had another, greater, purpose.

"The mounts look right," Raph told her, a measuring line in

his hand. "You think they used that machine to bring the generator here?"

Shirly tossed down a muddy rag, and a cleaner one was tossed up. Worker and shadow had a rhythm like the humming of pistons.

"I think the spare generator is meant to help that digger *leave,*" she told Raph. What she didn't understand was why anyone would send off their backup power source, even for a short time. It would put the entire silo at the whim of a breakdown. They may as well have found a motor crumbling into a solid ball of rust on the other side of the wall. It was difficult to imagine anyone agreeing with the plans coalescing in her mind.

A rag arced through the air and splashed into a bucket of brown water. Kali didn't throw another up. She was staring toward the entrance of the generator room. Juliette followed the shadow's gaze and felt a flush of heat. There, among the black and soiled men and women of Mechanical, an unblemished young man in brilliant silver stood, asking someone for directions. A man pointed, and Lukas Kyle, head of IT, her lover, started off in Juliette's direction.

"Get the backup generator serviced," Juliette told Raph, who visibly stiffened. He seemed to know where this was going. "We need to put her in just long enough to see what that digger does. We've been meaning to unhook and clean out the exhaust manifolds anyway."

Raph nodded, his jaws clenching and unclenching. Juliette slapped his back and didn't dare glance up at Shirly as she strode off to meet Lukas.

"What're you doing down here?" she asked him. She had spoken to Lukas the day before, and he had neglected to mention the visit. His aim was to corner her.

Lukas pulled up short and frowned—and Juliette felt awful

for the tone. There was no embrace, no welcoming handshake. She was too wound up from the day's discoveries, too tense.

"I should ask the same thing," he said. His gaze strayed to the crater carved out of the far wall. "While you're digging holes down here, the head of IT is doing the mayor's work."

"Then nothing's changed," Juliette said, laughing, trying to lighten the mood. But Lukas didn't smile. She rested her hand on his arm and guided him away from the generator and out into the hall. "I'm sorry," she told him. "I was just surprised to see you. You should've told me you were coming. And listen . . . I'm glad to see you. If you need me to come up and sign some things, I'm happy to. If you need me to give a speech or kiss a baby, I'll do that. But I told you last week that I was going to find some way to get my friends out. And since you vetoed my walking back over the hills—"

Lukas's eyes widened at the flippant heresy. He glanced around the hall to see if others were around. "Jules, you're worrying about a handful of people while the rest of the silo grows uneasy. There are murmurs of dissent all through the Up Top. There are echoes of the last uprising you stirred, only now they're aimed at us."

Juliette felt her skin warm. Her hand fell from Lukas's arm. "I wanted no part of that fight. I wasn't even *here* for it."

"But you're here for this one." His eyes were sad, not angry, and Juliette realized the days were as long for him in the Up Top as they were for her down in Mechanical. They'd spent less time talking in the past week than they had while she'd been in Silo 17. They were nearer to one another and in danger of growing apart.

"What would you have me do?" she asked.

"To start with, don't dig. Please. Billings has fielded a dozen complaints from neighbors speculating about what will happen. Some of them are saying that the outside will come to us. A priest from the Mids is holding two Sundays a week now to warn of the dangers, of this vision of his where the dust fills the silo to the brim and thousands die—"

"Priests—" Juliette spat.

"Yes, priests, with people marching from the Top and the Deep both to attend his Sundays. When he finds it necessary to hold three of them a week, we'll have a mob."

Juliette ran her fingers through her hair, rock and rubble tumbling out. She looked at the cloud of fine dust guiltily. "What do people think happened to me outside the silo? My cleaning? What are they saying?"

"Some can scarcely believe it," Lukas said. "It has the makings of legend. Oh, in IT we know what happened, but some wonder if you were sent to clean at all. I heard one rumor that it was an election stunt."

Juliette cursed under her breath. "And news of the other silos?"

"I've been telling others for years that the stars are suns like our own. Some things are too big to comprehend. And I don't think rescuing your friends will change that. You could march your radio friend up to the bazaar and say he came from another silo, and people would just as likely believe you."

"Walker?" Juliette shook her head, but she knew he was right. "I'm not after my friends to prove what happened to me, Luke. This isn't about me. They're living with the dead over there. With ghosts."

"Don't we as well? Don't we dine on our dead? I'm begging you, Jules. Hundreds will die for you to save a few. Maybe they're better off over there."

She took a deep breath and held it a pause, tried her best not to feel angry. "They're not, Lukas. The man I aim to save is half mad from living on his own all these years. The kids over there are having kids of their own. They need our doctors and they need our help. Besides . . . I promised them."

He rewarded her pleas with sad eyes. It was no use. How do you make a man care for those he's never met? Juliette expected the impossible of him, and she was just as much to blame. Did she truly care for the people being poisoned twice on Sundays? Or any of the strangers she had been elected to lead but had never met?

"I didn't want this job," she told Lukas. It was hard to keep the blame out of her voice. Others had wanted her to be mayor, not her. Though not as many as before, it seemed.

"I didn't know what I was shadowing for either," Lukas countered. He started to say something else, but held his tongue as a group of miners exited the generator room, a cloud of dust kicked up from their boots.

"Were you going to say something?" she asked.

"I was going to ask that you dig in secret if you have to dig at all. Or leave these men to it and come—"

He bit off the thought.

"If you were about to say home, this is my home. And are we really no better than the last of them who were in charge? Lying to our people? Conspiring?"

"I fear we are worse," he said. "All they did was keep us alive."

Juliette laughed at that. "Us? They elected to send you and me to die."

Lukas let out his breath. "I meant everyone else. They worked to keep everyone else alive." But he couldn't help it: he cracked a smile while Juliette continued to laugh. She smeared the tears on her cheeks into mud.

"Give me a few days down here," she said. It wasn't a question; it was a concession. "Let me see if we even have the means to dig. Then I'll come kiss your babies and bury your dead—though not in that order, of course."

Lukas frowned at her morbidness. "And you'll tamp down the heresies?"

She nodded. "If we dig, we'll do it quietly." To herself, she wondered if such a machine as she'd uncovered could dig any way but with a growl. "I was thinking of going on a slight power holiday, anyway. I don't want the main generator on a full load for a while. Just in case."

Lukas nodded, and Juliette realized how easy and necessary the lies felt. She considered telling him right then of another idea of hers, one she'd been considering for weeks, all the way back when she was in the doctor's office recovering from her burns. There was something she needed to do up top, but she could see that he was in no mood to be angered further. And so she told him the only part of her plan that she thought he'd enjoy.

"Once things are underway down here, I plan to come up and stay for a while," she said, taking his hand. "Come home for a while."

Lukas smiled.

"But listen here," she told him, feeling the urge to warn. "I've seen the world out there, Luke. I stay up at night listening to Walk's radio. There are a lot of people just like us out there, living in fear, living apart, kept ignorant. I mean to do more than save my friends. I hope you know this. I mean to get to the bottom of what's out there beyond these walls."

The knot in Lukas's throat bobbed up and down. His smile vanished. "You aim too far," he said meekly.

Juliette smiled and squeezed her lover's hand. "Says the man who watches the stars."

Silo 17

5

"SOLO! MR. SOLO!"

The faint voice of a young child worked its way into the deepest of the grow pits. It reached all the way to the cool plots of soil where lights no longer burned and things no longer grew. There, Jimmy Parker sat alone atop the lifeless soil and near to the memory of an old friend.

His hands idly picked clumps of clay and crushed them into powder. If he imagined really hard, he could feel the pinprick of claws through his coveralls. He could hear Shadow's little belly rattling like a water pump. It got harder and harder to imagine as the young voice calling his name grew nearer. The glow of a flashlight cut through the last tangle of plants that the young ones called the Wilds.

"There you are!"

Little Elise made a heap of noise that belied her small size. She stomped over to him in her too-big boots. Jimmy watched her approach and remembered wishing long ago that Shadow could talk. He'd had countless dreams wherein Shadow was a boy with black fur and a rumbly voice. But Jimmy no longer had such dreams. Nowadays, he was thankful for the speechless years with his old friend.

Elise squirmed through the rails of the fence and hugged

Jimmy's arm. The flashlight nearly blinded him as she clutched it against his chest, pointing it up.

"It's time to go," Elise said, tugging at him. "It's time, Mr. Solo."

He blinked against the harsh light and knew that she was right. The youngest among them, little Elise settled more arguments than she started. Jimmy crushed another clump of clay in his hand, sprinkled the soil across the ground, and wiped his palm on his thigh. He didn't want to leave, but he knew they couldn't stay. He reminded himself that it would be temporary. Juliette said so. She said he could come back here and live with all the others who came over. There would be no lottery for a while. There would be lots of people. They would make his old silo whole again.

Jimmy shivered at the thought of so many people. Elise tugged his arm. "Let's go. Let's go," she said.

And Jimmy realized what he was scared of. It wasn't the leaving one day, which was still some time off. It wasn't him setting up home in the Deep, which was nearly pumped dry and no longer frightened him. It was the idea of what he might return to. His home had only grown safer as it had emptied; he had been attacked when it had started filling up again. Part of him just wanted to be left alone, to be Solo.

On his feet, he allowed Elise to lead him back to the landing. She tugged on his calloused hand and pulled him forward with spirit. Outside, she gathered her things by the steps. Rickson and the others could be heard below, their voices echoing up the shaft of quiet concrete. One of the emergency lights was out on that level, leaving a black patch amid the dull green. Elise adjusted the shoulder satchel that held her memory book and cinched the top of her backpack. Food and water, a change of clothes, batteries, a faded doll, her hairbrush—practically everything she owned. Jimmy held the shoulder strap so she could work her arm through, then picked up his own load. The voices of the others faded. The stairwell faintly shook and rang with their footsteps as they headed down, which seemed a fairly odd direction to go in order to get *out*.

"How long before Jewel comes for us?" Elise asked. She took Jimmy's hand, and they spiraled down side by side.

"Not long," Jimmy said, which was his answer for I-don't-know. "She's trying. It's a long way to go. You know how it took a long time for the water to go down and vanish?"

Elise bobbed her head. "I counted the steps," she said.

"Yes, you did. Well, now they have to tunnel their way through solid rock to get to us. That won't be easy."

"Hannah says there'll be dozens and dozens of people after Jewel comes."

Jimmy swallowed. "Hundreds," he said hoarsely. "Thousands, even."

Elise squeezed his hand. Another dozen steps went by, both of them quietly counting. It was difficult for either of them to count so high.

"Rickson says they aren't coming to rescue us, but that they want our silo."

"Yes, well, he sees the bad in people," Jimmy said. "Just like you see the good in them."

Elise looked up at Jimmy. Both of them had lost their count. He wondered if she could imagine what thousands of people would be like. He could barely remember himself.

"I wish he could see the good in people like me," she said.

Jimmy stopped before they got to the next landing. Elise clutched his hand and her swinging satchel and stopped with him. He knelt to be closer to her. When Elise pouted, he could see the gap left by her missing tooth.

"There's a bit of good in all people," Jimmy said. He squeezed Elise's shoulder, could feel a lump forming in his throat. "But there's bad as well. Rickson is probably more right than wrong at times."

He hated to say it. Jimmy hated to fill Elise's head with such things. But he loved her as though she were his own. And he wanted to give her the great steel doors she would need if the silo were to grow full again. It was why he allowed her to cut up the books inside the tin cans and take the pages she liked. It was why he helped her choose which ones were important. The ones he chose were the ones for helping her survive.

"You'll need to start seeing the world with Rickson's eyes," Jimmy said, hating himself for it. He stood and pulled her down the steps this time, no longer counting. He wiped his eyes before Elise noticed him crying, before she asked him one of her easy questions with no easy answers at all.

6

IT WAS DIFFICULT to leave the bright lights and comfort of his old home behind, but Jimmy had agreed to move down to the lower farms. The kids were comfortable there. They quickly resumed their work among the grow plots. And it was closer to the last of the dwindling floods.

Jimmy descended slick steps spotted with fresh rust and listened to the plopping tune of water hitting puddle and steel. Many of the green emergency lights had been drowned by the floods. Even those that worked held murky bubbles of trapped water. Jimmy thought about the fish that used to swim in what now was open air. A few had been found swimming around as the water retreated, even though he'd long ago thought he'd caught them all. Trapped in shallowing pools, they had proved too easy to catch. He had taught Elise how, but she had trouble getting them off the hook. She was forever dropping the slimy creatures back into the water. Jimmy jokingly accused her of doing it on purpose, and Elise admitted she liked catching them more than eating them. He had let her catch the last few fish over and over until he felt too sorry for the poor things to allow it to go on. Rickson and Hannah and the twins had been happy to put these desperate survivors out of their misery and into their bellies.

Jimmy glanced up beyond the rail overhead, picturing his bobber out there in the middle of the air. He imagined Shadow peering down and batting his paw at him, as if Jimmy were now the fish, trapped underwater. He tried to blow bubbles, but nothing came out, just the tickle of his whiskers against his nose.

Further down, a puddle gathered where the stairs bottomed out. The floor was flat here, wasn't sloped to drain. The floods were never meant to get so high. Jimmy flicked on his flashlight, and the beam cut through the dismal darkness deep inside Mechanical. An electrical wire snaked through the open passageway and draped across a security station. A tangle of hose traced along beside it before doubling back on itself. The cable and the hose knew the way to the pumps; they had been left behind by Juliette.

Jimmy followed their trail. His first time to the bottom of the stairs, he had found the plastic dome of her helmet. It was among a raft of trash and debris and sludge, all the foulness left over once the water was gone. He had tried to clean it up as much as he could, had found his small metal washers—the ones that anchored his old paper parachutes—like silver coins among the detritus. Much of the garbage from the floods remained. The only thing he had saved from it all was the plastic dome of her helmet.

The wire and hose turned down a flight of square steps. Jimmy followed them, careful not to trip. Water fell occasionally from the pipes and wires overhead and smacked him on the shoulder and head. The drops twinkled in the beam of his flashlight. Everything else was dark. He tried to imagine being down there when the place was full of water—and couldn't. It was scary enough while dry.

A smack of water right on the crown of his head, and then a tickle as the rivulet raced into his beard. "Mostly dry, I meant,"

Jimmy said, talking to the ceiling. He reached the bottom of the steps. It was only the wire now guiding him along, and tricky to see. He splashed through a thin film of water as he headed down the hall. Juliette said it was important to be there when the pump got done. Someone would have to be around to turn it on and off. Water would continue seeping in, and so the pump needed to do its job, but it was bad for the thing to run dry. Something called an "impeller" would burn, she had told him.

Jimmy found the pump. It was rattling unhappily. A large pipe bent over the lip of a well—Juliette had told him to be careful not to fall in—and there was a sucking, gurgling sound from its depths. Jimmy aimed the flashlight down and saw that the shaft was nearly empty. Just a foot or so of water thrown into turbulence by the fruitless pull of the great pipe.

He pulled his cutters out of his breast pocket and fished the wire out of the thin layer of water. The pump growled angrily, metal clanging on metal, the smell of hot electrics in the air, steam rising from the cylindrical housing that provided the power. Teasing apart the two joined wires, Jimmy severed one of them with his cutters. The pump continued to run for a breath but slowly wound itself down. Juliette had told him what to do. He stripped the cut wire back and twisted the ends. When the basin filled again, Jimmy would have to short out the starter switch by hand, just as she had done all those weeks ago. He and the kids could take turns. They would live above the levels ruined by the floods, tend the Wilds, and keep the silo dry until Juliette came for them.

Silo 18

7

THE ARGUMENT WITH Shirly about the generator went badly. Juliette got her way, but she didn't emerge feeling victorious. She watched her old friend stomp off and tried to imagine being in her place. It had only been a couple of months since her husband, Marck, had died. Juliette had been a wreck for a solid year after losing George. And now some mayor was telling the head of Mechanical that they were taking the backup generator. Stealing it. Leaving the silo at the whim of a mechanical failure. One tooth snaps off one gear, and all the levels descend into darkness, all the pumps fall quiet, until it can be fixed.

Juliette didn't need to hear Shirly argue the points. She could well enough name them herself. Now she stood alone in a dim hallway, her friend's footsteps fading to silence, wondering what in the world she was doing. Even those around her were losing their trust. And why? For a promise? Or was she just being stubborn?

She scratched her arm, one of the scars beneath her coveralls itching, and remembered speaking with her father after almost twenty years of hardheaded avoidance. Neither of them had admitted how dumb they'd been, but it hung in the room like a family quilt. Here was their failing, the source of their drive to accomplish much in life and also the cause of the damage they so often left behind—this injurious pride.

Juliette turned and let herself back into the generator room. A clanging racket along the far wall reminded her of more... unbalanced days. The sound of digging was not unlike the warped generator of her past: young and hot and dangerous.

Work was already underway on the backup generator. Dawson and his team had the exhaust coupling separated. Raph worked one of the large nuts on the forward mount with a massive wrench, separating the generator from its ancient mooring. Juliette realized she was really doing this. Shirly had every right to be pissed off.

She crossed the room and stepped through one of the holes in the wall, ducked her head under the rebar, and found Bobby at the rear of the great digger, scratching his beard. Bobby was a boulder of a man. He wore his hair long and in the tight braids miners enjoyed, and his charcoal skin hid the efforts of dark digging. He was in every way his friend Raph's antithesis. Hyla, his daughter and also his shadow, stood quietly at his elbow.

"How goes it?" Juliette asked.

"How goes it? Or how goes this machine?" Bobby turned and studied her a moment. "I'll tell you how this rusted bucket goes. She's not one for turning, not like you need. She's aimed straight as a rod. Not meant to be guided at all."

Juliette greeted Hyla and sized up the progress on the digger. The machine was cleaning up well, was in remarkable shape. She placed a hand on Bobby's arm. "She'll steer," she assured him. "We'll place iron wedges along the wall here on the right-hand side." She pointed to the place. Overhead floodlights from the mines illuminated the dark rock. "When the back end presses on these wedges, it'll force the front to the side." With one hand representing the digger, she pushed on her wrist with the other, cocking her hand to show how it would maneuver.

Bobby reluctantly grumbled his agreement. "It'll be slow going, but that might work." He unfolded a sheet of fine paper, a schematic of all the silos, and studied the path Juliette had drawn. She had stolen the layout from Lukas's hidden office, and her proposed dig traced an arc from Silo 18 to Silo 17, generator room to generator room. "We'll have to wedge it downward as well," Bobby told her. "She's on an incline like she's itchin' to go up."

"That's fine. What's the word on the bracing?"

Hyla studied the two adults and twisted a charcoal in one hand, held her slate in the other. Bobby glanced up at the ceiling and frowned.

"Erik's not so keen on lending what he's got. He says he can spare girders enough for a thousand yards. I told him you'd be wanting five or ten times that."

"We'll have to pull some out of the mines, then." Juliette nodded to Hyla and her slate, suggesting she write that down.

"You mean to start wars down here, do you?" Bobby tugged on his beard, clearly agitated. Hyla stopped scratching on the slate and looked from one of her superiors to the other, not sure what to do.

"I'll talk to Erik," she told Bobby. "When I promise him the pile of steel girders we'll find in the other silo, he'll cave."

Bobby lifted an eyebrow. "Bad choice of words."

He laughed nervously while Juliette gestured to his daughter. "We'll need thirty-six beams and seventy-two risers," she said.

Hyla glanced guiltily at Bobby before jotting this down.

"If this thing moves, it's gonna make a lot of dirt," Bobby said. "Hauling the tailings from here to the crusher down in the mines is gonna make a mess and take as many men as the digging."

The thought of the crushing room where tailings were

ground to powder and vented to the exhaust manifold stirred painful memories. Juliette aimed her flashlight at Bobby's feet, trying not to think of the past. "We won't be expelling the tailings," she told him. "Shaft six is almost directly below us. If we dig straight down, we hit it."

"You mean to fill number six?" Bobby asked, incredulous.

"Six is nearly tapped out anyway. And we double our ore the moment we reach this other silo."

"Erik's gonna blow a gasket. You aren't forgettin' anybody, are you?"

Juliette studied her old friend. "Forgetting anybody?"

"Anyone you're neglecting to piss off."

Juliette ignored the jab and turned to Hyla. "Make a note to Courtnee. I want the backup generator fully serviced before it's brought in. There won't be room to pull the heads and check the seals once it's fitted in here. The ceiling will be too low."

Bobby followed as Juliette continued her inspection of the digger. "You'll be here to look after that, won't you?" he asked. "You'll be here to couple the genset to this monster, right?"

She shook her head. "Afraid not. Dawson will be in charge of that. Lukas is right, I need to go up and make the rounds—"

"Bullshit," Bobby said. "What's this about, Jules? I've never seen you leave a project in half like this, not even if it meant working three shifts."

Juliette turned and gave Hyla that look that all children and shadows know to mean their ears aren't welcome. Hyla stayed back while the two old friends continued on.

"My being down here is causing unrest," Juliette told Bobby, her voice quiet and swallowed by the vastness of the machine around them. "Lukas did the right thing to come get me." She shot the old miner a cold look. "And I'll beat you senseless if that gets back to him."

He laughed and showed his palms. "You don't have to tell me. I'm married."

Juliette nodded. "It's best you all dig while I'm elsewhere. If I'm to be a distraction, then let me be a distraction." They reached the end of a void that the backup generator would soon fill. It was so clever, this arrangement, keeping the delicate engine out where it would be used and serviced. The rest of the digger was just steel and grinding teeth, gears packed tight with grease.

"These friends of yours," Bobby said. "They're worth all this?"

"They are." Juliette studied her old friend. "But this isn't just for them. This is for us too."

Bobby chewed on his beard. "I don't follow," he said after a pause.

"We need to prove this works," she said. "This is only the beginning."

Bobby narrowed his eyes at her. "Well, if it ain't the beginning of one thing," he said, "I would hazard to say it spells the end of another."

8

Juliette paused outside Walker's workshop and knocked before entering. She had heard tell of him being out and about during the uprising, but this was a cog whose teeth refused to align with anything in her head. As far as she was concerned, it was mere legend, a thing to be disbelieved because it hadn't been seen with her own eyes—similar, she reckoned, to how her jaunt between silos didn't compute for most people. A rumor. A myth. Who was this woman mechanic who claimed to have seen another land? Stories such as these were dismissed—unless legend took seed and sprouted religion.

"Jules!" Walker peered up from his desk, one of his eyes the size of a tomato through his magnifiers. He pulled the lens away, and his eye shrank back to normal. "Good, good. So glad you're here." He waved her over. There was the smell of burning hair in the room, as if the old man had been leaning over his soldering work while careless of his long gray locks.

"I just came to transmit something to Solo," she said. "And to let you know I'll be away for a few days."

"Oh?" Walker frowned. He slotted a few small tools into his leather apron and pressed his soldering iron into a wet sponge. The hiss reminded Juliette of an ill-tempered cat who used to live in the pump room, fussing at her from the darkness. "That Lukas fellow pulling you away?" Walker asked.

Juliette was reminded that Walker was no friend to open spaces, but he was a friend to porters. And they were friendly with his coin.

"That's part of it," she admitted. She pulled out a stool and sank against it, studied her hands, which were scraped and stained with grease. "The other part is that this digging business is going to take a while, and you know how I get when I sit still. I've got another project I've been thinking on. It's going to be even less popular than this one here."

Walker studied her for a moment, glanced up at the ceiling, and then his eyes widened. Somehow, he knew precisely what she was planning. "You're like a bowl of Courtnee's chili," he whispered. "Making trouble at both ends."

Juliette laughed, but also felt a twinge of disappointment that she was so transparent. So predictable.

"I haven't told Lukas yet," she warned him. "Or Peter."

Walker scrunched up his face at the second name.

"Billings," she said. "The new sheriff."

"That's right." He unplugged his soldering iron and dabbed it against the sponge again. "I forget that ain't your job no more."

It hardly ever was, she wanted to say.

"I just want to tell Solo that we're nearly underway with the digging. I need to make sure the floods are under control over there." She gestured to his radio, which could do far more than broadcast up and down a single silo. Like the radio in the room beneath IT's servers, this unit he had built was capable of broadcasting to other silos.

"Sure thing. Shame you aren't leaving in a day or two. I'm almost done with the portable." He showed her a plastic box a little larger than the old radios she and the deputies used to wear on their hips. It still had wires hanging loose and a large external battery attached. "Once I get done with it, you'll be able to switch channels with a dial. It piggybacks the repeaters up and down both silos."

She picked the unit up gingerly, no clue what he was talking about. Walker pointed to a dial with thirty-two numbered positions around it. This she understood.

"Just got to get the old rechargeables to play nice in there. Working on the voltage regulation next."

"You are amazing," Juliette whispered.

Walker beamed. "Amazing are the people who made this the first time. I can't get over what they were able to do hundreds of years ago. People weren't as dumb back then as you'd like to believe."

Juliette wanted to tell him about the books she'd seen, how the people back then seemed as if they were from the future, not the past.

Walker wiped his hands on an old rag. "I warned Bobby and the others, and I think you should know too. The radios won't work so well the deeper they dig, not until they get to the other side."

Juliette nodded. "So I heard. Courtnee said they'll use runners just like in the mines. I put her in charge of the dig. She's thought of just about everything."

Walker frowned. "I heard she wanted to rig this side to blow as well, in case they hit a pocket of bad air."

"That was Shirly's idea. She's just trying to come up with reasons not to dig. But you know Courtnee, once she sets her mind to something, it gets done."

Walker scratched his beard. "As long as she don't forget to feed me, we'll be fine."

Juliette laughed. "I'm sure she won't."

"Well, I wish you luck on your rounds."

"Thanks," she said. She pointed to the large radio set on his workbench. "Can you patch me through to Solo?"

"Sure, sure. Seventeen. Forgot you didn't come down here to chat with me. Let's call your friend." He shook his head. "Have to tell you, from talking to him, he's one odd fellow."

Juliette smiled and studied her old friend. She waited to see if he was joking—decided he was being perfectly serious—and laughed.

"What?" Walker asked. He powered the radio on and handed her the receiver. "What did I say?"

Solo's update was a mixed bag. Mechanical was dry, which was good, but it hadn't taken as long as she'd thought for the flood to pump out. It might be weeks or months to get over there and see what they could salvage, and the rust would set in immediately. Juliette pushed these distant problems out of her mind and concentrated on the things she could lay a wrench on.

Everything she needed for her trip up fit in a small shoulder bag: her good silver coveralls, which she'd barely worn; socks and underwear, both still wet from washing them in the sink; her work canteen, dented and grease-stained; and a ratchet and driver set. In her pockets she carried her multi-tool and twenty chits, even though hardly anyone took payment from her since she turned mayor. The only thing she felt she was missing was a decent radio, but Walker had scrapped two of the functioning units to try and build a new one, and it wasn't ready yet.

With her meager belongings and a feeling like she was abandoning her friends, she left Mechanical behind. The distant clatter from the digging followed her through the hallways and out into the stairwell. Passing through security was like crossing some mental threshold. It reminded her of leaving that airlock all those weeks ago. Like a stopper valve, some things seemed to allow passage in only one direction. She feared how long it might be before she returned. The thought made it difficult to breathe.

She slowly gained height and began passing others on the stairwell, and Juliette could feel them watching her. The glares of people she had once known reminded her of the wind that had buffeted her on the hillside. Their distrustful glances came in gusts—just as quickly, they looked away.

Before long, she saw what Lukas had spoken of. Whatever goodwill her return had wrought—whatever wonder people held for her as someone who had refused to clean and managed to survive the great outside—was crumbling as sure as the concrete being hammered below. Where her return from the outside had brought hope, her plans to tunnel beyond the silo had engendered something else. She could see it in the averted gaze of a shopkeep, in the protective arm a mother wrapped around her child, in the whispers that came and just as suddenly went. Juliette was causing the opposite of hope. She was spreading fear.

A handful of people did acknowledge her with a nod and a "Mayor" as she passed them on the stairwell. A young porter she knew stopped and shook her hand, seemed genuinely thrilled to see her. But when she paused at the lower farms on one-twenty-six for food, and when she sought a bathroom three levels further up, she felt as welcomed as a greaser in the Up Top. And yet she was still among her own. She was their mayor, however unloved.

These interactions gave her second thoughts about seeing Hank, the deputy of the Down Deep. Hank had fought in the uprising and had seen good men and women on both sides give up their lives. As Juliette entered the deputy station on one-twenty, she wondered if stopping was a mistake, if she should just press on. But that was her young self afraid of seeing her father, her young self who buried her head in projects in order to avoid the world. She could no longer be that person. She had a responsibility to the silo and its people. Seeing Hank was the right thing to do. She scratched a scar on the back of her hand and bravely strode into his deputy station. She reminded herself that she was the mayor, not a prisoner being sent to clean.

Hank glanced up from his desk as she entered. The deputy's eyes widened as he recognized her—they had not spoken nor seen each other since she got back. He rose from his chair and took two steps toward her, then stopped, and Juliette saw the same mix of nerves and excitement that she felt and realized she shouldn't have been afraid of coming, that she shouldn't have avoided him until now. Hank reached out his hand timidly, as if worried she might refuse to shake it. He seemed ready to pull it back if it offended. Whatever heartache she had brought him, he still seemed pained at having followed orders and sending her to clean.

Juliette took the deputy's hand and pulled him into an embrace.

"I'm sorry," he whispered, his voice giving out on him.

"Stop that," Juliette said. She let go of the lawman and took a step back, studied his shoulder. "I'm the one who should be apologizing. How's your arm?"

He shrugged his shoulder in a circle. "Still attached," he said. "And if you ever dare apologize to me, I'll have you arrested."

"Truce, then," she offered.

Hank smiled. "Truce," he said. "But I do want to say—"

"You were doing your job. And I was doing the best I could. Now leave it."

He nodded and studied his boots.

"How are things around here? Lukas said there's been grumbling about my work below."

"There's been some acting up. Nothing too serious. I think most people are busy enough patching things up. But yeah, I've heard some talk. You know how many requests we get for transfer out of here and up to the Mids or the Top. Well, I've been getting ten times the normal. Folks don't want to be near what you've got going on, I'm afraid."

Juliette chewed her lip.

"Part of the problem is lack of direction," Hank said. "Don't want to shoulder you with this, but me and the boys down here don't have a clear idea which way is up right now. We aren't getting dispatches from Security like we used to. And your office . . ."

"Has been quiet," Juliette offered.

Hank scratched the back of his head. "That's right. Not that you've been exactly quiet yourself. We can sometimes hear the racket you're making out on the landing."

"That's why I'm visiting," she told him. "I want you to know that your concerns are my concerns. I'm heading up to my office for a week or two. I'll stop by the other deputy stations as well. Things are going to improve around here in a lot of ways."

Hank frowned. "You know I trust you and all, but when you tell people around here that things are going to improve, all they hear is that things are going to change. And for those who are breathing and count that as a blessing, they take that to mean one thing and one thing only."

Juliette thought of all she had planned, in the Up Top as well as the Down Deep. "As long as good men like you trust me, we'll be fine," she said. "Now, I've got a favor to ask."

"You need a place to stay the night," Hank guessed. He waved at the jail cell. "I saved your room for you. I can turn down the cot—"

Juliette laughed. She was happy that they could already joke about what had moments ago been a discomfort. "No," she said. "Thanks, though. I'm supposed to be up at the Mids farms by lights out. I have to plant the first crop in a new patch of soil being turned over." She waved her hand in the air. "It's one of those things."

Hank smiled and nodded.

"What I wanted to ask is that you keep an eye on the stairwell for me. Lukas mentioned there were grumbles up above. I'm going up to soothe them, but I want you to be on the alert if things go sour. We're short-staffed below, and people are on edge."

"You expecting trouble?" Hank asked.

Juliette considered the question. "I am," she said. "If you need to take a shadow or two, I'll budget it."

He frowned. "I normally like having chits thrown my way," he said. "So why does this make me feel uncomfortable?"

"Same reason I'm happy to pay," Juliette said. "We both know you're getting the busted end of the deal."

9

LEAVING THE DEPUTY'S office, Juliette climbed through
levels that had seen much of the fighting, and she noticed once
more the silo's wounds of war. She rose through ever-worsening
reminders of the battles that had been waged in her absence,
saw the marks left behind from the fighting, the jagged streaks
of bright silver through old paint, the black burns and pock-
marks in concrete, the rebar poking through like fractured bone
through skin.

She had devoted most of her life to holding that silo together,
to keeping it running. This was a kindness repaid by the silo as it
filled her lungs with air, gave rise to the crops, and claimed the
dead. They were responsible for one another. Without people,
this silo would become as Solo's had: rusted and fairly drowned.
Without the silo, she would be a skull on a hill, looking blankly
to the cloud-filled skies. They needed each other.

Her hand slid up the rail, rough with new welds, her own
hand a mess of scars. For much of her life, they had kept each
other going, she and the silo. Right up until they'd damn near
killed each other. And now the minor hurts in Mechanical she
had hoped to repair one day—squealing pumps, spitting pipes,
leaks from the exhaust—all paled before the far worse wreck-
age her leaving had caused. In much the same way that the oc-

casional scars—reminders of youthful missteps—were now lost beneath disfigured flesh, it seemed that one large mistake could bury all the minor ones.

She took the steps one at a time and reached that place where a bomb had ripped a gap in the stairs. A patchwork of metal stretched across the ruin, a web of bar and rail scavenged from landings that now stood narrower than before. Names of those lost in the blast were written here and there in charcoal. Juliette treaded carefully across the mangled metal. Higher up, she saw that the doors to Supply had been replaced. Here, the fighting had been especially bad. The cost these people in yellow had paid for siding with hers in blue.

A Sunday was letting out as Juliette approached the church on ninety-nine. Floods of people spiraled down toward the quiet bazaar she had just passed. Their mouths were pressed tight from hours of serious talk, their joints as stiff as their pressed coveralls. Juliette filed past them and took note of the hostile glances.

The crowds thinned by the time she reached the landing. The small temple was wedged in among the old hydroponic farms and worker flats that used to serve the Deep. It was before her time, but Knox once explained how the temple had sprouted on ninety-nine. It was when his own dad was a boy and protests had arisen over music and plays performed during Sundays. Security had sat back while the protestors swelled into an encampment outside the bazaar. People slept on the treads and choked the stairway until no one could pass. The farm one level up was ravaged in supplying food to these masses. Eventually, they took over much of the hydroponics level. The temple on twenty-eight set up a satellite office, and now that satellite on ninety-nine was bigger than the temple that had sprouted it.

Father Wendel was on the landing as Juliette rounded the last turn. He stood by the door, shaking hands and speaking briefly with each member of his congregation as they left the Sunday service. His white robes fairly emitted a light of their own. They shone much like his bald head, which glistened from the effort of preaching to the crowds. Between head and robes, Wendel seemed to sparkle. Especially to Juliette, who had just left a land of smudge and grease. She felt dirty just seeing such unblemished cloth.

"Thank you, Father," a woman said, bowing slightly, shaking his hand, a child balanced on her hip. The little one's head lolled against her shoulder in perfect slumber. Wendel rested a hand on the child's head and said a few words. The woman thanked him again, moved on, and Wendel shook the next man's hand.

Juliette made herself invisible against the rail while the last handful of churchgoers filed past. She watched a man pause and press a few clinking chits into Father Wendel's open palm. "Thank you, Father," he said, this farewell a chant of sorts. Juliette could smell what she thought was goats on the old man as he filed past and wound his way up, probably back to the pens. He was the last one to leave. Father Wendel turned and smiled at Juliette to let her know he'd been aware of her presence.

"Mayor," he said, spreading his hands. "You honor us. Did you come for the elevens?"

Juliette checked the small watch she wore around her wrist. "This wasn't the elevens?" she asked. She was making good time up the levels.

"It was the tens. We added another Sunday. The toppers come down for late service."

Juliette wondered why those who lived up top would travel so far. She had timed her walk to miss the services entirely, which was probably a mistake. It would be smart for her to hear what was being said that so many found alluring.

"I'm afraid I can only stop for a quick visit," she said. "I'll catch a Sunday on my way back down?"

Wendel frowned. "And when might that be? I heard you were returning to the work God and his people chose you for."

"A few weeks, probably. Long enough to get caught up."

An acolyte emerged on the landing with an ornate wooden bowl. He showed Wendel its contents, and Juliette heard the chits shift against one another. The boy wore a brown cloak, and when he bowed to Wendel, she saw the center of his scalp had been shaved. When he turned to leave, Wendel grabbed the acolyte's arm.

"Pay your respects to your mayor," he said.

"Ma'am." The acolyte bowed. His face showed no expression. Dark eyes under full and dark brows, his lips colorless. Juliette sensed that this young man spent little time outside of the church.

"You don't have to ma'am me," she told him politely. "Juliette." She extended a hand.

"Remmy," the boy said. A hand emerged from his cloak. Juliette accepted it.

"See to the pews," Wendel said. "We have another service yet."

Remmy bowed to both of them and shuffled away. Juliette felt pity for the boy, but she wasn't sure why. Wendel peered across the landing and seemed to listen for approaching traffic. Holding the door, he waved Juliette inside. "Come," he said. "Top up your canteen. I'll bless your journey."

Juliette shook her canteen, which sloshed nearly empty. "Thank you," she said. She followed him inside.

Wendel led her past the reception hall and waved her into the lower chapel, where she'd attended a few Sundays years prior. Remmy busied himself among the rows of benches and chairs, replacing pillows and laying out announcements handwritten on narrow strips of cheap paper. She caught him watching her as he worked.

"The gods miss you," Father Wendel said, letting her know that he was aware how long it'd been since she'd attended a Sunday. The chapel had expanded since she last remembered it. There was the heady and expensive smell of sawdust, of newly shaped wood made from claimed doors and other ancient timbers. She rested her hand on a pew that must've been worth a fortune.

"Well, the gods know where to find me," she answered, taking her hand off the pew. She smiled as she said this, meant it lightly, but saw a flash of disappointment on the father's face.

"I sometimes wonder if you aren't hiding from them as best you can," he said. Father Wendel nodded toward the stained glass behind the altar. The lights behind the glass were full-bright, shards of color thrown against the floor and ceiling. "I read your announcements for every birth and every death up there in my pulpit, and I see in them that you give credit in all things to the gods."

Juliette wanted to say that she didn't even write those announcements. They were written for her.

"But I sometimes wonder if you even believe in the gods, the way you take their rules so lightly."

"I believe in the gods," Juliette said, her temper stoked by this accusation. "I believe in the gods who created this silo. I do. And all the other silos—"

Wendel flinched. "Blasphemy," he whispered, his eyes wide as if her words could kill. He threw a look at Remmy, who bowed and moved toward the hall.

"Yes, blasphemy," Juliette said. "But I believe the gods made the towers beyond the hills and that they left us a way to discover, a way out of here. We have uncovered a tool in the depths of this silo, Father Wendel. A digging machine that could take us to new places. I know you disapprove, but I believe the gods gave us this tool, and I mean to use it."

"This digger of yours is the devil's work, and it lies in the devil's deep," Wendel said. The kindness had left his face. He patted his forehead with a square of fine cloth. "There are no gods like those you speak of, only demons."

This was his sermon, Juliette saw. She was getting his elevens. The people came far to hear this.

She took a step closer. Her skin was warm with anger. "There may be demons among my gods," she agreed, speaking his tongue. "The gods I believe in . . . the gods I worship were the men and women who built this place and more like it. They built this place to protect us from the world they destroyed. They were gods and demons, both. But they left us space for redemption. They meant us to be free, Father, and they gave us the means." She pointed to her temple. "They gave me the means right here. And they left us a digger. They did. There is nothing blasphemous about using it. And I've seen the other silos that you continue to doubt. I've been there."

Wendel took another step back. He rubbed the cross hanging around his neck, and Juliette caught Remmy peeking around the edge of the door, his dark brows casting shadows over his dark eyes.

"We should use all the tools the gods gave us," Juliette said. "Except for the one you wield, this power to make others fear."

"Me?" Father Wendel pressed one palm to his chest. With his other hand, he pointed at her. "*You* are the one spreading fear." He swept his hand at the pews and beyond to the tight rows of mismatched chairs, crates, and buckets at the back of the room. "They crowd in here three Sundays a day to wring their hands over the devil's work you do. Children can't sleep at night for fear that you'll kill us all."

Juliette opened her mouth, but the words would not come. She thought of the looks on the stairwell, thought of that mother pulling her child close, people she knew who no longer said hello. "I could show you books," she said softly, thinking of the shelves that held the Legacy. "I could show you books, and then you'd see."

"There's only one book worth knowing," Wendel said. His eyes darted to the large, ornate tome with its gilded edges that sat on a podium by the pulpit, that sat under a cage of bent steel. Juliette remembered lessons from that book. She'd seen its pages with those occasional and cryptic sentences peeking out amid bars of censored black. She also noticed the way the podium was welded to the steel decking, and not expertly. Fat puckers of paranoid welds. The same gods expected to keep men and women safe couldn't be trusted to look after one book.

"I should leave you to get ready for your elevens," she said, feeling sorry for her outburst.

Wendel uncrossed his arms. She could sense that they had both gone too far and that both knew it. She had hoped to allay doubts and had only worsened them.

"I wish you'd stay," Wendel told her. "At least fill your canteen."

She reached behind her back and unclipped the canteen. Remmy returned with a swish of his heavy brown cloaks, the shaved circle on his head glimmering with perspiration. "I will, Father," Juliette said. "Thank you."

Wendel nodded. He waved to Remmy and said nothing else to her as his acolyte drew water from the chapel fountain. Not a word. His earlier promise to bless her journey had gone forgotten.

10

JULIETTE PARTICIPATED IN a ceremonial planting at the Mids farm, had a late lunch, and continued her laconic pace up the silo. By the time she reached the thirties, the lights were beginning to dim, and she found herself looking forward to a familiar bed.

Lukas was waiting for her on the landing. He smiled a greeting and insisted on taking her shoulder bag, however light.

"You didn't have to wait for me," she said. But in truth, she found it sweet.

"I just got here," he insisted. "A porter told me you were getting close."

Juliette remembered the young girl in light blue coveralls who'd overtaken her in the forties. It was easy to forget that Lukas had eyes and ears everywhere. He held the door open, and Juliette entered a level packed with conflicting memories and feelings. Here was where Knox had died. Here was where Mayor Jahns had been poisoned. Here was where she had been doomed to clean and where doctors had patched her back up.

She glanced toward the conference room and remembered being told that she was mayor. That was where she had suggested to Peter and Lukas that they tell everyone the truth:

that they were not alone in the world. She still thought it a good idea, despite their protestations. But maybe it was better to *show* people rather than tell them. She imagined families taking a grand journey to the Down Deep the way they used to hike up to gaze at the wallscreen. They would travel to her world, thousands of people who had never been, who had no idea what the machines that kept them alive looked like. They would travel down to Mechanical so that they could then pass through a tunnel and see this other silo. On the way, they might marvel at the main generator that now hummed, perfectly balanced. They could marvel at the hole in the ground her friends had made. And then they could contemplate the thrill of filling an empty world so very much like their own, remaking it how they saw fit.

The security gate beeped as Lukas scanned his pass, and Juliette returned from her daydreams. The guard behind the gate waved at her, and Juliette waved back. Beyond him, the halls of IT sat quiet and empty. Most of the workers had gone home for the night. With no one there, Juliette was reminded of Silo 17. She imagined Solo walking around the corner, half a loaf of bread in his hand, crumbs caught in his beard, a happy grin on his face as he spotted her. That hall looked just like this hall, except for the busted light that dangled from its wires in Silo 17.

These two sets of memories jumbled in her head as she followed Lukas back to his private residence. Two worlds with the same layout, two lives lived, one here and one there. The weeks spent with Solo felt like an entire lifetime, such was the bond that formed between two people under strain. Elise might dart out of that office where the kids had set up their home and cling to Juliette's leg. The twins would be arguing over found spoils around the bend. Rickson and Hannah would be stealing a kiss in the dark and whispering of another child.

"—but only if you agree."

Juliette turned to Lukas. "What? Oh, yes. That's fine."

"You didn't hear a word of that, did you?" They reached his door, and he scanned his badge. "It's like you're off in another world sometimes."

Juliette heard concern in his voice, not anger. She took her bag from him and stepped inside. Lukas turned on the lights and threw his ID on the dresser by the bed. "You feeling okay?" he asked.

"Just tired from the climb." Juliette sat on the edge of the bed and untied her laces. She worked her boots off and left them in their usual place. Lukas's apartment was like a second home, familiar and cozy. Her own apartment on level six was a foreign land. She had seen it twice but had never spent a night there. To do so would be to fully accept her role as mayor.

"I was thinking about having a late dinner delivered." Lukas rummaged in his closet and brought out the soft cloth robe that Juliette loved to pull on after a hot shower. He hung it from the hook on the bathroom door. "Do you want me to run you a bath?"

Juliette took a heavy breath. "I reek, don't I?" She sniffed the back of her hand and tried to nose the grease. There was the acidic hint of her cutting torch, the spice of exhaust fumes from the digger—a perfume as tattooed on her flesh as the markings oilmen cut and inked into their arms. All this, despite the fact that she had showered before she left Mechanical.

"No—" Lukas appeared hurt. "I just thought you'd enjoy a bath."

"In the morning, maybe. And I might skip dinner. I've been snacking all day." She smoothed the sheets beside her. Lukas smiled and sat down next to her on the bed. His face bore an expectant grin, that glow in his eyes she saw after they made love—but the look dissipated with her next words: "We need to talk."

His face fell. His shoulders sagged. "We're not going to register, are we?"

Juliette seized his hand. "No, that's not it. Of course we are. Of course." She pressed his hand to her chest, remembering a love that she'd kept hidden from the Pact once before and how that had wrenched her in half. She would never make that mistake again. "It's about the digging," she said.

Lukas took a deep breath, held it for a moment, then laughed. "Only that," he said, smiling. "Amazing that your digging could come as the lesser of two harms."

"I have something else I want to do that you aren't going to like."

He raised an eyebrow. "If this is about trying to spread news of the other silos, about telling people what's out there, you know where Peter and I stand on that. I don't think those words are safe. People won't believe you, and those who do will want to cause trouble."

Juliette thought of Father Wendel and how people could believe amazing things crafted from mere words, how beliefs could form from books. But perhaps they had to *want* to believe those things. And maybe Lukas was right that not everyone would want to believe the truth.

"I'm not going to tell them anything," she told Lukas. "I want to *show* them. There's something I want to do up top, but it requires help from you and your department. I'm going to need some of your men."

Lukas frowned. "I don't like the sound of that." He rubbed her arm. "Why don't we discuss it tomorrow? I just want to enjoy having you here with me tonight. One night where we aren't working. I can pretend I'm just a server tech and you can be . . . not the mayor."

Juliette squeezed his hand. "You're right. Of course. And maybe I should jump in the shower real quick—"

"No, stay." He kissed her neck. "You smell like you. Shower in the morning."

She relented. Lukas kissed her neck again, but when he moved to unzip her coveralls, she asked him to douse the lights. For once, he didn't complain as he often did about not being able to see her. Instead, he left the bathroom light on and shut the door most of the way, leaving the barest of glows. As much as she loved being naked with him, she didn't like to be seen. The patchwork of scars made her look like the slices of mine-shaft that cut through granite: a web of white rock standing out from the rest.

But as unattractive as they were to the eyes, they were sensitive to the touch. Each scar was like a nerve ending rising from her own Deep. When Lukas traced them with his fingers—like an electrician following a diagram of wires—wherever he touched was a wrench across two battery terminals. Electricity fluttered through her body as they held each other in the darkness and he explored her with his hands. Juliette could feel her skin grow warm. This would not be a night where they fell fast asleep. Her designs and dangerous plans began to fade under the gentle pressure of his soft touch. This would be a night for traveling back to her youth, of *feeling* rather than thinking, back to simpler times—

"That's strange," Lukas said, stopping what he was doing.

Juliette didn't ask what was strange, hoping he'd forget it. She was too proud to tell him to keep touching her like that.

"My favorite little scar is gone," he said, rubbing a spot on her arm.

Juliette's temperature soared. She was back in the airlock, such was the heat. It was one thing to silently touch her wounds, another to name them. She pulled her arm away and rolled over, thinking this would be a night for sleep after all.

"No, here, let me see," he begged.

"You're being cruel," Juliette told him.

Lukas rubbed her back. "I'm not, I swear. May I please see your arm?"

Juliette sat up in the bed and pulled the sheets over her knees. She wrapped her arms around herself. "I don't like you mentioning them," she said. "And you shouldn't have a favorite." She nodded toward the bathroom, where a faint glow of light leaked out from the cracked door. "Can we please shut that or turn out the light?"

"Jules, I swear to you, I love you just the way you are. I've never seen you any other way."

She took that to mean that he'd never seen her naked before her wounds, not that he'd always found her beautiful. Getting out of bed, she moved to douse the bathroom light herself. She dragged the sheet behind her, leaving Lukas alone and naked on the bed.

"It was on the crook of your right arm," Lukas said. "Three of them crossed and made a little star. I've kissed it a hundred times."

Juliette doused the light and stood alone in the darkness. She could still feel Lukas gazing at her. She could feel people gawking at the scars even when she was fully clothed. She thought of George seeing her like that—and a lump rose in her throat.

Lukas appeared next to her in the pitch black, his arm around her, a kiss lighting on her shoulder. "Come back to bed," he said. "I'm sorry. We can leave the light out."

Juliette hesitated. "I don't like you knowing them so well," she said. "I don't want to be one of your star charts."

"I know," he said. "I can't help it. They're a part of you, the only you I've ever known. Maybe we should have your father take a look—?"

She pulled away from him, only to click the light back on. She studied the crook of her arm in the mirror, first her right arm and then her left, thinking he must be wrong.

"Are you sure it was there?" she asked, studying the web of scars for some bare patch, some piece of open sky.

Lukas took her tenderly by the wrist and elbow, lifted her arm to his mouth, and kissed it.

"Right there," he said. "I've kissed it a hundred times."

Juliette wiped a tear from her eye and laughed in that mix of gasp and sigh that comes from a sad burst of emotion. Locating a particularly offensive knot of flesh, a welt that ran right around her forearm, she showed it to Lukas, forgiving him if not believing him.

"Do this one next," she said.

Silo 1

11

THE SILICON-CARBON BATTERIES the drones ran on were the size of toaster ovens. Charlotte judged each one to weigh between thirty and forty pounds. They had been pulled from two of the drones and wrapped in webbing taken from one of the supply crates. Charlotte gripped one battery in each hand and took lunging squats in a slow lap around the warehouse, her thighs screaming and quivering, her arms numb.

A trail of sweat marked her progress, but she had a long way to go. How had she let herself get so out of shape? All the running and exercise during basic, just to sit at a console and fly a drone, to sit on her butt and play war games, to sit in a cafeteria and eat slop, to sit and read.

She'd gotten overweight, is what. And it hadn't bothered her until she'd woken up in this nightmare. She'd never felt the urge to get up and move around until someone had frozen her stiff for a few hundred years. Now she wanted the body back that she remembered. Legs that worked. Arms that weren't sore just from brushing her teeth. Maybe it was silly of her, thinking she could go back, be who she once was, return to a world she remembered. Or maybe she was being impatient with her recovery. These things took time.

She made it back around to the drones, a full lap. That she

could complete a circuit of the room meant progress. It'd been a few weeks since her brother had woken her, and the routine of eating, exercising, and working on the drones was beginning to seem normal. The insane world she had been woken up to was starting to feel real. And that terrified her.

She lowered the batteries to the ground and took a series of deep breaths. Held them. The routine of military life had been similar. It had prepared her for this, was all that kept her from going crazy. Being cooped up was not new. Living in the middle of a desert wasteland where it wasn't safe to go out was not new. Being surrounded by men she ought to fear was not new. Stationed in Iraq during the Second Iranian War, Charlotte had grown accustomed to these things, to not leaving base, to not wanting to leave her bunk or a bathroom stall. She was used to this struggle to keep sane. It was mental as much as physical exercise that was required.

She showered in one of the stalls down from drone control, toweled off, sniffed each of her three sets of coveralls, and decided it was time to prod Donny into doing laundry again. She pulled on the least offensive of the three, hung the towel to dry from the foot of an upper bunk, and then made up her bed Air Force crisp. Donald had once lived in the conference room at the other end of the warehouse, but Charlotte had almost grown comfortable in the barracks with its ghosts. It felt like home.

Down the hall from the barracks stood a room of pilot stations. Most were covered in plastic sheets. There was a flat desk along the same wall that bore a mosaic of large monitors. It was here that the radio set was being pieced together. Her brother had gathered a jumble of spare parts one at a time from the lower storerooms. It might be decades or even centuries before anyone noticed they were gone.

Charlotte flicked on the light bulb she'd rigged over the table and powered up the set. She could already get quite a few stations. She tuned the knob until she heard static and left it there, waiting on voices. Until then, she pretended it was the sea rolling up onto a beach. Sometimes it was rain on a canopy of fat leaves. Or a crowd of people quietly talking in a dark theater. She pawed through the bin of parts Donald had amassed and looked for a better set of speakers, still needed a microphone or some way to transmit. She wished she was more mechanically inclined. All she knew how to do was plug things together. It was like assembling a rifle or a computer—she just joined anything that would mate and flicked on the power. It had only resulted in smoke the one time. What it mostly took was patience, which she didn't have a lot of. Or time, which she was drowning in.

Footsteps down the hall signaled breakfast. Charlotte turned down the volume and cleared room on the desk as Donny entered, a tray in his hands.

"Morning," she said, getting up to take the tray from him. Her legs felt wobbly from the workout. As her brother stepped into the spill of light from the dangling bulb, she noted his frown. "Everything okay?" she asked.

He shook his head. "We might have a problem."

Charlotte set the tray down. "What is it?"

"I ran into a guy I knew from my first shift. Was stuck on the lift with him. A handyman."

"That's not good." She lifted the dented metal cover from one of the plates. There was an electrical board and a coil of wire beneath. Also, the small driver she'd asked for.

"Your eggs are under the other one."

She set the lid aside and grabbed her fork. "Did he recognize you?"

"I couldn't tell. I kept my head down until he got off. But I knew him as well as I've known anyone in this place. It feels like yesterday that I borrowed tools from him, asked him to change a light for me. Who knows what it feels like for him. That might've been yesterday or a dozen years ago. Memory works weird in this place."

Charlotte took a bite of eggs. Donny had put a touch too much salt on them. She imagined him up there with the shaker, his hand trembling. "Even if he did recognize you," she said around a bite of food, "he might think you're on another shift as yourself. How many people know you as Thurman?"

Donald shook his head. "Not many. But still, this could come crashing down on us at any moment. I'm going to bring some food up from the pantry, more dry goods. Also, I went in and changed the clearance for your badge so you can access the lifts. And I double-checked that no one else could get down here. I'd hate for you to get trapped if something happened to me."

Charlotte moved her eggs around her plate. "I don't like thinking about that," she said.

"Another bit of a problem. The head of this silo is going off shift in a week, which will make things a little complicated. I'm relying on him to orient the next guy to my status. Things have been going a little too smoothly thus far—"

Charlotte laughed and took another bite of eggs. "Too smoothly," she said, shaking her head. "I'd hate to see rough. What's the latest on your favorite silo?"

"The IT head picked up today. Lukas."

Charlotte thought her brother sounded disappointed. "And?" she asked. "Learn anything new?"

"He managed to crack another server. It's more of the same data, everything about its residents, every job they've had, who they're related to, from birth to death. I don't understand how those machines go from that information to this ranked list. It seems like a bunch of noise, like there has to be something else."

He produced a sheet of folded paper, a new printout of the rankings of the silos. Charlotte cleared a space on the work-bench, and he smoothed the report.

"See? The order has changed again. But what determines that?"

She studied the report while she ate, and Donald grabbed one of his folders of notes. He spent a lot of time working in the conference room where he could spread things out and pace back and forth, but Charlotte preferred it when he sat at that drone station. He would sit there for hours sometimes, going through his notes while Charlotte worked on the radio, the two of them listening for chatter among the static.

"Silo Six is back on top again," she muttered. It was like reading the side of a cereal box while she ate, all those numbers that made little sense. One column was labeled *Facility,* which Donald said was what they used to call the silos. Beside each silo was a percentage like a massive dose of daily vitamins: *99.992%, 99.989%, 99.987%, 99.984%.* The last silo with a percentage read *99.974%.* Every silo below this was marked off or had *N/A* listed. Silos 40, 12, 17, and a handful of others were included in that latter category.

"You still think the one on top is the only one that gets to survive?" she asked.

"I do."

"Have you told these people you're talking to? Because they're way down the list."

He just looked at her and frowned.

"You haven't. You're just using them to help you figure all this out."

"I'm not using them. Hell, I saved that silo. I save it every day that I don't report what's going on over there."

"Okay," Charlotte said. She returned to her eggs.

"Besides, they probably figure they're using me. Hell, I think they get more out of our talks than I do. Lukas, the one who heads up their IT, he peppers me with all these questions about the way the world used to be—"

"And the mayor?" Charlotte turned and studied her brother closely. "What does she get out of it?"

"Juliette?" Donald thumbed through a folder. "She enjoys threatening me."

Charlotte laughed. "I would love to hear that."

"If you get that radio sorted, you might."

"And then you'll spend more time working down here? It would be good, you know. Lessen the risk of being recognized." She scraped her plate with her fork, not willing to admit the real reason she wanted him down there more was how empty the place felt when he was gone.

"Absolutely." Her brother rubbed his face, and Charlotte saw how tired he was. Her gaze fell back to the numbers while she ate.

"It makes it seem arbitrary, doesn't it?" she wondered aloud. "If these numbers mean what you think they mean. They're functionally equivalent."

"I doubt the people who planned all this look at it that way. All they need is one of them. It doesn't matter which one. It's like a bunch of spares in a box. You pluck one out, and all you care about is if it'll work. That's it. They just want to see everything is one hundred percent all the way down."

Charlotte couldn't believe that's what they had in mind. But Donny had shown her the Pact and enough of his notes to convince her. All the silos but one would be exterminated. Their own included.

"How long before the next drone is ready?" he asked.

Charlotte took a sip of juice. "Another day or two. Maybe three. I'm really going light with this one. Not even sure if it'll fly." The last two hadn't made it as far as the first. She was getting desperate.

"Okay." He rubbed his face again, his palms muffling his voice. "We're gonna have to decide before too long what we're gonna do. If we do nothing, this nightmare plays out for another two hundred years, and you and I won't last that long." He started to laugh, but it turned into a cough. Donald fished into his coveralls for his handkerchief, and Charlotte looked away. She studied the dark monitors while he had one of his fits.

She didn't want to admit this to him, but her inclination was to let it play out. It seemed as if a bunch of precision machines were in control of humanity's fate, and she tended to trust computers a lot more than her brother did. She had spent years flying drones that could fly themselves, that could make decisions on which targets to hit, could guide missiles to precise locations. She often felt less like a pilot and more like a jockey, a person on a beast that could race along on its own, that only needed someone there to occasionally take the reins or shout encouragement.

She glanced over the numbers on the report again. Hundredths of a percentage point would decide who lived and who died. And most would die. She and her brother would either be asleep or long dead by the time it happened. The numbers made this looming holocaust seem so damn . . . arbitrary.

Donald used the folder in his hand to point at the report. "Did you notice Eighteen moved up two spots?"

She had noticed. "You don't think you've become too . . . attached, do you?"

He looked away. "I have a history with this silo. That's all."

Charlotte hesitated. She didn't want to press further, but she couldn't help herself. "I didn't mean the silo," she said. "You seem . . . different each time you talk to her."

He took a deep breath, let it out slowly. "She was sent to clean," he said. "She's been outside."

For a moment Charlotte thought that was all he was going to say on the matter. As if this were enough, as if it explained everything. He was quiet a pause, his eyes flicking back and forth.

"No one is supposed to come back from that," he finally said. "I don't think the computers take this into account. Not just what she survived, but that Eighteen is hanging in there. By all accounts, they shouldn't be. If they make it through this . . . you wonder if they don't give us the best hope."

"*You* wonder," Charlotte said, correcting him. She waved the piece of paper. "There's no way we're smarter than these computers, brother."

Donald appeared sad. "We can be more compassionate than them," he said.

Charlotte fought the urge to argue. She wanted to point out that he cared about this silo because of the personal contact. If he knew the people behind any of the other silos—if he knew their stories—would he root for them? It would be cruel to suggest this, however true.

Donald coughed into his rag. He caught Charlotte staring at him, glanced at the bloodstained cloth, put it away.

"I'm scared," she told him.

Donald shook his head. "I'm not. I'm not afraid of this. I'm not afraid of dying."

"I know you're not. That's obvious, or you would see someone. But you have to be afraid of something."

"I am. Plenty. I'm afraid of being buried alive. I'm afraid of doing the wrong thing."

"Then do nothing," she insisted. She nearly begged him right then to put a stop to this madness, to their isolation. They could go back to sleep and leave this to the machines and to the God-awful plans of others. "Let's not do anything," she pleaded.

Her brother rose from his seat, squeezed her arm, and turned to leave. "That might be the worst thing," he quietly said.

12

THAT NIGHT, CHARLOTTE awoke from a nightmare of flying. She sat up in her cot, springs crying out like a nest of birds, and could still feel herself swooping down through the clouds, the wind on her face.

Always dreams of flying. Dreams of falling. Wingless dreams where she couldn't steer, couldn't pull up. A plummeting bomb zeroing in on a man with his family, a man turning at the last minute to shield his eyes against the noonday sun, a glimpse of Charlotte's father and mother and brother and herself before impact and loss of signal—

The nest of birds beneath her fell quiet. Charlotte untangled her fists from the sheets, which were damp with all that dreams wrung from terrified flesh. The room hung heavy and somber around her. She could feel the empty bunks all around, that sense that her fellow pilots had been summoned away in the night, leaving her alone. She rose and padded across the hall to the bathroom, feeling her way and sliding the switches up just a fraction to keep the lights dim. She understood sometimes why her brother had lived in the conference room at the other end of the warehouse. Shadows of un-people stalked those halls. She could feel herself pass through the ghosts of the sleeping.

She flushed and washed her hands. There was no going

back to her bunk, no chance of returning to sleep, not after that dream. Charlotte tugged on a pair of the red coveralls Donny had brought her, one of three colors, a little variety for her locked-up life. She couldn't remember what the blue or gold ones were for, but she remembered reactor red. The red coveralls had pouches and slots for tools. She wore them while working, and so they were rarely the cleanest. Loaded up, the coveralls weighed near on twenty pounds, and they rattled as she walked. She zipped up the front and made her way down the hallway.

Curiously, the lights in the warehouse were already on. It had to be in the middle of the night. She was good about turning them off, and nobody else had access to that level. Her mouth suddenly dry, she crept towards the nearby drones under their tarps, the sound of whispers leaking from the shadows.

Beyond the drones—near the tall shelves with boxes of spares and tools and emergency rations—a man knelt over the still form of another. The figure turned at the sound of her jangling tools.

"Donny?"

"Yeah?"

A flush of relief. The sprawling body beneath her brother wasn't a body at all. It was a puffy suit laid out with its arms and legs spread, an empty and lifeless form.

"What time is it?" she asked, rubbing her eyes.

"Late," he said. He dabbed his forehead with the back of his sleeve. "Or early, depending. Did I wake you?"

Charlotte watched as he shifted his body to block her view of the suit. Flopping one leg up, he began to fold the outfit in on itself. A pair of shears and a roll of silvery tape sat by his knees, a helmet, gloves, and a bottle like a dive tank nearby. A pair of boots as well. The fabric whispered as it moved; it was this that she had mistaken for voices.

"Hm? No, you didn't wake me. I got up to go to the bathroom. Thought I heard something."

It was a lie. She had come out to work on a drone in the middle of the night, anything to stay awake, to stay grounded. Donald nodded and pulled a rag from his breast pocket. He coughed into this before stuffing it away.

"What're you doing up?" she asked.

"I was just going through some supplies." Donny made a pile out of the suit parts. "Some things they needed above. Didn't want to risk sending someone else down for them." He glanced at his sister. "You want me to fetch you something hot for breakfast?"

Charlotte hugged herself and shook her head. She hated the reminder of being trapped on that level, needing him to get her things. "I'm getting used to the rations in the crates," she told him. "The coconut bars in the MREs are growing on me." She laughed. "I remember hating them during basic."

"I really don't mind getting you something," Donny said, obviously looking for an excuse to get out of there, some way to change topics. "And I should have the last of what we need for the radio soon. I put in a requisition for a microphone, which I can't find anywhere else. There's one in the comm room that's acting up, which I might steal if nothing else works."

Charlotte nodded. She watched her brother stuff the suit back into one of the large plastic containers. There was something he wasn't telling her. She recognized when he was holding something back. It was what big brothers did.

Crossing to the nearest drone, she pulled the tarp off and laid out a wrench set on the forward wing. She had always been clumsy with tools, but weeks of work on the drones, of persistence if not patience, and she was getting the hang of how they were put together. "So what do they need the suit for?" she asked, forcing herself to sound nonchalant.

"I think it's something to do with the reactor." He rubbed the back of his neck and frowned. Charlotte allowed the lie to echo a bit. She wanted her brother to hear it.

Opening the skin of the drone's wing, Charlotte remembered coming home from basic training with new muscles and weeks of competitive fierceness forged among a squad of men. This was before she'd let herself go while on deployment. Back then, she'd been a wiry and fit teenager, her brother off at graduate school, and his first teasing remark about her new physique had landed him on the sofa, his arm pinned behind his back, laughing and teasing her further.

Laughing, that is, until a sofa cushion had been pressed to the side of his face, and Donny had squealed like a stuck pig. Fun and games had turned into something serious and scary, her brother's fear of being buried alive awakening something primal in him, something she never teased him for and never wanted to see again.

Now she watched as he sealed the bin with the suit inside and slid it back under a shelf. It wasn't needed elsewhere in the silo, she knew. Donald fumbled for his rag, and his coughing resumed. She pretended to be fixated on the drone while he had his fit. Donny didn't want to talk about the suit or the problem with his lungs, and she didn't blame him. Her brother was dying. Charlotte knew her brother was dying, could see him like she saw him in her dreams, turning at the last minute to shield his eyes against the noonday sun. She saw him the way she saw every man in that last instant of their lives. There was Donny's beautiful face on her screen, watching the inevitable fall from the sky.

He was dying, which is why he wanted to stockpile food for her and make sure she could leave. It was why he wanted to make sure she had a radio, so she would have someone to talk to. Her brother was dying, and he didn't want to be buried, didn't want to die down there in that pit in the ground where he couldn't breathe.

Charlotte knew damn well what the suit was for.

Silo 18

13

AN EMPTY CLEANING suit lay spread across the workbench, one of its arms draped over the edge, elbow bent at an
unnatural angle. The unblinking visor of the detached helmet
gazed silently up at the ceiling. The small screen inside the helmet had been removed to leave a clear plastic window out on
the real world. Juliette leaned over the suit, occasional drops of
sweat smacking its surface, as she tightened the hex screws that
held the lower collar onto the fabric. She remembered the last
time she'd built a suit like this.

Nelson, the young IT tech in charge of the cleaning lab, labored at an identical bench on the other side of the workshop.
Juliette had selected him as her assistant for this project. He
was familiar with the suits, young, and didn't appear to be
against her. Not that the first two criteria mattered.

"The next item we need to discuss is the population report," Marsha said. The young assistant—an assistant Juliette
had never asked for—juggled a dozen folders until she found
the right one. Recycled paper lay strewn across the neighboring workbench, turning an area for building things into a
lowly desk. Juliette glanced up and watched as Marsha shuffled through a folder. Her assistant was a slight girl just out of
her teens, graced with rosy cheeks and dark hair in tight coils.

Marsha had been the assistant to the last two mayors, a short but tumultuous span of time. Like the gold ID card and the apartment on level six, she had come with the job.

"Here it is," Marsha said. She bit her lip and scanned the report, and Juliette saw that it was printed on one side only. The amount of paper her office went through and repulped could afford to feed an apartment level for a year. Lukas had once joked that it was to keep the recyclers in business. The chance he was right had kept her from laughing.

"Can you hand me those gaskets?" Juliette asked, pointing to Marsha's side of the workbench.

The young girl pointed to a bin of lock washers. And then an assortment of cotter pins. Finally, her hand drifted over the gaskets. Juliette nodded. "Thanks."

"So, we're under five thousand residents for the first time in thirty years," Marsha said, returning to her report. "We've had a lot of . . . passings." Juliette could feel Marsha glance up at her, even as she concentrated on seating the gasket into the collar. "The lottery committee is calling for an official count, just so we can get a sense of—"

"The lottery committee would perform a census every week if they could." Juliette rubbed oil onto the gasket with her finger before seating the other side of the collar.

Marsha laughed politely. "Yes, well, they want to hold another lottery soon. They asked for another two hundred numbers."

"Numbers," Juliette grumbled. Sometimes she thought that was all Lukas's computers were good for, a bunch of tall machines to pull numbers from their whirring butts. "Did you tell them my idea about an amnesty? They do know we're about to double our space, right?"

Marsha shifted uncomfortably. "I told them," she said. "And I told them about the extra space. I don't think they took it so well."

Across the workshop, Nelson looked up from the suit he was working on. It was just the three of them in the old lab where people had once been outfitted to die. Now they were working on something else, a different reason to send people outside.

"Well, what did the committee say?" Juliette asked. "They do know that when we reach this other silo, I'm going to need people to come with me and get it up and running again. The population here is going to dip."

Nelson bent back to his work. Marsha closed the folder on the population report and looked at her feet.

"What did they say to my idea of suspending the lottery?"

"They didn't say anything," Marsha said. She glanced up, and the overhead lights caught the wet film across her eyes. "I don't think many of them believe in your other silo."

Juliette laughed and shook her head. Her hand was trembling as she set the last lock screw into the collar. "It doesn't really matter what the committee believes, does it?" Though she knew this was true of her as well. It was true of anyone. The world out there was the way it was no matter how much doubt or hope or hate a person breathed into it. "The dig is underway. They're clearing three hundred feet a day. I suppose the lottery committee will just have to make the trip down to see for themselves. You should tell them that. Tell them to go see."

Marsha frowned and made a note. "The next thing on the agenda..." She grabbed her ledger. "There's been a rash of complaints about—"

There was a knock at the door. Juliette turned, and Lukas entered the Suit Lab, smiling. He waved at Nelson, who saluted back with a 3/8 wrench. Lukas seemed unsurprised to see Marsha there. He clasped her shoulder. "You should just move that big wooden desk of hers down here," he joked. "You've got the porting budget for it."

Marsha smiled and tugged at one of her dark springs. She looked around the lab. "I really should," she said.

Juliette watched her young assistant blush in Lukas's presence and laughed to herself. The helmet locked into the collar with a neat click. Juliette tested the release mechanism.

"Do you mind if I borrow the mayor?" Lukas asked.

"No, I don't mind," Marsha said.

"I do." Juliette studied one of the suit's sleeves. "We're way behind schedule."

Lukas frowned. "There is no schedule. You set the schedule. And besides, have you even gotten permission for this?" He stood beside Marsha and crossed his arms. "Have you even told your assistant what you're planning?"

Juliette glanced up guiltily. "Not yet."

"Why? What're you doing?" Marsha lowered her ledger and studied the suits for what seemed the first time.

Juliette ignored her. She glared at Lukas. "I'm behind schedule because I want to get this done before they complete the dig. They've been on a tear. Hit some soft soil. I'd really like to be down there when they punch through."

"And I'd like for you to be at that meeting today, which you're going to miss if you don't get a move on."

"I'm not going," Juliette said.

Lukas shot a look at Nelson, who set down his wrench, gathered Marsha, and slid out the door. Juliette watched them leave and realized her young Lukas had more authority than she gave him credit for.

"It's the monthly town hall," Lukas said. "The first since your election. I told Judge Picken you'd be there. Jules, you've gotta play mayor or you won't *be* one for much longer —"

"Fine." She raised her hands. "I'm not mayor. I so decree it." She scrawled the air with a driver. "Signed and stamped."

"Not fine. What do you think the next person will make of all this?" He waved his hand at the workbenches. "You think you'll be able to play these games? This room will go right back to what it was built for in the first place."

Juliette bit down the urge to snap at him, to tell him these weren't games she was playing, that it was something far worse.

Lukas looked away from whatever face she was making. His eyes settled on the stack of books piled up by the cot she had brought in. She slept there sometimes when the two of them were disagreeing or when she just needed a place to be alone. Not that she'd slept much recently. She rubbed her eyes and tried to remember the last time she'd gotten four hours in a row. Her nights were spent welding in the airlock. Her days were spent in the Suit Lab or down behind the comm hub. She didn't really sleep anymore—she just passed out here and there.

"We should keep those locked up," Lukas said, indicating the books. "Shouldn't keep them out."

"No one would believe them if they opened them," Juliette said.

"For the paper."

She nodded. He was right. She saw information; others would see money. "I'll take them back down," she promised, and the anger drained away like oil from a cracked casing. She thought of Elise, who had told her over the radio of a book she was making, a single book from all her favorite pages. Juliette needed a book like that. Except where Elise's was probably full of pretty fish and bright birds, Juliette's would catalog darker things. Things in the hearts of men.

Lukas took a step closer. He rested a hand on her arm. "This meeting—"

"I hear they're thinking about a revote," Juliette said, cutting him off. She wiped a loose strand of hair off her face, tucked it behind her ear. "I'm not going to be mayor for long anyway. Which is why I need to get this done. By the time everyone votes again, it shouldn't matter."

"Why? Because you'll be the mayor of a different silo by then? Is that your plan?"

Juliette rested a hand on the domed helmet. "No. Because I'll have my answers by then. Because people will see by then. They'll believe me."

Lukas crossed his arms. He took a deep breath. "I've got to get down to the servers," he said. "If no one's there to answer the call, the lights eventually start flashing in the offices and everyone asks what the hell they're for."

Juliette nodded. She'd seen it for herself. She also knew that Lukas liked the long talks behind the server as much as she did. Except that he was better at it. All her talks led to arguments. He was good at smoothing things over, figuring things out.

"Please tell me you'll go to the meeting, Jules. Promise me you'll go."

She scanned the suit on the other table to see how far along Nelson was. They'd need one more suit for the extra person in the second airlock. If she worked through the night and all day tomorrow—

"For me," he pleaded.

"I'll go."

"Thank you." Lukas glanced at the old clock on the wall, its red arms visible behind hazed plastic. "I'll see you for dinner?"

"Sure."

He leaned forward and kissed her on the cheek. When he turned to go, Juliette began arranging her tools on the leather pad, setting them aside for later. She picked up a clean cloth and wiped her hands. "Oh, and Luke?"

"Yeah?" He paused at the door.

"Tell that fucker I said hello."

14

LUKAS LEFT THE Suit Lab and headed toward the server room on the other side of thirty-four. He passed a tech room that sat empty. The men and women who used to work in there now took up slack in the Down Deep and in Supply where mechanics and workers had lost their lives. People from IT sent to replace those they'd killed.

Juliette's friend Shirly had been left in charge of the aftermath down in Mechanical. She was forever complaining to his office about skeleton shifts, and then complaining again when Lukas reassigned anyone to help. What did she want from him? People, he supposed. Just not his people.

A handful of techs and security personnel standing outside the break room fell silent as Lukas approached. He waved, and hands went up politely. "Sir," someone said, which made him cringe. The chatter resumed only after he rounded the corner, and Lukas remembered being in on conversations like that as his former boss had stormed past.

Bernard. Lukas used to think he understood what it meant to be in charge. You did what you wanted. Decisions were arbitrary. You were cruel for the sake of being cruel. And now he found himself agreeing to worse things than he had ever imagined. Now he knew about a world of such horrors, that maybe men of his ilk weren't suited to lead. It wasn't a thing he could ever say out loud, but perhaps a revote would be for the best. Juliette would make a great lab tech there in IT. Soldering and welding weren't all that different, just matters of scale. And then he tried to imagine her building a suit for someone to clean in, or her sitting idly by while they took orders from another silo on how many births were allowed that week.

It was more likely that a new mayor would mean time apart. Or that he would have to file for a transfer to Mechanical and learn to turn a wrench. From head of IT to a third-shift greaser. Lukas laughed. He coded open the server room door and thought there might be something romantic about that, giving up his job and life to be with her. Maybe something more romantic than going up at night to hunt for stars. He would have to get used to Juliette bossing him around, but that wouldn't be a stretch. Enough degreaser, and her old room down there could be livable. As he wove his way through the servers, he thought of how he had lived in far worse, right there beneath his feet. It was being together that mattered.

The lights overhead weren't yet blinking. He was early or the man named Donald was late. Lukas made his way toward the far wall, passing by several servers with their sides off and wires streaming out. With Donald's help, he was figuring out how to fully access the machines, see what was on them. Nothing exciting yet, but he was making progress.

He stopped at the comm server, which had been his home within a home some lifetime ago. Now it was a different sort of conversation he fell into behind that server. It was a different sort of person on the other end of the line.

One of the rickety wooden chairs from below had been brought up. Lukas remembered climbing the ladder and pushing it ahead of him, Juliette yelling at him that they should lower a rope, the two of them arguing like young porters. Beside the chair, a stack of book tins made a side table of sorts. One of the Legacy books was splayed out on top. Lukas made himself comfortable and picked up the book. He had marked pages by creasing the corners. There were small dots in the margins where he had questions. He flipped through the book and scanned the material while he waited on the call.

What once had been boring about the books was now all he cared about. During his imprisonment—his Rite—he had been forced to read the parts of the Order on human behavior. Now he pored over these sections. And Donald, the voice on the other end of the line, had him fairly convinced that these were more than mere stories, these Robbers Cave boys and Milgrams and Skinners. Some of these things had truly happened.

He had graduated from these stories to find even more lessons in the Legacy books. It was the history of the old world that now commanded his attention. Episodic uprisings had occurred over thousands of years. He and Jules argued over whether or not there could be an end to such cyclic violence. The books suggested such hope was folly. And then Lukas had discovered an entire chapter on the dangers of an uprising's aftermath, the very situation in which they now found themselves. He read about men with strange names—Cromwell, Napoleon, Castro, Lenin—who fought to liberate a people and then enslaved them into something even worse.

They were legends, Juliette insisted. Myths. Like the ghouls parents use to make their children behave. She saw those chapters to mean that tearing a world down was a simple affair; the gravity of human nature tugged willingly. It was the building up afterward that proved complex. It was what to replace injustice with that very few gave thought to. Always with the tearing down, she said, as if the scraps and ashes could be pieced back together.

Lukas disagreed. He thought, and Donald said, that these stories were real. Yes, the revolutions were painful. There would always be a period when things were worse. But eventually, they get better. People learn from their mistakes. This is what he had tried to convince her of one night after a call from Donald had kept them up through the dim time. Jules, of course, had to get in the last word. She had taken him up to the cafeteria and had pointed to the glow over the horizon, to the lifeless hills, to the rare glint of sunlight on decrepit towers. "Here is your world made better," she had told him. "Here is man well learned from his mistakes."

Always with the last word, though Lukas had more to say. "Maybe this is the bad time that comes *before,*" he had whispered into his coffee. And Juliette, for her part, had pretended not to hear.

The pages beneath Lukas's fingers pulsed red. He glanced up at the lights overhead, now flashing with the incoming call. There was a buzzing from the comm server, a blinking indicator over the very first slot. He gathered the headset and untangled the cord, slotted it into the receiver.

"Hello?" he said.

"Lukas." The machine removed all intonation from the voice, all emotion. Except for disappointment. That it was not Juliette who answered elicited a letdown that could be felt if not quite heard. Or perhaps it was all in Lukas's head.

"Just me," he said.

"Very well. Just so you know, I have pressing matters here. Our time is short."

"Okay." Lukas found his place in the book. He skipped down to where they'd previously left off. These talks reminded him of his studies with Bernard, except now he had graduated from the Order to the Legacy. And Donald was swifter than Bernard, more open with his answers. "So . . . I wanted to ask you something about this Rousseau guy—"

"Before we do," Donald said, "I need to implore you again to stop with the digging."

Lukas closed the book on his finger, marking his place. He was glad Juliette had agreed to attend the Town Hall. She got animated whenever this topic came up. Because of an old threat she'd made, Donald seemed to think they were digging toward him, and she made Lukas vow to leave the lie alone. She didn't want them finding out about her friends in 17 or her plans to rescue them. Lukas found the ruse uncomfortable. Where Juliette distrusted this man—who had warned them both that their home could be shut down at any time through mysterious means—Lukas saw someone trying to help them at some cost to himself. Jules thought Donald was scared for his own life. Lukas thought Donald was frightened for *them*.

"I'm afraid that the digging will have to continue," Lukas said. He nearly blurted out: *She won't stop,* but best for there to be some sense of solidarity.

"Well, my people can pick up the vibrations. They know something is happening."

"Can you tell them we're having trouble with our generator? That it's misaligned again?"

There was a disappointed sigh that the computers couldn't touch. "They're smarter than that. What I've done is ordered them not to waste their time looking into it, which is all I can do. I'm telling you, nothing good can come of this."

"Then why are you helping us? Why stick your neck out? Because that's what it seems like you're doing."

"My job is to see that you don't die."

Lukas studied the inside of the server tower, the winking lights, the wires, the boards. "Yeah, but these conversations, going through these books with me, calling every single day like clockwork, why do you do it? I mean . . . what is it that you get out of these conversations?"

There was a pause on the other end of the line, a rare lack of surety from the steady voice of their supposed benefactor.

"It's because . . . I get to help you remember."

"And that's important?"

"Yes. It's important. It is to me. I know what it feels like to forget."

"Is that why these books are here?"

Another pause. Lukas felt that he was stumbling accidentally toward some truth. He would have to remember what was being said and tell Juliette later.

"They are there so that whoever inherits the world—whoever is chosen—will know . . ."

"Know what?" Lukas asked desperately. He feared he was going to lose him. Donald had trod near to this in prior conversations, but had always pulled away.

"To know how to set things right," Donald said. "Look, our time is up. I need to go."

"What did you mean about inheriting the world?"

"Next time. I need to go. Stay safe."

"Yeah," Lukas said. "You too—"

But his headphone had already clicked. The man who somehow knew so much about the old world had signed off.

15

JULIETTE HAD NEVER attended a Town Hall before. Like sows giving birth, she knew such things took place, but had never felt the urge to witness the spectacle. Her first time would be while as mayor, and she hoped it would be her last.

She joined Judge Picken and Sheriff Billings on the raised platform while residents spilled from the hallway and found their seats. The platform they'd put her on reminded her of the stage in the bazaar, and Juliette remembered her father comparing these meetings to plays. She never took him to mean that as a compliment.

"I don't know any of my lines," she whispered cryptically to Peter Billings.

The two of them sat close enough that their shoulders touched. "You'll do fine," Peter said. He smiled at a young woman in the front row, who wiggled her fingers back at him, and Juliette saw that the young sheriff had met someone. Life was continuing apace.

She tried to relax. She studied the crowd. A lot of unfamiliar faces out there. A few she recognized. Three doors led in from the hallway. Two of the doors opened on aisles that sliced through the rows of ancient benches. The third aisle was pressed against the wall. They divided the room into thirds,

much as less-well-defined boundaries partitioned the silo. Juliette didn't have to be told these things. The people making
their way inside made it obvious.

The Up Top benches in the center of the room were already
packed, and more people stood behind the benches at the back
of the hall, people she recognized from IT and from the cafeteria. The Mids benches off to one side were half full. Juliette
noticed most of these residents sat close to the aisle, as near to
the center as possible. Farmers in green. Hydroponic plumbers.
People with dreams. The other side of the room was nearly bare.
This was for the Down Deep. An elderly couple sat together in
the front row of this section, holding hands. Juliette recognized
the man, a bootmaker. They had come a long way. Juliette kept
waiting for more residents of the Deep to show, but it was too
much of a hike. And now she recalled how distant these meetings seemed while working in the depths of the silo. Often, she
and her friends only heard what was being discussed and what
rules were being passed after it had already happened. Not only
was it a far climb, but most of them were too busy surviving the
day-to-day to trudge anywhere for a discussion on tomorrows.

When the flow of residents became a trickle, Judge Picken
rose to begin the meeting. Juliette prepared to be bored half
to death by the proceedings. A quick talk, an introduction, and
then they would listen to what ailed the people. Promise to
make it better. Get right back to doing the same things.

What she needed to do was get back to work. There was so
much that needed accomplishing up at the airlock and down in
the Suit Lab. The last thing she wanted to do was listen to minor
grievances, a call for a revote, or anyone bitching about her digging. She suspected what was serious to others would feel minor to her. There was something about being sent to one's death
and surviving a baptism of fire upon one's return that pushed
most squabblings into the deepest recesses of one's mind.

Picken banged his gavel and called the meeting to order. He welcomed everyone and ran down the prepared docket. Juliette squirmed on her bench. She gazed out into the crowd and saw that the vast majority were gazing right back at her rather than watching the judge. She only caught the end of Picken's last sentence because of her name: "—hear from your mayor, Juliette Nichols."

He turned and waved her up to the podium. Peter patted her on the knee for encouragement. As she walked to the podium, the metal decking creaked beneath her boots where it wasn't screwed down tight. That was the only sound. And then someone in the audience coughed. And there was a rustling among the benches as bodies lurched back into motion. Juliette gripped the podium and marveled at the mix of colors facing her, the blues and whites and reds and browns and greens. Scowls above them, she saw. Angry people from all walks of life. She cleared her throat and realized how unprepared she was. She had hoped to say a few words, to thank the people for their concerns, to assure them that she was working tirelessly to forge a new and better life for them. Just give her a chance, she wanted to say.

"Thank you—" she began, and Judge Picken tugged on her arm and pointed to the microphone attached to the podium. Someone in the back shouted that they couldn't hear. Juliette swiveled the microphone closer and saw that the faces in the crowd were the same as those along the stairwell. They were wary of her. Awe, or something like it, had eroded into suspicion.

"I'm here today to listen to your questions. Your concerns," she said, the loudness of her voice startling her. "Before I do, I'd like to say a few things about what we hope to accomplish this year—"

"Did you let poison in here?" someone yelled from the back.

"Excuse me?" Juliette asked. She cleared her throat.

A lady stood up, a baby in her arms. "My child's had a fever ever since you returned!"

"Are the other silos real?" someone shouted.

"What was it like out there?"

A man bolted up from the Mids benches, his face ruddy with rage. "What're you doin' down there that's causing so much noise—?"

A dozen others stood and began shouting as well. Their questions and complaints forged a single noise, an engine of anger. The packed center section spilled outward into the aisles as people needed room to point and wave for attention. Juliette saw her father, standing in the very back, noticeable for his placid demeanor, his worried frown.

"One at a time—" Juliette said. She held her palms out. The crowd lurched forward, and then a shot rang out.

Juliette flinched.

There was another loud bang right beside her, and the gavel was no longer limp in Judge Picken's hand. The wooden disc on the podium leapt and spun as he pounded it back into place, over and over. Deputy Hoyle lurched out of a trance by the door and swam through the crowds in the aisle, urging everyone back into their seats and to hold their tongues. Peter Billings was up from the bench yelling for everyone to be calm as well. Eventually, a tense silence fell over the crowd. But something was whirring in these people. It was like a motor not yet running but one that wanted to, an electrical buzz just beneath the surface, humming and holding back. Juliette chose her words carefully.

"I can't tell you what it's like out there—"

"Can't or won't?" someone asked. This person was silenced by a glare from Deputy Hoyle, who ranged the aisle. Juliette took a deep breath.

"I can't tell you because we don't know." She raised her hands to hold the crowd still a moment. "Everything we've been told about the world beyond our walls has been a lie, a fabrication—"

"How do we know *you're* not the one lying?"

She sought the voice among the crowd. "Because I'm the one admitting that we don't know a damned thing. I'm the one who came here today to tell you that we should go out and see for ourselves. With fresh eyes. With real curiosity. I'm proposing that we do what has never been done, and that's to go and take a sample, to bring back a taste of the air out there and see what's wrong with the world—"

Outbursts from the back drowned out the rest of her sentence. People were up out of their seats again, even as others reached to restrain them. Some were curious now. Some were even more outraged. The gavel barked, and Hoyle loosed his baton and waved it at the front row. But the crowd was beyond calming. Peter stepped forward, a hand on the butt of his gun.

Juliette backed away from the podium. There was a squeal from the speakers as Judge Picken knocked the microphone with his arm. The wooden puck was lost, leaving him to bang on the podium itself, which Juliette saw was marked with half-moon frowns and smiles from past attempts at restoring calm.

Deputy Hoyle had to back up against the stage as the crowd lurched forward, many of them with questions still, most with unbridled fury. Spittle foamed on quivering lips. Juliette heard more accusations, saw the lady with her baby who blamed Juliette for some sickness. Marsha ran to the back of the stage and threw open a metal door painted to look like real wood—and Peter waved Juliette inside, back to the Judge's chambers. She didn't want to go. She wanted to calm these people down, to tell them she meant well, that she could fix this if they would just let her try. But she was being dragged back, past a cloakroom of dark robes that hung like shadows, steered down a hall where pictures of past judges hung askew, to an old metal desk painted to resemble the door.

The shouts were sealed off behind them. The door banging with fists for a moment, Peter cursing. Juliette collapsed into an old leather chair repaired with tape and held her face in her hands. Their anger was her anger. She could feel herself directing it toward Peter and Lukas, who had made her mayor. She could feel herself directing it toward Lukas for begging her to leave the digging and come up top, for making her come to this meeting. As if this rabble could be appeased.

A burst of noise filtered down the hall as the door opened for a moment. Juliette expected Judge Picken to join them. She was surprised to see her father instead.

"Dad."

She rose from the old chair and crossed the room to greet him. Her father wrapped his arms around her, and Juliette found that place in the center of his chest where she could remember finding comfort as a child.

"I heard you might be here," her father whispered.

Juliette didn't say anything. As old as she felt, the years melted away to have him there, to have his arms around her.

"I also heard what you're planning, and I don't want you to go."

Juliette stepped back to study her father. Peter excused himself. The noise from outside wasn't as loud this time when the door cracked, and Juliette realized Judge Picken had allowed her father passage, was out there calming the crowd. Her dad had seen those people react to her, had heard what people had said. She fought back a sudden welling of tears.

"They didn't give me a chance to explain—" she started, swiping at her eyes. "Dad, there are other worlds out there like our own. It's crazy to sit here, fighting amongst ourselves, when there are other worlds—"

"I'm not talking about the digging," her father said. "I heard what you're planning up top."

"You heard . . ." She wiped her eyes again. "Lukas—" she muttered.

"It wasn't Lukas. That technician, Nelson, came by for a check-up, asked me if I was going to be on standby in case anything went wrong. I had to pretend to know what he was talking about. I assume you were going to announce your plans out there just now?" He glanced toward the cloakroom.

"We need to know what's out there," Juliette said. "Dad, they haven't been trying to make it better. We don't know the first thing—"

"Then let the next cleaner see. Let them sample when they're sent out. Not you."

She shook her head. "There won't be anymore cleaning, Dad. Not while I'm mayor. I won't send anyone out there."

He placed a hand on her arm. "And I won't let my daughter go."

She pulled away from him. "I'm sorry," she said. "I have to. I'm taking every precaution. I promise."

Her father's face hardened. He turned his hand over and gazed at his palm.

"We could use your help," she said, hoping to bridge any new rift she feared she was creating. "Nelson's right. It would be nice to have a doctor on the team."

"I don't want any part in this," he said. "Look what happened to you the last time." He glanced at her neck, where the suit's metal collar had left a hook of a scar.

"That was the fire," Juliette told him, adjusting her coveralls.

"And the next time it'll be something else."

They studied one another in that chamber where people were quietly judged, and Juliette felt a familiar temptation to run away from conflict. It was countered by a new desire to bury her face in her father's chest and sob in a way that women her age weren't allowed, that mechanics never could.

"I don't want to lose you again," she told her dad. "You're the only family I've got left. Please support me in this."

It was difficult to say. Vulnerable and honest. A part of Lukas now lived inside of her—this was something he had imparted.

Juliette waited for the reaction and saw her father's face relax. It may have been her imagination, but she thought he moved a step closer, let down his guard.

"I'll give you a check-up before and after," he said.

"Thank you. Oh, speaking of a check-up, there's something else I wanted to ask you about." She worked the long sleeve of her coveralls up her forearm and studied the white marks along her wrist. "Have you ever heard of scars going away with time? Lukas thought—" She looked up at her father. "Do they ever go away?"

Her father took a deep breath and held it awhile. His gaze drifted over her shoulder and far away.

"No," he said. "Not scars. Not even with time."

Silo 1

16

CAPTAIN BREVARD WAS nearly through his seventh shift. Only three more to go. Three more shifts of sitting behind security gates reading the same handful of novels over and over until the yellowed pages gave up and fell out. Three more shifts of whipping his deputies at table tennis—a new deputy on each shift—and telling them that it'd been forever since he'd last played. Three more shifts of the same old food and the same old movies and the same old everything else bland that greeted him when he woke. Three more. He could make it.

Silo 1's Security chief now counted down shifts much as he had once counted down years to retirement. *Let them be uneventful,* was his mantra. The blandness was good. Vanilla was the taste of passing time. Such was his thought as he stood before an open cryopod splattered with dried blood, a foul taste very un-vanilla-like in his mouth.

A pop of blinding light erupted from Deputy Stevens's camera as the young man took another shot of the pod's interior. The body had been removed hours ago. A med tech had been servicing a neighboring pod when he noticed a smear of blood on the lid of this one. He had cleaned half the smear away before he realized what it was. Brevard now studied the tracks that the med tech's cleaning rag had left behind. He took another bitter sip of coffee.

His mug had lost its steam. It was the cold air in that warehouse of bodies. Brevard hated it down there. He hated waking up naked in that place, hated being brought back down and put to sleep, hated what the room did to his coffee. He took another sip. Three shifts left, and then retirement, whatever that meant. Nobody thought along that far. Only to their next shift.

Stevens lowered his camera and nodded toward the exit. "Darcy's back, sir."

The two officers watched as Darcy, the night guard, crossed the hall of cryopods. Darcy had been first on the scene early that morning, had woken Deputy Stevens, who had woken his superior. Darcy had then refused to slag off and get some sleep as ordered. He had instead accompanied the body up to Medical and had volunteered to wait on test results while the other men went over the crime scene. Darcy now waved a piece of paper a bit too enthusiastically as he headed their way.

"I can't stand this guy," Stevens whispered to his chief.

Brevard took a diplomatic sip of his coffee and watched his night guard approach. Darcy was young—late twenties, early thirties—with blond hair and a permanent, goofy grin. Just the sort of inexperienced person police forces loved to place on night shifts when all the bad shit went down. It wasn't logical, but it was tradition. Experience won you deep sleep for when the crazies were out.

"You won't believe what I've got," Darcy said, twenty paces away and more than a touch overeager.

"You've got a match," Brevard said dryly. "The blood on the lid goes with the pod." He nearly added that what Darcy most certainly *didn't* have was a hot cup of coffee for him or Stevens.

"That's part of it," Darcy said, appearing vexed. "How'd you know?" He took a few deep breaths and handed over the report.

"Because matches are exciting," Brevard said, accepting the sheet. "You wave a match in the air like you've got something to say. Lawyers and jury members get excited over a match." *And rookies,* he wanted to add. He wasn't sure what Darcy did before orientation, but it wasn't police work. Glancing down at the report, Brevard saw a standard DNA match, a series of bars lined up with one another, lines drawn between the bars where they were identical. And these two were identical, the DNA on file for the pod and the blood sample taken from the lid.

"Well, there's more," Darcy said. The night guard took another deep breath. He had obviously run down the hall from the lift. "Lots more."

"We think we've got it pieced together," Stevens said with confidence. He nodded toward the open cryopod. "It's pretty clear that a murder took place here. It started—"

"Not a murder," Darcy interjected.

"Give the deputy a chance," Brevard said, lifting his mug. "He's been looking at this for hours."

Darcy started to say something but caught himself. He rubbed under his eyes, seemed exhausted, but nodded.

"Right," Stevens said. He pointed his camera at the cryopod. "Blood on the lid means the struggle began out here. The man we found inside must've been subdued by our killer after a fight, that's how his blood got on the lid. And then he was tossed inside his own cryopod. His hands were bound, I'm assuming at gunpoint, because I didn't note any marks around the wrists, no other sign of struggle. He was shot once in the chest." Stevens pointed to the streaks and spots of blood on the inside of the lid. "We've got splatter here, indicating the victim was sitting up. But the way it ran suggests the lid was shut immediately after. And the coloration tells me that this likely happened on our shift, certainly within the past month."

Brevard watched Darcy's face the entire time, saw how it

scrunched up in disagreement. The kid thought he knew better than the deputy.

"What else?" Brevard asked Stevens, prodding his second-in-command along further.

"Oh, yes. After murdering the victim, our perp inserted an IV and a catheter to keep the body from decomposing, so we're looking at someone with medical training. He might, of course, still be on this shift. Which is why we thought it best to discuss this down here and not around the med team. We'll want to question them one at a time."

Brevard nodded and took a sip of coffee. He waited on the night guard's reaction.

"It wasn't murder," Darcy said, exasperated. "Do you guys want to hear what else I have? For starters, the blood on the lid matches the database entry for the *pod,* just like you said, but it doesn't match the victim. The guy inside is someone else."

Brevard nearly spat out his coffee. He wiped his moustache with his hand. "What?" he asked, not sure that he'd heard correctly.

"The blood on the outside was mixed with saliva. It came from a second person. Doc said it was probably a cough, maybe a chest wound. So our suspect is likely injured."

"Wait. So who's the guy we found in the pod?" Stevens asked.

"They're not sure. They ran his blood, but it seems his records have been tampered with. The guy this pod is registered to, he shouldn't be on the executive wing at all. Should've been in Deep Freeze. And the blood from the *inside* of the lid matches a partial record from the executive files, which would place him in here somewhere—"

"Partial record?" Brevard asked.

Darcy shrugged. "The files are all kinds of fouled up. According to Doctor Whitmore."

"Ah," Deputy Stevens said, snapping his fingers. "I've got it. I know what happened here." He pointed his camera at the pod. "There's a struggle out here, okay? A guy who doesn't want to be put under. He manages to break free, knows how to hack the—"

"Hold up," Brevard said, raising a hand. He could see on Darcy's face that there was more. "Why do you keep insisting this wasn't a murder? We've got a gunshot wound, blood splatter, a closed lid, no weapon, a man with his hands bound, and blood on the lid of this pod, whoever the hell it's registered to. Everything about this screams murder."

"That's what I've been trying to tell you," Darcy said. "It wasn't murder because the guy was plugged in. He was plugged in the entire time, even before he was shot. And the pod was still on and running. This Troy fellow—or whoever it is that we pulled out of there—he's still alive."

17

THE THREE MEN left the pod behind and headed for the medical wing and the operating room. Brevard's mind raced. He didn't need this crap on one of his shifts. This was not vanilla. He imagined the reports he would have to write after this, how much fun it would be to brief the next captain.

"Do you think we should get the Shepherd involved?" Stevens asked, referring to the head executive up on the administration wing, a man who kept mostly to himself.

Brevard scoffed. He coded open the Deep Freeze door and led the men out into the hallway. "I think this is a little below his pay grade, don't you? Shepherd has entire silos to worry about. You can see how it wears on him, how he keeps himself locked up. It's our job to handle cases like this. Even murder."

"You're right," Stevens said.

Darcy, still winded, labored to keep up.

They rode the lift up two levels. Brevard thought about how the body with the gun wound had felt as he had inspected it. The man had been as cold as a stiff in a morgue, but then weren't they all when they first woke up? He thought about all the damage the freezing and thawing produced, how the machines in their blood were supposed to keep them patched together, cell by cell. What if those little machines could do the same for a gunshot wound?

The lift opened on sixty-eight. Brevard could hear voices from the OR. It was difficult to let go of the theories that'd been percolating between him and Stevens for the past hour. It was hard to let go and adapt to everything Darcy had told them. The idea of records being tampered with made this a much more complex problem. Only three shifts to go, and now all this. But if the victim was indeed alive, catching their perp was all but guaranteed. If he was in any condition to talk, he could ID the man who shot him.

The doctor and one of his assistants were in the waiting room outside the little-used OR. Their gloves were off, the doctor's gray hair wild and unkempt as if he'd been running his fingers through it. Both men appeared exhausted. Brevard glanced through the observation window and saw the same man they'd pulled from the pod. He was lying as if asleep, his color completely different, tubes and wires snaking inside a pale blue paper gown.

"I hear we've had an extraordinary turnaround," Brevard said. He crossed to the sink and dumped his coffee down the drain, looked around for a fresh pot and didn't see one. He would've taken on another shift right then for a hot mug, a pack of smokes, and permission to burn them.

The doctor patted his assistant on the arm and gave him instructions. The young man nodded and fished in his pocket for a pair of gloves before backing his way through the door and into the operating room. Brevard watched him check the machines hooked up to the man.

"Can he talk?" Brevard asked.

"Oh, yes," Dr. Whitmore said. He scratched his gray beard. "We had quite the scene up here when he came to. The patient is much stronger than he appears."

"And not quite as dead," Stevens said.

Nobody laughed.

"He was very animated," Dr. Whitmore said. "He insisted his name wasn't Troy. This was before I ran the tests." He nodded at the piece of paper Brevard was now carrying.

Brevard looked to Darcy for confirmation.

"I was using the john," Darcy admitted sheepishly. "I wasn't here when he woke up."

"We gave him a sedative. And I took a blood sample in order to ID him."

"What did you come up with?" Brevard asked.

Dr. Whitmore shook his head. "His records have been expunged. Or so I thought." Taking a plastic cup from one of the cabinets, he ran some water from the sink and took a swig. "They were coming up partials because I don't have access to them. Just rank and cryo level. I remembered seeing this before on my very first shift. It was another guy from the executive wing, and then I remembered where you found this gentleman."

"The executive wing," Brevard said. "But this wasn't his pod, right?" He remembered what Darcy had told him. "The blood on the lid matches the pod, but the man inside is someone else. Wouldn't that suggest someone used their own pod in order to stash a body?"

"If my hunch is correct, it's worse than that." Dr. Whitmore took another sip of water and ran his fingers through his hair. "The name on the executive pod, Troy, matches the swab I took from the lid, but that man should be in Deep Freeze right now. He was put under over a century ago and hasn't been woken up since."

"But that was his blood on the lid," Stevens said.

"Which means he *has* been woken up since," Darcy pointed out.

Brevard glanced at his night-shift officer and realized he'd misjudged the young man. That was the blasted thing about working these shifts with different people every time. You couldn't really get to know anyone, couldn't gauge their worth.

"So the first thing I did was look in the medical records for any strange activity in the Deep Freeze. I wanted to see if anyone had ever been disturbed from there."

Brevard felt uneasy. The doctor was doing all of his work for him. "Did you find anything?" he asked.

Dr. Whitmore nodded. He waved toward the terminal on the waiting room desk. "There has been activity in the Deep Freeze initiated by this office. Not on my shift, mind you. But twice now, people have been woken up from coordinates that place them there. One of them was in the middle of the old Deep Freeze, that storehouse from before orientation."

The doctor paused to allow this to sink in.

It took Brevard a moment. His sleep-deprived night guard proved a hair quicker.

"A woman?" Darcy asked.

Dr. Whitmore frowned. "It's hard to say, but that's my suspicion. I don't have access to this person's records for some reason. I sent Michael down to check, to get a visual on who's in there."

"We could be dealing with a murder of passion," Stevens said.

Brevard grunted in agreement. He was already thinking the same thing. "Say there's a man who can't handle the loneliness. He's been waking up his wife in secret, would probably have to be an administrator to have access. Someone finds out, a non-executive, and so he has to kill the man. But . . . he gets killed instead—" Brevard shook his head. It was getting too complicated. He was too decaffeinated for this.

"Here's the kicker," Dr. Whitmore said.

Brevard groaned in anticipation. He regretted having dumped out his cold coffee. He waved for the news.

"There's been one other case of someone pulled from Deep Freeze, and this guy, I *do* have access to his records." Dr. Whitmore scanned the three security officers. "Anyone wanna guess the guy's name?"

"His name is Troy," Darcy said.

The doctor snapped his fingers, his eyes wide with surprise. "Bingo."

Brevard turned to his night guard. "And how the hell did you come up with that?"

Darcy shrugged. "Everyone loves a match."

"So let me get this straight," Brevard said. "We've got a rogue killer from the Deep Freeze knocking off an administrator, taking his place and likely his codes, and waking up women." The chief turned to Stevens. "Okay, I think you're right. It's time to get Shepherd involved. This just hit his pay grade."

Stevens nodded and turned toward the door. But there was a slap of hurrying boots out in the hall before he could leave. Michael, one of the medical assistants who had helped remove the body from the pod, flew around the corner in a lather and out of air. Resting his hands on his knees, he took several deep breaths, his eyes on his boss.

"I said be quick," Dr. Whitmore said. "I didn't mean for you to race."

"Yessir—" Michael took a series of deep breaths. "Sirs, we've got a problem." The medical assistant looked to the men from Security and grimaced.

"What is it?" Brevard asked.

"It was a woman," Michael said, nodding. "Sure enough. But the readout on her pod was flashing, so I ran a quick check." He scanned their faces, his eyes wild, and Brevard knew. He knew, but someone else beat him to it.

"She's dead," Darcy said.

The assistant nodded vigorously, his hands on his knees. "Anna," he muttered. "The name on the pod was Anna."

The man in the OR with no name tested his restraints, his old and sinewy arms bulging. Dr. Whitmore begged the gentleman to hold still. Captain Brevard stood on the other side of the gurney. He could smell the odor of a man newly awakened, a man left for dead. Wild eyes sought him out among those gathered. The man who had been shot seemed to recognize Brevard as the one in charge.

"Unloose me," the old man said.

"Not until we know what happened," Brevard told him. "Not until you're better."

The leather cuffs around the old man's wrists squeaked as he tested them. "I'll be better when I'm off this damn table."

"You've been shot," Dr. Whitmore said. He rested a hand on his patient's shoulder to calm him.

The old man lowered his head to his pillow, his eyes traveling from doctor to security officer and back again. "I know," he said.

"Do you remember who did it?" Brevard asked.

The man nodded. "His name's Donald." His jaw clenched and unclenched.

"Not Troy?" Brevard asked.

"That's what I meant. Same guy." Brevard watched the old man's hands squeeze into twin fists and then relax. "Look, I'm one of the Heads of this silo. I demand to be released. Check my records—"

"We'll get this sorted out—" Brevard started to say.

The restraints creaked. "Check the damn records," the old man said again.

"They've been tampered with," Brevard told him. "Can you tell us your name?"

The man lay still for a moment, muscles relaxing. He stared up at the ceiling. "Which one?" he asked. "My name is Paul. Most people call me by my last name, Thurman. I used to go by Senator—"

"Shepherd," Captain Brevard said. "Paul Thurman is the name of the man they call Shepherd."

The old man narrowed his eyes. "No, I don't think so," he said. "I've been called a number of things in my time, but never that."

Silo 17

18

THE EARTH GROWLED. Beyond the walls of the silo, the earth grumbled and the noise steadily grew.

It had begun as a distant thrum a few days ago, had sounded like a hydroponics pump kicking on at the end of a long run of pipe, a vibration that could be felt between the pads of one's feet and the slick metal floor. And then yesterday it had morphed into a steady quake that travelled up Jimmy's knees and bones and into his clenched teeth. Above him, drops of water shivered from pipes, a light drizzle splashing into puddles that had not yet fully dried from the vanishing floods.

Elise squealed and patted the top of her head as she was struck with a drop. She glanced up with a gapped smile and watched for more of the bombardment.

"That's an awful racket," Rickson said. He played his flashlight across the far wall of the old generator room where the noise seemed to originate.

Hannah clapped her hands together and told the twins to get away from the wall. Miles—at least Jimmy thought it was Miles; he could hardly tell the twins apart—had his ear pressed to the concrete, his eyes closed, his mouth agape in concentration. His brother Marcus tugged him back toward the others, face lit up with excitement.

"Get behind me," Jimmy said. His feet tingled from the vibrations. He could feel the noise in his chest as some unseen machine chewed through solid rock.

"How much longer?" Elise asked.

Jimmy tousled her hair and enjoyed the embrace of her worried arms around his waist. "Soon," he told her. The truth was, he didn't know. They'd spent the past two weeks keeping the pump running and Mechanical dry. That morning, they had woken up to find the noise of the digging intolerable. The racket had gotten worse throughout the day, and still the blank wall stood solid before them, still the light rain from wet and shivering pipes continued. The twins splashed in puddles, growing impatient. The baby, inexplicably, slept peacefully in Hannah's arms. They'd been there for hours, listening to the grumbles grow, waiting for something to happen.

The end of the long wait was presaged by mechanical sounds interspersed amid the racket of crushing rock. A squeal of metal joints, the clang of fearsome teeth, the size and breadth of the din becoming confusing as it came from everywhere all at once, from the floor and ceiling and the walls on all sides. Puddles were thrown into chaos. Water flew up from the ground as well as falling from above. Jimmy nearly lost his footing.

"Step back," he yelled over the clamor. He shuffled away from the wall with Elise attached to his hip, the others obeying, wide-eyed and arms out for balance.

A section of concrete fell away, a flat sheet the size of a man. It sloughed off and fell straight down, crumbling into rubble as it hit. Dust filled the air—it seemed to emanate from within the wall itself, concrete releasing powder like a great exhalation.

Jimmy took a few more steps back, and the kids followed, worry replacing excitement. It no longer sounded like an approaching machine—it sounded like hundreds of them. They were everywhere. They were in their chests.

The din reached a furious peak, more concrete falling away, metal screaming as if beaten, great clangs and shots of sparks, and then the great digger broke through, a crack and then a gash appearing in a circular arc like a shadow racing across the wall.

The size of the cut put the noise into perspective. Cutting teeth burst through from the ceiling, spun down beneath the floor, then rose back up on the other side. Iron rods jutted out where they'd been severed. There was the smell of burning metal and chalk. The digger was coming through the wall of level one-forty-two and chewing up a good bit of the concrete above and below. It was boring a hole bigger than a silo level was tall.

The twins whooped and hollered. Elise squeezed Jimmy's ribs so hard he had to work to breathe. The baby stirred in Hannah's arms, but its cries could barely be heard over the tumult. Another great spin from the teeth, another lap from ceiling to floor, and they broke through more fully and revealed themselves to be more like wheels, dozens of discs spinning within a larger disc. A boulder fell from the ceiling and tumbled across the floor toward the larger of the two generators. Jimmy expected the silo itself to come raining down around them.

A light bulb overhead shattered from the vibrations, a glitter of glass amid the drizzle of trapped flood water. "Back!" Jimmy yelled. They were clear across the wide generator room from the digger, but everywhere felt too close. The ground shook, making it difficult to stand. Jimmy felt suddenly afraid. This thing would keep coming, would bore straight through the silo and carry on; it was out of control—

The chewing disc entered the room, sharpened wheels spinning and screaming in the air, rock thrown up on one side and crumbling down from the other. The violence lessened. The squealing of dry metal joints grew less deafening. Hannah cooed to her child, rocking her arms back and forth, eyes wide and fixed on this intrusion into their home.

Somewhere, shouts emerged. They leaked through the falling rock. The rotating disc slowed to a halt, while some of the smaller wheels spun a while longer. Their edges revealed themselves as shiny and new where their battle through the earth had worn them bare. A length of rebar was wrapped around one like a knotted bootlace.

A respite of silence grew. The child fell still once more. A distant clatter and hum—the digger's rumbling belly perhaps—was the only sound.

"Hello?"

A shout from around the digger.

"Yeah, we're through," another voice called. A woman's voice.

Jimmy swept up Elise, who hugged his neck and locked her ankles around his waist. He ran toward the wall of studded steel before him.

"Hey!" Rickson called as he hurried after.

The twins raced along as well.

Jimmy couldn't breathe. It wasn't Elise squeezing him this time—it was the idea of *visitors*. Of people not to be afraid of. Someone he could run *to* rather than from.

Everyone felt it. They raced, grinning, toward the digger's maw.

Between the gap in the wall and the silent disc, an arm emerged, a shoulder, a woman climbing up from the cut tunnel that dipped below the floor.

She pushed herself to her knees, stood up straight, and brushed her hair from her face.

Jimmy pulled up. The group stopped a dozen paces away. A woman. A stranger. She stood in their silo, smiling, covered in dust and grime.

"Solo?" she asked.

Her teeth flashed. She was pretty, even covered in dirt. She walked toward the group and tugged off a pair of thick gloves while someone else crawled out from behind the digger's teeth. An outstretched hand. The baby crying. Jimmy shook the woman's hand, mesmerized by her smile.

"I'm Courtnee," the woman said. She swept her gaze over the children, her smile widening. "You must be Elise." She squeezed the young girl's shoulder, which caused the grip around Jimmy's neck to tighten.

A man emerged from behind the digger, pale as fresh paper with hair just as white, and turned to survey the wall of cutting teeth.

"Where's Juliette?" Jimmy asked, hiking Elise higher on his hip.

Courtnee frowned. "Didn't she tell you? She went outside."

PART II
OUTSIDE

Silo 18

19

JULIETTE STOOD IN the airlock while gas was pumped in around her. The cleaning suit crinkled against her skin. She felt none of the fear from the last time she was sent out, but none of the deluded hope that drove many to exile. Somewhere between pointless dreams and hopeless dread was a desire to know the world. And, if possible, make it better.

The pressure in the airlock grew, and the folds of her suit found every raised scar across her body, wrinkles pressing where wrinkles had once burned. It was a million pricks from a million gentle needles, every sensitive part of her touched all at once, as if this airlock remembered, as if it knew her. A lover's apology.

Clear plastic sheets had been hung over the walls. These began to ripple as they were forced tight around pipes, around the bench where she'd been dressed. Not long now. If anything, she felt excitement. Relief. A long project coming to an end.

She pulled one of the sample containers off her chest and cracked the lid, gathering some of the inert argon for a reference. Screwing the lid back on, she heard a dull and familiar thud within the recesses of the great outer door. The silo opened, and a wisp of fog appeared as pressurized gas pushed its way through, preventing the outside from getting in.

The fog swelled and swirled around her. It pushed at her back, urging her along. Juliette lifted a boot, stepped through the thick outer doors of Silo 18 and was outside once again.

The ramp was just as she remembered it: a concrete plane rising up through the last level of her buried home and toward the surface of the earth. Trapped dirt made slopes of hard corners, and streaks and splatters of mud stained the walls. The heavy doors thumped together behind her, and a dispersing fog rose up toward the clouds. Juliette began her march up the gentle rise.

"You okay?"

Lukas's soft voice filled her helmet. Juliette smiled. It was good to have him with her. She pinched her thumb and finger together, which keyed the microphone in her helmet.

"No one has ever died on the ramp, Lukas. I'm doing just fine."

He whispered an apology, and Juliette's smile widened. It was a different thing altogether to venture out with this support behind her. Much different than being exiled while shamed backs were turned, no one daring to watch.

She reached the top of the ramp, and a feeling of *rightness* overtook her. Without the fear or the digital lies of an electronic visor, she felt what she suspected humans were *meant* to feel: a heady rush of disappearing walls, of raw land spread out in every direction, of miles and miles of open air and tumbling clouds. Her flesh tingled from the thrill of exploration. She had been here twice before, but this was something new. This had purpose.

"Taking my first sample," she said, pinching her glove.

She pulled another of the small containers from her suit. Everything was numbered just like a cleaning, but the steps had changed. Weeks of planning and building had gone into this, a flurry of activity up top while her friends tunneled through the earth. She cracked the lid of the container, held it aloft for a count of ten, and then screwed the cap back on. The top of the vessel was clear. A pair of gaskets rattled inside, and twin strips of heat tape were affixed to the bottom. Juliette pressed waxy sealant around the lip of the lid, making it airtight. The numbered sample went into a flapped pouch on her thigh, joining the one from the airlock.

Lukas's voice crackled through the radio: "We've got a full burn in the airlock. Nelson is letting it cool down before he goes in."

Juliette turned and faced the sensor tower. She fought the urge to lift her hand, to acknowledge the dozens of men and women who were watching on the cafeteria's wallscreen. She looked down at her chest and tried to clear her mind, to remember what she was supposed to do next.

Soil sample. She shuffled away from the ramp and the tower toward a patch of dirt that maybe hadn't seen footsteps in centuries. Kneeling down—the undersuit pinching the back of her knee—she scooped dirt using the shallow container. The soil was packed hard and difficult to dig up, so she brushed more of the surface soil onto the top, filling the dish.

"Surface sample complete," she said, pinching her glove. She screwed the lid on carefully and pressed the ring of wax before sliding it into a pouch on her other thigh.

"Good going," Lukas said. He was probably aiming for encouragement. All she could hear was his intense worry.

"Taking the deep sample next."

She grabbed the tool with both hands. She had built the large T on the top while wearing bulky suit gloves to make sure the grip would be right. With the corkscrew end pressed against the earth, she twisted the handle around and around, leaning her weight into her arms to force the blades through the dense soil.

Sweat formed on her brow. A drop of perspiration smacked her visor and trembled into a little puddle as her arms jerked with effort. A caustic and stiff breeze buffeted her suit, pushing her to the side. When the tool penetrated all the way to the tape mark on the handle, she stood and pulled the T-bar, using her legs.

The plug came free, an avalanche of deep soil spilling off and crumbling into the dry hole. She slid the case over the plug and locked it into place. Everything had the fit and polish of Supply's best. She stowed the tool back in its pouch, slung it around onto her back, and took a deep breath.

"Good?" Lukas asked.

She waved at the tower. "I'm good. Two more samples left. How far along is the airlock?"

"Lemme check."

While Lukas saw how the preparations for her return were going, Juliette trudged toward the nearest hill. Her old footsteps had been worn away by a light rain, but she remembered the path well. The crease in the hill stood like an inviting stairway, a ramp on which two forms still nestled.

She stopped at the base of the hill and pulled out another container with gaskets and heat tape inside. The cap came off easily. She held it up to the wind, allowing whatever blew inside to become trapped. For all they knew, these were the first tests made of the outside air. Reams and reams of bogus reports from previous cleanings had been nothing but numbers used to uphold and justify fears. It was a charade of progress, of efforts being made to right the world, when all they ever cared about was selling the story of how wrong it was.

The only thing more impressive to Juliette than the depths of the conspiracy had been the speed and relief with which its mechanisms had crumbled within IT. The men and women of level thirty-four reminded her of the children of Silo 17, frightened and wide-eyed and desperate for some adult they could cling to and trust. This foray of hers to test the outside air was looked upon with suspicion and fear elsewhere in the silo, but in IT, where they had pretended to do this work for generations, the chance to truly investigate had been seized by many with wild abandon.

Damn!

Juliette slapped the cover on the container. Her mind had wandered; she had forgotten to count to ten, had probably gone twice that.

"Hey, Jules?"

She squeezed her fingers together. "Yeah?" Releasing the mic, she locked the lid tight, made sure it said "2" on the top, and sealed the edges. She put it away with the other container, cursing her inattention.

"The airlock burn is complete. Nelson went in afterward to get things ready for you, but they're saying it's gonna be a while to charge the argon again. Are you sure you're feeling okay?"

She took a moment to survey herself and give an honest answer. A few deep breaths. Wiggled her joints. Looked up at the dark clouds to make sure her vision and balance were normal.

"Yeah. I feel fine."

"Okay. And they are going to go with the flames when you come back. It looks like they really might've been necessary. We were getting some strange readings in the airlock before you left. As a precaution, Nelson is getting a scrub-down in the inner lock right now. We'll have everything prepped for you as fast as we can."

Juliette didn't like the sound of any of that. Her passage through the Silo 17 airlock had been terrifying, but with no lasting consequences. Dumping soup on herself had been enough to survive. The theory they had been working under was that conditions outside weren't as bad as they'd been led to believe, and that the flames were more a deterrent against not leaving the airlock than an actual necessity for cleansing the air. The challenge with this mission of hers was getting back inside without enduring another burn or another stint in the hospital. But she couldn't put the silo at risk, either.

She squeezed her fingers together, thinking suddenly of all that was at stake. "Is there still a crowd up there watching?" she asked Lukas.

"Yeah. There's a lot of excitement in the air. People can't believe this is happening."

"I want you to clear them out," she said.

She let go of her thumb. There was no reply.

"Lukas? Do you read me? I want you to get everyone down to at least level four. Clear out anyone not working on this, okay?"

She waited.

"Yeah," Lukas said. There was a lot of noise in the background. "We're doing that right now. Trying to keep everyone calm."

"Tell them it's just a precaution. Because of the readings in the airlock."

"Doing that."

He sounded winded. Juliette hoped she wasn't causing a panic for no reason.

"I'm going to get the last sample," she said, focusing on the task at hand. They had prepared for the worst. Everything was going to be okay. She was thankful for the crude sensors they'd installed in the airlock. The next time out, she hoped to install a permanent array on the tower. But she couldn't get too far ahead of herself. She approached one of the cleaners at the base of the hill.

The body they'd chosen belonged to Jack Brent. It had been nine years since he'd been sent to clean, having gone mad after his wife's second miscarriage. Juliette knew very little else about him. And that had been her main criterion for the final sample.

She made her way to what was left of the body. The old suit had long turned a dull gray like the soil. What once was a metallic coating flaked away like old paint. The boots were eaten thin, the visor chipped. Jack lay with his arms folded across his chest, legs straight and parallel, almost as if he had taken a nap and had never gotten up. More like he had lain down to gaze at the clear blue sky in his visor.

Juliette pulled the last box out, the one marked "3", and knelt beside the dead cleaner. It spooked her to think that this would've been her fate were it not for Scottie and Walker and the people of Supply who had risked so much. She lifted the sharp blade out of the sample box and cut a square patch from the suit. Setting the blade on the cleaner's chest, she picked up the sample and dropped it into the container. Holding her breath, she grabbed the blade, careful not to nick her own suit, and sliced into the rotted undersuit where it had been exposed across the cleaner's belly.

This last sample had to be prised out with the blade. If there was any flesh inside or gathered with it, she couldn't tell. Everything was thankfully dark beneath the torn and dilapidated suit. But it seemed like nothing but soil in there, blown in amongst the dry bones.

She put the sample in the container and left the blade by the cleaner, no longer needing it and not wanting to risk handling it any further with the bulky gloves. She stood and turned toward the tower.

"You okay?"

Lukas's voice sounded different. Muffled. Juliette exhaled, felt a little dizzy from holding her breath so long.

"I'm fine."

"We're almost ready for you. I'd start heading back."

She nodded, even though he probably couldn't see her at that distance, not even with the tall wallscreens magnifying the world.

"Hey, you know what we forgot?"

She froze and studied the tower.

"What is it?" she asked. "Forgot what?" Sweat trickled down her cheek, tickling her skin. She could feel the lace of scars at the back of her neck where her last suit had melted against her.

"We forgot to send you out with a pad or two," Lukas said. "There's already some build-up visible in here. And you know, while you're out there . . ."

Juliette glared at the tower.

"I'm just saying," Lukas said. "You maybe could have, you know, given it a bit of a cleaning—"

20

JULIETTE WAITED AT the bottom of the ramp. She remembered the last time she'd done this, standing in the same place with a blanket of heat tape Solo had made, wondering if she'd run out of air before the doors opened, wondering if she'd survive what awaited her inside. She remembered thinking Lukas was in there, and then struggling with Bernard instead.

She tried to shake those memories free. Glancing down at her pockets, she made sure the flaps on all the pouches were tightly sealed. Every step of the upcoming decontamination flitted through her mind. She trusted that everything would be in place.

"Here we go," Lukas radioed. Again, his voice was hollow and distant.

On cue, the gears in the airlock door squealed, and a plume of pressurized argon spilled through the gap. Juliette threw herself into the mist, an intense sensation of relief accompanying the move indoors.

"I'm in. I'm in," she said.

The doors thumped shut behind her. Juliette glanced at the inner airlock door, saw a helmet on the other side of the glass porthole, someone peering in, watching. Moving to the ready bench, she opened the airtight box Nelson had installed in her absence. Needed to be quick. The gas chambers and the flames were all automated.

Ripping the sealed pouches off her thighs, she placed them inside. She unslung the borer with its sample and added that as well, then pushed the lid shut and engaged the locks. The practice run-through had helped. Moving in the suit felt comfortable. She had lain in bed at night thinking through each step until they were habit.

Shuffling across the small airlock, she gripped the edge of the immense metal tub she'd welded together. It was still warm from the last bout of flames, but the water Nelson had topped it up with had sapped much of the heat. With a deep and pointless breath, she lowered herself over the edge.

The water flooded against her helmet, and Juliette felt the first real onrush of fear. Her breath quickened. Being outside was nothing like being underwater again. The floods were in her mouth; she could feel herself taking tiny gulps of air, could taste the steel and rust from the steps; she forgot what she was supposed to be doing.

Glimpsing one of the handles at the bottom of the tub, she reached for it and pulled herself down. One boot at a time, she found the bar welded at the other end of the tub and slipped her feet under, held herself to the bottom, trusting that her back was covered. Her arms ached as she strained against the suit's buoyancy. And even through her helmet and beneath that water, she could hear displaced fluid splashing over the lip and onto the airlock floor. She could hear the flames kick on and roar and lick at the tub.

"Three, four, five—" Lukas counted, and a painful memory flashed before her, the dull green emergency lights, the panic in her chest—

"Six, seven, eight—"

She could almost taste the oil and fuel from that final gasp as she emerged, alive, from the flooded depths.

"Nine, ten. Burn complete," he said.

Letting go of the handles and kicking her boots free, she bobbed to the boiling surface, the heat of the water felt through her suit. She fought to get her knees and boots beneath her. Water splashed and steamed everywhere. She feared the longer this next step took, the more the air could attach itself to her, contaminating the second airlock.

She hurried to the door, boots slipping dangerously, the locking wheel already spinning.

Hurry, hurry, she thought to herself.

It opened a crack. She tried to dive through, slipped, landed painfully on the door's jamb. Several gloved hands grabbed at her as she clawed her way forward, the two suited technicians yanking her through before slamming the door shut.

Nelson and Sophia—two of the former suit techs—had brushes ready. They dipped them into a vat of blue neutralizing agent and began scrubbing Juliette down before turning to themselves and each other.

Juliette turned her back and made sure they got that as well. She went to the vat and fished out the third brush, turned and started scrubbing Sophia's suit. And saw that it wasn't Sophia in there.

She squeezed her glove mic. "What the hell, Luke?"

Lukas shrugged, a wince of guilt on his face. She imagined he couldn't stand the thought of someone else risking themselves. Or probably just wanted to be there by the airlock door in case something went wrong. Juliette couldn't blame him; she would've done the same thing.

They scrubbed the second airlock while Peter Billings and a few others looked on from the sheriff's office. Bubbles from the cleaning fluid floated up in the air, then trembled toward the vents where the air inside the new airlock was being pumped into the first. Nelson worked on the ceiling, which they'd kept low on purpose. Less air inside. Less volume. Easier to reach. Juliette searched Nelson's face for any sign of trouble from his time in the inner airlock and blamed the flush and sweat on his energetic scrubbing.

"You've got perfect vacuum," Peter said, using the radio in his office. Juliette motioned to the others, drew her hand across her neck, then closed her fist. They both nodded and went back to scrubbing. While new air was cycled in from the cafeteria, they went over each other one more time, and Juliette finally had a moment to revel in the fact that she was back. Back inside. They had done it. No burns, no hospitals, no contamination. And now they would hopefully learn something.

Peter's voice filled her helmet again: "We didn't want to tell you while you were suiting up, but the dig punched through to the other side about half an hour ago."

Juliette felt a surge of both elation and guilt. She should've been down there. The timing was abysmal, but she had felt her window of opportunity closing there in the Up Top. She resigned herself to being happy for Solo and the kids, relieved by the end of their long ordeal.

The second airlock—with the sealed glass door she'd fashioned from a shower stall—began to open. Behind her, a bright light bloomed inside the old airlock, and the small porthole glowed red. A second round of flames surged and raged in the small room, bathing the spoiled walls, charring the very air, boiling off the water Juliette had spilled on the floor, and throwing the vat into a cauldron of raging steam.

Juliette waved the others out of the new airlock while she eyed the old one warily, remembering. Remembering being in there. Lukas came back and tugged her along, through the door and into the former jail cell where they stripped down to their undersuits for yet another round of showering. As she peeled off the soaking layers, all Juliette could think about was the sealed and fireproof box on the ready bench. She hoped it was worth the risk, that the answers to a host of cruel questions were tucked away, safely inside.

Silo 17

21

THE GREAT DIGGING machine stood quiet and still. Dust fell from where it had chewed through the ceiling, and the large steel teeth and spinning discs gleamed from their journey through solid rock. Between the discs, the digger's face was caked with dirt, debris, torn lengths of rebar, and large rocks. By the edge of the machine, where it jutted out into the heart of Silo 17, there was a black crack that connected two very different worlds.

Jimmy watched as strangers spilled from one of those worlds into his. Burly men with dark beards and yellow smiles, hands black with grease, stepped through and squinted up at the rusted pipes overhead, the puddles on the ground, the calm and quiet organs of a silo that had long ago rumbled and now sat deathly still.

They clasped Jimmy's hand, called him Solo, and squeezed the terrified children. They told him Jules said hello. And then they adjusted the lights on their helmets, which threw golden cones before them, and went splashing off into Jimmy's home.

Elise clutched Jimmy's leg as another group of miners and mechanics squeezed past. Two dogs bounded with them, stopped to sniff at the puddles, then at a trembling Elise, before following their owners. Courtnee—Juliette's friend—finished instructing a group before returning to Jimmy and the kids. Jimmy watched her move. Her hair was lighter than Juliette's, her features sharper, she wasn't quite as tall, but she had that same fierceness. He wondered if all the people from this other world would be the same: the men bearded and covered in soot, the women wild and resourceful.

Rickson rounded up the twins while Hannah cradled her crying baby and tried to soothe it back to sleep. Courtnee handed Jimmy a flashlight.

"I don't have enough lights for all of you," she said, "so you'll want to stick close together." She held her hand over her head. "The tunnel is high enough, just mind the support columns. And the ground is rough, so go slow and stick to the center."

"Why can't we stay here and have the doctor come to us?" Rickson asked.

Hannah shot him a look as she bounced the baby on her hip.

"It's much safer where we're taking you," Courtnee said, glancing around at walls slick and corroded. The way she looked at Jimmy's home made him feel defensive. They'd been getting along just fine for some time now.

Rickson flashed Jimmy a look like he had his own doubts about it being safer on the other side. Jimmy knew what he was scared of. Jimmy had heard the twins talking, and the twins had heard the older kids whispering. Hannah would have to get an implant in her hip like their mothers had. Rickson would be assigned a color and a job other than fending for his family. The young couple were just as wary of these adults as Jimmy was.

Despite their fears, they donned hard hats borrowed from those pouring into their world, clung to one another, and squeezed through the gap. Beyond the digger's teeth, there was a dark tunnel like the Wilds when all the lights were off. But there was a coolness, and an echo to their voices different than the Wilds. The earth seemed to swallow them as Jimmy tried to keep up with Courtnee, and the kids tried to keep up with him.

They entered a metal door and passed through the long digging machine, which was warm inside. Down a narrow corridor, people squeezing past in the other direction, and finally out another door and back into the cool and dark of the tunnel. Men and women shouted to one another, lights dancing from their helmets as they wrestled with piles of rubble that climbed toward the ceiling and out of sight. Rocks shifted and clattered. There were mounds of them on either side, leaving a precarious pathway in the center. Workers filed past, smelling of mud and sweat. There was a boulder taller than Jimmy that the foot traffic had to bend around.

It felt odd to walk straight ahead in one direction like that. They walked and walked without ever bumping into a wall or bending back around. It was unnatural. That lateral void was more frightening than the darkness with its occasional lights. It was scarier than the veil of dust drifting from the ceiling or the occasional rock tumbling down from the piles. It was worse than the strangers bumping past them in the dark, or the steel beams in the middle of the passage that leapt up from the swirling shadows. It was the eeriness of there being nothing to stop them. Walk and walk and walk in one direction, no end to it all.

Jimmy was used to the up-and-down of the spiral staircase. That was normal. This was not. And yet he stumbled along across the rough surface of the chewed rock, past men and women calling to one another in the flash-beam-studded darkness, between piles of earth crowding the narrow center. They overtook men and women carrying parts of machines and lengths of steel taken from his silo, and Jimmy wanted to say something to them. Elise sniffled and said she was scared. Jimmy scooped her up and let her cling to his neck.

The tunnel went on and on. Even when a light could be seen at the end, a rough square of light, it took countless steps to make that bright maw grow larger. Jimmy thought of Juliette walking this far in the outside. It seemed impossible that she had survived such an ordeal. He had to remind himself that he had heard her voice dozens of times since, that she had really done it, had gone off for help and had kept her promise to come back for him. Their two worlds had been made one.

He dodged another steel column in the center of the tunnel. Aiming his flashlight up, he could see the overhead beams these columns supported. The loose rocks crumbling down gave Jimmy new cause for alarm, and he found himself less reluctantly following Courtnee. He pressed forward, toward the promise of light ahead, forgetting what he was leaving behind and where he was going and thinking only about getting out from underneath the tenuously held earth.

Far behind them, a loud crack sounded out, followed by the rumble of shifting rock and then shouts from workers to get out of the way. Hannah brushed past him. He set Elise down, and she and the twins rushed ahead, dancing in and out of the beam of Courtnee's flashlight. Streams of people filed past, lights affixed to their hard hats, heading toward Jimmy's home. He patted his chest reflexively, feeling for the old key that he had put on before leaving the server room. His silo was unprotected. But the fear he could sense in the kids somehow made him stronger. He wasn't as terrified as they were. It was his duty to be strong.

The tunnel came to a blessed end, the twins scampering out first. They startled the gruff men and women in their dark blue coveralls with knee patches of grease and their leather aprons slotted with tools. Eyes grew wide on faces white with chalk and black from soot. Jimmy paused at the mouth of the tunnel and let Rickson and Hannah out first. All work ceased at the sight of the bundle cradled in Hannah's arms. One of the women stepped forward and lifted a hand as if to touch the child, but Courtnee waved her back and told the rest to return to their work. Jimmy scanned the crowd for Juliette, even though he'd been told she was up top. Elise begged to be carried again, her tiny hands stretched up in the air. Jimmy adjusted his pack and obliged, ignoring the pain in his hip. The bag around Elise's neck banged his ribs with its heavy book.

He joined the procession of little ones as they wove through the walls of workers frozen in place, workers who tugged their beards and scratched their heads and watched him as if he were a man from some fictional land. And Jimmy felt at his core that this was a grave mistake. Two worlds had been united, but they were not anything alike. Power surged here. Lights burned steady, and it was crowded with grown men and women. It smelled different. Machines rumbled rather than sat quiet. And the long decades of growing older sloughed off him in a sudden panic as Jimmy hurried to catch up with the others, just one of a number of frightened youth, emerging from shadows and silence into the bright and crowded and noisy.

Silo 18

22

A SMALL BUNKROOM HAD been set up for the kids, with a private room down the hall for Jimmy. Elise was unhappy with the arrangements and clung to one of his hands with both of hers. Courtnee told them she had food being sent down and then they could shower. A stack of clean coveralls sat on one of the bunks, a bar of soap, a few worn children's books. But first, she introduced a tall man in the cleanest pale red coveralls Jimmy could ever remember seeing.

"I'm Dr. Nichols," the man said, shaking Jimmy's hand. "I believe you know my daughter."

Jimmy didn't understand. And then he remembered that Juliette's last name was Nichols. He pretended to be brave while this tall, clean-shaven man peered into his eyes and mouth. Next, a cold piece of metal was pressed to Jimmy's chest, and this man listened intently through his tubes. It all seemed familiar. Something from Jimmy's distant past.

Jimmy took deep breaths as he was told. The children watched warily, and he realized what a model he was for them, a model for normalcy, for courage. He nearly laughed—but he was supposed to be breathing for the doctor.

Elise volunteered to go next. Dr. Nichols lowered himself to his knees and checked the gap of her missing tooth. He asked about fairies, and when Elise shook her head and said she'd never heard of such a thing, a dime was produced. The twins rushed forward and begged to be next.

"Are fairies real?" Miles asked. "We used to hear noises in the farm where we grew up."

Marcus wiggled in front of his brother. "I saw a fairy for real one day," he said. "And I lost twenty teeth when I was young."

"You did?" Dr. Nichols asked. "Can you smile for me? Excellent. Now open your mouth. Twenty teeth, you say."

"Uh-huh," Marcus said. He wiped his mouth. "And every one of them growed back except for the one Miles knocked out."

"It was an accident," Miles complained. He lifted his shirt and asked to have his breaths heard. Jimmy watched Rickson and Hannah huddle together around their infant as they studied the proceedings. He also noted that Dr. Nichols, even as he looked over the two boys, couldn't stop glancing at the baby in Hannah's arms.

The twins were given a dime each after their check-up. "Dimes are good luck for twins," Dr. Nichols said. "Parents put two of these under their pillows in the hopes of having such healthy boys as you."

The twins beamed and scrutinized the coins for any sign of a faded face or portion of a word to suggest they were real. "Rickson used to be a twin too," Miles said.

"Oh?" Dr. Nichols shifted his attention to the older kids sitting side by side on the lower bunk.

"I don't want to take the implant," Hannah said coolly. "My mother had the implant, but it was cut out of her. I don't want to be cut."

Rickson wrapped an arm around her and held her close. He narrowed his eyes at the tall doctor, and Jimmy felt nervous.

"You don't have to take the implant," Dr. Nichols whispered, but Jimmy saw the way he glanced at Courtnee. "Do you mind if I listen to your child's heartbeat? I just want to make sure it's nice and strong—"

"Why wouldn't it be?" Rickson asked, thrusting his shoulders back.

Dr. Nichols studied the boy a moment. "You met my daughter, didn't you? Juliette."

He nodded. "Briefly," he said. "She left soon after."

"Well, she sent me down here because she cares about your health. I'm a doctor. I specialize in children, the youngest of them. I think your child looks very strong and healthy. I just want to be sure." Dr. Nichols held up the metal disc at the end of his hearing tubes and pressed his palm against it. "There. So it'll be nice and warm. Your boy won't even know I'm taking a listen."

Jimmy rubbed his chest where his breathing had been checked and wondered why the doctor hadn't warmed it for *him*.

"For a dime?" Rickson asked.

Dr. Nichols smiled. "How about a few chits, instead?"

"What's a chit?" Rickson asked, but Hannah was already adjusting herself on the bunk so the doctor could have a look.

Courtnee rested a hand on Jimmy's shoulder while the check-ups continued. Jimmy turned to see what she needed.

"Juliette wanted me to call her as soon as you all were over here. I'll be back to check on you in a little while—"

"Wait," Jimmy said. "I'd like to come. I want to speak with her."

"Me too," said Elise, pressing against his leg.

Courtnee frowned. "Okay," she said. "But let's be quick, because you all need to eat and get freshened up."

"Freshened up?" Elise asked.

"If you're going to go up and see your new home, yeah."

"New home?" Jimmy asked.

But Courtnee had already turned to go.

Jimmy hurried out the door and down the hall after Courtnee. Elise grabbed her shoulder bag, the one that held her heavy book, and scampered along beside him.

"What did she mean about a new home?" Elise asked. "When are we going back to our real home?"

Jimmy scratched his beard and wrestled with truth and lies. *We may never go home,* he wanted to say. *No matter where we end up, it may never feel like home again.*

"I think this will be our new home," he told her, keeping his voice from cracking. He reached down and rested his wrinkled hand on her thin shoulder, felt how fragile she was, this flesh that words could crack. "It'll be our home for a time, at least. Until they make our old home better." He glanced ahead at Courtnee, who did not look back.

Elise stopped in the middle of the hallway and peered over her shoulder. When she turned back, the dim lights of Mechanical caught the water in her eyes. Jimmy was about to tell her not to cry when Courtnee knelt down and called Elise over. Elise refused to budge.

"Do you want to come with us to call Juliette and talk with her on the radio?" Courtnee asked.

Elise chewed on her finger and nodded. A tear rolled down her cheek. She clutched the bag with her book in it, and Jimmy remembered kids from another lifetime who used to cling to dolls in the same way.

"After we make this call and you get freshened up, I'll get you some sweetcorn from the pantry. Would you like that?"

Elise shrugged. Jimmy wanted to say that none of the kids

had ever tasted sweetcorn before. He had never heard of the stuff himself. But now he wanted some.

"Let's go call Juliette together," Courtnee said.

Elise sniffed and nodded. She took Jimmy's hand and peered up at him. "What's sweetcorn?" she asked.

"It'll be a surprise," Jimmy said, which was the dead truth.

Courtnee led them down the hall and around a bend. It took a moment for the twists and turns to remind Jimmy of the dark and wet place he'd left behind. Beyond the fresh paint and the humming lights, past the neat wires and the smell of fresh grease, lay a labyrinth identical to the rusted bucket he'd explored the past two weeks. He could almost hear the puddles squish beneath his feet, hear that screaming pump he tended suck at an empty basin—but that was a real noise at his feet. A loud yip.

Elise screamed, and at first Jimmy thought he'd stepped on her. But there at his feet was a large brown rat with a fearsome tail, crying and turning circles.

Jimmy's heart stopped. Elise screamed and screamed, but then he realized it was his voice he was hearing. Elise's arms were latched around his leg, making it difficult to turn and flee. And meanwhile, Courtnee bent over with laughter. Jimmy nearly fainted as Courtnee scooped the giant rat off the ground. When the thing licked at her chin, he realized it wasn't a rat at all but a dog. A juvenile. He'd seen grown dogs in the Mids of his silo when he was a boy, but had never seen a pup. Elise loosened her grip when she saw that the animal meant no harm.

"It's a cat!" Elise cried.

"That's no cat," Jimmy said. He knew cats.

Courtnee was still laughing at him when a young man careened around the corner, panting, summoned no doubt by Jimmy's startled screeches.

"There you are," he said, taking the animal from Courtnee. The pup clawed at the man's shoulder and tried to bite his earlobe. "Damn thing." The mechanic swatted the pup's face away. He gripped it by the scruff of its neck, its legs pawing at the air.

"Is that more of them?" Courtnee asked.

"Same litter," the man said.

"Conner was to put them down weeks ago."

The man shrugged. "Conner's been digging that damn tunnel. But I'll get on him about it." He nodded to Courtnee and marched back the way he'd come, the animal dangling from its scruff.

"Gave you a fright," Courtnee said, smiling at Jimmy.

"Thought he was a rat," Jimmy said, remembering the hordes of them that'd taken over the lower farms.

"We got overrun with dogs when some people from Supply hunkered down here," Courtnee said. She led them down the hall in the direction the man had gone. Elise, for once, was scampering out in front. "They've been busy ever since making more dogs. Found a litter of them myself in the pump room, beneath the heat exchangers. A few weeks ago, another was discovered in the tool lock-up. We'll be finding them in our beds soon enough, damn things. All they do is eat and make mess all over the place."

Jimmy thought of his youth in the server room, eating raw beans out of a can and shitting on the floor grates. You couldn't hate a living thing for . . . living, could you?

The hall ahead came to a dead end. Elise was already exploring to the left as if she were looking for something.

"Walker's workshop is this way," Courtnee said.

Elise glanced back. There was a yip from somewhere, and she turned and carried on.

"Elise," Jimmy called.

She peeked into an open door before disappearing inside. Courtnee and Jimmy hurried after.

When they turned the corner, they found her standing over a parts crate, the man from the hallway placing something back inside. Elise gripped the edge of the crate and bent forward. Yipping and scratching leaked out of the plastic bin.

"Careful, child." Courtnee hurried her way. "They bite."

Elise turned to Jimmy. One of the squirming animals was in her arms, a pink tongue flashing out.

"Put it back," Jimmy said.

Courtnee reached for the animal, but the man corralling the pups already had it by its neck. He dropped the puppy back in with the others and kicked the lid shut with a bang.

"I'm sorry, boss." He slid the crate aside with his foot while Elise made plaintive noises.

"Are you feeding them?" Courtnee asked. She pointed to a pile of scraps on an old plate.

"Conner is. Swear. They're from that dog he took in. You know how he is about the thing. I told him what you said, but he's been putting it off."

"We'll discuss it later," Courtnee said, her eyes darting at young Elise. Jimmy could tell she didn't want to discuss what needed doing in front of the child. "C'mon." She guided Jimmy to the door and back into the hall. He in turn pulled a complaining child after him.

23

A FAMILIAR AND UNPLEASANT odor awaited them at their destination. It was the smell of hot electrics like the humming servers and the stench of unwashed men. For Jimmy, it was a noseful of his old self and his old home. An earful of it too. There was a hiss of static—a familiar, ghostly whisper like his radios made. He followed Courtnee into a room of workbenches and the wreck of countless projects underway or abandoned, it was difficult to tell which.

There was a scattering of computer parts on a counter by the door, and Jimmy thought how his father would have lectured to see them so poorly arranged. A man in a leather smock turned from one of the far benches, a smoking metal wand in his hand, tools studding his chest and poking out of a hundred pockets, a grizzled beard and a wild look in his eyes. Jimmy had never seen such a man in all his life.

"Courtnee," the man said. He pulled a bright length of silver wire from his lips, set the wand down, and waved the smoke from his face. "Is it dinner?"

"It's not yet lunch," Courtnee told him. "I want you to meet two of Juliette's friends. They're from the other silo."

"The other silo." Walker adjusted a lens down over one eye and squinted at his visitors. He got up slowly from his stool.

"I've spoken with you," he said. He wiped his palm on the seat of his coveralls and extended his hand. "Solo, right?"

Jimmy stepped forward and accepted Walker's hand. The two men chewed their beards and studied each other for a moment. "I prefer Jimmy," he said at last.

Walker nodded. "Yes, yes. That's right."

"And I'm Elise." She waved. "Hannah calls me Lily, but I don't like being called Lily. I like Elise."

"It's a good name," Walker agreed. He tugged on his beard and rocked back on his heels, studying her.

"They were hoping to get in touch with Jules," Courtnee said. "And I was supposed to call her and let her know they're here. Is she . . . did everything go okay?"

Walker seemed to snap out of a trance. "What? Oh. Oh, yes." He clapped his hands. "Everything went, it seems. She's back inside."

"What did she go out for?" Jimmy asked. He knew Juliette had been working on something but not what. Just some Project she never wanted to discuss over the radio because she didn't know who might be listening.

"She went to see what was out there, apparently," Walker said. He grumbled something and eyed the open door to his workshop with a scrunched-up nose. He apparently didn't believe this was a valid reason for going anywhere. After an uncomfortable pause, he dropped his gaze to his desk. His old hands deftly lifted an unusual-looking radio, one bristling with knobs and dials. "Let's see if we can raise her," he said.

He called for Juliette, and someone else answered. They said to wait a moment. Walker held the radio out to Jimmy, who took it from him, familiar enough with how they worked.

A voice crackled out of the air: "Yes? Hello—?"

It was Juliette's voice. Jimmy squeezed the button.

"Jules?" He glanced at the ceiling and realized that for the first time in forever, she was above him somewhere, the two of them back under the same top. "Are you there?"

"Solo!" And he didn't correct her. "You're with Walker. Is Courtnee there?"

"Yes."

"Great. That's great. I'm so sorry I wasn't there. I'll be down as soon as I can. They're making up a place for the kids near the farms, more like home. I've just got this . . . one little project to finish first. It should only be a few days."

"It's okay," Jimmy said. He smiled nervously at Courtnee and felt very young all of a sudden. In truth, a few days felt like a very long time. He wanted to see Jules or go home. Or both. "I want to see you soon," he added, changing his mind. "Don't let it be too long."

A burst of static. The sound of radio waves thinking. "It won't be. I promise. Did you see my dad? He's a doctor. I sent him down to check on you and the kids."

"We saw him. He's here." Jimmy glanced down at Elise, who was tugging him toward the door, probably thinking of sweet-corn.

"Good. You said Courtnee was there. Can you put her on?"

Jimmy handed the radio over and saw that his hand was trembling. Courtnee took it. She listened to Juliette say something about the great stairway, and Courtnee updated her on the dig. There was talk of bringing the radio up so Jules could have it, an argument between them on why her father wasn't up top to make sure she and someone named Nelson were okay, a lot that Jimmy didn't understand. He tried to follow along, but his mind wandered. And then he realized Elise was nowhere to be seen.

"Where did that child get off to?" he asked. He ducked down and peered beneath the tool bench, saw nothing but a pile of parts and broken machines. He stood and checked behind one of the tall counters. It was a bad time for playing Hide and Find. He checked the far corner, and a cool taste of panic rose in his throat. Elise was quick to disappear back in his silo, was prone to distraction, just wandered off toward anything shiny or the slightest waft of fruit-smells. But here . . . with strangers and places he didn't know. Jimmy lumbered across the room and peeked between the benches and behind the cluttered shelves, every second cranking up the sound of his heartbeat in his ears.

"She was just—" Walker started to say.

"I'm right here," Elise called. She waved from the hallway, was standing just outside the door. "Can we get back to Rickson? I'm hungry."

"And I promised you sweetcorn," Courtnee said, smiling. Her conversation with Juliette was done. She had missed Jimmy's minute or two of complete and utter panic. On the way to the door, she handed him the strange radio. "Jules wants you to take this with you."

Jimmy accepted it gingerly.

"She said it might be a day or two, but she'll see you at your new place by the lower farms."

"I'm really hungry," Elise called out impatiently. Jimmy laughed and told her to be polite, but his stomach was grumbling too. He joined her in the hallway and saw that she had her large memory book out of her shoulder bag. She clutched it tightly to her chest. Loose and colorful pages she had yet to sew in jutted out at odd angles.

"Follow me," Courtnee said, leading them down the hall. "You are going to love Mama Jean's sweetcorn."

Jimmy felt certain this was true. He hurried along after Courtnee, eager to eat and then see Jules. Behind him, little

Elise trailed along at her own pace. She cradled her large book in both arms—humming quietly to herself because she didn't know how to whistle—her shoulder bag kicking and squirming and making noises of its own.

24

JULIETTE ENTERED THE airlock to retrieve the samples; she could feel the heat from the earlier fire—or else she was imagining it. It could've been her temperature going up inside the suit. Or it may simply have been the sight of that sealed container on the ready bench, its lid now discolored from the lick of flames.

She checked the container with the flat of her glove. The material on her palm didn't grow tacky and stick to the metal; it felt cool to the touch. Over an hour of scrubbing down, changing into new suits, cleaning both airlocks, and now there was a box of clues. A box of outside air, of soil and other samples. Clues, perhaps, to all that was wrong with the world.

She retrieved the box and joined the others beyond the second airlock. A large lead-lined trunk was waiting, its joints sealed, the interior padded. The welded sample box was nestled inside. After the lid was shut, Nelson added a ring of caulk, and Lukas helped Juliette with her helmet. With it off, she realized how labored her breathing had become. Wearing that suit was starting to get to her.

She wiggled out of it while Peter Billings sealed all of the airlocks. His office adjacent to the cafeteria had been a construction site for the past week, and she could tell he would be glad for everyone to be gone. Juliette had promised to remove the inner lock as soon as possible, but that there would most likely be more excursions before that happened. First, she wanted to see about the small pockets of outside air she'd brought into the silo. And it was a long way down to the Suit Lab on thirty-four.

Nelson and Sophia went ahead of them to clear the stairwell. Juliette and Lukas followed after, one hand each on either side of the trunk like porters on a tandem. Another violation of the Pact, Juliette thought. People in silver, porting. How many laws could she break now that she was in a position to uphold them all? How clever could she be in justifying her actions?

Her thoughts drifted from her many hypocrisies to the dig far below, to the news that Courtnee had punched through, that Solo and the kids were safe. She hated that she couldn't be down there with them, but at least her father was. Initially reluctant to play any role in her voyage outside, her father had then resisted leaving her to see to the kids instead. Juliette had convinced him they had taken enough precautions that a check-up of her health was unnecessary.

The trunk swayed and banged against the rail with a jarring clang, and she tried to concentrate on the task at hand.

"You okay back there?" Lukas called.

"How do porters do this?" she asked, switching hands. The weight of the lead-lined trunk pulled down, and its bulk was in the way of her legs. Lukas was lower down and able to walk in the center of the stairway with his arm straight by his side — much more comfortable-looking. She couldn't manage anything similar from higher up. At the next landing, she made Lukas wait while she removed the belt threaded through the waist of her coveralls and tied this to the handle, looping it over her shoulder the way she'd seen a porter do. This allowed her to walk to the side, the weight of the box leaning against her hip, just how they carried those black bags with bodies to be buried.

After a level, it almost grew comfortable, and Juliette could see the appeal of porting. It gave one time to think. The mind grew still while the body moved. But then the thought of black bags and what she and Lukas were porting, and her thoughts found a dark shadow to lie still in.

"How're you doing?" she asked Lukas after two turns of complete silence.

"Fine," he said. "Just wondering what we're carrying here, you know? What's inside the box."

His mind had found similar shadows.

"You think this was a bad idea?" she asked.

He didn't answer. It was hard to tell if that was a shrug, or if he was adjusting his grip.

They passed another landing. Nelson and Sophia had taped the doors off, but faces watched from behind dirty glass. Juliette spotted an elderly woman holding a bright cross against the glass. As she turned, the woman rubbed the cross and kissed it, and Juliette thought of Father Wendel and the idea that she was bringing fear, not hope, to the silo. Hope was what he and the church offered, some place to exist after death. Fear came from the chance that changing the world for the better could possibly make it worse.

She waited until they were beneath the landing. "Hey, Luke?"

"Yeah?"

"Do you ever wonder what happens to us after we're gone?"

"I know what happens to us," he said. "We get slathered in butter and chewed off the cob."

He laughed at his own joke.

"I'm serious. Do you think our souls join the clouds and find some better place?"

His laughter stopped. "No," he said after a long pause. "I think we simply stop being."

They descended a turn and passed another landing, another

door taped off and sealed as a precaution. Juliette realized their voices were drifting up and down a quiet and empty stairwell.

"It doesn't bother me that I won't be around one day," Lukas said after a while. "I don't stress about the fact that I wasn't here a hundred years ago. I think death will be a lot like that. A hundred years from now my life will be just like it was a hundred years ago."

Again, he adjusted his grip or shrugged. It was impossible to say.

"I'll tell you what does last forever." He turned his head to make sure she could hear, and Juliette braced for something corny like "love" or something unfunny like "your casseroles."

"What lasts forever?" she obliged, sure to regret it but sensing that he was waiting for her to ask.

"Our decisions," he said.

"Can we stop a moment?" Juliette asked. There was a burn where the strap rubbed across her neck. She set her end down on a step, and Lukas held his half to keep the trunk level. She checked the knot and stepped around to switch shoulders. "I'm sorry—'our decisions'?" She had lost him.

Lukas turned to face her. "Yeah. Our actions, you know? They last forever. Whatever we do, it'll always be what we did. There's no taking them back."

This wasn't the answer she was expecting. There was sadness in his voice as he said these things, that box resting against his knee, and Juliette was moved by the utter simplicity of his answer. Something resonated, but she wasn't sure what it was. "Tell me more," she said. She looped the strap around her other shoulder and readied to lift it again. Lukas held the rail with one hand and seemed content to rest there a moment longer.

"I mean, the world goes around the sun, right?"

"According to you." She laughed.

"Well, it does. The Legacy and the man from Silo One confirm it."

Juliette scoffed as if neither could be trusted. Lukas ignored her and continued.

"That means we don't exist in one place. Instead, everything we do is left in . . . like a trail out there, a big ring of decisions. Every action we take—"

"And mistake."

He nodded and dabbed at his forehead with his sleeve. "And every mistake. But every good thing we do as well. They are immortal, every single touch we leave behind. Even if nobody sees them or remembers them, that doesn't matter. That trail will always be what happened, what we did, every choice. The past lives on forever. There's no changing it."

"Makes you not want to fuck up," Juliette said, thinking on all the times she had, wondering if this box between them was one more mistake. She saw images of herself in a great loop of space: fighting with her father, losing a lover, going out to clean, a great spiral of hurts like a journey down the stairs with a bleeding foot.

And the stains would never wash out. That's what Lukas was saying. She would always have hurt her father. Was that the way to phrase it? Always have had. It was immortal tense. A new rule of grammar. *Always have had* gotten friends killed. *Always have had* a brother die and a mother take her own life. *Always have had* taken that damn job as sheriff.

There was no going back. Apologies weren't welds; they were just an admission that something had been broken. Often between two people.

"You okay?" Lukas asked. "Ready to go on?"

But she knew he was asking more than if her arm was tired. He had this ability to spot her secret worries. He had a keen vision that allowed him to glimpse the smallest pinprick of hurt through heavy clouds.

"I'm fine," she lied. And she searched her past for some noble deed, for a bloodless tread, for any touch on the world that had left it a brighter place. But when she had been sent to clean, she had refused. Always have had refused. She had turned her back and walked off, and there was no chance of going back and doing it any other way.

Nelson was waiting for them in the Suit Lab. He was already prepped and in his second suit, but with his helmet off. The suit Juliette wore outside and the two used to scrub her down had been left in the airlock. Only the radios installed in the collars had been saved. They were as precious as people, Juliette had joked. Nelson and Sophia had already installed them in this pair of suits; Lukas would have a third radio in the hall.

The trunk went on the floor by a cleared workbench; Juliette and Lukas both shook sensation and blood back into their arms. "You've got the door?" she asked Lukas.

He nodded and threw a last frowning glance at the trunk. Juliette could tell he would rather stay and help. He squeezed her arm and kissed her on the cheek before leaving and closing the door. Juliette sat on her cot and squeezed herself into yet another suit and could hear him and Sophia working seal tape around the door. The vents overhead had already been double-bagged. Juliette reckoned there was far less air in the container than she had allowed inside Silo 17—and she had survived that ordeal—but they were still taking every precaution. They were acting as if even one of those containers had enough poison in it to kill everyone in the silo. It was a condition Juliette had insisted upon.

Nelson zipped up her back and folded the velcro flap over, sealing it tight. She tugged on her gloves. Both of their helmets clicked into place. To give them plenty of air and time, she had pulled an oxygen bottle from the acetylene kit. The flow of air was regulated with a small knob, and the overflow spilled out through a set of double valves. Testing the set-up, Juliette had found they could go for days on the trickle of air from the shared tank.

"You good?" she asked Nelson, testing the volume on her radio.

"Yeah," he said. "Ready."

Juliette appreciated the rapport they had developed, the rhythm of two mechanics on the same shift working the same project night after night. Most of their conversations regarded the project, challenges to overcome, tools to pass back and forth. But she had also learned that Nelson's mother used to work with her father, was a nurse before moving down to the Deep to become a doctor. She also learned that Nelson had built the last two cleaning suits, had fitted Holston before cleaning, had just missed being assigned to her. Juliette had decided that this project was as much for his absolution as hers. He had put in long hours that she didn't think she could expect from anyone else. They were both looking to make things right.

Selecting a flat driver from the tool rack, she began scraping caulk from around the lid of the trunk. Nelson chose another driver and worked his side. When their efforts met, she checked with him, and they pried the lid open to reveal the metal container from the airlock bench. Lifting this out, they rested it on a cleared work surface. Juliette hesitated. From the walls, a dozen cleaning suits looked down on them in silent disapproval.

But they had taken all precautions. Even ludicrous ones. The suits they were wearing had been stripped down of all the excess padding, making it easier to work. The gloves as well. Every concession Lukas had asked for, she had provided. It'd been like Shirly with the backup generator and the dig, going so far as to throttle back the main genny to reduce the power load, even rigging the tunnel with blast charges in case of contamination, whatever it took to allow the project to move forward.

Juliette snapped back to the present as she realized Nelson was waiting on her. She grabbed the lid and hinged it open, pulled out the samples. There were two of air, one control sample of argon from the airlock, one each of surface and deep soil, and one of desiccated human remains. They were each placed on the workbench, and then the metal container was set aside.

"Where do you want to start?" Nelson asked. He grabbed a small length of steel pipe with a piece of chalk slotted into the end, an improvised writing device for gloved hands. A blackboard slate stood ready on the bench to take notes.

"Let's start with the air samples," she said. It had already been several hours in getting the samples down to the lab. Her private fear was that there'd be nothing left of the gaskets by now, nothing to observe. Juliette checked the labels on the containers and found the one marked "2." It'd been taken near the hills.

"There's irony here, you know," Nelson said.

Juliette took the sample container from him and peered through the clear plastic top. "What do you mean?"

"It's just . . ." He turned and checked the clock on the wall and scratched the time onto the slate, glanced back guiltily at Juliette. "Being allowed to do this, to see what's out there, to even talk about it. I mean, I put your suit together. I was lead tech on the sheriff's suit." He frowned behind his clear dome. Juliette could see a shine on his brow. "I remember helping him get dressed."

It was his third or fourth awkward attempt at an apology, and Juliette appreciated it. "You were just doing your job," she assured him. And then she thought about how powerful that sentiment was, how far down a nasty road that could take a person, shuffling along and simply doing their job.

"But the irony is that this room—" He waved a glove at the suits peering down from the walls. "Even my mom thought this room was here to help people, help cleaners survive for as long as possible, help explore the outside world that nobody's supposed to talk about. And finally, here we are. More than talking about it."

Juliette didn't say anything, but he was right. It was a room of both hope and dread. "What we yearn to find and what's out there are two different things," she eventually said. "Let's stay focused."

Nelson nodded and readied his chalk. Juliette shook the first sample container until the two gaskets inside separated. The durable one from Supply was perfectly whole. The yellow marks on the edge were still there. The other gasket was in far worse shape. Its red marks were already gone, the edges eaten away by the air inside the container. The same was true of the two samples of heat tape adhered to the bottom. The square piece from Supply was intact. She had cut the one from IT into a triangle in order to tell them apart. It had a small hole eaten through it.

"I'd say an eighth gone on the sample two gasket," Juliette said. "One hole in the heat tape three millimeters across. Both Supply samples appear fine."

Nelson wrote her observations down. This was how she had decided to measure the toxicity of the air, by using the seals and heat tape designed to rot out there and compare it to the ones she knew would last. She passed him the container so he could verify and realized that this was their first bit of data. This was confirmation as great as her survival on the outside. The equipment pulled from the cleaning suit storage bays was meant to fail. Juliette felt chills at the momentous nature of this first step.

Already, her mind raced with all the experiments to perform next. And they hadn't yet opened the containers to see what the air inside was like.

"I confirm an eighth of wear on the gasket," Nelson said, peering inside the container. "I would go two and a half mils on the tape."

"Mark two and a half," she said. One way she would change this next time would be to keep their own slates. Her observations might affect his and vice versa. So much to learn. She grabbed the next sample while Nelson scratched his numbers.

"Sample one," she said. "This one was from the ramp." Peering inside, she spotted the whole gasket that had to be from Supply. The other gasket was half worn. It had nearly pinched all the way through in one place. Tipping the container upside down and rattling it, she was able to get the gasket to rest against the clear lid. "That can't be right," she said. "Let's see that lamp."

Nelson swiveled the arm of the worklight toward her. Juliette aimed it upward, bent over the workbench, and twisted her body and head awkwardly to peer past the dilapidated gasket toward the shiny heat tape beyond.

"I . . . I'd say half wear on the gasket. Holes in the heat tape five . . . no, six mils across. I need you to look at this."

Nelson marked down her numbers before taking the sample. He returned the light to his side of the bench. She hadn't expected a huge difference between the two samples, but if one sample was worse, it should be the one from the hills, not the ramp. Not where they were pumping out good air.

"Maybe I pulled them out in the wrong order," she said. She grabbed the next sample, the control. She'd been so careful outside, but she did remember her thoughts being scrambled. She had lost count at one point, had held one of the canisters open too long. That's what it was.

"I confirm," Nelson said. "A lot more wear on these. Are you sure this one was from the ramp?"

"I think I screwed up. I held one of them open too long. Dammit. We might have to throw those numbers out, at least for any comparison."

"That's why we took more than one sample," Nelson said. He coughed into his helmet, which fogged the dome in front of his face. He cleared his throat. "Don't beat yourself up."

He knew her well enough. Juliette grabbed the control sample, cursing herself under her breath, and wondered what Lukas was thinking out there in the hall, listening in on his radio. "Last one," she said, rattling the container.

Nelson waited, chalk poised above the slate. "Go ahead."

"I don't . . ." She aimed the light inside. She rattled the container. Sweat trickled down her jaw and dripped from her chin. "I thought this was the control," she said. She set the sample down and grabbed the next container, but it was full of soil. Her heart was pounding, her head spinning. None of this made sense. Unless she'd pulled the samples out in the wrong order. Had she screwed it all up?

"Yeah, that's the control sample," Nelson said. He tapped the canister she'd just checked with his length of pipe. "It's marked right there."

"Gimme a sec," she said. Juliette took a few deep breaths. She peered inside the control sample once again, which had been collected inside the airlock. It should have captured nothing but argon. She handed the container to Nelson.

"Yeah, that's not right," he said. He shook the container. "Something's not right."

Juliette could barely hear. Her mind raced. Nelson peered inside the control sample.

"I think . . ." He hesitated. "I think maybe a seal fell out when you opened the lid. Which is no big deal. These things happen. Or maybe . . ."

"Impossible," she said. She had been careful. She remembered seeing the seals in there. Nelson cleared his throat and placed the control sample on the workbench. He adjusted the worklight to point directly down into it. Both of them leaned over. Nothing had fallen out, she was sure of it. But then, she had made mistakes. Everyone was capable of them—

"There's only one seal in there," Nelson said. "I really think maybe it fell—"

"The heat tape," Juliette said. She adjusted the light. There was a flash from the bottom of the container where a piece of tape was stuck. The other piece was gone. "Are you telling me that an adhered piece of tape fell out as well?"

"Well then, containers are out of order," he said. "We have them backwards. This makes perfect sense if we got them all backwards. Because the one from the hill isn't quite as worn as the ramp sample. That's what it is."

Juliette had thought of that, but it was an attempt to match what she thought she knew to what she was seeing. The whole point of going out was to confirm suspicions. What did it mean that she was seeing something completely different?

And then it hit her like a wrench to the skull. It hit her like a great betrayal. A betrayal by a machine that was always good to her, like a trusted pump that suddenly ran backwards for no apparent reason. It hit her like a loved one turning his back while she was falling, like some great bond that wasn't simply taken away but never truly existed.

"Luke," she said, hoping he was listening, that he had his radio on. She waited. Nelson coughed.

"I'm here," he answered, his voice thin and distant. "I've been following."

"The argon," Juliette said, watching Nelson through both of their domes. "What do we know about it?"

Nelson blinked the sweat from his eyes.

"Know what?" Lukas said. "There's a periodic table in there somewhere. Inside one of the cabinets, I think."

"No," Juliette said, raising her voice so she could be sure he heard. "I mean, where does it come from? Are we even sure what it is?"

Silo 1

25

THERE WAS A rattle in Donald's chest, a flapping of some loosely connected thing, an internal alarm that his condition was deteriorating—that he was getting worse. He forced himself to cough, as much as he hated to, as much as his diaphragm was sore from the effort, as much as his throat burned and muscles ached. He leaned forward in his chair and hacked until something deep inside him tore loose and skittered across his tongue, was spat into his square of fetid cloth.

He folded the cloth rather than look and collapsed back into his chair, sweaty and exhausted. He took a deep, less-rattly breath. Another. A handful of cool gasps that didn't quite torture him. Had anything ever felt so great as a painless breath?

Glancing around the room in a daze, he absorbed all that he had once taken for granted: remnants of meals, a deck of cards, a butterflied paperback with browned pages and striated spine— signs of shifts endured but not suffered. He was suffering. He suffered the wait before Silo 18 answered. He studied the schematic of all the other silos that he fretted over. Dead worlds is what he saw. All of them would die except for one. There was a tickle in his throat, and he knew for certain that he would be dead before he decided anything, before he found some way to help or choose or steer the project off its suicidal course. He was the only one who knew or cared—and his knowledge and compassion would be buried with him.

What was he thinking, anyway? That he could fix things? That he could put right a world he had helped destroy? The world was long past fixing. The world was long past setting to right. One glimpse of green fields and blue skies from a drone, and his mind had tumbled out of sorts. Now it'd been so long since that one glimpse that he'd begun to doubt it. He knew how the cleanings worked. He knew better than to trust the vision of some machine.

But foolish hope had him there, in that comm room, reaching out once more. Foolish hope had him dreaming of a stop to it all, some way to let these silos full of people live their own lives, free of all this meddling. It was curiosity as well, wanting to know what was going on in those servers, the last great mystery, one he could explore only with the help of this IT Head he had inducted himself. Donald just wanted answers. He longed for truth and for a painless death for himself and for Charlotte. An end to shifts and dreams. A final resting place, perhaps, up on that hill with a view of Helen's grave. It wasn't too much to hope for, he didn't think.

He checked the clock on the wall. They were late to answer. Fifteen minutes already. Something was happening. He watched the second hand jitter around and realized the entire operation, all of the silos, was like a giant clock. The whole thing ran on automatic. It was winding down.

Invisible machines rode the winds around the planet, destroying anything human, returning the world to wilderness. The people buried underground were dormant seeds that would have to wait another two hundred years before they sprouted. Two hundred years. Donald felt his throat begin to tickle once more and wondered if he had two *days* in him.

At that moment, he only had fifteen minutes. Fifteen minutes before the operators would come back on shift. These sessions of his had grown regular. It was not unusual to clear everyone out for classified discussions, but it was beginning to seem suspicious that he did it every day at the same exact time. He could see the way they looked at one another as they took their mugs and filed out. Probably thought it was some romance. Donald often felt as if it were a romance of sorts. A romance of olden times and truth.

Now he was being stood up. Half of this session had been wasted on listening to the line buzz and go unanswered. Something was happening over there. Something bad. Or maybe he was on edge from the reports of a dead body found in his own silo, some murder the folks in Security were looking into. It was strange that this barely stirred him. He cared more about other silos, had lost all empathy for his own.

There was a click in his ringing headset. "Hello?" he asked, his voice tired and weak. He trusted the machines to make him sound stronger.

There was no reply, just the sound of someone breathing. But that was good enough for an introduction. Lukas never failed to say hello.

"Mayor," he said.

"You know I don't like being called that," she said. She sounded winded, as though she'd been running.

"You prefer Juliette?"

Silence. Donald wondered why he preferred to hear from her. Lukas, he was fond of. He had been there when the young man took his Rite, and Donald admired his curiosity, his study of the Legacy. It filled him with nostalgia to talk about the old world with Lukas. It was a therapy of sorts. And Lukas was the one helping him pry the lid off those servers to study their contents.

With Juliette, the allure was something different. It was the accusations and abuse, which he knew he fully deserved. It was the harsh silences and the threats. There was some part of Donald that wanted her to come end him before his cough could. Humiliation and execution—that was his path to exoneration.

"I know how you're doing it," Juliette finally said, fire in her voice. Venom. "I finally understand. I figured it out."

Donald peeled his headset from one ear and wiped a trickle of sweat. "What do you understand?" he asked. He wondered if Lukas had uncovered something in one of the servers, something to set Juliette off.

"The cleanings," she spat.

Donald checked the clock. Fifteen minutes were going to slip by in a hurry. The person reading that novel would be back soon, as well as the techs in the middle of that game of cards. "I'm happy to talk about the cleanings—"

"I've just been outside," she told him.

Donald covered his microphone and coughed. "Outside where?" he asked. He thought of the tunnel she claimed to be digging, the racket they had been making over there that had recently gone silent. He thought she meant she'd been beyond the boundaries of her silo.

"*Outside* outside. The hills. The world the ancients left behind. I took samples."

Donald leaned forward in his seat. She meant to threaten him, but all he heard was a promise. She meant to torture him, but all he felt was excitement. *Outside*. And to take samples. He dreamed of such a venture. Dreamed of discovering what he had breathed out there, what they had done to the world, if it was getting better or worse. Juliette must think *he* held the answers, but he had nothing but questions.

"What did you find?" he whispered. And he damned the machines that would make him sound disinterested, that would make him sound as if he knew. Why couldn't he just say that he had no idea what was wrong with the world or with himself and please, please help him? Help each other.

"You aren't sending us out there to clean. You're sending something else. I'll tell you what I found—"

To Donald, her voice was the entire universe. The weight of the soil overhead vanished, as did the solidness beneath his feet. It was just him in a bubble, and that voice.

"—we took two samples and another from the airlock that should've been inert gas. We took a sample from the ramp and one from the hills."

Suddenly, he was the silent one. His coveralls clung to him. He waited and waited, but she outlasted him. She wanted him to beg for it. Maybe she knew how lost he was.

"What did you find?" he asked again.

"That you're a lying sack of ratshit. That everything we've been told, any time we've trusted you, we've been fools. We take for granted everything you show us, everything you tell us, and none of it's true. Maybe there were no ancients. You know these goddamn books over here? Burn them all. And you let Lukas believe this crap—"

"The books are real," Donald said.

"Ratshit. Like the argon? Is the argon real? What the hell are you pumping into the airlocks when we go out to clean?"

Donald repeated her question in his head. "What do you mean?" he asked.

"Stop with the games. I know what's going on now. When you send us outside, you pump our airlocks full of something that eats away at us. It takes the seals and gaskets first, and then our bodies. You've got it down to a science, haven't you? Well, I found the camera feeds you hid. I cut them weeks ago. Yeah, that was me. And I saw the power lines coming in. I saw the pipes. The gas is in the pipes, isn't it?"

"Juliette, listen to me—"

"Don't you say my name like you know me. You don't know me. All these talks, telling me how my silo was built like you built it yourself, telling Lukas about a disappeared world like you'd seen it with your own eyes. Were you trying to get us to like you? To think you were our friend? Saying you want to help us?"

Donald watched the clock tick down. The techs would be back soon. He'd have to yell at them to get out. He couldn't leave the conversation like this.

"Stop calling us," Juliette said. "The buzzing and the flashing lights, it's giving us headaches. If you keep doing this every day, I'm going to start tearing shit down, and I've got enough to worry about."

"Listen . . . Please—"

"No, you listen. You are cut off from us. We don't want your cameras, your power, your gas. I'm cutting it all. And no one will ever clean from here again. No more of this bullshit argon. The next time I go out, it'll be with clean air. Now fuck off and leave us to it."

"Juliette—"

But the line was dead.

Donald pulled his headset off and threw it against the desk. Playing cards scattered, and the book fell from its perch, losing someone's place.

Argon? What the hell had come over her? The last time she'd been so angry was when she said she had found some machine, threatened to come after him. But this was something else. Argon. Pumped out with a cleaning. He had no idea what she was talking about. Pumped out with a cleaning—

A bout of dizziness struck him, and Donald sank back into his chair. His coveralls were damp with sweat. He clutched a bloody rag and remembered a fog-filled airlock. He remembered stumbling down a ramp with a jostling crowd, crying for

Helen, the vision of bomb blasts seared in his retinas, Anna and Charlotte tugging him along, while a white cloud billowed out around him.

The gas. He knew how the cleanings went. There was gas to pressurize the airlock. Gas to push against the outside air. Gas to push *out*.

"The dust is in the air," Donald said. He leaned against the counter, his knees weak. The nanos eating away at mankind, they were loosed on the world with every cleaning, little puffs like clockwork, tick-tock with each exile.

The headphones sat there quietly. "I am an ancient," Donald said, using her words. He grabbed the headphones from the desk and repeated into the microphone, loudly, "I am an ancient! I did this!"

He sagged once more against the desk, catching himself before he fell. "I'm sorry," he muttered. "I'm sorry, I'm sorry." Louder, yelling it: "I'm sorry!"

But nobody was listening.

26

CHARLOTTE WORKED THE aileron on the drone's left wing up and down. There was still a bit of play in the cables that guided the flap. She grabbed a work rag hanging from the drone's tail and dabbed the back of her neck. Reaching into her tool bag, she chose a medium driver. Beneath the drone lay a scattering of parts, everything she could find inside that the drone didn't need. The bombing computer, the munitions mounts from the wings, the release servos. She'd taken out every camera but one, had even stripped out some of the bracing struts that helped the drone pull up to a dozen Gs. This would be a straight flight, no stress on the wings. They would go low and fast this time, not caring if the drone was spotted. It was important to see further, to make sure, to verify. Charlotte had spent a week working on the blasted thing, and all she could think about was how quickly the last two had broken down and how lucky that first flight now seemed.

Lying on her back, she worked her shoulders and hips and squirmed beneath the tail of the drone. The access panel was already open, the cables exposed. Every panel would get a fine bead of caulk before it went back together, sealing the machine against the dust. *This'll work,* she told herself as she adjusted the servo arm holding the cable. It would have to. Seeing her brother, the state he was in, had her thinking they didn't have another flight in them. It would be all or nothing. It wasn't just the coughing—he now seemed to be losing his mind.

He had come back from his latest call and had forgotten to bring her dinner. He had also forgotten the last part for the radio he had promised. Now he paced around the drone while she worked, mumbling to himself. He paced down the hall to the conference room and dug through his notes. He stomped back toward the drone, coughing and picking up a conversation she didn't feel a part of.

"—their fear, don't you see? We do it with their fear."

She peeked out from under the drone to see him waving his hands in the air. He looked ashen. There were specks of blood on his coveralls. It was almost time to throw in the towel, get in that lift, turn them both in. Just so he would see someone.

He caught her looking at him.

"Their fear doesn't just color the world they see," he said, his eyes wild. "They poison the world with it. It's a toxin, this fear. They send their own out to clean, and that poisons the world!"

Charlotte didn't know how to respond. She wiggled back out to work the aileron again, thinking of how much faster this would go with two people. She considered asking for his help, but her brother couldn't seem to stand still, much less hold a wrench.

"And this got me thinking, about the gas. I mean, I should have known, right? We pump it into their homes when we're done with them. That's how we end their existence. It's all the same gas. I've done it." Donald walked in a tight circle, jabbing his chest with his finger. He coughed into the crook of his arm. "God knows I've done it. But that's not the only thing!"

Charlotte sighed and pulled her driver back out. Still a touch too loose.

"Maybe they can twist this around, you know?" He began to

wander back to the conference room. "They turned off their cameras. And there was that silo that turned off its demolitions. Maybe they can turn off the gas—"

His voice trailed off with him. Charlotte studied the hallway at the back of the warehouse. The light spilling from the conference room danced with his shadow as he paced back and forth among his notes and charts, walking in circles. They were both stuck in circles. She could hear him cursing. His erratic behavior reminded her of their grandmother, who had gone ungracefully. This would be how she remembered him when he was gone: coughing up blood and babbling nonsense. He would never be Congressman Keene in a pressed suit, never her older and competent brother, never again.

While he agonized over what to do, Charlotte had her own ideas. How about they wake everyone up like Donald had done for her? There were only a hundred or so men on shift at any one time. There were thousands of women asleep. Many thousands. Charlotte thought of the army she could raise. But she wondered if Donny was right—if they would refuse to fight their fathers and husbands and brothers. It took a strange kind of courage to do that.

The light down the hall wavered again with shadows. Pacing back and forth, back and forth. Charlotte took a deep breath and worked the flap on the wing. She thought about his other idea to set the world straight, to clear the air and free the imprisoned. Or at least to give them all a chance. An equal chance. He had likened it to knocking down borders in the old world. There was some saying he repeated about those who had an advantage and wanted to keep it, about the last ones up pulling the ladder after them. "Let's lower the ladders," he had said more than once. Don't let the computers decide. Let the people.

Charlotte still didn't get how that might work. And neither, obviously, did her brother. She wiggled back under the drone and tried to imagine a time when people were born into their jobs, when they had no choice. First sons did what their fathers did. Second sons went to war, to the sea, or to the Church. Any boy who followed was left on his own. Daughters went to the sons of others.

Her wrench slipped off the cable stay—her knuckles banging the fuselage. Charlotte cursed and studied her hand, saw blood welling up. She sucked on her knuckle and remembered another injustice that had once given her pause. She remembered being on deployment and feeling grateful that she was born in the States, not in Iraq. A roll of the dice. Invisible borders drawn on maps that were as real as the walls of silos. Trapped by circumstance. What life you lived was divined by some calculus of your people, your leaders, like computers tallying your fate.

She crawled out once again and tried the wing. The play in the cable was gone. The drone was in the best condition Charlotte could make her. She gathered the wrenches she would no longer need and began slotting them into her tool bag when there was a ding at the end of the shelves, off toward the lifts.

Charlotte froze. Her first thought was of food. The ding meant Donny bringing her food. But her brother's shadow could be seen down the hall.

She heard a lift door slide open. Someone was running. Several someones. Boots rang out like thunder, and Charlotte risked yelling Donald's name. She shouted it down the hall once before rushing around the drone and grabbing the tarp. She spun the tarp like a fisherman's net across the wide wings and the scattering of parts and tools. Had to hide. Hide her work and then herself. Donny had heard her. He would hide as well.

The tarp drifted to the ground on a cushion of trapped air; it billowed out and settled. Charlotte turned toward the hallway to run to Donny just as men spilled from the tall shelves. She fell to the ground at once, certain she'd been spotted. Boots clomped past. Gripping the edge of the tarp, she lifted it slowly and curled her knees against her body. She used her shoulder and hip to wiggle underneath the tarp to join the drone. Donny had heard her call out. He would hear the boots and hide in the bathroom attached to the conference room, hide in the shower. Somewhere. They couldn't know they were down there. How had these people gotten in? Her brother said he had the highest access.

The running receded. They were heading straight to the back of the warehouse, almost as if they knew. Voices nearby. Men talking. Slower footsteps shuffling past the drone. Charlotte thought she heard Donny cry out as he was discovered. Crawling on her belly, she scooted beneath the drone to the other edge of the tarp. The voices were fading, slow footsteps walking past. Her brother was in trouble. She remembered a conversation from a few days prior and wondered if he'd been recognized in the lift. A handyman had seen him. The darkness beneath the tarp closed in around her at the thought of being left alone, of him being taken. She relied on him. She was going crazy enough locked in that warehouse with him to keep her company. Without him—she didn't want to imagine.

Resting her chin on the cool steel plating, she slid her arms forward and lifted the tarp with the backs of her hands. A low sliver of the world was exposed. She could see boots dangerously close. She could smell oil on the decking. Ahead of her, it looked like a man having a hard time walking, another man in silver coveralls helping to support him, their feet shuffling along as if with a single mind.

Beyond them, a hallway was thrown into brightness; all the overhead lights Donny preferred to leave off were now on. Charlotte sucked in her breath as her brother was pulled from the conference room. One of the men in the bright silver coveralls punched him in the ribs. Her brother grunted, and Charlotte felt the blow to her own side. She dropped the tarp with one hand and covered her mouth in horror. The other hand trembled as it lifted the tarp further, not wanting to see but needing to. Her brother was hit again, but the shuffling man waved an arm. She could hear a feeble voice commanding them to stop.

The two men in silver held her brother down on the ground and did as they were told. Charlotte forgot to breathe as she watched the man who shuffled along as if weak—watched him march into the lit hallway. He had white hair as brilliant as the bulbs overhead. He labored to walk, leaned on the young man beside him, arm draped across his back, until he came to a stop by her brother.

Charlotte could see Donny's eyes. He was fifty meters away, but she could see how wide they were. Her brother stared up at this old and feeble man, didn't look away even as he coughed, a bad fit from the blow to his ribs, drowning out something being said by the man who could barely stand.

Her brother tried to speak. He said something over and over, but she couldn't hear. And the thin man with the white hair could barely stand, could barely stand but could still swing his boots. The young man beside him propped him up, and Charlotte watched, cowed and trembling, as a leg was brought back over and over before lashing forward, a heavy boot slamming into her brother with ferocious might, Donny's own legs scrambling to shield himself, hugging his shins as two men pinned him to the ground, giving him nowhere to hide from kick after brutal, stomping, and angry kick.

Silo 18

27

"ARE YOU SURE you should be digging around in there?" Lukas asked.

"Hold the light still," Juliette said. "I've got one more to go."

"But shouldn't we talk about this?"

"I'm just looking, Luke. Except that right now, I can't see a damn thing."

Lukas adjusted the light, and Juliette crawled forward. It was the second time she'd explored beneath the floor grates at the bottom of the server room ladder. It was here that she'd traced the camera feeds over a month ago, soon after Lukas made her mayor. He had shown her how they could see anywhere within the silo, and Juliette had asked who else could see. Lukas had insisted no one until she found the feeds disappearing through a sealed port where the outer edge of the silo wall should be. She remembered seeing other lines in that bundle. Now she wanted to make sure.

She worked the last screw on the cover panel. It came off, exposing the dozens of wires she'd cut, each of them bursting with hundreds of tiny filaments like silver strands of hair. Running parallel to the bundles were thick cables that reminded her of the main feeds from the two generators in Mechanical. There were also two copper pipes buried in there.

"Have you seen enough?" Lukas asked. He crouched down behind her where the floor grating had been removed and aimed the light over her shoulder.

"In the other silo, this level still has power. All of thirty-four has full power with no generator running." She tapped the thick cables with her driver. "The servers over there are still humming as well. And some of the survivors tapped into that power to run pumps and things up and down the silo. I think all that juice comes from here."

"Why?" Lukas asked. He played the light across the bundle and seemed more interested now.

"Because they needed the power for the pumps and grow lights," Juliette said, amazed she had to spell it out.

"No, why are they providing this power in the first place?"

"Maybe they don't trust us to keep things running on our own. Or maybe the servers require more juice than we can generate. I don't know." She leaned to the side and peered back at Lukas. "What I want to know is why they left it running after they tried to kill everyone. Why not shut it off with everything else?"

"Maybe they did. Maybe your friend hacked in here and turned it back on."

Juliette laughed. "No. Not Solo—"

There was a voice down the hall. The crawl space grew dark as Lukas spun the flashlight around. There shouldn't have been anyone else down there.

"It's the radio," he said. "Let me see who it is."

"The flashlight," Juliette called out—but he was already gone. His boots rang and faded down the hallway.

Juliette reached ahead of herself and felt for the copper pipes. They were the right size. Nelson had shown her where the argon tanks were kept. There was a pump and filter mechanism that was supposed to draw a fresh supply of argon from deep within the earth, similar to how the air handlers worked. But now Juliette knew to trust nothing. Pulling out the floor panels and the wall panels behind the tanks, she had discovered two lines feeding into the gas tanks separate from the supply system. A supply system she now suspected did absolutely nothing. Just like with the gaskets and heat tape, the second power feed, the visor of lies, everything had a false front. The truth lay buried beneath.

Lukas stomped back toward her. He knelt down, and the light returned to the crawlspace.

"Jules, I need you to get out of there."

"Please hand me the flashlight," she told him. "I can't see shit." This was going to be another argument like when she'd cut the camera feeds. As if she would cut these pipes without knowing what was in them—

"I need you to get out here. I . . . please."

And she heard it in his voice. Something was wrong. Juliette looked back and caught an eyeful of flashlight.

"One sec," she said. She wiggled back toward him on her palms and the toes of her boots until she reached the open access panel. She left her multi-tool behind.

"What is it?" She sat up and stretched her back, untied her hair, gathered the loose ends, and began tying it back. "Who was that?"

"Your father—" Lukas began.

"Something wrong with my father?"

He shook his head. "No, that was him that called. It . . . one of the kids is gone."

"Missing?" But she knew that wasn't what he meant. "Lukas, what happened?" She stood and dusted off her chest and knees, headed toward the radio.

"They were on their way up to the farms. There was a crowd heading down. One of the kids went over the rails—"

"Fell?"

"Twenty levels," Lukas said.

Juliette couldn't believe this. She grabbed the radio and pressed a palm against the wall, suddenly dizzy. "Who was it?"

"He didn't say."

Before she squeezed the mic, she saw that the set had been left on channel 17 from the last time she'd called Jimmy. Her dad must've been using Walker's new portable. "Dad? Do you read me?"

She waited. Lukas held out his canteen, but Juliette waved him away.

"Jules? Can I get back to you? Something else has just come up."

Her father sounded shaken. There was a lot of static in the line. "I need to know what's going on," she told him.

"Hold on. Elise—"

Juliette covered her mouth.

"—we've lost Elise. Jimmy went looking for her. Baby, we had a problem coming up. There was a crowd heading down. An angry crowd. They knew who I had with me. And Marcus went over the rails. I'm sorry—"

Juliette felt Lukas's hand on her shoulder. She wiped her eyes. "Is he—?"

"I haven't made my way down yet to check. Rickson got hurt in the scuffle. I'm tending to him. Hannah and Miles and the baby are fine. We're at Supply right now. Look, I really need to go. We can't find Elise, and Jimmy took off after her. Someone said they saw her heading up. I don't want you to do anything, but I thought you'd want to know about the boy."

Her hand trembled as she squeezed the mic. "I'm coming down. You're at Supply on one-ten?"

There was a long pause. She knew he was debating whether

or not to argue with her about heading that way. The radio popped as he gave up without a fight.

"I'm at one-ten, yeah. I'm heading down to see about the boy. I'll leave Rickson and the others here. I told Jimmy to bring Elise back here once he finds her."

"Don't leave them there," Juliette said. She didn't know whom they could trust, where they might be safe. "Take them with you. Dad, get them back to Mechanical. Get them home." Juliette wiped her forehead. The entire thing was a mistake. Bringing them over was a mistake.

"Are you sure?" her father asked. "The crowd we ran into. I think they were heading that way."

28

ELISE WAS LOST in the bizarre. She had heard someone call it that, and it was the right name for the place, a place of crowds beyond imagining, a land so wildly strange that its name barely did it justice.

How she found herself there was a bit bewildering. Her puppy had disappeared in a great confrontation of strangers—more people than she thought could exist at one time—and she had chased up the steps after it. One person after another had pointed helpfully upward. A woman in yellow said she saw a man with a dog heading toward the bizarre. Elise had gone up ten levels until she'd reached landing one-hundred.

There had been two men on the landing blowing smoke from their noses. They had said someone just passed through with a dog. They had waved her inside.

Level one-hundred in her home was a scary wasteland of narrow passages and empty rooms scattered with trash and debris and rats. Here it was all of that but full of people and animals and everyone shouting and singing. It was a place of bright colors and awful smells, of people breathing smoke in and out, smoke they held in their fingers and kept going with small sparks of fire. There were men who wore paint on their faces. A woman dressed all in red with a tail and horns who had waved Elise inside a tent, but Elise had turned and ran.

She ran from one fright to another until she was completely lost. There were knees everywhere to bump into. No longer looking for Puppy, now she just wanted out. She crawled beneath a busy counter and cried, but that got her nowhere. It did give her a terribly close view of a fat and hairless animal that made noises like Rickson snoring, though. This animal was led right by her with a rope around its neck. Elise dried her eyes and pulled her book out, looked through pictures until she could name it a pig. Naming things always helped. They weren't nearly so scary after that.

It was Rickson who got her moving again, even though he wasn't there. Elise could hear his loud voice booming through the Wilds telling her there was nothing to be afraid of. He and the twins used to send her on errands through the pitch black when she was just old enough to walk. They would send her for blackberries and plums and delicacies near the stairs when there were people still around to fear. "The littlest ones are the safest," Rickson used to tell her. That was years ago. She wasn't so little anymore.

She put her book away and decided that the dark Wilds with their leafy fingers brushing her neck and the clicking of pumps and chattering teeth were worse than painted people leaking smoke from their noses. With her face chapped from crying, she crawled out from beneath the counter and jostled among the knees. Always turning right—which was the trick to getting through the Wilds in the dark—she found herself in a smoky hallway with loud hisses and a smell in the air like boiling rat.

"Hey, kid, you lost?"

A boy with short-cropped hair and bright green eyes studied her from the edge of a booth. He was older than her, but not by

much. As big as the twins. Elise shook her head. She reconsid-
ered and nodded.

The boy laughed. "What's your name?"

"Elise," she said.

"That's a different name."

She shrugged, not sure what to say. The boy caught her eyeing a man beyond him as he lifted strips of sizzling meat with a
large fork.

"You hungry?" the boy asked.

Elise nodded. She was always hungry. Especially when she
was scared. But maybe that was because she got scared when
she went out looking for food, and she went out looking for food
when she was hungry. Hard to remember which came first. The
boy disappeared behind the counter. He came back with a thick
piece of meat.

"Is it rat?" Elise asked.

The boy laughed. "It's pig."

Elise scrunched up her face, remembering the animal that
grunted at her earlier. "Does it taste like rat?" she asked, full of
hope.

"You say that louder and my dad'll have your hide. You want
some or not?" He handed the strip of meat over. "I'm guessing
you don't have two chits on you."

Elise accepted the meat and didn't say. She took a small bite,
and little bursts of happiness exploded in her mouth. It was better than rat. The boy studied her.

"You're from the Mids, aren't you?"

Elise shook her head and took another bite. "I'm from Silo
Seventeen," she said, chewing. Her mouth was full of saliva.
She eyed the man cooking the strips of meat. Marcus and Miles
should be there to try some.

"You mean level seventeen?" The boy frowned. "You don't
look like a topper. No, too dirty to be a topper."

"I'm from the other silo," Elise said. "West of here."

"What's a westophere?" the boy asked.

"West. Where the sun sets."

The boy looked at her funny.

"The sun. It comes up in the east and sets in the west. That's why maps point up. They point up at north." She thought about pulling her book out and showing him the maps of the world, explaining how the sun went around and around, but her hands were covered in grease, and anyway the boy didn't seem interested. "They dug over and rescued us," she explained.

At this, the boy's eyes went wide. "The dig. You're from the other silo. It's real?"

Elise finished the strip of pig and licked her fingers. She nodded.

The boy shoved a hand at her. Elise wiped her palm on her hip and grabbed it with her own.

"My name's Shaw," he said. "You want another piece of pig? Come under the counter. I'll introduce you to my father. Hey, Pa, I want you to meet someone."

"I can't. I'm looking for Puppy."

Shaw scrunched up his face. "Puppy? You'd want the next hall over." He nodded the direction. "But c'mon, pig is much better. Dog is chewy like rat, and puppy is just more expensive than dog but tastes the same."

Elise froze. The pig that went by earlier with a rope around its neck, maybe that one was a pet. Maybe they ate pets, just like Marcus and Miles always wanted to keep a rat for fun, even when everyone else was hungry. "They eat puppy?" she asked this boy.

"If you've got the chits, sure." Shaw grabbed her hand. "Come back to the grill with me. I want you to meet my dad. He says you all aren't real."

Elise pulled away. "I've got to find my puppy." She turned

and scurried through the crowd in the direction the boy had nodded.

"Whaddya mean, *your* puppy—?" he yelled after her.

Around a line of stalls, Elise found another smoky hall. More smells like rat on a stick over an open flame. An old woman wrestled with a bird, two angry wings flapping from her fists. Elise stepped in poop and nearly slipped. The strangeness all around melted with the thought of her puppy gone. She heard someone yell about a dog, and searched for the voice. An older boy, probably Rickson's age, was holding up a piece of red meat, a giant piece with white stripes that looked like bones. There was a pen there and signs with numbers on them. People from the crowd stopped to peer inside. Some of them pointed inside the pen and asked questions.

Elise fought through them toward the sound of yipping. There were live dogs in the pen. She could see through the slats and almost over the top when she was on her tiptoes. A huge animal the size of a pig lunged at the fence and growled at her, and the fence shook. It was a dog, but with a rope around its jaw so it couldn't open. Elise could feel its hot breath blowing out its nose. She scooted out of everyone's way and around the side.

There was a smaller pen in the back. Elise went past the counter to where two young men tended a smoking grill. Their backs were turned. They took something from a woman and handed her a package. Elise grabbed the top of the smaller fence and peered over. There was a dog on its side with five—no, six little animals eating at its belly. She thought they were rats at first, but they were the tiniest of puppies. They made Puppy seem like a grown dog. And they weren't eating the dog—they were sucking like Hannah's baby did at her breast.

Elise was so fixated on the tiny critters that she didn't see the animal at the base of the fence lunge at her until it was too late. A black nose and a pink tongue bounced up and caught her on the jaw. She peered directly down the other side of the fence and saw Puppy, who bounded up at her again.

Elise cried out. Reaching over the fence, she had both hands on the animal, when someone grabbed her from behind.

"Don't think you can afford that one," one of the men behind the counter said.

Elise squirmed in his grip and tried to keep a hold of Puppy.

"Easy now," the man said. "Let it go."

"Let *me* go!" Elise cried.

Puppy slipped from her grasp. Elise wiggled loose, the shoulder strap of her bag yanked over her head. She fell at the man's feet and got back up, reached for Puppy again.

"Well, now," she heard the man say.

Elise reached over the fence and grabbed her pet again. Puppy's feet scratched at the fence to help. His front paws draped over her shoulder, a wet tongue in her ear. Elise turned to find a man towering over her, a bloody white piece of fabric tied over his chest, her Memory Book in his hands.

"What's this?" he asked, thumbing through the pages. A few of the loose papers shuffled free and he grabbed at them frantically.

"That's my book," Elise said. "Give it back."

The man peered down at her. Puppy licked her face.

"Trade you for that one," he said, pointing at Puppy.

"They're both mine," she insisted.

"Naw, I paid for that runt. But this'll do." He weighed her book in his hands, then reached down and steered Elise out of the booth and back toward the crowded hall.

Elise reached for the book. Her bag was being left behind. Puppy nipped her on the hand and nearly squirmed free. She was crying, she realized, as she squealed for the man to give her back her things. He showed his teeth and grabbed her by the hair, was angry now. "Roy! Come grab this runt."

Elise screeched. The boy from outside yelling "dog" to every-one who passed by headed toward her. Puppy was nearly free. She was losing her grip again, and the man was going to rip out her hair.

She lost Puppy, and Elise squealed as the man lifted her off the ground. Then there was a flash, like a dog pouncing, but it was brown coveralls rather than brown fur that flew past, and the large man let out a grunt and fell to the ground. Elise went spilling after.

He no longer had a grip on her hair. Elise saw her bag. Her book. She grabbed both, clutched a handful of loose pages. Shaw was there, the boy who fed her pig. He scooped up Puppy and grinned at Elise.

"Run," he said, flashing his teeth.

Elise ran. She danced away from the boy in the hall and bounced off people in the crowd. Looking over her shoulder, she saw Shaw running after her, Puppy clutched to his chest upside down, paws in the air. The crowd rattled and made room as the men from the stall came after them.

"This way!" Shaw yelled, laughing, as he overtook Elise and turned a corner. Tears streamed from her eyes, but Elise was laughing too. Laughing and terrified and happy to have her book and her pet and getting away and this boy who was nicer to her than the twins. They dashed beneath another of the counters—the smell of fresh fruit—and someone yelled at them. Shaw ran through a dark room with unmade beds, through a kitchen with a woman cooking, then back out into another stall. A tall man with dark skin shook a spatula at them, but they were already out among the crowds, running and laughing and danc-ing between—

And then someone in the crowd snatched him up. Large and powerful hands jerked the boy into the air. Elise stumbled. Shaw kicked and screamed at this man, and Elise looked up and saw that it was Solo holding him. He smiled down at Elise through his thick beard.

"Solo!" Elise squealed. She grabbed his leg and squeezed.

"This boy got something of yours?" he asked.

"No, he's a friend. Put him down." She scanned the crowd for any sign of the men chasing them. "We should go," she told Solo. She squeezed his leg once more. "I want to go home."

Solo rubbed her head. "And that's just where we're heading."

29

ELISE LET SOLO carry her bag and her book while she clutched Puppy. They made their way through the crowds, out of the bizarre, and back to the stairwell. Shaw trailed after them, even after Solo told the boy to get back to his family. And as Elise and Solo made their way down the stairwell to find the others, she kept glancing back to catch sight of Shaw in his brown coveralls, peeking from around the central post or through the rails of a landing higher up. She thought about telling Solo that he was still there, but she didn't.

A few levels below the bizarre, a porter caught up to them and delivered a message. Jewel was heading down and looking for them. She had half the porters hunting for Elise. And Elise never knew that she'd been missing.

Solo made her drink from his canteen while they waited at the next landing. She then poured a small puddle into his old and wrinkled hands, and Puppy took grateful sips. It took what felt like forever for Jewel to arrive, but when she did, it was in a thunder of hurrying boots. The landing shook. Jewel was all sweaty and out of breath, but Solo didn't seem to care. The two of them hugged, and Elise wondered if they'd ever let go. People came and went from the landing and gave them funny looks as they passed. Jewel was smiling and crying both when they finally released each other. She said something to Solo, and it was his turn to cry. Both of them looked at Elise, and she could see that it was secrets or something bad. Jewel picked her up next and kissed her on the cheek and hugged her until it was hard to breathe.

"It's gonna be okay," she told Elise. But Elise didn't know what was wrong.

"I got Puppy back," she said. And then she remembered that Jewel didn't know about her new pet. She looked down to see Puppy peeing on Jewel's boot, which must be like saying hello.

"A dog," Jewel said. She squeezed Elise's shoulder. "You can't keep her. Dogs are dangerous."

"She's not dangerous!"

Puppy chewed on Elise's hand. Elise pulled away and rubbed Puppy's head.

"Did you get her from the bazaar? Is that where you went?" Jewel looked to Solo, who nodded. Jewel took a deep breath. "You can't take things that don't belong to you. If you got it from a vendor, it'll have to go back."

"Puppy came from the Deep," Elise said. She bent down and wrapped her arms around the dog. "He came from Mechanical. We can take him back there. But not to the bizarre. I'm sorry I took him." She squeezed Puppy and thought about the man holding up the red meat with the white ribs. Jewel turned to Solo again.

"It didn't come from the bazaar," he confirmed. "She plucked it from a box down in Mechanical."

"Fine. We'll straighten this out later. We need to catch up with the others."

Elise could tell that all of them were tired, including her and Puppy, but they set out anyway. The adults seemed eager to get down, and after seeing the bizarre Elise felt the same way. She told Jewel she wanted to go home, and Jewel said that's where they were heading. "We ought to make things how they used to be," Elise told them both.

For some reason that made Jewel laugh. "You're too young to be nostalgic," she said.

Elise asked what nostalgic meant, and Jewel said, "It's where you think the past was better than it really was, only because the present sucks so bad."

"I get nostalgic a lot," Elise declared.

And Jewel and Solo both laughed at that. But then they looked sad after. Elise caught them looking at each other like this a lot, and Jewel kept wiping at her eyes. Finally, Elise asked them what was wrong.

They stopped in the middle of the stairway and told her. Told her about Marcus, who had slipped over the rails when that crazy crowd had knocked her down and Puppy had gotten away. Marcus had fallen and died. Elise looked at the rails beside her and didn't see how Marcus could slip over rails so high. She didn't understand how it had happened, but she knew it was like when their parents had gone off and never came back. It was like that. Marcus would never come laughing through the Wilds again. She wiped her face and felt awful for Miles, who wasn't a twin anymore.

"Is that why we're going home?" she asked.

"It's one of the reasons," Jewel said. "I never should've brought you here."

Elise nodded. There was no arguing with that. Except she had Puppy now, and Puppy had come from here. And no matter what she told Jewel, Elise wasn't giving him back.

Juliette allowed Elise to lead the way. Her legs were sore from the run down; she had nearly lost her footing more than once. Now she was eager to see the kids together and home, couldn't stop blaming herself for what had happened to Marcus. The levels went by full of regrets, and then there was a call on the radio.

"Jules, are you there?"

It was Shirly, and she sounded upset. Juliette pulled the radio from her belt. Shirly must've been with Walker, using one of his sets. "Go ahead," she said. She kept a hand on the rail and followed Elise and Solo. A porter and a young couple squeezed by heading in the other direction.

"What the hell is going on?" Shirly asked. "We just had a mob come through here. Frankie got overrun at the gates. He's in the infirmary. And I've got another two or three dozen people heading through this blasted tunnel of yours. I didn't sign on for this."

Juliette figured it was the same group that led to Marcus's death. Jimmy turned and eyed the radio and its news. Juliette turned down the volume so Elise couldn't hear.

"What do you mean by *another* two or three dozen? Who else is over there?" Juliette asked.

"Your dig team, for one. Some mechanics from third shift who should be sleeping but want to see what's on the other side. And the planning committee you sent."

"The planning committee?" Juliette slowed her pace.

"Yeah. They said you sent them. Said it was okay to inspect the dig. Had a note from your office."

Juliette remembered Marsha saying something about this before the Town Hall. But she had been busy with the suits.

"Did you not send them?" Shirly asked.

"I may have," Juliette admitted. "But this other group, the mob, my dad and them had a run-in on their way down. Someone fell to their death."

There was silence on the other end. And then: "I heard we

had a fall. Didn't know it was related. I tell you, I'm this close to pulling everyone back and shutting this down. Things are out of hand, Jules."

I know, Juliette thought. But she didn't broadcast this. Didn't utter it out loud. "I'll be there soon. On my way now."

Shirly didn't respond. Juliette clipped the radio to her belt and cursed herself. Jimmy hung back to speak with her, allowing Elise to walk further ahead.

"I'm sorry about all of this," Juliette told him.

The two of them walked in silence for a turn of the staircase.

"The people in the tunnel, I saw some of them taking what's not theirs," Jimmy said. "It was dark when they brought us over, but I saw people carrying pipe and equipment from my silo back to this one. Like it was the plan the whole time. But then you said we were going to rebuild my home. Not use it for spares."

"I did. I do. I do mean to rebuild it. As soon as we get down there, I'll talk to them. They aren't taking spares."

"So you didn't tell them it was okay?"

"No. I . . . I may have told them it made sense to come get you and the kids, that the extra silo would mean certain . . . redundancies—"

"That's what a spare is."

"I'll talk to them. I promise. Everything will be all right in the end."

They walked in silence for a while.

"Yeah," Solo finally said. "You keep saying that."

Silo 1

30

CHARLOTTE AWOKE IN darkness, damp with sweat. Cold. The metal decking was cold. Her face was sore from it resting so long on the steel. She worked a half-dead arm from beneath her and rubbed her face, felt the marks there from the diamond plating.

The attack on Donny returned like a dimly remembered dream. She had curled up and waited. Had somehow held back her tears. And whether exhausted from the effort or terrified of moving, she had eventually succumbed to sleep.

She listened for footsteps or voices before cracking the tarp. It was pitch black outside. As black there as under the drone. Like a chick from a nest, she crawled out from beneath the metal bird, her joints stiff, a weight on her chest, a terrible solitude all around her.

Her worklight was somewhere beneath the tarp. She uncovered the drone and patted around, felt some tools, knocked over and noisily scattered a ratchet set. Remembering the drone's headlamp, she felt inside an open access panel, found the test switch, and pressed it. A golden carpet was thrown out in front of the bird's beak. It was enough to find her worklight.

She grabbed this and a large wrench as well. She was no longer safe. A mortar had flown into camp and had leveled a tent, had taken a bunkmate. Another could come whistling down at any time.

She aimed her flashlight toward the lifts, afraid of what they could disgorge without warning. In the silence, she could hear her heartbeat. Charlotte turned and headed for the conference room, for the last place she'd seen him.

There was no sign of struggle on the floor. Inside the conference room, the table was still scattered with notes. Maybe not as many as before. And the several bins scattered among the chairs were gone. Someone had done a poor job of cleaning up. Someone would be back.

Charlotte doused the lights and turned to go. Stepping through the place where he'd been attacked, she saw this time the splattered blood on the wall. She felt the sobs she'd wrestled down before falling asleep rise up to seize her throat, constricting it, wondered if her brother was still alive. She could see the man with the white hair standing there, kicking and kicking, an unholy rage in him. And now she had no one. She hurried through the dark warehouse toward the glowing drone. Pulled from sleep, shown a frightening world, and now she'd been left alone.

The light from the drone's beak spilled across the floor and illuminated a door.

Not quite alone.

Charlotte gathered her wits. She reached into the access panel and turned the drone's headlamp off. She carefully rearranged the tarp. It would no longer do to leave things amiss—she must always assume she might have visitors. With her worklight bobbing, she made for the door, stopped, went back for her tool bag. The drone was now a distant priority. With her tools and light, she hurried past the barracks and to the end of the hall, into the flight room. The workbench on the far wall held a radio pieced together over the weeks. It worked. She and her brother had listened to the chatter from distant worlds. Maybe there was a way to make it transmit. She pawed through the spare parts he had left for her, searching. If nothing else, she could listen. Maybe she could find out what they'd done to him. Maybe she could hear from him—or reach out to another soul.

31

WITH EVERY COUGH, Donald's ribs exploded into a thousand splinters. This shrapnel pierced his lungs and his heart and sent a tidal wave up his spinal column. He was convinced this was taking place inside his body, these bombs of bone and nerve. Already, he missed the simple torture of burning lungs and searing throat. His bruised and cracked ribs now made a mockery of old torments. Yesterday's misery had become nostalgic fondness.

He lay on his cot, bleeding and bruised, having given up on escape. The door was sound, and the space above the ceiling panels led nowhere. He didn't think he was on the admin levels. Maybe Security. Perhaps residential. Or someplace he wasn't familiar with. The hallway outside remained eerily quiet. It could be the middle of the night. Banging on the door was brutal on his aching ribs, and shouting hurt his throat. But the worst pain was imagining what he'd dragged his sister into, what would become of her. When the guards or Thurman came back, he should tell them she was down there, beg for them to be merciful. She had been like a daughter to Thurman, and Donald was the only one to blame for waking her up. Thurman would see that. He would put her back under where she might sleep until the end came for them all. It would be for the best.

Hours passed. Hours of bruised swelling and feeling his pulse throb in a dozen places. Donald tossed and turned, and day and night became even less distinguishable in that buried crypt. A feverish sweat overtook him, one born of regret and fear more than infection. He had nightmares of frozen pods set ablaze, of fire and ice and dust, of flesh melting and bone turning to powder.

Falling in and out of sleep, he had another dream. A dream of a cold night on a wide ocean, of a ship sinking beneath his feet, the deck trembling from the savagery of the sea. Donald's hands were frozen to the wheel of the ship, his breath a fog of lies. Waves lapped over the rails as his command sank deeper and deeper. And all around him on the water were lifeboats ablaze. All the women and children burned out there, screaming, trapped in lifeboats shaped like cryopods that were never meant to reach the shore.

Donald saw that now. He saw it awake—panting, coughing, sweating—as well as in his dreams. He remembered thinking once that the women had been set aside so that there would be nothing to fight over. But the opposite was true. They were there to give the rest of them something to fight *for*. Someone to save. It was for them that men worked these dark shifts, slept through these dark nights, dreaming of what would never be.

He covered his mouth, rolled over in bed, and coughed up blood. Someone to save. The folly of man—the folly of the blasted silos he had helped to build—this assumption that things needed saving. They ought to have been left on their own, both people and the planet. Mankind had the right to go extinct. That's what life did: it went extinct. It made room for the next in line. But individual men had often railed against the natural order. They had their illegally cloned children, their nano treatments, their spare parts, and their cryopods. Individual men like those who did this.

Approaching boots signaled a meal, an end to the interminable nightmare of being asleep with wild thoughts and lying awake with bodily pain. It had to be breakfast, because he was starving. It meant he'd been up for much of the night. He expected the same guard who'd delivered his last meal, but the door cracked open to reveal Thurman. A man in Security silver stood behind him, unsmiling. Thurman entered alone and shut the door, confident that Donald posed no threat to him. He appeared better, fitter, than he had the day before. More time awake, perhaps. Or a flood of new doctors loosed in his bloodstream.

"How long are you keeping me here?" Donald asked, sitting up. His voice was scratchy and distant, the sound of autumn leaves.

"Not long," Thurman said. The old man dragged the trunk away from the foot of the bed and sat on it. He studied Donald intently. "You've only got a few days to live."

"Is that a medical diagnosis? Or a sentencing?"

Thurman raised an eyebrow. "It's both. If we keep you here and leave you untreated, you will die from the air you breathed. We're putting you under, instead."

"God forbid you put me out of my misery."

Thurman seemed to consider this. "I've thought about letting you die in here. I know the pain you're in. I could fix you or let you break all the way down, but I don't have the heart for either."

Donald tried to laugh, but it hurt too much. He reached for the glass of water on the tray and took a sip. A pink spiral of blood danced on the surface as he lowered the glass.

"You've been busy this last shift," Thurman said. "There are drones and bombs missing. We've woken up a few of the people who went into freeze recently to piece together your handiwork. Do you have any idea what you've risked?"

There was something worse than anger in Thurman's voice. Donald couldn't place it at first. Not disappointment. It wasn't any form of rage. The rage had drained from his boots. This was something subdued. It was something like fear.

"What I've risked?" Donald asked. "I've been cleaning up your mess." He sloshed water as he saluted his old mentor. "The silos you damaged. That silo that went black all those years ago. It was still there—"

"Silo Forty. I know."

"And Seventeen." Donald cleared his throat. He grabbed the heel of bread from the tray and took a dry bite, chewed until his jaws ached, chased it with blood-smeared water. He knew so much that Thurman didn't. This occurred to him in that moment. All the talks with the people of 18, the time spent poring over drawings and notes, the weeks of piecing things together, of being in charge. He knew in his present condition that he was no match for Thurman in a fight, but he still felt the stronger of the two. It was his knowledge that made him feel that way. "Seventeen wasn't dead," he said before taking another bite of bread.

"So I've learned."

Donald chewed.

"I'm shutting down Eighteen today," Thurman said quietly. "What that facility has cost us . . ." He shook his head, and Donald wondered if he was thinking of Victor, the head of heads, who had blown his own head off over an uprising that took place there. In the next moment, it occurred to him that the people he'd placed so much hope in were now gone as well. All the time spent smuggling parts to Charlotte, dreaming of an end to the silos, hope of a future under blue skies, all for nothing. The bread felt stale as he swallowed.

"Why?" he asked.

"You know why. You've been talking to them, haven't you?

What did you think was going to become of that place? What were you thinking?" The first hints of anger crept into Thurman's voice. "Did you think they were going to save you? That any of us can be saved? What the hell were you thinking?"

Donald didn't plan on answering, but a response came as reflexively as a cough: "I thought they deserved better than this. I thought they deserved a chance—"

"A chance for what?" Thurman shook his head. "It doesn't matter. It doesn't matter. We planned for enough." He muttered this last to himself. "The shame is that I have to sleep at all, that I can't be here to manage everything. It's like sending drones up when you need to be there yourself, your hand on the yoke." Thurman made a fist in the air. He studied Donald a while. "You're going under first thing in the morning. It's a far cry from what you deserve. But before I'm rid of you, I want you to tell me how you did it, how you ended up here with my name. I can't let that happen again—"

"So now I'm a threat." Donald took another pull of water, flooding the tickle in his throat. He tried to take a deep breath, but the pain in his chest made him double over.

"You aren't, but the next person who does this might be. We tried to think of everything, but we always knew the biggest weakness, the biggest weakness of any system, was a revolt from the top."

"Like Silo Twelve," Donald said. He remembered that silo falling as a dark shadow emerged from its server room. He had witnessed this, had ended that silo, had written a report. "How could you not expect what happened there?" he asked.

"We did. We planned for everything. It's why we have spares. It's why we have the Rite, a chance to try a man's soul, a box to put our ticking time bombs in. You're too young to understand this, but the most difficult task mankind ever tried to master—and that we never quite managed—was how to pass supreme

power from one hand to the next." Thurman spread his arms.
His old eyes sparkled, the politician in him reawakened. "Until
now. We solved it here with the cryopods and the shifts. Power
is temporary, and it never leaves the same few hands. There is
no transfer of power."

"Congratulations," Donald spat. And he remembered suggesting to Thurman once that he could be President, and Thurman had suggested it would be a demotion. Donald saw that
now.

"Yes. It was a good system. Until you managed to subvert it."

"I'll tell you how I did it if you answer something for me."
Donald covered his mouth and coughed.

Thurman frowned and waited for him to stop. "You're dying," he said. "We'll put you in a box so you can dream until the
end. What could you possibly want to know?"

"The truth. I have so much of it, but still a few holes. They
hurt more than the holes in my lungs."

"I doubt that," Thurman said. But he seemed to consider the
offer. "What is it you want to know?"

"The servers. I know what's on them. All the details of everyone's lives in the silos, where they work, what they do, how long
they live, how many kids they have, what they eat, where they
go, everything. I want to know what it's for."

Thurman studied him. He didn't say anything.

"I found the percentages. The list that shuffles. It's the
chances that these people survive when they're set free, isn't it?
But how does it know?"

"It knows," Thurman said. "And that's what you think the silos do?"

"I think there's a war playing out, yes. A war between all
these silos, and only one will win."

"Then what do you need from me?"

"I think there's something else. Tell me, and I'll tell you how

I took your place." Donald sat up and hugged his shins while a coughing fit ravaged his throat and ribs. Thurman waited until he was done.

"The servers do what you say. They keep track of all those lives, and they weigh them. They also decide the lotteries, which means we get to shape these people in a very real way. We increase our odds, allow the best to thrive. It's why the chances keep improving the longer we're at this."

"Of course." Donald felt stupid. He should have known. He had heard Thurman say over and over that they left nothing to chance. And wasn't a lottery just that?

He caught the look Thurman was giving him. "Your turn," he said. "How'd you do it?"

Donald leaned back against the wall. He coughed into his fist while Thurman looked on, wide-eyed and silent. "It was Anna," Donald said. "She found out what you had planned. You were going to put her under after she was done helping you, and she feared she would never wake up again. You gave her access to the systems so she could fix your problem with Forty. She set it up so that I would take your place. And she left a note asking for my help, left it in your inbox. I think she wanted to ruin you. To end this."

"No," Thurman said.

"Oh, yes. And I woke up and didn't understand what she was asking of me. I found out too late. And in the meantime, there were still problems with Silo Forty. When I woke up and started this shift, Forty—"

"Forty was already taken care of," Thurman said.

Donald rested his head back and stared at the ceiling. "They made you think so. Here's what I think. I think Silo Forty hacked the system, that's what Anna found. They hacked their camera feeds so we couldn't know what was going on, a rogue head of IT, a revolt from the top, just like you said. The cutting of the camera feeds was when they went black. But before that, they hacked the gas lines so we couldn't kill them. And before that, they hacked the bombs meant to bring down their silos in case any of this happened. They worked their way backwards. By the time they went black, they were in charge. Like me. Like what Anna did for me."

"How could they—?"

"Maybe she was helping them, I don't know. She helped me. And somehow word spread to others. Or maybe by the time Anna was done saving your ass, she realized they were right and we were wrong. Maybe she left Silo Forty alone in the end to do whatever they pleased. I think she thought they might save us all."

Donald coughed, and thought of all the hero sagas of old, of men and women struggling for righteousness, always with a happy ending, always against impossible odds, always bullshit. Heroes didn't win. The heroes were whoever *happened* to win. History told their story—the dead didn't say a word. All of it was bullshit.

"I bombed Silo Forty before I understood what was going on," Donald said. He gazed at the ceiling, feeling the weight of all those levels, of the dirt and the heavy sky. "I bombed them because I needed a distraction, because I didn't care. I killed Anna because she brought me here, because she saved my life. I did your job for you both times, didn't I? I put down two rebellions you never saw coming—"

"No." Thurman stood. He towered over Donald.

"Yes," Donald said. He blinked away welling tears, could feel a hole in his heart where his anger toward Anna once lay. All that was there now was guilt and regret. He had killed the one who had loved him the most, had fought for the things that were right. He had never stopped to ask, to think, to talk.

"You started this uprising when you broke your own rules,"

he told Thurman. "When you woke her up, you started this. You were weak. You threatened everything, and I fixed it. And goddamn you to hell for listening to her. For bringing me here. For turning me into this!"

Donald closed his eyes. He felt the tickle of escaping tears as they rolled down his temples, and the light through his lids quivered as Thurman's shadow fell over him. He braced for a blow. He tilted his head back, lifted his chin, and waited. He thought of Helen. He thought of Anna. He thought of Charlotte. And remembering, he started to tell Thurman about his sister and where she was hiding before those blows landed, before he was struck as he deserved to be for helping these monsters, for being their unwitting tool at every turn. He started to tell Thurman about Charlotte, but there was a brightening of light through his lids, the slinking away of a shadow, and the slamming of an angry door.

Silo 18

32

LUKAS SENSED SOMETHING was wrong before he slotted the headphones into the jack. The red lights above the servers throbbed red, but it was the wrong time of day. The calls from Silo 1 came like clockwork. This call had come in the middle of dinner. The buzzing and flashing lights had moved to his office and then to the hallway. Sims, the old Security chief, had tracked Lukas down in the break room to let him know someone was getting in touch, and Lukas's first thought was that their mysterious benefactor had a warning for them. Or maybe he was calling to thank them for finally stopping with the digging.

There was a click in his headset as the connection was made. The lights overhead stopped their infernal blinking. "Hello?" he said, catching his breath.

"Who is this?"

Someone different. The voice was the same, but the words were wrong. Why wouldn't this person know who he was?

"This is Lukas. Lukas Kyle. Who is this?"

"Let me speak to the head of your silo."

Lukas stood up straight. "I am the head of this silo. Silo Eighteen of World Order Operation Fifty. Who am I speaking to?"

"You're speaking to the man who dreamed up that World Order. Now get me the head. I have here a . . . Bernard Holland."

Lukas nearly blurted out that Bernard was dead. Everyone knew Bernard was dead. It was a fact of life. He had watched him burn rather than go out to clean, watched him burn rather than allow himself to be saved. But this man didn't know that. And the complexities of life on the other end of that line, that infallible line, caused the room to wobble. The gods weren't omnipotent. Or they didn't sup around the same table. Or the one who called himself Donald was more rogue than even Lukas had believed he might be. Or — as Juliette would claim if she were there — these people were fucking with him.

"Bernard is . . . ah, he is indisposed at the moment."

There was a pause. Lukas could feel the sweat bead up on his forehead and neck, the heat of the servers and the conversation getting to him.

"How long before he's back?"

"I'm not sure. I can, uh, try to get him for you?" His voice lilted at the end of what shouldn't have been a question.

"Fifteen minutes," the voice said. "After that, things are going to go very badly for you and everyone over there. Very badly. Fifteen minutes."

The line clicked dead before Lukas could object or argue for more time. Fifteen minutes. The room continued to wobble. He needed Jules. He would need someone to pretend to be Bernard — maybe Nelson. And what had this man meant when he said he had dreamed up the World Order? That wasn't possible.

Lukas hurried to the ladder and raced down. He grabbed the portable radio from the charging rack and scrambled back up the ladder. He would call Juliette on his way to tracking down Nelson. A different voice would win him some time until he could sort this out. In a way, this was a call he'd always expected, someone wanting to know what in the hell was going on in their silo, but it had never come. He had expected it, and now it took him by surprise.

"Jules?" He reached the top of the ladder and tried the radio. What if she didn't answer? Fifteen minutes. And then what? How bad could they really make it for them in the silo? The other voice—Donald—had tossed around dire and vacuous warnings from time to time. But this felt different. He tried Juliette again. His heart shouldn't be pounding so. He opened the server room door and raced down the hall.

"Can I call you back?" Jules asked, the radio in his palm crackling with her voice. "I've got a nightmare down here. Five minutes?"

Lukas was breathing hard. He dodged around Sims in the hallway, who spun to watch him go. Nelson would be in the Suit Lab. Lukas squeezed the transmit button. "Actually, I could use some help right now. Are you still on your way down?"

"No, I'm here. Just left the kids with my dad. I'm heading to Walker's to get a battery. Are you running? You're not coming down here, are you?"

Deep breaths. "No, I'm looking for Nelson. Someone called, said they need to speak to Bernard, that there would be trouble for us otherwise. Jules—I've got a bad feeling about this."

He rounded the bend and saw that the door to the Suit Lab was open. Strips of seal tape fluttered around the jamb.

"Calm down," Juliette told him. "Take it easy. Who did you say called? And why are you looking for Nelson?"

"I was going to have him talk to this guy, pretend he's Bernard, at least to buy us some time. I don't know who's calling. It sounds like the same guy, but it's not."

"What did he say?"

"He said to get Bernard, said he was the one who dreamed up Operation Fifty. Dammit, Nelson's not here." Lukas glanced around the workbenches and tool cabinets. He remembered passing Sims. The old Security chief had clearance to the server room. Lukas left the Suit Lab and rushed back down the hall.

"Lukas, you aren't making any sense."

"I know, I know. Hey, I'll call you back. I need to catch Sims—"

He jogged down the hallway. Offices flew past, most of them empty, workers who had transferred out of IT or those at dinner. He spotted Sims turning a corner toward the security station.

"Sims!"

The Security chief peered back around the corner, stepped into the hall, and studied Lukas as he ran at him. Lukas wondered how many minutes had passed, how strict this man was going to be.

"I need your help," he said. He pointed to the server room door, which stood at the junction of the two halls. Sims turned and studied the door with him.

"Yeah?"

Lukas entered his code and pushed the door open. Inside, the lights were back to throbbing red. No way it'd been fifteen minutes already. "I need a huge favor," he told Sims. "Look, it's . . . complicated, but I need you to talk to someone for me. I need you to pretend to be Bernard. You knew him well enough, right?"

Sims pulled up. "Pretend to be who?"

Lukas turned and grabbed the larger man's arm, urged him along. "No time to explain. I just need you to answer this guy's questions. It's like a drill. Just be Bernard. Tell yourself that you're Bernard. Act angry or something. And get off the line as quickly as you can. In fact, say as little as possible."

"Who am I talking to?"

"I'll explain afterward. I just need you to get through this.

Fool this guy." He guided Sims to the open server and handed him the headphones. Sims studied them as though he'd never seen a pair. "Just put those over your ears," Lukas said. "I'm going to plug you in. It's like a radio. Remember, you are Bernard. Try to sound like him, okay? Just be him."

Sims nodded. His cheeks were red, a bead of sweat running down his brow. He looked ten years younger and nervous as hell.

"Here you go." Lukas slotted the cord into the jack, thinking that Sims was probably even better for this than Nelson. This would buy them some time until he could figure out what was going on. He watched as Sims flinched, must've heard a greeting in the headphones.

"Hello?" he asked.

"Confident," Lukas hissed. The radio in his hand crackled with Juliette's voice, and he turned down the volume, didn't want it overheard. He would have to call her back.

"Yes, this is Bernard." Sims talked through his nose, high and tight. It sounded more like a man doing a woman's voice than a fair approximation of the former silo head. "This *is* Bernard," Sims said again, more insistently. He turned to Lukas and pleaded with his eyes, looked absolutely helpless. Lukas waved his hand in a small circle. Sims nodded as he listened to something, then pulled the headset off.

"Okay?" Lukas hissed.

Sims held the headset out to Lukas. "He wants to speak to you. I'm sorry. He knows it isn't him."

Lukas groaned. He tucked the radio under his arm, Juliette's voice tiny and distant, and pulled on the headset, slick with sweat.

"Hello?"

"You shouldn't have done that."

"Bernard is . . . I couldn't reach him."

"He's dead. Was it an accident, or was he murdered? What's going on over there? Who's in charge? We've got no feeds over here."

"I'm in charge," Lukas said. He was painfully aware that Sims was studying him. "Everything is just fine over here. I can have Bernard call you—"

"You've been talking with someone over here."

Lukas didn't respond.

"What did he tell you?"

Lukas glanced at the wooden chair and the pile of books. Sims followed his gaze, and his eyes widened at the sight of so much paper.

"We've been talking about population reports," Lukas said. "We put down an uprising. Yes, Bernard was injured during the fighting—"

"I have a machine here that tells me when you're lying."

Lukas felt faint. It seemed impossible, but he believed the man. He turned around and collapsed into the chair. Sims studied him warily. His Security chief could tell that things weren't right.

"We're doing the best we can," Lukas said. "Everything's in order over here. I am Bernard's shadow. I passed the Rite—"

"I know. But I think you've been poisoned. I'm very sorry, son, but this is something I should have done a long time ago. It's for the good of everyone. I truly am sorry." And then, cryptically and softly, almost as if to someone else, the voice uttered the words: "Shut them down."

"Wait—" Lukas said. He turned to Sims, and now they looked helplessly at one another. "Let me—"

Before he could finish, there was a hissing sound above him. Lukas glanced up to find a white cloud billowing down from the vents. An expanding mist. He remembered exhaust fumes like this from long ago, back when he was locked inside the server room and the people in Mechanical tried to divert gas to choke him out. He remembered the feeling that he was going to suffocate inside that room. But this fog was different. It was thick and sinister.

Lukas pulled his undershirt over his mouth and yelled for Sims to come with him. They both dashed through the server room, dodging between the tall black machines, avoiding the cloud where they could. They got to the door that led out to IT, which Lukas figured was airtight. The red light on the panel blinked happily. Lukas didn't remember locking the door. Holding his breath, he punched in his code and waited for the light to turn green. It didn't. He punched it in again, concentrating, feeling lightheaded from not enough air, and the keypad buzzed and blinked at him with its red and solitary eye.

Lukas turned to Sims to complain and saw the large man peering down at his palms. His hands were covered in blood. Blood was pouring from Sims's nose.

33

Juliette cursed the radio and finally let Walker have a try. Courtnee watched them both with concern. Lukas had come through a couple of times, but all they'd heard was the patter of boots and the hissing of his breathing or some kind of static.

Walker examined the portable. The radio had grown needlessly complex with the knobs and dials he'd added. He fiddled with something and shrugged. "Looks okay to me," he said, tugging on his beard. "Must be on the other end."

One of the other radios on the bench barked. It was the large unit he'd built, the one with the wire dangling from the ceiling. There was a familiar voice followed by a burst of static: "Hello? Anyone? We've got a problem down here."

Juliette raced around the workbench and grabbed the mic before Walker or Courtnee could. She recognized that voice. "Hank, this is Juliette. What's going on?"

"We've got . . . ah, reports from the Mids of some kind of vapor leak. Are you still in that area?"

"No, I'm down in Mechanical. What kind of vapor leak? And from where?"

"In the stairwell, I think. I'm out on the landing right now and don't see anything, but I hear a racket above me. Sounds like a ton of traffic. Can't tell if it's heading up or down. No fire alarm, though."

"Break. Break."

It was another voice cutting in. Juliette recognized it as Peter. He was calling for a pause in the chatter so he could say something.

"Go ahead, Peter."

"Jules, I've got some kind of leak up here as well. It's in the airlock."

Juliette looked to Courtnee, who shrugged. "Confirm that you have smoke in the airlock," she said.

"I don't think it's smoke. And it's in the airlock you added, the new one. Wait. No . . . that's strange."

Juliette found herself pacing between Walker's workbenches. "What's strange? Describe what you're seeing." She imagined an exhaust leak, something from the main generator. They would have to shut it down, and the backup was gone. Fuck. Her worst nightmare. Courtnee frowned at her, was probably thinking the same thing. Fuck, fuck.

"Jules, the yellow door is open. I repeat, the inner airlock door is wide open. And I didn't do it. It was locked just a bit ago."

"What about the smoke?" Juliette asked. "Is it getting worse? Stay low and cover your face. You'll want a wet rag or something—"

"It's not smoke. And it's inside the new door you welded up. That door is still shut. I'm looking through the glass right now. The smoke is all inside there. And I . . . I can see through the yellow door. It's wide open. It's . . . holy shit—"

Juliette felt her heart race. The tone of his voice. She couldn't remember Peter ever uttering a cuss word in all the time she'd known him, and she'd known him through the worst of it. "Peter?"

"Jules, the outer door is open. I say again, the outer airlock door is wide open. I can see straight through the airlock and to . . . what looks like a ramp. I think I'm looking outside. Gods, Juliette, I'm looking straight outside—"

"I need you to get out of there," Juliette said. "Leave everything as it is and get out. Shut the cafeteria door behind you. Seal it up with something. Tape or caulk or something from the kitchen. Do you read?"

"Yes. Yes." His voice was labored. Juliette recalled Lukas telling her something bad was about to happen. She looked to Walker, who still had the new portable in his hand. She needed the old portable. She shouldn't have let him modify the thing. "I need you to raise Luke," she said.

Walker shrugged helplessly. "I'm trying," he said.

"Jules, this is Peter again. I've got traffic heading my way up the stairs. I can hear them. Sounds like half the silo. I don't know why they're heading this way."

Juliette thought of what Hank had said about hearing traffic on the stairwell. If there was a fire, everyone was supposed to man a hose or get to a safe level and wait for assistance. Why would people be running *up*?

"Peter, don't let them near the office. Keep them away from the airlock. Don't let them through."

Her mind whirled. What would she do if she were up there? Have to get in there with a suit on and shut those doors. But that would mean opening the new airlock door. The new airlock door! It shouldn't be there. Forget the sign of smoke, the outside air was now attached to the silo. The outside air—

"Peter?"

"Jules—I . . . I can't stay here. Everyone's acting crazy. They're in the office, Jules. I . . . I don't want to shoot anyone—I can't."

"Listen to me. The vapor. It's the argon, isn't it?"

"It . . . maybe. Yeah. It looked like that. I only saw it fill the airlock the once, when you went out. But yeah—"

Juliette felt her heart sink, her head spin. Her boots no longer touched the floor as she hovered, empty inside, numb and half-deaf. The gas. The poison. The seal missing from the sample canister. That fucker in Silo 1 and his threats. He'd done it. He was killing them all. A thousand useless plans and schemes flitted through Juliette's mind, all of them hopeless and too late. Far too late.

"Jules?"

She squeezed the mic to answer Peter, and then realized the voice was coming from Walker's hands. It was coming from the portable radio.

"Lukas," she gasped. Her vision blurred as she reached for the other radio.

34

"JULES? GODDAMMIT. My volume was down. Can you hear me?"

"I hear you, Lukas. What the hell is going on?"

"Shit. Shit."

Juliette heard clangs and bangs.

"I'm okay. I'm okay. Shit. Is that blood? Okay, gotta get to the pantry. Are you still with me?"

Juliette realized she wasn't breathing. "Are you talking to me? What blood?"

"Yeah, I'm talking to you. Fell down the ladder. Sims is dead. They're doing it. They're shutting us down. My stupid nose. I'm going in the pantry—" The feed turned into static.

"Lukas? Lukas!" She turned to Walker and Courtnee, both watching with wide and wet eyes.

"—no good. Cam't geb recebtion in there." Lukas's voice was garbled as though he were pinching his nose or holding back a sneeze. "Baby, you've gotta seal yourselb off. Can't stob my nose—"

Panic surged through Juliette. Shutting them down. The threats of ending them with the push of a button. Ending them. A silo like Solo's. Maybe a second flitted by, two seconds, and in that brief flash she recalled him telling her stories of the way his silo fell, the rush up top, the spilling out into the open air, the bodies piling up that she had waded through years later. All in an instant, she was transported back and forth through time. This was Silo 17's past; she was witnessing the fall of that silo as it played out in her home. And she had seen their grim future, had seen what was to come of her world. She knew how this ended. She knew that Lukas was already dead.

"Forget the radio," she told him. "Lukas, I want you to forget the radio and seal yourself in that pantry. I'm going to save as many as I can."

She grabbed the other radio, which was tuned to her silo. "Hank, do you read me?"

"Yes—?" She could hear him panting. "Hello?"

"Get everyone down to Mechanical. Everyone you can and as fast as you can. Now."

"I feel like I should be going up," Hank said. "Everyone is storming up."

"No!" Juliette screamed into her radio. Walker startled and dropped the other radio's microphone. "Listen to me, Hank. Everyone you can. Down here. Now!"

She cradled the radio in both hands, glanced around the room to see what else she should grab.

"Are we sealing off Mechanical?" Courtnee asked. "Like before?"

Courtnee must've been thinking about the steel plating welded across security during the holdout. The scars of those joints were still visible, the plating long gone.

"No time for that," Juliette said. She didn't add that it might all be pointless. The air could already be spoiled. No telling how long it took. A part of her mind wanted to focus on all that lay above her, all that she couldn't save, the people and the things as well. Everything good and needed in the world that was now out of reach.

"Grab anything crucial and let's go." She looked to the two of them. "We need to go right now. Courtnee, get to the kids and get them back to their silo—"

"But you said . . . that mob—"

"I don't care about them. Go. And take Walk with you. See that he gets to the dig. I'll meet you there."

"Where are you going?" Courtnee asked.

"To get as many others as I can."

The hallways of Mechanical were strangely devoid of panic. Juliette ran through scenes of normalcy, of people walking to and from their shifts, trolleys of spare parts and heavy pumps, a shower of sparks from someone welding, a flickering flashlight and a passer-by tapping it with their fist. The radio had brought word to her ahead of time. No one else knew.

"Get to the dig," she shouted to everyone she passed. "That's an order. Now. Now. Go."

There was a delayed response. Questions. Excuses. People explained where they were heading, that they were busy, that they didn't have time right then.

Juliette saw Dawson's wife, Raina, who would've been just coming off shift. Juliette grabbed her by the shoulders. Raina's eyes widened, her body stiffened, to be handled like that.

"Get to the classroom," Juliette told her. "Get your kids, get all the kids, and get them through the tunnel. Now."

"What the hell's going on?" someone asked. A few people jostled by in the narrow passageway. One of Juliette's old hands from first shift was there. A crowd was forming.

"Get to the fucking dig," Juliette shouted. "We've got to clear out. Grab everyone you can, your kids, anything you think you need. This is not a drill. Go. Go!"

She clapped her hands. Raina was the first to turn and run, pushing herself through the packed corridor. Those who knew her best leapt into action soon after, rounding up others. Juliette raced toward the stairwell, shouting as she did for everyone to get to the other silo. She vaulted over the security gates, the guard on duty looking up with a startled "Hey!" Behind her, she could hear someone else yelling for everyone to follow, to get moving. Ahead of her, the stairway itself trembled. She could hear welds singing and loose struts rattling. Over this, she could hear the sound of boots stomping her way.

Juliette stood at the bottom of the stairwell and peered up through that wide gap between the stairs and the stairwell's concrete wall. Various landings jutted out overhead, wide bands of steel that became narrow ribbons higher up. The shaft receded into darkness. And then she saw the white clouds like smoke higher up. Maybe from the Mids.

She squeezed the radio.

"Hank?"

No response.

"Hank, come back."

The stairway hummed with the harmonics of heavy but distant traffic. Juliette stepped closer and rested a hand on the rail. It vibrated, numbing her hand. The clanging of boots grew louder. Looking up, she could see hands sliding down the rail above her, could hear voices shouting encouragement and confusion.

A handful of people from the one-thirties spilled down the last turn and seemed confused about where to go next. They had the bewildered look of people who had never known that the stairway ended, that there was this floor of concrete below their homes. Juliette yelled at them to head inside. She turned and shouted into Mechanical for someone to show them the way, to let them through security. They stumbled past, most of them empty-handed, one or two with children clutched to their chests or towed behind, or with bundles cradled in their arms.

They spoke of fire and smoke. A man shuffled down, holding a bloody nose. He insisted that they should be heading up, that they should all be heading up.

"You," Juliette said, grabbing the man by the arm. She studied his face, the crimson dripping from his knuckles. "Where are you coming from? What happened?" She indicated his nose.

"I fell," he said, uncovering his face to talk. "I was at work—"

"Okay. That's fine. Follow the others." She pointed. Her radio barked with a disembodied voice. Shouting. An unholy din. Juliette moved away from the stairs and covered one ear, pressed the radio to the other. It sounded vaguely like Peter. She waited until he was done.

"Can barely hear you!" she yelled. "What's going on?"

She covered her ear again and strained for his words. "—getting through. To the outside. They're getting out—"

Her back found the concrete of the stairwell. She slid down into a crouch. A few dozen people scampered down the stairs. Some stragglers in the yellow of Supply joined them, clutching a few things. Hank arrived, finally, directing traffic, shouting at those who seemed eager to turn back, to head in the other direction. A handful of people from Mechanical came out to help. Juliette concentrated on Peter's voice.

"—can't breathe," he said. "Cloud coming in. I'm in the galley. People pouring up. Everyone. Acting crazy. Falling over. Everyone dead. The outside—"

He gasped and wheezed between every other word. The radio clicked off. Juliette screamed into the handset a few times, but she couldn't raise him. Gazing up the stairwell, she saw the fog overhead. The smoke pouring out into the stairway seemed to thicken. It grew more and more dense as Juliette watched, horrified.

And then something dark punched through—a shadow amid the white. It grew. There was a scream, a terrible peal as it flew down and down, past the landings, on the other side of the stairwell, and then a thudding boom as a person slammed into the deck. The violence of the impact was felt in Juliette's boots.

More screams. This time from those nearby, those dozens spilling down the stairwell, the few who had made it. They crawled over one another in a dash for Mechanical. And the white smoke, it descended down the stairwell like a hammer.

35

JULIETTE FOLLOWED THE others into Mechanical—she was the last one through. The arms on one of the security gates had been busted backward. A crowd surged over the gates while some hopped sideways through the gap. The guard who was meant to prevent this helped people down on the other side and directed them where to go.

Juliette threw herself over and hurried through the crowd toward the bunkroom where the kids had been put up. Someone was clattering around in the break room as she passed, hopefully looting needed things. *Hopefully looting*. The world had gone suddenly mad.

The bunkroom was empty. She assumed Courtnee had already gotten there. No one was getting out of Mechanical, anyway. And it was probably already too late. Juliette doubled back down the hall and headed for the winding stairs that penetrated the levels of Mechanical. She surged with a packed crowd down to the generator room and the site of the dig.

There were piles of tailings and chunks of concrete studded with rebar around the oil rig, which continued to bob its head up and down as if it knew the sad ways of the world, as if depressedly resigned to what was happening, as if saying: "Of course. Of course."

More tailings and rubble from the dig formed piles inside the generator room, everything that hadn't yet been shoveled down the shaft to mine six. There was a scattering of people, but not the crowds Juliette had hoped. The great crowds were likely dead. And then a fleeting thought, an urge to laugh and feel ridiculous, the idea that the smoke was nothing, that the airlock up top had held, that everything was okay and that her friends would soon rib her about this panic she had caused.

But this hope vanished as quickly as it came. Nothing could cut through the metallic fear on her tongue, the sound of Peter's voice telling her that the airlock was wide open, that people were collapsing, Lukas telling her that Sims was dead.

She pushed through the crowd pouring into the tunnel and called out for the children. Then she spotted Courtnee and Walker. Walker was wide-eyed, his jaw sagging. Juliette saw the crowds through his eyes and realized the burden she had left Courtnee with, the challenge of dragging this recluse once again from his lair.

"Have you seen the kids?" she yelled over the crowd.

"They're already through!" Courtnee yelled back. "With your father."

Juliette squeezed her arm and hurried into the darkness. There were lights flashing ahead—the few who had battery-powered flashlights, those with miner's hats on—but between these beams were wide swaths of pitch black. She jostled with the invisible others who materialized solidly out of shadow. Rocks clattered down from the piles of tailings to either side; dust and debris fell from the ceiling, eliciting shrieks and curses. The passage was narrow between the rows of rubble. The tunnel had been made for a handful of people to pass through, no more. Most of the massive hole bored through the earth had been left full of the scraps the digging had generated.

Where logjams formed, some people attempted to scamper

up and along the tops of these piles. This just pushed heaps of dirt and rock down on those between, filling the tunnel with screams and curses. Juliette helped dig someone out and urged everyone to stay in the center, not to shove, even as someone practically climbed over her back.

There were others who tried to turn back, afraid and confused and distrusting of this dark run in a straight line. Juliette and others yelled for them to continue on. A nightmare formed of bumping into the support beams hastily erected in the center of the tunnel, of crawling on hands and knees over tall piles from partial cave-ins, of a baby crying at the top of its lungs somewhere. The adults did a better job of dampening their sobs, but Juliette passed by dozens crying. The journey felt interminable, as if they would crawl and stumble through that tunnel for the rest of time, until the poisonous air caught them from behind.

A jam of foot traffic formed ahead, people shoving at each others' backs, and flashlight beams played over the steel wall of the digger. The end of the tunnel. The access door at the back of the machine was open. Juliette found Raph standing by the door with one of the flashlights, his pale face aglow in the darkness, eyes wide and white.

"Jules!"

She could barely hear him over the voices echoing back and forth in the dark shaft. She made her way to him, asked him who had already passed through.

"It's too dark," he said. "They can only get through one at a time. What the hell is going on? Why all the people? We thought you said—"

"Later," she told him, hoping there would be a later. She doubted it. More likely, there would be piles of bodies at both ends of this silo. That would be the great difference between 17 and 18. Bodies at both ends. "The kids?" she asked, and as soon as she did, she wondered why with all the dead and dying she would concentrate on so few. The mother she never was, she suspected. The primal urge to look after her brood when far more than that was in peril.

"Yeah, quite a few kids came through." He paused and shouted directions to a couple who didn't want to enter the metal door at the back of this digger. Juliette could hardly blame them. They weren't even from Mechanical. What did these people think was going on? Just following the panicked shoutings of others. Probably thought they were lost in the mines. It was a wild experience even for Juliette, who had scaled hills and seen the outside.

"What about Shirly?" Juliette asked.

He aimed his flashlight inside. "Saw her for sure. I think she's in the digger. Directing traffic."

She squeezed Raph's arm, looked back at the writhing darkness of shadowy forms behind her. "Make sure you get through," she told him, and his pale face nodded his consent.

Juliette squeezed into the queue and entered the back of the digger. Cries and shouts rattled within like children screaming into empty soup cans. Shirly was at the back of the power plant, directing the shuffling and shoving mass of people through a crack in the darkness so narrow that everyone had to turn sideways. The lights that'd been rigged up inside the digger to work the tailings were off, the backup generator idle, but Juliette could feel the residual heat from it having been run. She could hear the clicking of metal as it cooled. She wondered if Shirly had been operating the unit in order to move the machine and its power plant back toward Silo 18. She and Courtnee had been arguing over where the digger belonged.

"What the hell?" Shirly asked Juliette when she spotted her.

Juliette felt like bursting into tears. How to explain what she feared, that this was the end of everything they'd ever known? She shook her head and bit her lip. "We're losing the silo," she finally managed. "The outside's getting in."

"So why send them this way?" Shirly had to yell over the clamor of voices. She pulled Juliette to the other side of the generator, away from all the shouting.

"The air is coming down the stairwell," Juliette said. "There's no stopping it. I'm going to seal off the dig."

Shirly chewed on this. "Take down the supports?"

"Not quite. The charges you wanted rigged up—"

Shirly's face hardened. "Those charges are rigged from the other side. I rigged them to seal off *this* side, to seal off *this* silo, to protect us from the air over *here*."

"Well, now all we *have* is the air over here." Juliette passed Shirly the radio, which was all she'd taken from her home. Shirly cradled it in her arms. She balanced it atop her flashlight, which bloomed against Juliette's chest. In the light that spilled back, Juliette could see a mask of confusion on her poor friend's face. "Watch over everyone," Juliette told her. "Solo and the kids—" She eyed the generator. "The farms here are salvageable. And the air—"

"You're not going to—" Shirly started.

"I'll make sure the last of them get through. There were a few dozen behind me. Maybe another hundred." Juliette grasped her old friend's arms. She wondered if they were still friends. She wondered if there was still that bond between them. She turned to go.

"No."

Shirly grabbed Juliette's arm, the radio falling and clattering to the floor. Juliette tried to yank free.

"I'll be damned," Shirly shouted. She spun Juliette around. "I'll be goddamned if you're leaving me to this, in charge of this. I'll be goddamned—"

There were cries somewhere, from a child or an adult, it was impossible to tell. Just a cacophony of confused and terrified voices echoing in the packed confines of that great steel machine. And in the darkness, Juliette couldn't see the blow coming, couldn't see Shirly's fist. She just felt it on her jaw, marveled at the bright flash of light in the pitch black, and then remembered nothing for a while.

She came to moments or minutes later—it was impossible to tell. Curled up on the steel deck of the digger, the voices around her subdued and far away, she lay still while her face throbbed.

Fewer people. Just the ones who'd made it, and they were moving on through the bowels of the digger. She had been out for a minute or two, it seemed. Maybe longer. Much longer. Someone called her name, was looking for her in the black, but she was invisible curled up on the far side of the generator in the shadow of shadows. Someone called her name.

And then a great boom in the distance. It was like a sheet of three-inch steel falling and banging next to her head. A great rumble in the earth, a tremor felt right through the digger, and Juliette knew. Shirly had gone to the control room and had taken her place. She had set off the charges meant to protect her old home from this new one. She had doomed herself with the others.

Juliette wept. Someone called her name, and Juliette realized it was coming from the radio near her head. She reached for it numbly, her senses scrambled. It was Lukas.

"Luke," she whispered, squeezing the transmit button. His voice meant he was outside the steel locker, the airtight pantry full of food. She thought of Solo surviving for decades on those cans. Lukas could too, if anyone could. "Get back inside," she said, sobbing. "Seal yourself off." She cradled the radio in both hands and remained curled up on the deck.

"I can't," Lukas said. There was coughing, an agonizing wheeze. "I had to . . . had to hear your voice. One last time." The next bout of coughing could be felt in Juliette's own chest, which was full to bursting. "I'm done, Jules. I'm done . . ."

"No." She cried this to herself, and then squeezed the radio. "Lukas, you get inside that pantry right now. Lock it and hold on. Just hold on—"

She listened to him cough and struggle to find his voice. When it came, it was a rattle. "Can't. This is it. This is it. I love you, Jules. I love you . . ."

The last was a whisper, barely more than static. Juliette wept and slapped the floor and screamed at him. She cursed him. She cursed herself. And through the open door of the digger, a cloud of dust billowed in on a cool breeze, and Juliette could taste it on her tongue, on her lips. It was the dry chalk of crushed rock, the remnants of Shirly's blast far down the tunnel, the taste of everything she had ever known . . . dead.

PART III

HOME

Silo 1

36

CHARLOTTE LEANED AWAY from the radio, stunned. She stared at the crackling speaker, listened to the hiss of static, and played the scene over and over in her head. An open door, toxic air leaking in, people dying, a stampede, a silo gone. A silo her brother had labored to save was gone.

Her hand trembled as she reached for the dial. Flipping through channels, she heard other voices from other silos, little snippets of conversation and silence with no context, proof that elsewhere, life continued apace:

"—second time this month this has happened. You let Carol know—"

"—if you'll hold it for me until I get there, I'd sure appre—"

"..."

"—roger that. We have her in custody now—"

Bouts of static between these conversations held the place of silos full of dead air. Silos full of the dead.

Charlotte dialed back to 18. The repeaters were still working up and down that silo; she could tell from the hiss. She listened for that voice to return, the woman calling for everyone to head to the bottom levels. Charlotte had heard someone say her name. It was strange to think she'd heard the voice of this woman her brother was obsessed with, this rogue mayor as he called her, this cleaner-come-home.

It could've been someone else, but Charlotte didn't think so. Those were commands from someone in charge. She imagined a woman huddling down in the depths of a distant silo, some-place dark and lonely, and felt a sudden kinship. What she wouldn't give to be able to transmit rather than just listen, some way to reach out.

Leaning forward, she rubbed the side of the radio where the mic would wire up. It was suspicious that her brother saved this part for last. Almost as if he didn't trust her not to speak with someone. Almost as if he wanted her simply to listen. Or maybe it was himself he was worried about. Perhaps he didn't trust what he would do if he could broadcast his thoughts over the air. This wasn't the heads of the silos listening in, this was any-one with a radio.

Charlotte patted her chest and felt for the ID he had given her, and images flashed before her of a boot rising and falling, of a wall and a floor spotted with blood. In the end, he hadn't been given a chance. But she had to do something. She couldn't sit there listening to static forever, listening to people die. Donny said her ID would work the lifts. The urge to take action was overpowering.

She powered the radio down and covered it with the sheet of plastic. She arranged the chair so it appeared undisturbed and studied the drone control room for signs of habitation. Back at her bunk, she opened her trunk and studied the outfits. She chose reactor red. It fitted her more loosely than the others. Pulling it out, she inspected the name patch. *Stan*. She could be a Stan.

She got dressed and went to the storeroom. There was plenty of grease to be had from the disassembled drone. She collected some on her palm, searched one of the supply bins for a cap, and went to the bathroom. The men's room. Charlotte used to enjoy putting on make-up. That seemed like a different lifetime, a different person. She remembered moving from playing video games to trying to be pretty, shading her cheeks so they didn't look so chubby. This was before basic training made her lean and hard for a brief time. It was before two tours of duty helped her to regain her natural body, get used to that body, accept it, even love it.

She used the grease to deaccentuate her cheekbones. A little on her eyebrows made them appear fuller. A foul-tasting smear on her lips so they weren't so red. It was the opposite of any make-up job she'd ever applied. She stuffed her hair inside the cap and pulled the brim down low, adjusted her coveralls until those looked like folds of fabric rather than breasts.

It was a pathetic disguise. She saw through it immediately. But then, she knew. In a world where women weren't allowed, would any suspect? She wasn't sure. She couldn't know. She longed for Donny to be there so she could ask him. She imagined him laughing at her, which was nearly enough to make her cry.

"Don't you fucking cry," she told the mirror, dabbing at her eyes. She was worried what the crying might do to her make-up. But the tears came anyway. They came and disturbed nothing. They were drops of water gliding over grease.

There was a schematic somewhere. Charlotte searched Donny's folder of notes by the radio and didn't see it. She tried the conference room where her brother had spent much of his time poring through boxes of files. The place was a wreck. Most of his notes had been hauled off. They must be planning on coming back for the rest, probably in the morning. Or they could arrive right then, and Charlotte would have to explain what she was doing there:

"I was sent down here to retrieve . . . uh . . ." Her lowered voice sounded ridiculous. She shuffled through the opened folders and loose pages and tried again, this time with her normal voice just slightly flattened. "I was told to take this to recycling," she explained to nobody. "Oh? And what level is recycling on?" she asked herself. "I have no fucking clue," she admitted. "That's why I'm looking for a map."

She found a map. It wasn't the right one, though. A grid of circles with red lines radiating out to a single point. She only knew it was a map because she recognized the layout with its grid of letters down the side and numbers across the top. The Air Force had once assigned daily targets on grids like these. She would grab a bagel and coffee in the mess hall, and then a man and his family from D-4 would die in a fiery maelstrom. Break for lunch. Ham and cheese on rye.

Charlotte recognized the circles laid out across the grid. It was the silos. She had flown three drones over depressions in hills just like this. The red lines were odd. She traced one with her finger. They reminded her of flight lines. They extended off every silo except for the one near the center, which she thought might be the one she was in. Donald had shown her this layout once on the big table, the one now buried under the loose pages. She folded the map and stuffed it into her breast pocket and kept looking.

The Silo 1 schematic she had seen before seemed lost, but she found the next best thing. A directory. It listed personnel by rank, shift assignment, occupation, living level, and work level. It was the size of a phone book for a small town, a reminder of how many people were taking turns running the silo. Not people—*men*. Scanning the names, Charlotte saw that it was all men. She thought of Sasha, the only other woman who'd gone through boot camp with her. Strange to think that Sasha was dead, that all the men in her regiment, everyone from flight school, all of them were dead.

She found the name of a reactor mechanic and his work level, looked for a pen amid the chaos, found one, and jotted the level number down. Administration, she discovered, was on level thirty-four. A comms officer worked on the same level, which sucked. She hated to think of the comm room right down the hall from the people who ran the joint. A security officer worked on twelve. If Donny was being held, maybe he'd be there. Unless they'd put him back to sleep. Unless he was in whatever passed for a hospital there. Cryo was down below, she thought. She remembered coming up the lift after he'd woken her. She found the level for the main cryo office by locating someone who worked there, but that probably wasn't where the bodies were kept. Was it?

Her notes became a mess of scribbles, a rough outline of what was where above and below her. But where to start in her search? She couldn't find mention of the supply and spares rooms her brother had been raiding, probably because no one actually worked on those levels. Starting over on a fresh piece of paper, she drew a cylinder and made the best schematic she could, filling in the floors she knew from Donny's routine and the ones from the directory. Starting with the cafeteria at the very top, she worked her way down to the cryo office, which was as far down as her notes took her. The empty levels were her best bet. Some of those would be storerooms and warehouses. But the lift could just as easily open to a roomful of men playing cards—or whatever it was they did to kill the time while they killed the world. She couldn't just roll the dice; she needed a plan.

She studied the map and considered her options. One place for sure would have a mic, and that was the comm room. She checked the clock on the wall. Six twenty-five. Dinnertime and end of shift, lots of people moving about. Charlotte touched her face where she had smudged grease to dull her cheekbones. She wasn't thinking straight, probably shouldn't go anywhere until after eleven. Or was it better to be lost in a jostling crowd? What was out there? She paced and debated. "I don't know, I don't know," she said, testing her new voice. It sounded like she had a cold. That was the best way to sound male: like she had a cold.

She returned to the storeroom and studied the lift doors. Someone could burst out right then, and her decision would be made for her. She should wait until later. Returning to the drones, she pulled the tarp off the one she'd been working on and studied the loose panels and scattering of tools. Glancing back at the conference room, she saw Donny curled there on the floor, trying to fend off the kicks with his shins, two men holding him down, a man who could barely stand landing sickening blows.

Picking up a driver, Charlotte slotted it into one of the tool pouches on her coveralls. Not sure what to do, she got to work on the drone, killing time. She would go out later that night when there were fewer people up and less chance of being spotted. First, she would get the next machine ready to fly. Donny wasn't there—his work lay unfinished—but she could soldier on. She could piece things back together, one bolt and one nut at a time. And that night, she would go out and find the part she needed. She would win back her voice and reach out to those people in that stricken silo, if any of them were still alive.

37

THE ARRIVING LIFT struck midnight. Well, five past midnight. That's when Charlotte finally built up enough nerve to venture out, and the lift sent a ding echoing through the armory.

The doors rattled open, and she stepped inside memories of a lost place and time, memories of a normal world where lifts took people to and from work. Clutching the ID card Donny had given her, she felt another pang of doubt. The doors began to close. Charlotte stuck her boot out and allowed the doors to slam against her foot, and the lift opened again. She waited for alarms to sound as the doors tried to close a second time. Maybe she should get off the damn thing and make up her mind, let the lift be on its way, grab another in an hour or two. The doors pinched her boot tentatively, and then retreated, like a monster considering whether to eat her. Charlotte decided she had delayed long enough.

She pressed her ID card to the reader and watched its eye blink green, then pressed the button for level thirty-four. Admin and comms. The lion's den. The doors seemed to sigh gratefully as they finally met. The floors began to flash by.

Charlotte checked the back of her neck and felt a few loose strands of hair. She tucked them into her cap. Admin was a risk—she would stand out in red coveralls meant for the reactor level—but it would be even more awkward to show up where she seemed to belong while not knowing her way around or what she was supposed to do. She patted her pockets to make sure she had her tools, made sure they were visible. They were her cover. Hidden inside a large pouch on her hip, a pistol from one of the storage bins sagged conspicuously. Charlotte's heart raced as the levels flew past. She tried to imagine the world outside that Donald had described, the dry and lifeless wasteland. She imagined the lift going all the way up and opening on those barren hills, the wind howling inside the lift. It might be a relief.

No passengers joined her on the way up. It was a good decision, going this time of night. Thirty-six, thirty-five, and then the lift slowed. The doors opened on a hallway, the lights beyond harsh and bright. She doubted her disguise immediately. A man looked up from a gate a dozen paces distant. There was nothing familiar about this world, nothing like her home of the past few weeks. She tugged the brim of her hat down, aware that it didn't match her coveralls. The important thing was confidence, which she felt none of. Be brash. Direct. She told herself that the days here were full of sameness. Everyone would see what they expected to see. She approached the man and his gate and held out her ID.

"You expected?" the man asked. He pointed to the scanner on her side of the gate. Charlotte swiped the card, not knowing what might happen, fully prepared to run, to pull out the pistol, to surrender, or some confusing mix of all three.

"We're showing a, uh... power drain on this level." Her pretend-sick voice sounded ludicrous to her own ears. But then, she knew her voice better than anyone—she told herself that was why it sounded funny. It might sound normal to someone else. She also hoped a power drain made as little sense to this man as it did to her. "I was sent up to check the comm room. You know where it is?"

A question for him. Tickle his male ego for directions. Charlotte felt a rivulet of sweat run down the nape of her neck and wondered if there were anymore loose strands of hair. She fought the urge to check. Lifting her arm might tighten her coveralls across her chest. Sizing up the large man, she pictured him grabbing her and slamming her to the ground, hands the size of small plates pummeling her.

"Comms? Of course. Yeah. Down the hall to the end, turn left. Second door on your right."

"Thanks." Tipping her hat allowed her to keep her head down. She pushed through the bars with a clack and the tick of some invisible counter.

"Forgetting something?"

She turned. Her hand fell to the pouch by her leg.

"Need you to sign the work log." The guard held out a worn digital tablet, its screen a haze of curling scratches.

"Right." Charlotte took the plastic stylus hanging from a cord of wire repaired with tape. She studied the entry box in the center of the screen. There was a place to write the time and a place to sign her name. She filled in the time and glanced at her chest, already forgetting. Stan. Her name was Stan. She scrawled this messily, tried to make it look casual, handed him the tablet and stylus.

"See you on your way out," the guard said.

Charlotte nodded and hoped her way out would prove just as uneventful.

She followed his directions down the main hall. There was more activity, more sounds than she expected at that time of night. There were lights on in a few of the offices, the squeak of chairs and filing cabinets and keyboards clattering. A door opened down the hall, and a man stepped out, pulled the door shut behind him. Charlotte saw his face, and her legs went numb. She staggered a few steps on stalks of bone and meat, wobbly. Dizzy. Nearly fell.

She lowered her head and scratched the back of her neck, disbelieving. But it was Thurman. Slimmer and older-looking. And then images of Donny curled in a ball and being beaten half to death flooded back. The hallway blurred behind a coat of tears. The white hair, the tall frame. How had she not recognized him then?

"You're a ways from home, aren't you?" Thurman asked.

His voice was sandpaper. It was a familiar scratch. As familiar as her mother's or her father's voice would've been.

"Checking a power drain," Charlotte said, not stopping or turning, hoping he meant her coveralls and not her gender. How could he not hear that it was her voice? How could he not recognize her gait, her frame, the bare patch of skin on the back of her neck, that few square inches of exposed flesh, anything to betray her?

"See to it," he said.

She walked a dozen paces. Two dozen. Sweating. Feeling drunk. She waited until she was at the end of the hall, just starting to make the turn, before glancing back toward the security station. Thurman was there in the distance, speaking with the guard, his white hair like the bare sun. Second door on the right, she reminded herself. She was in danger of forgetting the guard's directions to the comm room, such was the pounding of her heart and the racing of her mind. She took a deep breath and reminded herself why she was there. Seeing Thurman and realizing it was he who had laid into Donny had stunned her. But there was no time for processing that. A door stood before her. She tested the knob, then stepped inside.

• • •

A lone man sat inside the comm room, staring at a bank of monitors and flashing indicators. He turned in his seat as Charlotte entered, a mug in his hand, a great belly wedged between the armrests. Fine wisps of hair had been combed across an otherwise bald head. He peeled back one of the cups from his ear and lifted his eyebrows questioningly.

There had to be half a dozen radio units scattered across the U-shaped arrangement of workbenches and comfortable chairs. An embarrassment of riches. Charlotte just needed one part.

"Yeah?" the radio operator asked.

Charlotte's mouth felt dry. One lie had gotten her past the guard; she had one more fib prepared. She cleared her mind of having seen Thurman in the hallway, of images of him kicking her brother.

"Here to fix one of your units," she said. She pulled a driver from a pocket and briefly imagined having to fight this man, felt a surge of adrenaline. She had to stop thinking like a soldier. She was an electrician. And she needed to get him talking so that she wasn't. "Which is the one with the bum mic?" She waved her driver across the units. Years of piloting drones and working with computers had taught her one thing: there was always a problem machine. Always.

The radio operator narrowed his eyes. He studied her for a moment, then glanced around the room. "You must mean number two," he said. "Yeah. The button's sticky. I'd given up on anyone taking a look." The chair squeaked as he leaned back and locked his fingers behind his head. His armpits were dark stains. "Last guy said it was minor. Not worth replacing. Said to use it until it gave out."

Charlotte nodded and went to the machine he had indicated. It was too easy. She attacked the side panel with her driver, her back to the operator.

"You work down on the reactor levels, right?"

She nodded.

"Yeah. Ate across from you in the cafeteria a while back."

Charlotte waited for him to ask her name again or to resume some conversation he'd had with a different tech. The driver slipped out of her sweaty palm and clattered on the desk. She scooped it back up. She could feel the operator watching her work.

"You think you'll be able to fix it?"

She shrugged. "I need to take it with me. Should have it back tomorrow." She pulled the side panel off and loosened the screw holding the microphone's cord to the casing. The cord itself unplugged from a board inside the machine. On second thought, she undid this board and pulled it out as well. Couldn't remember if she had one installed already, and it made her look as though she really knew what the hell she was doing.

"You'll have it tomorrow? That's great. Really appreciate this."

Charlotte gathered the parts and stood up straight. Pinching the brim of her hat was enough of a goodbye; she turned and headed out the door, leaving too hastily, she suspected. The side panel and screws had been left on the counter. A real tech would've put them back, wouldn't they? She wasn't sure. She knew a few pilots from a different life who would've laughed to have seen her pretending to be technically inclined, modding drones and building radios, putting grease rather than rouge on her face.

The operator said one last thing, but his words were pinched off as she pulled the door shut. She hurried down the hall and toward the main corridor, expecting to round the bend and find Thurman there with a handful of guards, wide shoulders blocking her way. She slotted the driver back into her pocket and coiled the microphone wire up, cradled it and the board to her chest. When she turned the corner, there was no one in the hall except the guard. It took what felt like hours to walk down that corridor to the security gate. It took days. The walls pressed in and throbbed with her heartbeat. Her coveralls clung to her damp skin. Tools rattled, and the gun weighed heavy at her hip. With each step, the lift doors somehow drew two steps further away from her.

She stopped at the gate, remembered the place on the slate to mark her time out, and made a show of checking the guard's clock before scratching the time.

"That was quick," the guard said.

She forced a smile but didn't look up. "Wasn't a big deal." She handed him the tablet and stepped through the clacking gates. Behind her, down the hall, someone closed an office door, boots squeaking on tile. Charlotte marched toward the lifts and jabbed the call button once, twice, wishing the damn thing would hurry. The lift dinged its arrival. There was a clomp of boots behind her.

"Hey!" someone yelled.

Charlotte didn't turn. She hurried inside the lift as someone else clacked through the security gates.

"Hold that for me."

38

A BODY SLAMMED AGAINST the lift doors, a hand jutting inside. Charlotte nearly screamed in fright, nearly slapped at the hand, but then the doors were opening, and a man crowded into the lift beside her, breathing hard.

"Going down, right?"

The name patch on his gray coveralls read *Eren*. He caught his breath while the doors closed. Charlotte's hand was trembling. It took two tries to scan her card. She reached for the button marked "54", but caught herself before pressing it. She had no business being on that level. No one did. The man was watching her, his own card out, waiting for her to decide.

What level for the reactor? She had it written down on a piece of paper inside one of her pockets, but she couldn't very well pull it out and study it. Suddenly, she could smell the grease on her face, could feel herself damp with sweat. Cradling the radio parts in one arm, she pressed one of the lowest levels, trusting that this man would get off before she did and she would have the lift to herself.

"Excuse me," he said, reaching in front of her to swipe his card. Charlotte could smell stale coffee on his breath. He punched the button for level forty-two, and the lift shivered into motion.

"Late shift?" Eren asked.

"Yeah," Charlotte said, keeping her head down and her voice low.

"You just waking up?"

She shook her head. "Night shift."

"No, I mean are you just coming out of freeze? Don't think I've seen you around. I'm the on-shift head right now." He laughed. "For another week, anyway."

Charlotte shrugged. It was boiling hot inside the lift. The numbers were counting down so damn slowly. She should've pressed a nearby floor, gotten off, and waited on the next lift. Too late, now.

"Hey, look at me," the man said.

He knew. He was standing so close. Too close for anything but suspicious scrutiny. Charlotte glanced up; she could feel her breasts press against her coveralls, could feel hair trailing out from her cap, could feel her cheekbones and stubble-free chin, everything that made her a woman, not least of which was her powerful revulsion at this strange man staring at her, this man who had her trapped and powerless in a small lift. She met his gaze, feeling all of this and more. Helpless and afraid.

"What the fuck?" the man said.

Charlotte threw her knee up between his legs, hoping to cripple him, but he turned his hips and jumped back. She caught him on the thigh, instead. She fumbled for the pistol—but the pouch was snapped shut. Never thought she'd need to draw it in a hurry. She got the pouch open and the pistol free as the man slammed into her, knocking the wind out of her lungs and the gun from her hand. The gun and the radio parts clattered to the floor. Boots squeaked as the two of them wrestled, but she was vastly overpowered. His hands gripped her wrists painfully. She screamed, her high-pitched voice a confession. The lift slowed to a stop on his level, and the doors dinged open.

"Hey!" Eren yelled. He tried to drag Charlotte through the doors, but she placed a boot on the panel and kicked off, attempting to wrench free of his grip. "Help!" he shouted over his shoulder and down the dim and empty hall. "Guys! Help!"

Charlotte bit his hand at the base of his thumb. There was a pop as her teeth punctured his flesh, and then the bitter taste of blood. He cursed and lost his grip on her wrist. She kicked him back through the door, lost her cap, felt her hair spill down to her neck as she reached for the gun.

The doors began to close, leaving the man out in the hallway. He lurched from his hands and knees and was back through the doors before they could bang shut. He slammed into Charlotte, and she hit the back wall as the lift continued its merry jaunt down the silo.

A blow caught her in the jaw. Charlotte saw a flash of bright light. She jerked her head back before the next punch landed. The man pressed her against the back of the lift, was grunting like a crazed animal, a sound of fury and terror and startlement. He was trying to kill her, this thing he couldn't understand. She had attacked him, and now he was trying to kill her. A blow to her ribs, and Charlotte cried out and clutched her side. She felt hands around her neck, squeezing, lifting her off the floor. Her palm settled on a driver slotted into her coveralls.

"Hold . . . still," the man grunted through clenched teeth.

Charlotte gagged. Couldn't breathe. Could barely make a sound. Her windpipe was being crushed. Driver in her right fist, she brought it up over his shoulder and slammed it at his face, hoping to scratch him, hoping to scare him, to make him let go. She drove it with all the strength she had left in her, with the last of her consciousness, as the dark tunnel of her vision began to iris shut.

The man saw the strike coming and turned his head to the side, eyes wide as he sought to avoid the blow. She missed his face. The driver buried itself in his neck instead. He lost his grip on her, and Charlotte felt the driver twist and tear inside his throat as she clung to it to keep from falling.

There was a flash of warmth on her face. The lift came to a sudden stop, and both of them fell to the ground. There was a gurgling sound, and the heat on Charlotte's face was the man's blood, which jetted out in crimson spurts. They both gasped for air. Beyond, there was laughter in a hallway, loud voices booming, a gleaming floor that reminded her of the medical wing in which she'd woken up.

She staggered to her feet. The man in gray who had attacked her kicked and squirmed on the ground, his life spilling out of his neck, his eyes wide and beseeching her—anyone—for help. He tried to speak, to cry out to the people down the hall, but it was little more than a gurgle. Charlotte stooped and grabbed him by the collar. The doors were closing. She jammed her boot between them, and they opened again. Tugging on the man— who slipped and slid in his own blood, heels slamming against the floor of the lift—she pulled him into the hallway, made sure his boots were free of the doors. The lift began to close again, threatening to leave her there with him. There was more laughter from a nearby room, a group of men cracking up over some joke. Charlotte dove for the closing doors, stuck her arm between them, and they opened once more. She staggered inside, numb and exhausted.

There was blood everywhere. Her boots slipped in the stuff. Looking at the horror on the ground, she realized something was missing. The pistol. Panic tightened her chest as she glanced up, the doors shuddering together a final time. There was a deafening bang from the gun, hate and fear in a dying man's eyes, and then she was thrown back, a fire erupting in her shoulder.

"Fuck."

Charlotte staggered across the lift, her first thought to get it moving, to flee. She could feel the man on the other side of the door, could picture him clutching his neck with one hand and holding that pistol in the other, could imagine him fumbling for the lift call button, leaving a smear of blood on the wall. She pressed a handful of buttons, marking them with blood, but none of the floors lit up. Cursing, she fumbled for her ID. One arm wouldn't respond. She reached awkwardly across herself with the other, dug the ID out, nearly dropped it, ran it through the scanner.

"Fuck. Fuck," she whispered, her shoulder on fire. She jabbed the button for fifty-four. Home. Her prison had become home, a safe place. By her feet lay the radio parts. The control board was cracked in half from someone's boot. She slid down to her heels, cradling her other arm, fighting the urge to pass out, and scooped up the microphone. She draped this by its cord around the back of her neck, left the other parts. There was blood everywhere. Some of it had to be hers. Reactor red. It blended right in with her coveralls. The lift rose, slowed to a stop, and opened on the dark supply room on fifty-four.

Charlotte staggered out, remembered something, and stepped back inside. She kicked the doors open as they tried to shut, was angry with them now. With her elbow, she tried to wipe the lift buttons clean. There was a smear of blood, a fingerprint, on button fifty-four, a sign pointing to where she had gone. It was no use. The doors again tried to close, and again she kicked them for their effort. Desperate, Charlotte bent and ran her palm through the man's spilled blood, returned to the panel, and covered every button with a great dose of the stuff. Finally, she scanned her ID and pressed the top level, sending the goddamn thing far away, as far away as she could. Staggering out, she collapsed to the ground. The doors began to close, and she was glad to let them.

39

THEY WOULD LOOK for her. She was a fugitive locked in a cage, in a single, giant building. They would hunt her down.

Charlotte's mind raced. If the man she attacked died there in the hallway, she might have until the end of shift before he was discovered and they started looking for her. If he found help, it could be hours. But they had to have heard the gun going off, right? They would save his life. She hoped they would save his life.

She opened a crate where she'd seen a medical kit. Wrong crate. It was the next one. She dug the kit out and undid her coveralls, tearing at the snaps. Wiggling her arms out, she saw the grisly wound. Dark red blood puckered from a hole in her arm and streaked down to her elbow. She reached around and winced as her fingers found the exit. Her arm was numb from the wound down. From the wound up, it was throbbing.

She tore a roll of gauze open with her teeth, then wrapped it under her armpit and around and around, sent the roll behind her neck and across her other shoulder to keep it all in place. Finally, another few laps across the wound. She'd forgotten a pad, a compress, didn't feel like doing it again. Instead, she just made the last wrap as tight as she could tolerate before cinching the end. As far as dressings went, it was a train wreck. Everything from basic training had gone out the window during the fight and after. Just impulse and reflex. Charlotte closed the lid on the bin, saw the blood left on the latch, and realized she'd have to think more clearly to get through this. She opened the case back up, grabbed another roll of gauze, and cleaned up after herself, then checked the floor outside the lifts.

It was a mess. She went back for a small bottle of alcohol, remembered where she'd seen a huge jug of industrial cleaner, grabbed that plus more gauze, wiped everything up. Took her time. Couldn't get in too big a hurry.

The bundle of soiled and stained cloth went back in the bin, the lid kicked shut. Satisfied with the condition of the floor, she hurried to the barracks. Her cot made it obvious that someone lived there. The other mattresses were bare. Before she fixed this, she stripped down, grabbed another pair of coveralls, and went to the bathroom. After washing her hands and face, and the bright spill of blood down her neck and between her breasts, she cleaned the sink and changed. The red coveralls went into her footlocker. If they looked in there, she was screwed.

She pulled the covers off her bed, grabbed her pillow, and made sure everything else was straight. Back in the warehouse, she opened the hangar door on the drone lift and threw her things inside. She went to the shelves and gathered rations and water, added this. Another small medical kit. Inside the bin of first-aid gear, she discovered the microphone, which she must've dropped earlier while grabbing the gauze. This and two flashlights and a spare set of batteries went inside the lift as well. It was the last place anyone would look. The door was practically invisible unless you knew what to search for. It only came up to her knees and was the same color as the wall.

She considered crawling inside right then, would just need to outlast the first thorough search of the level. They would concentrate on the shelving units, the stacks, and think the place was clear, move on to the many other warrens in which she could be hiding. But before she waited that out, there was the microphone coiled up that she had worked so hard to acquire. There was the radio. She had a few hours, she told herself. This wouldn't be the first place they'd check. Surely she had a few hours.

Dizzy from lack of sleep and loss of blood, she made her way to the flight control room and pulled the plastic sheet from the radio. Patting her chest, she remembered she'd changed coveralls. And besides, that driver was gone. She searched the bench for another, found one, and removed the panel from the side of the unit. The board she wasn't sure about was already installed. It was a simple matter of plugging the microphone in. She didn't bother with affixing it to the side panel or closing anything up.

She checked the seating of the control boards. It was a lot like a computer, all the parts slotting together, but she was no electrician. She had no idea if there was anything else, anything missing. And no way in hell was she going on another run for parts. She powered up the unit and selected the channel marked "18".

She waited.

Adjusting the squelch, she brought enough static into the speakers to make sure the unit was on. There was no traffic on the channel. Squeezing the microphone put an end to the static, which was a good sign. Weary and hurting and fearful for herself as well as her brother, Charlotte managed a smile. The click of the microphone back through the speakers was a small victory.

"Can anyone read me?" she asked. She propped one elbow on the desk, her other arm hanging useless by her side. She tried again. "Anyone out there with ears on? Please come back."

Static. Which didn't prove anything. Charlotte could very well imagine the radios sitting miles away in this silo somewhere, all the operators around them slouched over, dead. Her brother had told her about the time he had ended a silo with the press of a button. He had come to her with his eyes shining in the middle of the night and told her all about it. And now this other silo was gone. Or maybe her radio wasn't broadcasting.

She wasn't thinking straight. Needed to troubleshoot before she jumped to conclusions. Reaching for the dial, she immediately thought of the other silo she and her brother had eavesdropped in on, this neighboring silo with a handful of survivors who liked to chat back and forth and play games like Hide and Find with their radios. If she remembered right, the mayor of 18 had somehow transmitted on this other frequency before. Charlotte clicked over to "17" to test her mic, see if anyone would respond, forgetting the late hour. She used her old call sign from the Air Force out of habit.

"Hello. Hello. This is charlie two-four. Anyone read me?"

She listened to static, was about to switch over to another channel when a voice broke through, shaky and distant:

"Yes. Hello? Can you hear us?"

Charlotte squeezed the microphone again, the pain in her shoulder momentarily gone, this connection with a strange voice like a shot of adrenaline.

"I hear you. Yes. You can read me okay?"

"What the hell is going on over there? We can't get through to you. The tunnel . . . there's rubble in the tunnel. No one will respond. We're trapped over here."

Charlotte tried to make sense of this. She double-checked the transmit frequency. "Slow down," she said and took a deep breath, took her own advice. "Where are you? What's going on?"

"Is this Shirly? We're stuck over here in this . . . other place. Everything's rusted. People are panicking. You've gotta get us out of here."

Charlotte didn't know whether to answer or simply power the unit down and try again later. It felt as though she had butted into the middle of a conversation, confusing one of the parties. Another voice chimed in, supporting her theory:

"That's not Shirly," someone said, a woman's voice. "Shirly's dead."

Charlotte adjusted the volume. She listened intently. For a moment, she forgot the man dying in the hallway below, the man she had stabbed, the wound in her arm. She forgot about those who must be coming after her, searching for her. She listened instead with great interest to this conversation on channel 17, this voice that sounded vaguely familiar.

"Who is this?" the first voice—the male voice—asked.

There was a pause. Charlotte didn't know whom he was asking, whom he expected an answer from. She lifted the microphone to her lips, but someone else answered.

"This is Juliette."

The voice was labored and weary.

"Jules? Where are you? What do you mean, Shirly's dead?"

Another burst of static. Another dreadful pause.

"I mean they're all dead," she said. "And so are we."

A burst of static.

"I killed us all."

Silo 17

40

JULIETTE OPENED HER eyes and saw her father. A white light bloomed and passed from one of her eyes to the other. Several faces loomed behind him, peering down at her. Light blue and white and yellow coveralls. What seemed a dream at first gradually coalesced into something real. And what was sensed as nothing more than a nightmare hardened into recollection: Her silo had been shut down. Doors had been opened. Everyone was dead. The last thing she remembered was clutching a radio, hearing voices, and declaring everyone dead. And she had killed them.

She waved the light away and tried to roll onto her side. She was on damp steel plating, someone's undershirt tucked under her head, not on a bed. Her stomach lurched, but nothing came out. It was hollow, cramping, heaving. She made gagging noises and spat on the ground. Her father urged her to breathe. Raph was there, asking her if she'd be all right. Juliette bit down the urge to yell at them all, to yell at the world to leave her the hell alone, to hug her knees and weep for what she'd done. But Raph kept asking if she was okay.

Juliette wiped her mouth with her sleeve and tried to sit up. The room was dark. She was no longer inside the digger. A lambent glow beat from somewhere, like an open flame, the smell of burning biodiesel, a homemade torch. And in the gloom, she saw the dance and swing of flashlights at the ends of disembodied hands and on miners' helmets as her people tended to one another. Small groups huddled here and there. A stunned silence sat like a blanket atop the scattered weeping.

"Where am I?" she asked.

Raph answered. "One of the boys found you in the back of that machine. Said you were curled up. They thought you were dead at first—"

Her father interrupted. "I'm going to listen to your heart. If you can take deep breaths for me."

Juliette didn't argue. She felt young again, young and miserable for breaking something, for disappointing him. Her father's beard twinkled with silver from Raph's flashlight. He plugged his stethoscope into his ears, and she knew the drill. She parted her coveralls. He listened as she swallowed deep gulps of air and let them out slowly. Above her, she recognized enough of the pipes and electrical conduit and exhaust ducts to locate herself. They were in the large pump facility adjacent to the generator room. The ground was wet because all this had been flooded. There must be water trapped above here, a slow leak somewhere, a reservoir gradually emptying. Juliette remembered all the water. She had donned a cleaning suit and had swum past this room in some long-ago life.

"Where are the kids?" she asked.

"They went with your friend Solo," her father said. "He said he was taking them home."

Juliette nodded. "How many others made it?" She took another deep breath and wondered who was still alive. She remembered herding all that she could through the dig. She had seen Courtnee and Walker. Erik and Dawson. Fitz. She remembered seeing families, some of the kids from the classrooms, and that young boy from the bazaar in shopkeep brown coveralls. But Shirly . . . Juliette reached up and gingerly touched her sore jaw. She could hear the blast and feel the rumbles in the ground again. Shirly was gone. Lukas was gone. Nelson and Peter. Her heart couldn't hold it all. She expected it to stop, to quit, while her father was listening to it.

"There's no telling how many made it," Raph said. "Everyone is . . . it's chaos out there." He touched Juliette's shoulder. "There was a group that came through a while back, before everything went nuts. A priest and his congregation. And then a bunch more came after. And then you."

Her father listened intently to her stubborn heartbeat. He moved the metal pad from one corner of her back to another, and Juliette took deep, dutiful breaths. "Some of your friends are trying to figure out how to turn that machine around and dig us out of here," her father said.

"Some are already digging," Raph told her. "With their hands. And shovels."

Juliette tried to sit up. The pain of all she'd lost was hammered by the thought of losing those who remained. "They can't dig," she said. "Dad, it's not safe over there. We have to stop them." She clutched his coveralls.

"You need to take it easy," he said. "I sent someone to fetch you some water—"

"Dad, if they dig, we'll die. Everyone over here will die."

There was silence. It was broken by the slap of boots. A light slashed the darkness up and down, and Bobby arrived with a dented tin canteen sloshing with water.

"We'll die if they dig us out," Juliette said again. She refrained from adding that they were all dead anyway. They were walking corpses in that shell of a silo, that home for madness and rust. But she knew she sounded just as mad as everyone else had, cautioning against digging because the air over here was supposed to be poison. Now they wanted to tunnel to their death as badly as she had wanted to tunnel to hers.

She drank from the canteen, water splashing from her chin to her chest, and considered the lunacy of it all. And then she remembered the congregation that'd come over to exorcise this poisoned silo's demons, or maybe to see the devil's work for themselves. Lowering the canteen, she turned to her father, a looming silhouette in the spill of light from Raph's flashlight.

"Father Wendel and his people," Juliette said. "Was that . . . ? They were the ones who came earlier?"

"They were seen heading up and out of Mechanical," Bobby said. "I heard they were looking for a place to worship. A bunch of the others went up to the farms, heard there was still something growing there. A lot of people are worried about what we'll eat until we get out of here."

"What we'll eat," Juliette muttered. She wanted to tell Bobby that they weren't getting out of there. Ever. It was gone. Everything they had known. The only reason she knew and they didn't is because she had stumbled through the piles of bones and over the mounds of the dead getting into this silo. She had seen what becomes of a fallen world, had heard Solo tell his story of dark days, had listened on the radio as those events played out all over again. She knew the threats, the threats that had now been carried out, all because of her daring.

Raph urged her to sip some more water, and Juliette saw in the flashlit faces around her that these survivors thought they were merely in a spot of trouble, that this was temporary. The truth was that this was likely all that remained of their people, this few hundred who had managed to get through, those lucky enough to live in the Deep, a startled mob from the lower Mids, a congregation of fanatics who had doubted this place. Now they were dispersing, looking to survive what they must hope would be over in a few days, a week, simply concerned with having enough to eat until they were saved.

They didn't yet understand that they *had* been saved. Everyone else was gone.

She handed the canteen back to Raph and started to get up. Her father urged her to stay put, but Juliette waved him off. "We have to stop them from digging," she said, getting to her feet. The seat of her coveralls was damp from the wet floor. There was a leak somewhere, pools of water trapped in the ceilings and the levels above them, slowly draining. It occurred to her that they would need to fix this. And just as quickly, she realized there was no point. Such planning was over. It was now about surviving the next minute, the next hour.

"Which way to the dig?" she asked.

Raph reluctantly pointed with his flashlight. She pulled him along, stopped short when she saw Jomeson, the old pump repairman, huddled against a wall of silent and rusted pumps, his hands cupped in his lap. Jomeson was sobbing to himself, his shoulders pumping up and down like pistons as he gazed into his hands.

Juliette pointed her father to the man and went to his side. "Jomes, are you hurt?"

"I saved this," Jomeson blubbered. "I saved this. I saved this."

Raph aimed his flashlight into the mechanic's lap. A pile of chits glimmered in his palms. Several months' pay. They clinked as his body shook, coins writhing like insects.

"In the mess hall," he said between sniffles and sobs. "In the mess hall while everyone was running. I opened the till. Cans and cans and jars in the larder. And this. I saved this."

"Shhh," Juliette said, resting a hand on his trembling shoulder. She looked to her father, who shook his head. There was nothing to be done for him.

Raph aimed the flashlight elsewhere. Further down, a

mother rocked back and forth and wailed. She clutched a baby to her chest. The child seemed to be okay, its small arm reaching up for its mother, its hand opening and closing, but making no noise. So much had been lost. Everyone had what they could carry and nothing more, just whatever they had grabbed. Jomeson sobbed for what he had grabbed as floodwater trickled from the ceiling, a silo weeping, all but the children crying.

41

JULIETTE FOLLOWED RAPH through the great digger and into the tunnel. They walked a long way over piles of rocks, scampered over avalanches of tailings cascading down from both sides, saw clothes, a single boot, and a half-buried blanket that'd been dropped. Someone's canteen lay forgotten, which Raph collected; he shook it and smiled when it sloshed.

In the distance, open flames bathed rock in orange and red, the raw meat of the earth exposed. A fresh pile of rubble sloped down from a full cave-in of the ceiling, the result of Shirly's sacrifice. Juliette pictured her friend on the other side of those rocks. She saw Shirly slumped over in the generator control room, asphyxiated or poisoned or simply disintegrating in the outside air. This image of a friend lost joined that of Lukas in his small apartment below the servers, his young and lifeless hand relaxed around a silent radio.

Juliette's radio had gone silent as well. There had been that brief transmission in the middle of the night from someone above them, a transmission that woke her up and that she had ended by announcing that everyone was dead. After that call, she had tried to reach Lukas. She had tried him over and over, but it hurt too much to listen to the static. She was killing herself and her battery by trying, had finally switched the unit off, had briefly considered calling on channel 1 to yell at the fucker who had betrayed her, but she didn't want them to know any of her people had survived, that there were more of them out there to kill.

Juliette vacillated between fuming over the evil of what they'd done and mourning the loss of those they'd taken. She leaned against her father and followed Raph and Bobby toward the clinks and thwacks and shouts of digging. Right then, she needed to buy time, to save what was left. Her brain was in survival mode, her body numb and staggering. What she knew for sure was that joining the two silos yet again would mean the death of them all. She had seen the white mist descending the stairwell, knew that this wasn't some harmless gas, had seen what was left of the gasket and heat tape. This was how they poisoned the outside air. It was how they ended worlds.

"Watch yer toes!" someone barked. A miner trundled by with a barrow of rubble. Juliette found herself walking up a sloping floor, the ceiling getting closer and closer. She could make out Courtnee's voice ahead. Dawson's too. Piles of tailings had been hauled away from the collapse to mark the progress already made. Juliette felt torn between the urge to warn Courtnee to stop what she was doing and the desire to jump forward and dig with her own hands, to bend her nails back as she clawed her way toward whatever had happened over there, death be damned.

"Okay, let's clear that top back before we go any further. And what's taking so long with the jack? Can we please get some hydraulics from the genset fed back here? Just because it's dark doesn't mean I can't see you dregs slackin'—"

Courtnee fell silent when she saw Juliette. Her face hardened, her lips pressed tight. And Juliette could sense her friend was wavering between slapping her and hugging her. It stung that she did neither.

"You're up," Courtnee said.

Juliette averted her gaze and studied the piles of stone and rock. Soot swirled and settled from the burning diesel torches. It made the cold air deep inside the earth feel dry and thin, and Juliette worried about the oxygen being burned and whether the sparse farms of Silo 17 could keep up with the demand. And what about all the new lungs—hundreds of pairs of them—sucking that oxygen down as well?

"We need to talk about this," Juliette said, waving at the cave-in.

"We can talk about what the hell happened here after we dig our way back home. If you want to grab a shovel—"

"This rock is the only thing keeping us alive," Juliette said.

Several of those digging had already stopped when they saw who was talking to Courtnee. Courtnee barked at them to get back to work, and they did. Juliette didn't know how to do this delicately. She didn't know how to do it at all.

"I don't know what you're getting at—" Courtnee started.

"Shirly brought the roof down and saved us. If you dig through this, we'll die. I'm sure of it."

"Shirly—?"

"Our home was poisoned, Court. I don't know how to explain it, but it was. People were dying up top. I heard from Peter and—" She caught her breath. "From Luke. Peter saw the outside. The *outside*. The doors had opened and people were dying. And Luke—" Juliette bit her lip until the pain cleared her thoughts. "The first thing I thought of was to get everyone over here, because I knew it was safe here—"

A bark of laughter from Courtnee. "Safe? You think it's . . . ?" She took a step closer to Juliette, and suddenly no one was digging. Juliette's father placed a hand on his daughter's arm and tried to pull her back, but Juliette held her ground.

"You think it's safe over here?" Courtnee hissed. "Where the hell are we? There's a room back there that looks a goddamn lot like our gen room, except that it's a rusted wreck. You think those machines will ever spin again? How much air do we have over here? How much fuel? What about food and water? I give us a few days if we don't get back home. That's a few days of dead-out digging, mostly by hand. Do you have any idea what you've done to us, bringing us over here?"

Juliette withstood the barrage. She welcomed it. She longed to add a few stones of her own.

"I did this," she said. She pulled away from her father and faced the diggers, whom she knew well. She turned and threw her voice down the dark pit from which she'd just come. "*I did this!*" she shouted at the top of her lungs, sending her words barreling toward those she'd damned and doomed. Again, she screamed: "*I did this!*" and her throat burned from the soot and the sting of the admission, her chest cracking open and raw with misery. She felt a hand on her shoulder, her father again. The only sounds, once her echoes died down, were the crackle and whisper of open flames.

"I caused this," she said, nodding. "We shouldn't have come here to begin with. We shouldn't. Maybe my digging is the reason they poisoned us, or my going outside, but the air over here is clean. I promised you all that this place was here and that the air was fine. And now I'm telling you, just as surely, that our home is lost. It is poisoned. Opened to the outside. Everyone we left behind—" She tried to catch her breath, her heart empty, her stomach in knots. Again, her father propped her up. "Yes, it was my fault. My prodding. That's why the man who did this—"

"Man?" Courtnee asked.

Juliette surveyed her former friends, men and women she

had worked alongside for years. "A man, yes. From one of the silos. There are fifty silos just like ours—"

"So you've told us," one of the diggers said gruffly. "So the maps say."

Juliette searched him out. It was Fitz, an oilman and former mechanic. "And do you not believe me, Fitz? Do you now believe that there are only two in all the universe and that they were this near to one another? That the rest of that map is a lie? I am telling you that I stood on a ridge and I saw them with my own eyes. While we stand here in this dark pit choking on fumes, there are tens of thousands of people going about their days, days like we once knew—"

"And you think we should be digging toward them?"

Juliette hadn't considered that. "Maybe," she said. "That might be our only way out of this, if we can reach them. But first we need to know who is over there and if it's safe. It might be as ruined as our silo. Or as empty as this one. Or full of people not at all happy to see us. The air could be toxic when we push through. But I can tell you that there are others."

One of those digging slid down the rubble to join the conversation. "And what if everything is fine on the other side of this pile? Aren't you the one who always has to go look and see?"

Juliette absorbed the blow. "If everything is fine over there, then they will come for us. We will hear from them. I would love for that to be true, for this to happen. I would love to be wrong. But I'm not." She studied their dark faces. "I'm telling you that there's nothing over there but death. You think I don't want to hope? I've lost . . . we've all lost people we love. I listened as men I loved and cared about breathed their last, and you don't think I want to get over there and see for myself? To bury them proper?" She wiped her eyes. "Don't you think for a moment that I don't want to grab a shovel and work three shifts until we're through to them. But I know that I would be burying those of us who are left. We would be tossing this dirt and these rocks right into our own graves."

No one spoke. Somewhere, gravity won a delicate struggle against a rock, and the loose stone tumbled with clacks and clatters toward their feet.

"What would you have us do?" Fitz asked, and Juliette heard an intake of air from Courtnee, who seemed to bristle at the thought of anyone taking advice from her ever again.

"We need a day or two to determine what happened. Like I said, there are a lot of worlds like our own out there. I don't know what they hold, but I know one of them seems to think it's in charge. They have threatened us before, saying they can push a button and end us, and I believe that's what they've done. I believe it's what they did to this other world as well." She pointed down the tunnel to Silo 17. "And yes, it may have been because we dared to dig or because I went outside looking for answers, and you can send me to clean for those sins. I will gladly go. I will clean and die in sight of you. But first, let me tell you what little I know. This silo we're in, it will flood. It is slowly filling even now. We need to power the pumps that keep it dry, and we need to make sure that the farms stay wet, the lights stay on, that we have enough air to breathe." She gestured to one of the torches set into the wall. "We're going through an awful lot of air."

"And where are we supposed to get this power? I was one of the first through to the other side. It's a heap of rust over there!"

"There's power up in the thirties," Juliette said. "Clean power. It runs the pumps and lights in the farms. But we shouldn't rely on that. We brought our own power with us—"

"The backup generator," someone said.

Juliette nodded, thankful to have them listening. For now, at least, they'd stopped digging.

"I'll shoulder the burden for what I've done," Juliette said, and the flames blurred behind a film of tears. "But someone else brought this hell on us. I know who it was. I've spoken with him. We need to survive long enough to make him and his people pay—"

"Revenge," Courtnee said, her voice a harsh whisper. "After all the people who died trying to get some measure of that when you left to clean—"

"Not revenge, no. Prevention." Juliette peered down the dark tunnel and into the gloom. "My friend Solo remembers when this world—his world—was destroyed. It wasn't gods that brought this upon us, but men. Men close enough to talk to by radio. And there are other worlds standing out there beneath their thumbs. Imagine if someone else had acted before now. We would have gone about our lives, never knowing the threat that existed. Our loved ones would be alive right now." She turned back to Courtnee and the others. "We shouldn't go after these people for what they did. No. We should go after them for what they're capable of doing. Before they do it again."

She searched her old friend's eyes for understanding, for acceptance. Instead, Courtnee turned her back on her. She turned away from Juliette and studied the pile of rubble they'd been clearing. A long moment passed, smoke filling the air, orange flames whispering.

"Fitz, grab that torch," Courtnee ordered. There was a moment's hesitation, but the old oilman complied. "Douse that thing," she told him, sounding disgusted with herself. "We're wasting air."

42

ELISE HEARD VOICES down the stairwell. There were strangers in her home. Strangers. Rickson used to frighten her and the twins into behaving by telling them stories of strangers, stories that made them never want to leave their home behind the farms. A long time ago, Rickson used to say, anyone you didn't know was out to kill you and take your things. Even some of those who *did* know you couldn't be trusted. That's what Rickson used to say late at night when the clicking timers made the grow lights go suddenly out.

Rickson told them the story over and over of how he was born because of two people in love—whatever that meant—and that his father had cut a poisoned pill out of his mother's hip, and that's how people had babies. But not all people had babies out of two people in love. Sometimes it was strangers, he said, who came and took whatever they wanted. It was men in those old days, and often what they wanted was for women to make babies, and so they cut poisoned pills right out of their flesh and the women had babies.

Elise didn't have a poisoned pill in her flesh. Not yet. Hannah said they grew in there late like grown-up teeth, which was why it was important to have babies as early as you could. Rickson said this weren't true at all, and that if you were born without a pill in your hip you'd never have one, but Elise didn't know what to believe. She paused on the stairs and rubbed her side, feeling for any bumps there. Tonguing the gap between her teeth in concentration, she felt something hard beneath her gums and growing. It made her want to cry, knowing her body could do foolish things like growing teeth and pills beneath her flesh without her asking. She called up the stairs for Puppy, who had squirmed loose again and had bounded out of sight. Puppy was bad like this. Elise was starting to wonder if puppies were a thing you could own or if they were always running away. But she didn't cry. She clutched the rail and took another step and another. She didn't want babies. She just wanted Puppy to stay with her, and then her body could do whatever it wanted.

A man overtook her on the stairs—it wasn't Solo. Solo had told her to stick close. "Tell *Puppy* to stick close," she would say when Solo caught up to her. It paid to have excuses ready like this. Like pumpkin seeds in pockets. This man overtaking her looked back at her over his shoulder. He was a stranger, but he didn't seem to want her things. He already had things, had a coil of the black and yellow wire that dipped from the ceiling in the farms that Rickson said never to touch. Maybe this man didn't know the rules. It was peculiar to see people she didn't know in her home, but Rickson lied sometimes and was wrong some other times and maybe he lied or was wrong with his scary stories and Solo had been right. Maybe it was a good thing, these strangers. More people to help out and make repairs and dig water trenches in the soil so all the plants got a good drink. More people like Juliette, who had come and made their home better, took them up to where the light was steady and you could heat water for a bath. Good strangers.

Another man spiraled into view with noisy boots. He had a sack bursting with green leaves, the smell of ripe tomatoes and blackberries trailing past. Elise stopped and watched him go.

That's too much to pick all at once, she could hear Hannah saying. Too much. More rules that nobody knew. Elise might have to teach them. She had a book that could teach people how to fish and how to track down animals. And then she remembered that all the fish were gone. And she couldn't even track down one puppy.

Thinking of fish made Elise hungry. She very much wanted to eat right at that moment, and as much as possible. Before there wasn't any left. This hunger was a feeling that came sometimes when she saw the twins eating. Even if she wasn't hungry, she would want some. A lot. Before it was all gone.

She trundled up the steps, her bag with her memory book knocking against her thigh, wishing she'd stayed with the others or that Puppy would just stay put.

"Hey, you."

A man on the next landing peered over the rails and down at her. He had a black beard, only not as messy as Solo's. Elise paused a moment, then continued up the stairs. The man and the landing disappeared from view as she twisted beneath them. He was waiting for her as she reached the landing.

"You get separated from the flock?" the man asked.

Elise cocked her head to the side. "I can't be in a flock," she said.

The man with the dark beard and bright eyes studied her. He wore brown coveralls. Rickson had a pair like them that he wore sometimes. That boy from the bizarre had coveralls like that.

"And why not?" the man asked.

"I'm not a sheep," said Elise. "Sheep make flocks, and there aren't any of them left."

"What's a sheep?" the man asked. And then his bright eyes flashed even brighter. "I seen you. You're one of the kids who lived here, aren't you?"

Elise nodded.

"You can join our flock. A flock is a congregation of people. The members of a church. Do you go to church?"

Elise shook her head. She rested her hand on her memory book, which had a page on sheep, how to raise them and how to care for them. Her memory book and this man disagreed. She felt a hollow in her stomach as she tried to sort out which of them to trust. She leaned toward her book, which was right about so much else.

"Do you want to come inside?" The man waved an arm at the door. Elise peered past him and into the darkness. "Are you hungry?"

Elise nodded.

"We're gathering food. We found a church. The others will be down from the farms soon. Do you want to come in, get something to eat or drink? I picked what I could carry. I'll share it with you." He placed a hand on her shoulder, and Elise found herself studying his forearm, which was thick with dark hair like Solo's but not like Rickson's. Her tummy grumbled, and the farms seemed so far away.

"I need to get Puppy," she said, her voice small in that vast stairwell, a tiny puff of fog in the cool air.

"We'll get your puppy," the man said. "Let's go inside. I want to hear all about your world. It's a miracle, you know. Did you know that you are a miracle? You are."

Elise didn't know this at all. It weren't in any of the books she'd made memories from. But she'd missed a lot of pages. Her stomach grumbled. Her stomach talked to her, and so she followed this man with the dark beard into the dark hall. There were voices ahead, a soothing and quiet mix of hums and whispers, and Elise wondered if this was what a flock sounded like.

Silo 1

43

CHARLOTTE WAS BACK to living in a box. A box, but without the cold, without the frosted window, and without the line of bright blue plunged deep into her vein. This box was missing those things and the chance of sweet dreams and the nightmare of waking. It was a plain metal box that dented and sang as she adjusted her weight.

She had made a tidy home of the drone lift, a metal container too low to sit up in, too dark for her to see her hand in front of her face, and too quiet to hear herself think. Twice she had lain there listening to boots on the other side of the door as men hunted for her. She stayed in the lift that night. She waited for them to come back, but they must have many levels to prowl.

She moved every few minutes in a fruitless attempt to make herself comfortable. She went once to use the bathroom when she couldn't hold it anymore, when she feared she would go in her coveralls. To flush or not to flush? Risk the noise or the evidence in the bowl? She flushed, and imagined pipes rattling in some far-off place, someone able to pinpoint where it was coming from.

At the end of the hall, she made sure they hadn't discovered the radio. She expected to find it missing, Donald's notes as well, but all was still there beneath the plastic sheet. Hesitating a moment, Charlotte gathered the folders. They were too valuable to lose. She hurried back to her hole and pushed her things into a corner. Curling up, she pictured boots landing on her brother.

She thought of Iraq. There were dark nights there, lying in her bunk, men coming and going on and off their shifts with whispers and the squeak of springs. Dark nights when she had felt more vulnerable than her drone ever did in the sky. The barracks had felt like an empty parking garage in the dead of night, footsteps in the distance, and her unable to find her car keys. Hiding in that small drone lift felt the same. Like sleeping at night in a darkened garage, in a barracks full of men, wondering what she might wake up to.

She slept little. With a flashlight cradled between her cheek and her shoulder, she went through Donald's folders, hoping the dry reading might help her nod off. In the silence, words and snippets of conversation from the radio returned to her. Another silo had been destroyed. She had listened to their panicked voices, to reports of outer doors being opened, reports of the gas her brother had said he could unleash on these people. She had heard Juliette's voice, heard her say that everyone was dead.

She found a small chart in one of the folders, a map of numbered circles with many of them crossed out. People lived in those circles, Charlotte thought. And now another of them was empty. One more X to scratch. Except Charlotte, like her brother, now felt some connection with these people. She had listened to their voices with him on the radio, had listened to Donald as he recounted his efforts to reach out to them, this one silo that was open to what he had to say, that was helping him hack into their computers to understand what was happening. She had asked him once why he didn't reach out to other silos, and he had said something about those in charge not being safe. They would have turned him in. Somehow, her brother and these people were all rebelling, and now they were gone. This was what happened to those who rebelled. Now it was just Charlotte in darkness and silence.

She flipped through her brother's notes, and her neck began to cramp from holding the flashlight like that. The temperature in the box rose until she was sweating in her coveralls. She couldn't sleep. This was nothing like that other box they put her in. And the more she read, the more she understood her brother's endless pacing, his desire to do something, to put an end to the system in which they were trapped.

Careful with the water and food, taking tiny sips and small bites, she stayed inside for what felt like days but may have been hours. When she needed to go to the bathroom again, she decided to sneak to the end of the hall and try the radio once more. The urge to pee was matched only by the need to know what was going on. There had been survivors. The people of 18 had managed to scamper over the hills and reach another silo. A handful had survived—but how long would they last?

She flushed and listened to the surge of reclaimed water gurgle through overhead pipes. Taking a chance, she went to the drone control room. She left the hall light off and uncovered the radio. There was nothing but static on 18. The same on 17. She turned through a dozen of the other channels until she heard voices and was sure the thing was working. Back to 17, she waited. She could wait forever, she knew. She could wait until they came and found her. The clock on the wall showed that it was just past three, the middle of the night, which she thought was a good thing. They might not be looking for her right then. But then nobody might be listening, either. She squeezed the mic anyway.

"Hello," she said. "Can anyone hear me?"

She nearly identified herself, where she was calling from,

but then wondered if the people in her silo were listening in as well, monitoring all the stations. And what if they were? They wouldn't know where she was transmitting from. Unless they could trace her through the repeaters. Maybe they could. But wasn't this one of the silos crossed off their list? They shouldn't be listening at all. Charlotte moved her tools out of the way and looked for the piece of paper Donny had brought her, the ranking of the silos. It listed at the bottom all of the silos that'd been destroyed—

"Who is this?"

A man's voice spilled from the radio. Charlotte grabbed the mic, wondering if this was someone in her silo transmitting on that frequency.

"I'm . . . Who is this?" she asked, unsure how to answer.

"You down in Mechanical? You know what time it is? It's the middle of the night."

Down in Mechanical. That was the layout of their silos, not hers. Charlotte assumed this was one of the survivors. She also assumed others might be listening in and decided to play it safe.

"Yes, I'm in Mechanical," she said. "What's going on over—I mean, up there?"

"I'm trying to sleep is what, but Court told us to keep this thing on in case she called. We've been wrestling with the water lines. People are staking claims in the farms, marking out plots. Who is this?"

Charlotte cleared her throat. "I'm looking for . . . I was hoping to reach your mayor. Juliette."

"She ain't here. I thought she was down with you. Try in the morning if it ain't an emergency. And tell Court we could use a few more bodies up here. A decent farmer if we've got one. And a porter."

"Uh . . . okay." Charlotte glanced at the clock again, seeing how long she'd have to wait. "Thanks," she said. "I'll try back."

There was no response, and Charlotte wondered why she felt the urge to reach out in the first place. There was nothing she could do for these people. Did she think there was something they could do for her? She studied the radio she'd built, the extra screws and wire scattered around the base, the collection of tools. It was a risk being out and about, but it felt less terrifying than being alone in the drone lift. The risk of discovery was far outweighed by the chance of contact. She would try again in a few hours. Until then, she would try to get some sleep. She covered the radio and considered her old cot in the barracks down the hall, but it was the windowless metal box that claimed her.

44

DONALD'S BREAKFAST ARRIVED with company. They had left him alone the previous day and made him skip a meal. He figured it was some sort of interrogation technique. Same with the boots stomping noisily past in the middle of the night, keeping him up. Anything to throw off his clock, perturb him, make him feel crazy. Or maybe that was day and this was the middle of the night and he hadn't skipped a meal at all. Hard to tell. He had lost track of time. There was a clean circle on the wall and a protruding screw where a clock had once stood.

Two men in security coveralls arrived with Thurman and breakfast. Donald had slept in his coveralls. He pulled his feet up on his cot while the three men packed into his small room. The two security officers regarded him suspiciously. Thurman handed him his tray, which held a plate of eggs, a biscuit, water, and juice. Donald was in incredible pain, but he was also starving. He searched for silverware and saw none, started eating the eggs with his fingers. Hot food made his ribs feel better.

"Check the ceiling panels," one of the security officers said. Donald recognized him. Brevard. He had been chief for almost as long as Donald had been up on shift. Donald could tell Brevard was not his friend.

The other man was younger. Donald didn't recognize him. He was usually up late to avoid being seen, knew the night guard better than these guys. The younger officer scampered on top of the dresser welded to the wall and lifted a ceiling panel. He pulled a flashlight from his hip and shined the light in all directions. Donald had a good idea of what the man was seeing. He had already checked.

"It's blocked," the young officer said.

"You sure?"

"It wasn't him," Thurman said. He had never taken his eyes off of Donald. Thurman waved at the room. "There was blood everywhere. He'd be covered in it."

"Unless he washed up somewhere and changed clothes."

Thurman frowned at the idea. He stood a few paces from Donald, who no longer felt hungry. "Who was it?" Thurman asked.

"Who was what?"

"Don't play dumb. One of my men was attacked, and someone dressed as a reactor tech logged through security right here on this level the same night. They came down this hall, looking for you is my guess. Went to comms, where I know you've been spending your time. There's no way you've been pulling this off on your own. You took someone in, maybe someone from your last shift. Who?"

Donald broke off a piece of biscuit and put it in his mouth to give his lips something to do. Charlotte. What was she doing? Ranging the silo in search of him? Going to comms? She was out of her mind if it was her.

"He knows something," Brevard said.

"I have no idea what you're talking about," Donald said. He took a sip of water and noticed his hand was shaking. "Who was attacked? Are they okay?" He thought of the possibility that it was his sister's blood they had found. What had he done, waking her up? Again, he thought of coming clean and telling them where she was hiding, just so she wouldn't be alone.

"It was Eren," Thurman said. "He got off the late shift, ran for the lift, and was found thirty floors down in a pool of blood."

"Eren's hurt?"

"Eren's dead," Brevard said. "A driver to his neck. One of the lifts is covered in his blood. I want to know where the man who did this—"

Thurman held up a hand, and Brevard fell silent. "Give us a minute," Thurman said.

The young officer standing on the dresser adjusted the ceiling panel until it fell back into place. He jumped down and wiped his hands on his thighs, leaving the dresser covered in lint and snowflakes of styrofoam. The two security men waited outside. Donald recognized one of the office workers passing by before the door shut, nearly called out, wondered what the hell everyone must have thought when they found out he wasn't who he had said he was.

Thurman reached into his breast pocket and procured a folded square of cloth, a fresh rag. He handed this to Donald, who accepted it gratefully. Strange what accounted for a gift. He waited for the need to cough, but it was a rare moment of respite. Thurman held out a plastic bag and kept it open for him. Donald realized what it was for and dug out his other rag, dropped the bloody mess into the bag.

"For analysis, right?"

Thurman shook his head. "There's nothing here we don't already know. Just a . . . gesture. I tried to kill you, you know. It was weak of me to try, and it was because I was weak that I didn't succeed. It turns out you were right about Anna."

"Is Eren really dead?"

Thurman nodded. Donald unfolded the cloth and folded it back up again. "I liked him."

"He was a good man. One of my recruits. Do you know who killed him?"

Donald now saw the cloth for what it was. Bad cop had become good cop. He shook his head. He tried to imagine Charlotte doing these things and couldn't. But then, he couldn't picture her flying drones and dropping bombs or doing fifty push-ups. She was an enigma locked away in his childhood, constantly surprising. "I can't imagine anyone I know killing a man like that. Other than you."

Thurman didn't react to this.

"When do I go under?"

"Today. I have another question."

Donald lifted the water from the tray and took a long pull. The water was cold. It was incredible how good water could taste. He should tell Thurman about Charlotte right then. Or wait until he was going under. What he couldn't do was leave her there alone. He realized Thurman was waiting on him. "Go ahead," he said.

"Do you remember Anna leaving the armory while you were up? I realize you were only with her for a brief time."

"No," Donald said. And it hadn't felt like a brief time. It had felt like a lifetime. "Why? What did she do?"

"Do you remember her talking about gas feeds?"

"Gas feeds? No. I don't even know what that means. Why?"

"We found signs of sabotage. Someone tampered with the feeds between Medical and Population Control." Thurman waved his hand, dismissing what he was about to say. "Like I said, I think you were right about Anna." He turned to leave.

"Wait," Donald said. "I have a question."

Thurman hesitated, his hand on the door.

"What's wrong with me?" Donald asked.

Thurman looked down at the red rag in the plastic bag. "Have you ever seen what the land looks like after a battle?" His voice had grown quiet. Subdued. "Your body is a battlefield now. That's what's going on inside of you. Armies with billions to a side are waging war with one another. Machines that mean to rip you apart and those that hope to keep you together. And their boots are going to turn your body into shrapnel and mud."

Thurman coughed into his fist. He started to pull the door open.

"I wasn't going over the crest that day," Donald said. "I wasn't going out there to be seen. I just wanted to die."

Thurman nodded. "I thought as much later. And I should've let you. But they sounded the alarm. I came up and saw my men struggling with suits and you halfway gone. There was a grenade in my foxhole and years of knowing what I'd do if that ever happened. I threw myself on it."

"You shouldn't have," Donald said.

Thurman opened the door. Brevard was standing on the other side, waiting.

"I know," he said. And then he was gone.

45

DARCY WORKED ON his hands and knees. He dunked his crimson rag into the bucket of red water and wrung it out until it was pink, then went back to scrubbing the mess inside the lift. The walls were already clean, the samples sent out for analysis. While he worked, he grumbled to himself in a mockery of Brevard's voice: "Take samples, Darcy. Clean this up, Darcy. Fetch me a coffee, Darcy." He didn't understand how fetching coffee and mopping up blood had become part of his job description. What he missed were the uneventful night shifts; he couldn't wait for things to get back to normal. Amazing what can begin to feel normal. He almost couldn't smell the copper in the air anymore, and the metallic taste was gone from his tongue. It was like those daily doses in the paper cups, the bland food every day, even the infernal buzzing from the lift with its doors jammed open. All these things to get used to until they disappeared. Things that faded into dull aches like memories from a former life.

Darcy didn't remember much of his old life, but he knew he was good at this job. He had a feeling he used to work security a long time ago, back in a world no one talked about, a world trapped in old films and reruns and dreams. He vaguely remembered being trained to take a bullet for someone else. He had one solid and recurring dream of jogging in the morning, the way the air cooled the sweat from his brow and neck, the chirping of birds, running behind some older man in sweatpants and noticing how this man was going bald. Darcy remembered an earpiece that grew slick and wouldn't stay in place, always falling out of his ear. He remembered watching crowds, the way his heart raced when balloons burst and relic scooters backfired, forever waiting for the chance to take a—

Bullet.

Darcy stopped scrubbing and dabbed his face with his sleeve. He stared at the crack between the floor and the wall of the lift where something bright was lodged, a little stone of metal. He tried to secure it with his fingers, but they wouldn't fit in the crack. A bullet. He shouldn't be touching it anyway.

The rag fell with a splash into the bucket. Darcy grabbed the sample kit from the hallway. The lift continued to buzz and buzz, hating this standing still, wishing it could go places. "Cool your jets," Darcy whispered. He pulled one of the sample bags from the small box inside the kit. The tweezers weren't where they were supposed to be. He dug in the bottom of the kit until he found them, cursed the men on other shifts with no respect for their colleagues. It was like living in a dorm, Darcy thought. No, not the right word, the right memory. Like living in a barracks. It was the semblance of order over an underlying mess. Crisp sheets with folded corners over stained mattresses. That's what this was, people not putting things back where they belonged.

He used the tweezers to grab the bullet and drop it into the plastic bag. It was slightly misshapen but not severely. Hadn't hit anything solid, but it'd hit something. Rubbing the bag around the bullet and holding it up to the light, he saw how a pink stain appeared on the plastic. There was blood on the bullet. He checked the floor to see if he'd slopped any of the bloody water near where the bullet had been wedged, if the blood had perhaps gotten there due to his carelessness.

It hadn't. The man they'd found dead had been stabbed in the neck, but a gun had been discovered nearby. Darcy had sampled the blood inside the lift in a dozen places. A med tech had picked the samples up, and Stevens and the chief had told him that all the samples matched the victim. But now Darcy very likely had a blood sample from the attacker, who was still at large. The man who'd killed Eren. A real clue.

He clutched the sample bag and waited for the express to arrive. He considered for a moment handing this over to Stevens, which would be protocol, but he had found the bullet, knew what it was, had been careful in collecting it. He ought to be the one to see the results.

The express arrived with a cheerful ding. An exhausted-looking man in purple coveralls guided a wheeled bucket out, steered it with the handle of a mop. Instead of calling in his find, Darcy had called down backup. The night custodian. The two men shook hands. Darcy thanked him for staying on shift late, said he owed him a big one. He took the man's place inside the express.

He only had to go down two levels. It felt crazy, taking the express two levels. What the silo needed was stairs. There were so many times he just needed to go up or down a single level and found himself waiting five minutes for a blasted lift. It made no sense. He sighed and pressed the button for the medical wing. Before the doors shut, he heard a wet slap from the mop next door.

Dr. Whitmore's office was crowded. Not with workers—it was just Whitmore and his two med techs busying about—but with bodies. Two extra bodies on slabs. One was the woman discovered dead the day before; Darcy remembered her name being Anna. The other was Eren, the former silo head. Whitmore was at his computer, typing up notes while the lab techs worked on the deceased.

"Sir?"

Whitmore turned. His eyes went from Darcy's face to his hands. "Whatcha got?"

"One more sample. On a bullet. Can you run it for me?"

Whitmore waved at one of the men in the operating room, who exited with his hands held by his shoulders.

"Can you run this for the officer?"

The lab tech didn't seem thrilled. He tugged his bloodstained gloves off with loud thwacks and threw them in the sink to be washed and sterilized. "Let's see it," he said.

The machine didn't take long. It beeped and whirred and made purposeful sounds, and then spit out a piece of paper in jittery fits. The tech reached for the results before Darcy could. "Yup. Got a match. It belongs to . . . Huh. That's weird."

Darcy took the report. There was the bar graph, that unique UPC code of a man's DNA. Amounts and percentages of various blood levels were written in inscrutable code: *IFG, PLT, Hgb*. But where the system should have listed the details of the matching personnel record, it simply said on one of the many lines: *Emer*. The rest of the bio fields were blank.

"Emer," the lab tech said. He crossed to the sink and began washing the gloves and his hands. "That's a weird name. Who would pick a name like that?"

"Where are those other results?" Darcy asked. "From earlier."

The tech nodded to the recycle bin at Dr. Whitmore's feet, who continued to clack away at his keyboard. Darcy sifted through the bin, found one of the results sheets from earlier. He held the two side by side.

"It's not a name," Darcy said. "That would be on the top line.

This is where the location should be." On the other report, the name Eren stood above a line listing the freeze hall and the co-ordinates of the dead man's storage pod. Darcy remembered what one of the smaller freeze halls was called.

"Emergency Personnel," he said with satisfaction. He had solved a small mystery. He smiled at the room, but the other men had already returned to their work.

Emergency Personnel was the smallest of the freeze halls. Darcy stood outside the metal door, his breath visible in the air and clouding the steel. He entered his code, and the keypad blinked red and buzzed its disapproval. He tried the master se-curity code next, and the doors clunked open and slid into the walls.

His heart raced with a mix of fear and excitement. It wasn't simply being on this trail of clues, it was where that trail was tak-ing him. Emergency Personnel had been set aside for the most extreme of cases, for those times when Security was deemed in-sufficient. Through a dense haze, he remembered a time when cops stepped aside while heavily armored men emerged from vans and took down a building with military precision. Had that been him? In a former, former life? He couldn't remember. And anyway, these men in the emergency hall were different. Many of them had been up and about recently. Darcy remem-bered from when he got on shift. They were pilots. He recalled seeing ripples in his mug of coffee one day and finding out that bombs had been dropped from drones. Moving from one pod to the next, he searched for an empty one. Someone had not gone back to sleep when they should have, he suspected. Or someone had been stirred to do bad things.

It was this last possibility that filled him with fear. Who had access to such personnel? Who had the ability to awaken them without anyone knowing? He suspected that no matter whom he reported his findings to, as those findings went up and up the chain of command, they would possibly reach the person or people responsible. It also occurred to him that the man who had been killed was the on-shift head of the entire silo, the head of all the silos. This was big. This was huge. A feud between silo heads? This could get him off coffee-brewing and blood-mopping duty forever.

He was two thirds of the way through the grid of cryopods, making a circuit back and forth, when he started to suspect that he might've been wrong. It was all so tenuous. He was playing at someone else's job. There wouldn't be anyone missing, no grand conspiracy, nobody up killing people—

And then he peered inside a pod with no face there, with no frost on the glass. A palm on the skin of the pod confirmed that it was off. It was the same temperature as the room: cool but not freezing. He checked the display, fearing that it would be off and blank as well, but it showed power. Just no name. Only a number.

Darcy pulled out his report pad and clicked a pen. Only a number. He suspected any name that went with the pod would be classified. But he had his man. Oh, he had his man. And even if he couldn't get a name, he knew where these pilots spent their time when they were on shift. He had a very good idea of where this missing man with his bullet wound might be hiding.

46

CHARLOTTE WAITED UNTIL morning before trying the radio again. This time, she knew what she wanted to say. She also knew her time was short. She had heard people outside the drone lift again that morning, looking for her.

Waiting until she was sure they were gone, she nosed about and saw that they'd cleaned out the rest of Donald's notes in the conference room. She went to the bathroom and took the time to change her bandage, found her arm a scabbed mess. At the end of the hall, she expected to find the radio missing, but the control room was undisturbed. They probably never looked under the plastic sheet, just assumed that everything in the room was part of the drone operations. She uncovered the radio, and the unit buzzed when she powered it on. She arranged Donny's folders across her scattering of tools.

Something Donny had told her came back. He had said they wouldn't live forever, the two of them. They wouldn't live long enough outside the pods to see the results of their actions. And that made it hard to know how best to act. What to do for these people, these three dozen or so silos that were left? Doing nothing doomed so many of them. Charlotte felt her brother's need to pace. She picked up the mic and considered what she was about to do, reaching out to strangers like this. But reaching out was better than just listening. The day before, she had felt like a 911 operator who could only listen while a crime was being committed, unable to respond, powerless to send help.

She made sure the knob was on seventeen, adjusted the volume and squelch until she was rewarded with a soft hiss of static. Somehow, a handful of people had survived the destruction of their silo. Charlotte suspected they had crossed overland. Their mayor—this Juliette her brother had spoken with—had proved it was possible. Charlotte suspected it was this that had drawn her brother's attention. She knew from the suit Donny had been working on that he had dreamed of escaping somehow. These people may have found a way.

She opened his folders and spread out her brother's discoveries. There was a ranking of the silos sorted by their chance of survival. There was a note from the Senator, this suicide pact. And the map of all the silos, not with X's but with the red lines radiating out to a single point. Charlotte arranged the notes and composed herself before making the call. She didn't care if she was discovered. She knew damn well what she wanted to say, what she thought Donny was dying to say but didn't know how.

"Hello, people of Silo Eighteen. People of Silo Seventeen. My name is Charlotte Keene. Can you hear me? Over."

She waited, a rush of adrenaline and a flood of nerves from broadcasting her name, for being so bold. She had very likely just poked the hornets' nest in which she hid. But she had truths to tell. She had been woken up by her brother into a nightmare, and yet she remembered the world from before, a world of blue skies and green grass. She had glimpsed that world with her drone. If she had been born into this, had never known anything else, would she want to be told? To be awoken? Would she want someone to tell her the truth? For a moment, the pain in her shoulder was forgotten. The throbbing was pushed aside by this mix of fear and excitement—

"I'm picking you up nice and clear," someone answered, a man's voice. "You're looking for someone on eighteen? I don't think anyone's up there. Who did you say this was?"

Charlotte squeezed the mic. "My name is Charlotte Keene. Who is this?"

"This is Tom Higgins, head of the Planning Committee. We're up here at the deputy station on seventy-five. We're hearing there's been some kind of collapse, that we shouldn't head back down. What's going on below?"

"I'm not below you," Charlotte said. "I'm in another silo."

"Say again. Who is this? Keene, you say? I don't recognize your name from the census."

"Yes, Charlotte Keene. Is your mayor there? Juliette?"

"You say you're in our silo? Is this someone from the Mids?"

Charlotte started to say something, realized how difficult this was going to be, but another voice cut in. A familiar voice.

"This is Juliette."

Charlotte leaned forward and adjusted the volume. She squeezed the mic. "Juliette, my name is Charlotte Keene. You've been speaking with my brother, Donny. Donald, I mean." She was nervous. She paused to wipe her palms on the leg of her coveralls. When she let go of the mic, the man from earlier could be heard talking on the same frequency:

"—heard our silo is gone. Can you confirm? Where are you?"

"I'm in Mechanical, Tom. I'll come see you when I can. Yes, our silo is gone. Yes, you should stay where you are. Now let me see what this person wants."

"What do you mean, 'gone'? I don't understand."

"Dead, Tom. Everyone is dead. You can tear up your fucking census. Now please stay off the air. In fact, can we change channels?"

Charlotte waited to hear what the man would say. And then she realized the mayor was speaking to her. She hurriedly squeezed the mic before the other voice could step on her transmission.

"I . . . uh, yes. I can transmit on all frequencies."

Again, the head of the planning committee, or whatever he'd called himself, stepped in: "Did you say dead? Was this your doing?"

"Channel eighteen," Juliette said.

"Eighteen," Charlotte repeated. She reached for the knob as a burst of questions spilled from the radio. The man's voice was silenced by a twist of Charlotte's fingers.

"This is Charlotte Keene on channel eighteen, over."

She waited. It felt as though a door had just been pulled tight, a confidant pulled inside.

"This is Juliette. What's this about me knowing your brother? What level are you on?"

Charlotte couldn't believe how difficult this was to get across. She took a deep breath. "Not level. Silo. I'm in Silo One. You've spoken with my brother a few times."

"You're in Silo One. Donald is your brother."

"That's right." And finally, it sounded as if this was established. It was a relief.

"Have you called to gloat?" Juliette asked. There was a sudden spark of life in her voice, a flash of violence. "Do you have any idea what you've done? How many people you've killed? Your brother told me he was capable of this, but I didn't believe him. I never believed him. Is he there?"

"No."

"Well, tell him this. And I hope he believes me when I say it: My every thought right now is how best to kill him, to make sure this never happens again. You tell him that."

A chill spread through Charlotte. This woman thought her brother had brought doom on them. Her palms felt clammy as she cradled the mic. She pressed the button, found it sticking, knocked it against the table until it clicked properly.

"Donny didn't . . . He may already be dead," Charlotte said, fighting back the tears.

"That's a shame. I guess I'll be coming for whoever's next in line."

"No, listen to me. Donny . . . it wasn't him who did this. I swear to you. Some people took him. He wasn't supposed to be talking to you at all. He wanted to tell you something and didn't know how." Charlotte released the mic and prayed that this was getting through, that this stranger would believe her.

"Your brother warned me he could press a button and end us all. Well, that button has been pressed, and my home has been destroyed. People I care about are now dead. If I wasn't coming after you bastards before, I sure as hell am now."

"Wait," Charlotte said. "Listen. My brother is in trouble. He's in trouble because he was talking to you. The two of us . . . we aren't involved in this."

"Yeah, right. You want us talking. Learn what you can. And then you destroy us. It's all games with you. You send us out to clean, but you're just poisoning the air. That's what you're doing. You make us fear each other, fear you, and so we send our own people out, and the world gets poisoned by our hate and our fear, doesn't it?"

"I don't—Listen, I swear to you, I don't know what you're talking about. I . . . this will be hard for you to believe, maybe, but I remember when the world out there was very different. When we could live and breathe out there. And I think part of it can be like that again. Is like that right now. That's what my brother wanted to tell you, that there's hope out there."

A pause. A heavy breath. Charlotte's arm was back to throbbing.

"Hope."

Charlotte waited. The radio hissed at her like an angry breath forced through clenched teeth.

"My home, my people, are dead and you would have me hope. I've seen the hope you dish out, the bright blue skies we pull down over our heads, the lie that makes the exiled do your bidding, clean for you. I've seen it, and thank God I knew to doubt it. It's the intoxication of nirvana. That's how you get us to endure this life. You promise us heaven, don't you? But what do you know of our hell?"

She was right. This Juliette was right. How could such a conversation as this take place? How did her brother manage it? It was alien races who somehow spoke the same tongue. It was gods and mortals. Charlotte was attempting to commune with ants, ants who worried about the twists of their warrens beneath the soil, not the layout of the wider land. She wouldn't be able to get them to see—

But then Charlotte realized this Juliette knew nothing of her own hell. And so she told her.

"My brother was beaten half to death," Charlotte said. "He could very well be dead. It happened before my own eyes. And the man who did it was like a father to us both." She fought to hold it together, to not let the tears creep into her voice. "I'm being hunted right now. They will put me back to sleep or they will kill me, and I don't know that there's a difference. They keep us frozen for years and years while the men work in shifts. There are computers out there that play games and will one day decide which of your silos is allowed to go free. The rest will die. All of the silos but one will die. And there's nothing we can do to stop it."

She fumbled through the folder for the notes, the list of the rankings, and couldn't find it through her blurred vision. She grabbed the map instead. Juliette was saying nothing, was likely just as confused by Charlotte's hell as Charlotte was by hers. But it needed to be said. These awful truths discovered needed to be told. It felt good.

"We . . . Donny and I were only ever trying to figure out how to help you, all of you, I swear. My brother . . . he had an affinity for your people." Charlotte let go of the mic so this person couldn't hear her cry.

"My people," Juliette said, subdued.

Charlotte nodded. She took a deep breath. "Your silo."

There was a long silence. Charlotte wiped her face with her sleeve.

"Why do you think I would trust you? Do you know what you all have done? How many lives you've taken? Thousands are dead—"

Charlotte reached to adjust the volume, to turn it back down.

"—and the rest of us will join them. But you say you want to help. Who the hell are you?"

Juliette waited for her to answer. Charlotte faced the hissing box. She squeezed the mic. "Billions," she said. "Billions are dead."

There was no response.

"We killed so many more than you could ever imagine. The numbers don't even make sense. We killed nearly everyone. I don't think . . . the loss of thousands . . . it doesn't even register. That's why they're able to do it."

"Who? Your brother? Who did this?"

Charlotte wiped fresh tears from her cheeks and shook her head. "No. Donny would never do this. It was . . . you probably don't have the words, the vocabulary. A man who used to be in charge of the world the way it once was. He attacked my brother. He found us." Charlotte glanced at the door, half expecting Thurman to kick it down and barge in, to do the same to her. She had poked the nest, she was sure of it. "He's the one who killed the world and your people. His name is Thurman. He was a . . . something like a mayor."

"Your mayor killed my world. Not your brother, but this other man. Did he kill this world that I'm standing in right now? It's been dead for decades. Did he kill it as well?"

Charlotte realized this woman thought of silos as the entire world. She remembered an Iraqi girl she spoke with once while attempting to get directions to a different town. That was a conversation in a different language about a different world, and it had been simpler than this.

"The man who took my brother killed the wider world, yes." Charlotte saw the memo in the folder, the note labeled *The Pact*. How to explain?

"You mean the world outside the silos? The world where crops grew aboveground and silos held seeds and not people?"

Charlotte let out a held breath. Her brother must've explained more than he let on.

"Yes. That world."

"That world has been dead for thousands of years."

"Hundreds of years," Charlotte said. "And we . . . we've been around a long time. I . . . I used to live in that world. I saw it before it was ruined. The people here in this silo are the ones who did it. I'm telling you."

There was silence. It was the sucking vacuum after a bomb. An admission, clearly stated. Charlotte had done it, what she thought her brother had always wanted to do. Admit to these people what they'd done. Paint a target. Invite retribution. All that they deserved.

"If this were true, I would want all of you dead. Do you understand me? Do you know how we live? Do you know what the world is like outside? Have you seen it?"

"Yes."

"With your own eyes? Because I have."

Charlotte sucked in a deep breath. "No," she admitted. "Not with my own eyes. With a camera. But I've seen further out than any, and I can tell you that it's better out there. I think you're right about us poisoning the world, but I think it's contained. I think there's a great cloud around us. Beyond this cloud is blue skies and a chance at a life. You have to believe me, if I could help you get free, make this right, I would in a heartbeat."

There was a long pause. A very long pause.

"How?"

"I'm not . . . I don't think I'm in a position to help. I'm only saying if I could, I would. I know you're in trouble over there, but I'm not in great shape over here. When they find me, they'll probably kill me. Or something like it. I've done . . ." She touched the driver on the bench, ". . . very bad things."

"My people will want me dead for the part I played in this," Juliette said. "They'll send me to clean, and I won't come back this time. So I guess we have something in common."

Charlotte laughed and wiped her cheeks. "I'm truly sorry," she said. "I'm sorry for the things you're going through. I'm sorry we did this to you all."

There was silence.

"Thank you. I want to believe you, believe that you and your brother weren't the ones who did this. Mostly because someone close to me wanted me to believe your brother was trying to help. So I hope you aren't in the way when I get over there. Now, these bad things you say you've done, have you done them to bad people?"

Charlotte sat up straight. "Yes," she whispered.

"Good. That's a start. And now let me tell you about the world out there. I've loved two men in all my life, and both of them tried to convince me of this, that the world was a good place, that we could make it better. When I found out about the diggers, when I dreamed about tunneling here, I thought this was the way. But it only made things worse. And those two men with all that hope bursting from their breasts? Both of them are dead. That's the world I live in."

"Diggers?" Charlotte asked. She tried to make sense of this. "You got to that other silo through the airlocks. Over the hills."

Juliette didn't answer at first. "I've said too much," she said. "I should go."

"No, wait. Help me understand. You tunneled from one silo to another?" Charlotte leaned forward and spread the notes out again, grabbed the map. Here was one of those puzzles that made no sense until a new rule or piece of information was made available. She traced one of the red lines out beyond the silos to a point labeled *SEED*.

"I think this is important," Charlotte said. She felt a surge of excitement. She saw how the game was supposed to play out, what was to become of this in two hundred years. "You have to believe me when I say this, but I am from the old world. I promise. I've seen it covered with crops that ... like you say, that grow aboveground. And the world outside that looks ruined, I don't think it stretches like that forever. I've seen a glimpse. And these diggers, you called them. I think I know what they're for. Listen to me. I have a map here that my brother thought was important. It shows a bunch of lines leading to this place marked S-E-E-D."

"Seed," Juliette said.

"Yeah. These lines look like flight lines, which never made sense. But I think they lead to a better place. I think the digger you found wasn't meant to go between silos. I think—"

There was a noise behind her. Charlotte had a difficult time processing it, even though she had expected it for hours, for days. She was so used to being alone, despite the fear that they were coming for her, the perfect knowledge that they were coming for her.

"You think what?" Juliette asked.

Turning, Charlotte watched the door to the drone control room fly open. A man dressed like those who had held her brother down stood in the hallway. He came at her, all alone, shouting for her to hold still, shouting for her to raise her hands. He trained a gun on her.

Juliette's voice spilled from the radio. She asked Charlotte to go on, to tell her what the diggers were for, to answer. But Charlotte was too busy complying with this man, holding one hand over her head and the other as high as the pain would allow. And she knew it was all over.

Silo 17

47

THE GENSET GRUMBLED to life. There was a rattle deep in the belly of the great digger, and then a string of lights flickered on in Silo 17's pump room, in the generator room, and down the main hall. There were whoops and applause from exhausted mechanics, and Juliette realized how important these small victories were. Light shone where once there was dark flood.

For her, every breath was a small victory. Lukas's death was a weight on her chest, as were the losses of Peter and Marsha and Nelson. Everyone in IT she had come to know and forgive was gone. The cafeteria staff. Practically anyone above Supply, all those who hadn't made a run for it. Weights on her chest, every one. She took another deep breath and marveled that breathing was still possible.

Courtnee had taken charge of the mechanics, stepping into the vacuum Shirly had left. She and her team were the ones stringing lights and wires and getting the pumps rigged and automated. Juliette moved about like a ghost. Only a handful seemed to see her. Just her father and a few of her closest friends, loyal to a fault.

She found Walker in the back of the digger, where the tight confines and reliable power made him feel closer to home. He looked over her radio and pronounced it both operational and out of juice. "I could rig up a charger in a few hours," he told her apologetically.

Juliette surveyed the conveyor belt, which had been swept free of dirt and rubble and now served as a workbench for both Walker and the dig team. Walker had several projects underway for Courtnee: pumps to respool and what looked like disassembled mining detonators. Juliette thanked him but told him she was heading up soon; there were chargers in the deputy stations as well as in IT on thirty-four.

Further down the conveyor belt, she noticed members of the dig team poring over a schematic. Juliette gathered the radio and her flashlight from Walker's station, patted him on the back, and joined them.

Erik, the old mine foreman, had a pair of dividers and was marking out distances on the schematic. Juliette squeezed in to get a closer look. It was the silo layout she'd brought down from IT all those weeks ago. It showed a grid of circles, a few of them crossed out. There were markings between two silos to show the route the digger had taken. The schematic had been used by the mining team to chart their way, buttressed by Juliette's best guess on which direction she had walked and how far.

"We could make it to number sixteen in two weeks," Erik calculated.

Bobby grunted. "C'mon. It took longer than that to get here."

"I'm relying on your extra incentive to get out of this place," Erik said.

Someone laughed.

"What if it ain't safe over there?" Fitz asked.

"It probably isn't," Juliette said.

Grime-covered faces turned to acknowledge her.

"You got friends in all of these?" Fitz asked. He practically sneered at her. Juliette could feel the tension among the group. Most of them had gotten their families through, their loved ones and kids and brothers and sisters. But not all.

Juliette squeezed between Bobby and Hyla and tapped one of the circles on the map. "I've got friends right here," she said.

Shadows swayed drunkenly across the map as the bulb overhead swung on its cord. Erik read the label on the circle Juliette had indicated. "Silo One," he said. He traced the three rows of silos between this location and where they currently stood. "That would take a lot longer."

"It's okay," she said. "I'm going alone."

Eyes went from the map to her. The only sound was the rumbling of the genset at the other end of the digger.

"I'll be going overland. And I know you need all the blast charges you can lay hands on, but I saw you had a few cases left over from the dig. I'd love to take enough to pop a hole in the top of this silo."

"What are you talking about?" Bobby asked.

Juliette leaned over the map and traced a path with her finger. "I'm going overland in a modified suit. I'm going to strap as many sticks of blast charge as I can to the door of this silo, and then I'm going to open that motherfucker like a soup can."

Fitz smiled a toothless smile. "What kind of friends you say you got over there?"

"The dead kind," Juliette said. "The people who did this to us live right there. They're the ones who make the world outside unlivable. I think it's time they live in it."

No one spoke for a beat. Until Bobby asked, "How thick are the airlock doors? I mean, you've seen 'em."

"Three, four inches."

Erik scratched his beard. Juliette realized half the men

around that table were doing some kind of figuring. Not a one of them was going to talk her out of this.

"It would take twenty to thirty sticks," someone said.

Juliette searched out the voice and saw a man she didn't recognize. Someone from the Mids who had made it down, maybe. But he was wearing a mechanic's coveralls.

"You all had one-inch plate welded up at the base of the stairwell. We used eight sticks to punch through it. I'd say plan on three to four times that."

"You're a transfer?" Juliette asked.

"Yes, ma'am." He nodded. And looking past the grime to his cropped hair and bright smile, Juliette thought she could see the Up-Topper in there. One of the men sent from IT to bolster the shifts in Mechanical. Someone who had blown open the barrier her friends had erected during the uprising. He knew what he was talking about.

Juliette looked to the others. "Before I go, I'll reach out to a few of these silos, see if any will harbor you. But I've got to warn you, the heads of these joints all work for these people. They'd as likely kill you when you come crashing through their walls as feed you. I don't know what's salvageable here, but you might be better off staying put. Imagine what we would've thought if a few hundred strangers cut their way inside our home and asked to be put up."

"We would've let them," Bobby said.

Fitz sneered. "Easy for you to say, you've got your two kids. What about those of us in the lottery?"

This got several people talking all at once. Erik slapped the conveyor belt with his hand to silence them. "That's enough," he said. He glared at those gathered. "She's right. We need to know where we're headed first. In the meantime, we can start staging. We're gonna want all the supports in the mines of this place, which means a lot of water to pump out and exploring to do."

"How exactly are we going to aim this thing?" Bobby asked. "She was a bitch to steer here. These things aren't fond of turning."

Erik nodded. "Already thought of that. We'll dig around it and give her room enough to spin in place. Court says it's possible to run a set of tracks at a time, a little forward on one side, a little back on the other. She'll creep around as long as there's no earth in the way."

Raph appeared at Juliette's side. He had been hanging back during the discussion. "I'm coming with you," he said.

Juliette realized it wasn't a question. She nodded.

When Erik was done explaining what they needed to do next, workers began to scatter. Juliette caught Erik's attention and showed him her radio. "I'm going to go see Courtnee and my dad before I leave, and I've got some friends that headed off to the farms. I'll have someone bring you down a radio as soon as I find another. And a charger. If I make contact with a silo that'll have you, I'll let you know."

Erik nodded. He started to say something, scanned the faces of those still milling about, then waved her to the side. Juliette handed her radio to Raph and followed.

A few paces away, Erik glanced around and waved her further along. And then further. Until they were at the far end of the tailings facility where the very last bulb swayed and flickered.

"I've heard what some of them are sayin'," Erik said. "I just want you to know it's ratshit, okay?"

Juliette scrunched up her face in confusion. Erik took a deep breath, eyed his workers in the distance. "My wife was working in the one-twenties when this went down. Everyone around her was running up, and as much as she felt the urge to join them, she headed straight down here to our kids. Was the only one on her level to make it. She fought a helluva crowd to get here. People were acting crazy."

Juliette squeezed his arm. "I'm glad she made it." She watched the dangling lights shine in Erik's eyes.

"Goddammit, Jules, listen to what I'm telling you. This morning, I woke up on a rusted sheet of plate steel, a crick in my neck I may live with for the rest of my life, two damn kids sleeping on me like a mattress, and my ass dead numb from the cold—"

Juliette laughed.

"—but Lesley is laying there watching me. Like she's been watching me a long while. And my wife looks around us at this rusted hellhole, and she says thank God we had this place to come to."

Juliette turned away and wiped at her eyes. Erik grabbed her arm and made her face him. He wasn't going to let her retreat like that.

"She hated this dig. Hated it. Hated me taking on a second shift, hated it because of my bitchin' and moanin' over the struts you made me pull, what we did to number six. Hated it because I hated it. You understand?"

Juliette nodded.

"Now, I know the fix we're in as well as most. I don't reckon we'll get anywhere with this next dig, but it'll give us something to do until our time comes. Until then, I'm going to wake up sore next to the woman I love, and if I'm lucky I'll do the same thing the next morning, and every one of those is a gift. This ain't hell. This is what comes before. And you gave us that."

Juliette wiped the tears from her cheeks. Some part of her hated herself for crying in front of him. Another part wanted to throw her arms around his neck and sob. She missed Lukas

more powerfully in that moment than she thought herself capable.

"I don't know about this fool's errand you're setting off on,
but you take whatever of mine you need. If that means more
digging with my bare hands, so be it. You get those fuckers. I
want to see them in hell by the time I get there."

48

JULIETTE FOUND HER father in the makeshift clinic he had set up in a cleared-out and rusted storeroom. Raylee, a second-shift electrician nine months pregnant, rested on a bedroll, her husband at her side, both of them with their hands on her belly. Juliette acknowledged the couple and realized their child would be the first—maybe ever—to be born in a different silo from its parents. That child would never know the gleaming Mechanical in which they worked and lived, would never travel up to the bazaar and hear music or see a play, may never gaze at a functioning wallscreen to know the outside world. And if it was a girl, she would face the danger of having children of her own like Hannah had, with no one to tell her otherwise.

"You setting off?" Juliette's father asked.

She nodded. "Just came to tell you goodbye."

"You say that like I'll never see you again. I'll be up to check on the kids once I get things sorted down here. Once we have our new arrival." He smiled at Raylee and her husband.

"Just goodbye for now," Juliette said. She had made the others swear not to tell anyone, especially Court and her father, about what she had planned. As she gave her father a final squeeze, she tried not to let her arms betray her.

"And just so you know," she told him, letting go, "those kids are the nearest thing I'll ever have to children of my own. So whenever I'm not there to look after them, if you can lend Solo a hand . . . Sometimes I think he's the biggest kid of the lot."

"I will. And I know. And I'm sorry about Marcus. I blame myself."

"Don't, Dad. Please don't. Just . . . look after them when I'm too busy to. You know how I can get into some fool project."

He nodded.

"I love you," she said. And then she turned to go before she betrayed herself and her plans any further. In the hallway, Raph shouldered a heavy bag. Juliette grabbed the other. The two of them walked beyond the current string of lights and into the near-darkness, neither of them employing their flashlights, the halls familiar enough, their eyes soon adjusting.

They passed through an unmanned security station. Juliette spotted the breathing hose doubling back on itself, remembered swimming through that very spot. Ahead, the stairwell glowed a dull green from resilient emergency lights, and she and Raph began the long slog up. Juliette had a list in her head of who she needed to see and what she needed to grab on the way. The kids would be in the lower farms, back at their old home. Solo as well. She wanted to see them, and then head up and grab a charger and hopefully another radio at the deputy station. If they were lucky and made good time, she'd be in her old home in the cleaning lab later that night, assembling one last suit.

"You remember to grab the detonators from Walker?" Juliette asked. She felt as though she was forgetting something.

"Yup. And the batteries you wanted. And I topped up our canteens. We're good."

"Just checking."

"How about for modding the suits?" Raph asked. "You sure you have everything up there you need? How many of them are left, anyway?"

"More than enough," Juliette said. She wanted to tell him right then that two suits would be more than enough. She was pretty sure Raph thought he was coming with her the whole way. She was steeling herself for that fight.

"Yeah, but how many? I'm just curious. Nobody was allowed to talk about those things before . . ."

Juliette thought of the stores between thirty-four and thirty-five, the in-floor bunkers that seemed to go on forever. "Two . . . maybe three hundred suits," she told him. "More than I could count. I only modded a couple."

Raph whistled. "That's enough for a few hundred years of cleanings, eh? Assuming you were sending 'em out one a year."

Juliette thought that was about right. And she supposed, now that she knew how the outside air got poisoned, that this was probably the plan: a steady flow of the exiled. Not cleaning, but doing the exact opposite. Making the world dirty.

"Hey, do you remember Gina from Supply?"

Juliette nodded, and the past tense was a busted knuckle. Quite a few from Supply had made it down, but Gina hadn't.

"Did you know we were seeing each other?"

Juliette shook her head. "I didn't. I'm sorry, Raph."

"Yeah."

They made a turn of the staircase.

"Gina did an analysis once of a bunch of spares. You know they had this computer just to tally everything, where it was located, how many were on order, all of that? Well, IT had burned through a few chips for their servers, bang, bang, bang, just one of those weeks where failures crop up all in a row—"

"I remember those weeks," Juliette said.

"Well, Gina wondered how long before they were gonna run out of these chips. This was one of those parts they couldn't make more of, you know? Intricate things. So she looked at the average failure rate, how many they had in the pens, and she came up with two hundred and forty-eight years."

Juliette waited for him to continue. "That number mean something?" she asked.

"Not at first, no. But the number got her curious because she'd run a similar report a few months prior, again out of curiosity, and the number had been close to that. A few weeks later, a bulb goes out in her office. Just a bulb. It winks out while she's working on something, and it got her thinkin'. You've seen the storehouse of bulbs they've got, right?"

"I haven't, actually."

"Well, they're vast. She took me down there once. And . . ."

Raph fell quiet for a few treads.

"Well, the storehouse is about half empty. So Gina runs the figures for a simple bulb for the whole silo and comes up with two hundred and fifty-one years' supply."

"About the same number."

"That's right. And now she's real curious—you'd have loved this about her—she started running reports like this in her spare time, big-ticket items like fuel cells and pregnancy implants and timer chips. And they all converge at right about two-fifty. And that's when she figures we've got that much time left."

"Two hundred and fifty years," Juliette said. "She told you this?"

"Yeah. Me and a few others over drinks. She was pretty drunk, mind you. And I remember . . ." Raph laughed. "I remember Jonny saying that she was remembering the hits and forgetting the misses, and speaking of forgetting the missus, he needed to get back to his. And one of Gina's friends from Supply says that people've been saying stuff like this since her grandmother was around, and they would always be saying that. But

Gina says the only reason this wasn't occurring to everyone at once is because it's early. She said to wait two hundred years or so, and people would be going down into empty caverns to get the last of everything, and then it would be obvious."

"I'm truly sorry she's not here," Juliette said.

"Me too." They climbed a few steps. "But that's not why I'm bringing this up. You said there were a couple hundred suits. Seems like the same count, don't it?"

"It was just a guess," Juliette told him. "I only went down there the couple of times."

"But it seems about right. Don't it seem like a clock ticking down? Either the gods knew how much to stock away, or they don't have plans for us past a certain date. Makes you feel like pig's milk, don't it? Anyhow, that's how it seems to me."

Juliette turned and studied her albino friend, saw the way the green emergency lights gave him a sort of eerie glow. "Maybe," Juliette said. "Gina may've been on to something."

Raph sniffed. "Yeah, but fuckit. We'll be long dead before then."

He laughed at this, his voice echoing up and down the stairs, but the sentiment made Juliette sad. Not just that everyone she knew would be dead before that date ever happened, but that this knowledge made it easier to stomach an awful and morbid truth: Their days were counted. The idea of saving anything was folly, a life especially. No life had ever been truly saved, not in the history of mankind. They were merely prolonged. Everything comes to an end.

49

THE FARMS WERE DARK, the overhead lights sleeping on their distantly clicking timers. Down a long and leafy hall, voices spilled as grow plots were claimed and those claims were just as quickly disputed. Things that were not owned by anyone became owned. It reminded Hannah of troubling times. She clutched her child to her chest and stuck close to Rickson.

Young Miles led the way with his dying flashlight. He beat it in his palm whenever it dimmed, which somehow coaxed more life out of it. Hannah glanced back in the direction of the stairwell. "What's taking Solo so long?" she asked.

Nobody answered. Solo had chased after Elise. It was common enough for her to run off after some distraction, but it was different with all these people everywhere. Hannah was worried.

The child in her arms wailed. It did this when it was hungry. It was allowed to. Hannah clamped down on her own complaints; she was hungry too. She adjusted the child, unhooked one strap of her overalls, and gave the infant access to her breast. The hunger was worse with the pressure of eating for two. And where crops had once brushed against her arms along that hall—where an empty stomach was one of the few things she never need fear—burgeoning plots stood startlingly empty. Ravaged. Owned.

Stalk and leaf rustled like paper as Rickson climbed over the rail and explored the second and third rows, hunting for a tomato or cucumber or any of the berries that had gone wild and had spread through the other crops, their curly arms twining around the stalks of their brethren. He returned noisily and pressed something into Hannah's hand, something small with a soft spot where it had rested on the ground for too long. "Here," he said, and went back to searching.

"Why would they take so much all at once?" Miles asked, digging for food of his own. Hannah sniffed the small offering from Rickson, which smelled vaguely like squash, but underripe. The voices in the distance lifted in argument. She took a small bite and recoiled at the bitter taste.

"They took so much because they aren't family," Rickson said. His voice leaked from behind dark plants that trembled from his passing.

Young Miles aimed his flashlight toward Rickson, who emerged from the rows of cornstalks empty-handed. "But we aren't family," Miles said. "Not really. And we never did this."

Rickson hopped over the rail. "Of course we're family," he said. "We live together and work together like families are supposed to. But not these people, haven't you seen? Seen how they dress differently so they can be told apart? They don't live together. These strangers will fight like our parents fought. Our parents weren't family, either." Rickson untied his hair and collected the loose strands around his face, then tied it all back up. His voice was hushed, his eyes peering into the darkness where voices argued. "They'll do like our parents and fight over food and women until there aren't any of them left. Which means we'll have to fight back if we want to live."

"I don't want to fight," Hannah said. She winced and pulled the baby away from her sore nipple, began working her overalls to switch breasts.

"You won't have to fight," Rickson said. He helped with her overalls.

"They left us alone before," Miles said. "We lived back here for years, and they came and took what they needed and didn't fight us. Maybe these people will do the same."

"That was a long time ago," Rickson said. He watched the baby settle into its mother's breast, then ranged down the railing and into the darkness to forage some more. "They left us alone because we were young and we were theirs. Hannah and I were your age. You and your brother were toddlers. No matter how bad the fighting got, they left us kids alone to live or die by our own devices. It was a gift, the way they abandoned us."

"But they used to come," Miles said. "And bring us things."

"Like Elise and her sister?" Hannah asked. And now she and Rickson had both brought up deceased siblings. That hall was full of the dead and gone, she realized, the plucked-from-above. "There will be fighting," she told Miles, who still didn't seem so sure. "Rickson and I aren't kids any longer." She rocked the baby in her arms, that suckling reminder of just how far from kids they had become.

"I wish they'd just leave," Miles said morosely. He banged the flashlight, which gave forth like a burped baby. "I wish it could all go back to normal. I wish Marcus was here. It don't feel right without him."

"A tomato," Rickson said, emerging victorious from the shadows. He held the red orb in the beam of Miles's light, which threw a blush across all their faces. A knife materialized. Rickson cut the vegetable into thirds, with Hannah getting hers first. Red juice like blood dripped from his hand, from Hannah's lips, and from the knife. They ate in relative quiet, the voices down the hall distant and scary, the knife dripping with life but capable of dripping with worse.

Jimmy cursed himself as he climbed the stairs. He cursed as he used to, with only himself to hear, with words that never had far to travel, moving from his lips to his own ears. He cursed himself and stomped around and around, sending vibrations up and down to mingle with others. Keeping an eye on Elise had turned into a bother. One glance in the other direction, and off she went. Like Shadow used to when all the grow lights popped on at once.

"No, not like Shadow," he mumbled to himself. Shadow had stayed underfoot most days. He had always been tripping over Shadow. Elise was something else.

Another level went past, alone and empty, and Jimmy remembered that this wasn't new. This wasn't sudden. Elise was forever coming and going however she liked. He had just never worried about her when the silo was empty. It made him reconsider what made a place dangerous. Maybe it wasn't the place at all.

"You!"

Jimmy rose to another landing, one-twenty-two. A man waved from the doorway. He had gold coveralls on, which meant something back when things had meaning. It was the first face Jimmy had seen in a dozen levels.

"Have you seen a girl?" Jimmy asked, ignoring the fact that this man seemed to have a question of his own. Jimmy held his hand at his hip. "This high. Seven years old. Missing a tooth." He pointed past his beard at his own teeth.

The man shook his head. "No, but you're the man who used to live here, right? The survivor?" The man had a knife in his hand, which flashed silver like a fish in water. The man in gold then laughed and peered beyond the landing's rail. "I guess we're all survivors, aren't we?" Reaching out, he took hold of one of the rubber hoses Jimmy and Juliette had affixed to the wall to carry off the floods. With a deft swipe of the knife, the hose parted. He began hauling up the lower part, which dangled free far below.

"That was for the floods—" Jimmy began.

"You must know a lot about this place," the man said. "I'm sorry. My name's Terry. Terry Harlson. I'm on the Planning Commi—" He squinted at Jimmy. "Hell, you don't know or care, do you? We're all from the same place to you."

"Jimmy," he said. "My name's Jimmy, but most people call me Solo. And that hose—"

"You have any idea where this power is coming from?" Terry jerked his head at the green lights that dotted the underside of the stairs. "We're up another forty levels from here. Radio there's got power. Some of these wires strung up all over the place got juice too. You do that?"

"Some of it," Jimmy said. "Some was already like that. A little girl named Elise came this way. Did you—?"

"I reckon the power's coming from above, but Tom told me to check down here. He says the power always came from below in our silo, should be the same in this one. Everything else is. But I saw the high-water mark down there where this place was full of water. I don't think power's been coming from there in a while. But you should know, right? This place got any secrets you can tell us about? Love to know about that power."

The hose lay in a coil at the man's feet. The knife was back out, glimmering in his hand. "You ever thought of being on a committee?"

"I need to find my friend," Jimmy said.

Another swipe, but the electrical cord put up more resistance. It was the copper at the center. The man held a loop of the black wire in his hand and sawed back and forth, great muscles bulging beneath an undershirt stained with sweat. After some exertion, the knife burst free, the cord severed in two.

"If your friend ain't with the men in the farms, she's probably up with the chanters. I passed them on my way down. They found a chapel." Terry jabbed the knife skyward before stuffing it away and looping wire around his arm.

"A chapel," Jimmy said. He knew the one. "Thank you, Terry."

"Only fair," the man said, shrugging. "Thanks for telling me where all this power comes from."

"The power—?"

"Yeah, you said it came from above. From level . . ."

"Thirty-four? I said that?"

The man smiled. "I believe you did."

50

ELISE HAD WATCHED the people in the bottom where the floods used to be—the ones who were working to dig their way out and get the power going, get the lights on. She had also seen people at the farms harvesting a bunch of food and figuring out how to get people fed. And now there was this third group of people arranging furniture and sweeping the floors and making things tidy. She had no clue what they were trying to do.

The nice man who had last seen Puppy was off to one side, speaking with another man in a white outfit who had a bald circle in the center of his head even though he looked too young to be bald. The outfit was strange. Like a blanket. Instead of two legs, it had only one, and it was big enough that it swirled around him and made it so you couldn't hardly see his feet. The nice man with the dark whiskers seemed to be arguing a point. The man in the white blanket just frowned and stood there. Now and then, one or both of them would glance at Elise, and she worried they were talking about her. Maybe they were talking about how to find Puppy.

The furniture grew into straight lines, all facing the same way. There weren't any tables like the rooms she used to eat in behind the farms, the places where she would hide under furniture and pretend she was a rat with a whole rat family, all of them talking and twitching their whiskers. Here, it was just chairs and benches facing a wall where a colorful glass picture stood with some of the glass broken out. A man in coveralls worked behind that wall, was visible through the broken glass and hazy behind the part that remained. He spoke to someone else, who passed a black cord through a door. They were working on something, and then a light burst on back there, throwing colorful rays across the room, and a few people moving furniture stopped and stared. Some of them whispered. It sounded like they were all whispering the same thing.

"Elise."

The man with the dark whiskers knelt down beside her. Elise startled and clutched her bag to her chest. "Yes?" she asked, her voice a whisper.

"Have you heard of the Pact?" the man asked. The other man with no hair on the center of his head and the white blanket around his shoulders stood behind, that same frown on his face. Elise imagined that he never smiled.

She nodded. "A pack is a bunch of animals, like deer and dogs and puppies."

The man smiled. "Pact, not pack." But it all sounded the same to Elise. "And dogs and puppies are the same animal."

She didn't feel like correcting him. She'd seen what dogs looked like in her book and in the bizarre, and they were scary. Puppies weren't scary.

"Where did you hear about deer?" the man in the white blanket asked. "Do you have children's books over here?"

Elise shook her head. "We have real books. I've seen deer. They're tall and funny with skinny legs, and they live in the woods."

The man with the whiskers in the orange coveralls didn't seem to care about deer. Not as much as the other man. Elise looked to the door, wondered where everyone she knew was. Where was Solo? He should've been helping her find Puppy.

"The Pact is a very important document," said the man in orange. She suddenly remembered his name was Mr. Rash. He had introduced himself, but she was bad with names. Only ever needed to know a few. Mr. Rash was very nice to her. "The Pact is like a book but only smaller," he was saying. "Similar to how you're like a woman but only smaller."

"I'm seven," Elise said. She wasn't small anymore.

"And you'll be seventeen before you know it." The man with the whiskers reached out and touched Elise's cheek. Elise pulled back, startled, which made the man frown. He turned and looked up at the man in the white blanket, who was studying Elise.

"What books were these?" the man in white asked. "The ones with these animals, they were here in this silo?"

Elise felt her hands drop to her bag and rest protectively there, rest on her Memory Book. She was pretty sure the page with the deer had gone into her book. She liked the things about the green world, the things about fishing and animals and the sun and stars. She bit her lip to keep from saying anything.

The man with the whiskers—Mr. Rash—knelt beside her. He had a sheet of paper and a purple stick of chalk in his hands. He set these on the bench by her leg and rested his hand on Elise's knee. The other man stepped closer.

"If you know of books in this place, it is your duty to God to tell us where they lie," the man in the blanket said. "Do you believe in God?"

Elise nodded. Hannah and Rickson had taught her about God and the night prayers. The world blurred around her, and Elise realized she had tears in her eyes. She swiped them away. Rickson hated it when she cried.

"Where are these books, Elise? How many of them are there?"

"A lot," she said, thinking of all the books she'd stolen pages out of. Solo had been so angry with her when he'd found out she was taking pictures and the how-tos from them. But the how-tos showed her a better way to fish, and then Solo had shown her how to stitch the pages in and out of books proper and they had fished together.

The man in the white blanket knelt down in front of her. "Are these books all over the place?"

"This is Father Remmy," Mr. Rash said, making room for the man with the bald patch and introducing him to Elise. "Father Remmy is going to guide us through these troubling times. We are a flock. We used to follow Father Wendel, but some leave the flock and some join. Like you."

"These books," Mr. Remmy said, who seemed young to be a father, didn't seem all that much older than Rickson. "Are they near us? Where might we find them?" He swept his hand from the wall to the ceiling, had a strange way of talking, a loud voice that could be felt in Elise's chest, a voice that made her want to answer. And his eyes—green like the flooded depths she and Solo used to fish in—made her want to tell the truth.

"All in one place," Elise said, sniffling.

"Where?" the man whispered. He was holding her hands, and the other man was watching this with a funny expression. "Where are the books? It is so important, my daughter. There is only one book, you know. All these others are lies. Now tell me where they are."

Elise thought of the one book in her bag. It was not a lie. But she didn't want this man touching her book. Didn't want him touching her at all. She tried to pull away, but his large hands gripped her more firmly. Something swam behind his eyes.

"Thirty-four," she whispered.

"Level thirty-four?"

Elise nodded, and his hands loosened on hers. As he pulled away, Mr. Rash moved closer and rested a hand on Elise's hand, covering the place the other man had hurt.

"Father, can we . . . ?" Mr. Rash asked.

The man with the bald circle nodded, and Mr. Rash picked up the piece of paper from the bench. One side was printed on. The other side had been written on by hand. There was a purple chalk, and Mr. Rash asked Elise if she could spell, if she knew her letters.

Elise bobbed her head. Her hand once again fell to her bag, guarding her book. She could read better than Miles. Hannah had made sure of that.

"Can you spell your name for me?" the man asked. He showed her the piece of paper. There were lines drawn at the bottom. Two names had already been signed. Another line was blank. "Right here," he said, indicating that line. He pressed the chalk into Elise's hand. She was reading some of the other words, but the writing was messy. It had been written quickly and on a rough surface. Plus, her vision was blurry. "Just your name," he said once more. "Show me."

Elise wanted to get away. She wanted Puppy and Solo and Jewel and even Rickson. She wiped her tears and swallowed a sob that was trying to choke her. If she did what they wanted, she would be free to go. There were more and more people in that room. Some of them were watching her and whispering. She heard a man say that someone else was lucky, that there were more men than women, that people would get left out if they weren't careful. They were watching her and waiting, and the furniture was now straight, the floors swept, some green leaves from plucked plants scattered around the stage.

"Right here," Mr. Rash said. He held her wrist and forced the chalk until it hovered over the line. "Your name." And everyone was watching. Elise knew her letters. She could read better than Rickson. But she could hardly see. She was a fish like she used to catch, under the water, looking up at all these hungry people. But she printed her name. She hoped it would make them go away.

"Good girl."

Mr. Rash bent forward and kissed her on the cheek. People started clapping. And then the man in the white blanket with the fascination for books chanted some words, that voice booming and pretty at the same time. His words felt deep within her chest as he pronounced someone in the name of the Pact, husband and wife.

PART IV

DUST

Silo 1

51

DARCY RODE THE lift up to the armory. He put the small bag with the bullet away and stuffed the blood results into his pocket, stepped out of the lift and fumbled for the wide bank of light switches. Something told him the pilot missing from the cryopod in Emergency Personnel was hiding on this level. It was the level where they'd found the man posing as the Shepherd. It was also where a handful of pilots had been stationed a month or so ago during a flurry of activity. He and Stevens and a few of the others had searched the level several times already, but Darcy had a feeling. It started with the fact that the lift required a security override before it would even bring him to that level.

Only a handful of top personnel and those in Security could manage that sort of override, and on his previous visits Darcy had seen why. Crates of munitions and ammo lined the shelves. There were tarps draped over what appeared to be military drones. Pyramids of bombs sitting on racks. Not anything you wanted the kitchen staff stumbling across when they came down for a can of powdered potatoes and jabbed the wrong button in the lift.

Previous searches hadn't turned up anyone else, but there had to be thousands of places among the tall shelves with their large plastic bins. Darcy peered into these shelves as the lights overhead flickered on. He imagined that he was this pilot, moments after he'd killed a man, arriving there in a lift splattered with blood, on the run and looking for a place to hide.

Crouching, he examined the polished concrete outside the lift. Stepping back and tilting his head, he studied the shine. There was a bit more gleam in front of the door. Perhaps it was from the uneven traffic, the shuffle of boots, the gradual wear. He lowered himself to the floor and took a deep sniff, noted the smell of leaves and pine trees, of lemon and a time forgotten, back when things grew and the world smelled fresh.

Someone had cleaned the floor here. Recently, he thought. He remained crouched and peered through the aisles of weapons and emergency gear, aware that he wasn't alone. What he should do is head straight for Brevard and bring in backup. There was a man in here capable of killing, someone from Emergency Personnel with military training, someone with access to every weapon in those crates. But this man was also wounded, hiding, and scared. And backup seemed like a bad idea.

It wasn't so much that Darcy was the one who had pieced this together and deserved the credit, it was his increasing certainty that these murders pointed straight to the top. The people involved in this were of the highest rank. Files had been tampered with, Deep Freeze disturbed, neither of which should've been possible. The people he reported to might be involved. And Darcy had stood there propping up the real Shepherd while the old man laid boots into his impostor. Nothing about that was protocol. That shit was personal. He knew the guy that took the beating, used to see him up late shifts all the time, had spoken with him now and then. It was hard to imagine that guy killing people. Everything was upside down.

Darcy pulled his flashlight off his hip and began to search the shelves. He needed something more than a bright light, something more than they assigned to night guards. There were designations on the bins from a different life, one barely remembered. He pried open the lids on several bins—the vacuum seals softly popping—before he found what he was looking for: An H&K .45, a pistol both modern and ancient. Top of the line when it rolled off the factory floor, but those factories were little more than memories. He slotted a clip into the weapon and hoped the ammo was good. He felt more confident with the firearm and crept through the storeroom with renewed purpose, not the cursory laps from the day before when eighty levels needed searching.

He peeked under each of the tarps. Beneath one, he found loose tools and scattered parts, a drone partly disassembled or being repaired. Recent work? It was impossible to tell. There was no dust, but there wouldn't be under the tarp. He walked the perimeter, looked for white foam pellets on the ground from any ceiling panels that may have been disturbed, checked the offices at the very back, looked for any places where the shelves might be scaled, any large bins high up. He headed toward the barracks and noticed the low metal hangar door for the first time.

Darcy made sure the safety was off. He gripped the handle on the door and threw it up, then crouched down and aimed his flashlight and pistol into the gloom.

He very nearly shot up someone's bedroll. There was a rumpled pile of pillows and blankets that looked at first like a person sleeping. He saw more of the folders like the ones he'd helped gather from the conference room. This was probably where the man they'd snagged had been hiding. He'd have to show Brevard and get the place cleaned up. He couldn't imagine living like that, like a rat. He shut the hangar and moved to the door down the wall, the one that led to the barracks. Opening it a crack, Darcy made sure the hall was clear. He moved quietly from room to room, sweeping each. No sign of habitation in the bunkrooms. The bathrooms were still and quiet. Eerie, almost. Leaving the women's, he thought he heard a voice. A whisper. Something beyond the doorway at the very end.

Darcy readied his pistol and stood at the end of the hall. He pressed his ear to the door and listened.

Someone talking. He tried the knob and found it unlocked, took a deep breath. Any sign of a man reaching for a weapon, and he would shoot. He could already hear himself explaining to Brevard what had happened, that he'd had a hunch, had followed a clue, didn't think to ask for backup, had come down and found this man wounded and bleeding. He drew first. Darcy had been protecting himself. One more dead body and another case closed. That was his line if this went badly. All this and more flashed through his mind as he threw the door open and raised his weapon.

A man turned from the end of the room. Darcy yelled for him to freeze as he shuffled closer, his training ingrained and coming as naturally as a heartbeat. "Don't move," he shouted, and the man raised his hands. It was a young man in gray coveralls, one arm over his head and the other held limply at his side.

And then Darcy saw that something was wrong. Everything was wrong. It wasn't a man at all.

"Don't shoot," Charlotte pleaded. She raised one hand and watched this man approach her, a gun aimed at her chest.

"Stand up and step away from the desk," the man said. His voice was unwavering. He gestured with his gun to indicate the wall.

Charlotte glanced at the radio. Juliette asked if she could hear her, asked her to finish what she was saying, but Charlotte didn't test this man by reaching for the transmit button. She eyed the scattering of tools, the drivers, the wire cutters, and remembered the gruesome fight from the day before. Her arm throbbed beneath the gauze wrapping. It hurt to raise her hand even to her shoulder. The man closed the distance between them.

"Both hands up."

His stance—the way he held his gun—reminded her of basic training. She did not doubt that he would shoot her.

"I can't raise it any more than this," she said. Again, Juliette pleaded for her to say something. The man eyed the radio.

"Who're you talking to?"

"One of the silos," she said. She slowly reached for the volume.

"Don't touch it. Against the wall. Now."

She did as he said. Her one consolation was the hope that he would take her to her brother. At least she would know what they'd done with him. Her days of isolation and worry had come to an end. She felt a twinge of relief to have been discovered.

"Turn around and face the wall. Place your hands behind your back. Cross your wrists."

She did this. She also turned to the side and glanced over her shoulder at him, caught a glimpse of a white plastic tie pulled from his belt. "Forehead on the wall," he told her. And then she felt him approach, could smell him, could hear him breathing, and thoughts of spinning around and putting up a fight evaporated as the tie cinched painfully around her wrists.

"Are there any others?" he asked.

She shook her head. "Just me."

"You're a pilot?"

Charlotte nodded. He gripped her elbow and spun her around. "What're you doing here?" Seeing the bandage on her arm, his eyes narrowed. "Eren shot you."

She didn't respond.

"You killed a good man," he said.

Charlotte felt tears well up. She wished he would just take her wherever they were going, put her back to sleep, let her see Donny, whatever came next. "I didn't want to," was her feeble defense.

"How did you get here? You were with the other pilots? It's just . . . women don't . . ."

"My brother woke me," Charlotte said. She nodded at the man's chest, where a Security emblem blazed. "You took him." And she remembered the day they came for Donny, a young man propping up Thurman. She recognized this man in front of her, and more tears came. "Is he . . . still alive?"

The man looked away for a moment. "Yes. Barely."

Charlotte felt tears track down her cheeks.

The man faced her again. "He's your brother?"

She nodded. With her arms strapped behind her, she couldn't wipe her nose, couldn't even reach her shoulder to wipe it on her coveralls. She was surprised this man had come alone, that he wasn't calling for backup. "Can I see him?" she asked.

"I doubt that. They're putting him back under today." He aimed his gun at the radio as Juliette again called for some response. "This isn't good, you know. You've put these people in danger, whoever you're talking to. What were you thinking?"

She studied this man. He looked to be her age, early thirties, looked more like a soldier than a cop. "Where are the others?" she asked. She glanced toward the door. "Why aren't you taking me in?"

"I will. But I want to understand something before I do. How did you and your brother . . . how did you get out?"

"I told you, he woke me." Charlotte glanced at the table where Donny's notes lay. She had left the folders open. The map was on top, the Pact memo visible. The security guard turned to see what she was looking at. He stepped away from her and rested a hand on one of the folders.

"So who woke your brother?"

"Why don't you ask him?" Charlotte was beginning to worry. Him not taking her in felt like a bad thing, like he was operating outside the rules. She had seen men in Iraq operate outside the rules. It was never to do anything good. "Please just take me to see my brother," she said. "I surrender. Just take me in."

He narrowed his eyes at her, then turned his attention back to the folders. "What is all this?" He picked up the map and studied it, set it down and picked up another piece of paper. "We pulled crates of this stuff out of the other room. What the hell are you two working on?"

"Just take me in," Charlotte begged. She was getting scared.

"In a minute." He studied the radio, found the volume, turned it down. He put his back to the desk and leaned against it, the pistol held casually by his hip. He was going to drop his pants, Charlotte realized. He was going to force her to her knees. He hadn't seen a woman in several hundred years, was wanting to understand how to wake them up. That's what he wanted. Charlotte considered running for the door, hoping he might shoot her, hoping he would either miss or hit her square—

"What's your name?" he asked.

Charlotte felt tears roll down her cheeks. Her voice quivered, but she managed to whisper her name.

"Mine's Darcy. Relax. I'm not going to hurt you."

Charlotte began to shake. It was exactly what she imagined a man would say before doing something vile.

"I just want to understand what the hell's going on before I turn you over. Because everything I've seen today suggests this is bigger than you and your brother. Bigger than my job. Hell, for all I know, the moment I take you up to the office, they're going to put me under and put you back to work down here."

Charlotte laughed. She turned her head and wiped the tears hanging from her jaw onto her shoulder. "Not likely," she said. And she began to suspect that this man really wasn't going to hurt her, that he was just as curious as he seemed. Her gaze drifted back to the folders. "Do you know what they have planned for us?" she asked.

"Hard to say. You killed a very important man. You shouldn't be up. They'll put you in Deep Freeze would be my guess. Alive or dead, I don't know."

"No, not what they're gonna do to me and my brother—what they have planned for all of us. What happens after our last shift."

Darcy thought for a moment. "I ... I don't know. Never thought about it."

She nodded to the folders beside him. "It's all in there. When I go back to sleep, it won't matter if I'm alive or dead. I'll never get up again. Neither will your sister or mom or wife or whoever they have here."

Darcy glanced at the folders, and Charlotte realized his not taking her in right away was an opportunity, not a problem. This is why they couldn't let anyone know the truth. If people knew, they wouldn't stand for it.

"You're making this up," Darcy said. "You don't know what will happen after—"

"Ask your boss. See what he says. Or your boss's boss. And keep asking. Maybe they'll give you a pod down in Deep Freeze next to mine."

Darcy studied her for a heartbeat. He set his pistol down and unbuttoned the top button on his coveralls. And then the next. He kept unbuttoning them down to his waist, and Charlotte knew she'd been right about what he planned to do. She prepared to jump him, to kick him between the legs, to bite him—

Darcy took the folders and slid them around his back, tucked them into his shorts. He began buttoning up his coveralls.

"I'll look into it. Now let's go." He picked up the gun and gestured toward the door, and Charlotte took a grateful breath. She walked around the drone control stations. Inside, she felt torn. She had wanted this man to take her in, but now she wanted to talk more. She had feared him, but now she wanted to trust him. Salvation seemed to come from being arrested, from being put back to sleep, and yet some other salvation seemed to lie within reach.

Her heart pounded as she was marched into the hallway. Darcy shut the door to the control room. She passed the bunkrooms and the bathrooms, waited at the end of the hall for him to open the door to the armory, her hands useless behind her back.

"I knew your brother, you know," Darcy said as he held the door for her. "He never seemed like the sort. Neither do you."

Charlotte shook her head. "I never wanted to hurt anyone. We were only ever after the truth." She passed through the armory and toward the lift.

"That's the problem with the truth," Darcy said. "Liars and honest men both claim to have it. It puts people in my position in something of a predicament."

Charlotte pulled to a stop. This seemed to startle Darcy, who took a step back and tightened his grip on his pistol. "Let's keep moving," he told her.

"Wait," Charlotte said. "You want the truth?" She turned and nodded at the drones beneath their tarps. "How about you stop trusting what people are telling you? Stop deciding who to believe with your gut. Let me show you. See what's out there for yourself."

52

DONALD'S SIDE WAS a sea of purples, blacks, and blues. He held his undershirt up, his coveralls hanging from his hips, and inspected his ribs in the bathroom mirror. In the center of the bruise there was a patch of orange and yellow. He touched this—barely a brush of his fingertips—and a jolt of electricity shot down his legs and into his knees. He nearly collapsed, and it took a moment to gather his breath. He lowered his shirt gingerly, buttoned his coveralls up, and hobbled back to his cot.

His shins hurt from protecting himself from Thurman's blows. There was a knot on his forearm like a second elbow. And every time a coughing fit seized him, he wanted to die. He tried to sleep. Sleep was a vehicle for passing the time, for avoiding the present. It was a trolley for the depressed, the impatient, and the dying. Donald was all three.

He turned out the light beside his cot and lay in the darkness. The cryopods and shifts were exaggerated forms of sleep, he thought. What seemed unnatural was more a matter of degree than of kind. Cave bears hibernated for a season. Humans hibernated each night. Daytime was a shift, each one endured like a quantum of life, all the short-term planning leading up to another bout of darkness, little thought given to stringing those days into something useful, some chain of valuable pearls. Just another day to survive.

He coughed, which brought bolts of agony to his ribs and flashes of light to his vision. Donald prayed to black out, to pass away, but the gods in charge of his fate were expert torturers. Just enough—but not too much. *Don't kill the man,* he could hear his wounds whispering to one another. *We need him alive so that he can suffer for what he's done.*

The coughing passed with the taste of copper on his lips, blood misting his coveralls—but he didn't care. He laid his head back, soaked in sweat from pain and exertion, and listened to the feeble groans escaping his lips.

Hours or minutes passed. Days. There was a rap at the door, the slide and click of a tumbler, someone flicking on the lights. It would be a guard with dinner or breakfast or some other meaningless designation of time of day. It would be Thurman to lecture him, to grill him, to take him and put him to sleep.

"Donny?"

It was Charlotte. The hall behind her was third-shift dim. As she came to him, a man filled the doorway, one of the security officers. They had discovered her and were locking her up as well. But they were giving him this moment at least. He sat up too quickly, nearly lost his balance, but their arms found one another, both of them wincing in the embrace.

"My ribs," Donald hissed.

"Watch my arm," his sister said.

She untangled herself and stepped back, and Donald was about to ask her what was wrong with her arm, but she pressed a finger to her lips. "Hurry," she said. "This way."

Donald peered past her to the man in the doorway. The guard gazed up and down the hallway, was more concerned about someone coming than about him or his sister escaping.

The ache in Donald's ribs lessened as he realized what was going on.

"We're leaving?" he asked.

His sister nodded and helped him stand. Donald followed her into the hall.

So many questions, but silence was paramount. Now wasn't the time. The security officer closed the door and locked it. Charlotte was already heading toward the lifts. Donald limped after her, barefoot, his left leg singing with every step. They were on the admin level. He passed the accounting offices where spares and supplies were managed; Records, where the major happenings of every silo were tallied and entered into the servers; Population Control, where so many of his reports had once originated. All the offices quiet at what must've been an early-morning hour.

The security station was unmanned. Beyond it, a lift was waiting for them, persistently buzzing in a hold state. Donald noted a strong odor of cleaning agent in the lift. Charlotte slammed the hold button back in, scanned her ID, and pressed the armory level. The guard slid through the closing doors sideways, and Donald noticed the gun in his hand. It wasn't for fear of being discovered by others that he was carrying that gun, Donald realized. They weren't quite free. The young man stood on the other side of the lift and watched him and his sister warily.

"I know you," Donald said. "You work the late shift."

"Darcy," the guard said. He didn't offer his hand. Donald thought of the empty security station and realized this man should've been there.

"Darcy, right. What's going on?" He turned to his sister. A gauze wrapping could be seen peeking out from her short-sleeved undershirt. "Are you okay?"

"I'm fine." She watched the floors light up and slide by with obvious trepidation. "We flew another drone." She turned to Donald, her eyes on fire. "It made it through."

"You saw it?" His wounds were forgotten; the man standing in the lift with the gun was forgotten. It had been so long since that first flight gave him a brief glimpse of blue skies that he had grown to doubt it, had come to think it had never happened at all. The other flights had failed, had never reached as far. The lift slowed as it approached the storehouse.

"The world isn't gone," Charlotte confirmed. "Just our piece of it."

"Let's get off the lift," Darcy said. He waved the gun. "And then I want to understand what the hell is going on. And look, I'm not above having you both locked up before the morning shift comes on. I'll deny we ever talked like this."

Just inside the armory, Donald took a deep, wheezing breath and patted his back pocket. He pulled out the cloth and coughed, bent over to reduce the strain on his ribs. He folded the cloth away quickly so Charlotte couldn't see.

"Let's get you some water," she said, looking to the storehouse of supplies.

Donald waved her off and turned to Darcy. "Why are you helping us?" he asked, his voice hoarse.

"I'm not helping you," Darcy insisted. "I'm hearing you out." He nodded to Charlotte. "Your sister has made some bold claims, and I did a little reading while she put her bird together."

"I gave him some of your notes," Charlotte said. "And the drone flight. He helped me launch it. I put her down in a sea of grass. Real grass, Donny. The sensors held out for another half hour. We just sat there and stared at it."

"But still," Donald said, looking to Darcy. "You don't know us."

"I don't know my bosses, either. Not really. But I saw the beating you took, and it didn't sit right with me. You two are

fighting for something, and it might be something bad, something I'm going to stop, but I've noticed a pattern. Any question
I ask outside of my duties, and the flow of information stops.
They want me to work the night shift and have a fresh pot on in
the morning, but I remember being something more in a different life. I was taught to follow orders, but only up to a point."

Donald nodded grimly. He wondered if this young man had
been deployed overseas. He wondered if he'd suffered from
PTSD, had been on any meds. Something had come back to him,
something like a conscience.

"I'll tell you what's going on here," Donald said. He led them
away from the lift doors and toward the aisle of supplies that
held canned water and MREs. "My old boss—the man you
watched give me this limp—explained some things. More than
he likely meant to. Most of this is what I've put together, but he
filled in some blanks."

Donald lifted the lid on one of the wooden crates his sister
had pried open. He winced in pain, and Charlotte rushed to
help him. He grabbed a can of water and popped the lid, took
a long swig while Charlotte pulled out two more cans. Darcy
switched his gun to his other hand to accept a can, and Donald felt the presence of crate after crate of guns around him. He
was sick of the things. Somehow, the fear of the one in Darcy's
hand was gone. The pain in his chest was a different sort of bullet wound. A quick death would be a blessing.

"We aren't the first people to try and help a silo," Donald said.
"That's what Thurman told me. And a lot more makes sense
now. C'mon." He led them off that aisle and down another. A
light flickered overhead. It would die soon. Donald wondered
if anyone would bother to replace it. He found the plastic crate
he was looking for hidden among a sea of others, tried to pull it
down, and felt a cry from his ribs. He sucked it up and hauled it

anyway, his sister helping with one hand, and together they carried it to the conference room. Darcy followed.

"Anna's work," he grunted, hefting the container onto the conference table while Darcy hit the lights. There was a schematic of the silos beneath a thick sheet of glass, and the glass was marked with old wax notes, scratched into illegibility by elbows and folders and glasses of whisky. All of his other notes were gone, but that was okay. He needed to look for something old, something from the past, from his previous shift. He pulled out several folders and flopped them onto the table. Charlotte began looking through them. Darcy remained by the door and glanced occasionally at the floor in the hall, which remained splattered with dried blood.

"There was a silo shut down a while back for broadcasting on a general channel. Not on my shift." He pointed to Silo 10 on the table, which bore the remnants of a red X. "A burst of conscience broadcast on a handful of channels, and then it was shut down. But it was Silo Forty that kept Anna busy for the better part of a year." He found the folder he was looking for, flipped it open. Seeing her handwriting blurred his vision. He hesitated, ran his hands across her words, remembering what he'd done. He had killed the one person trying to help him, the one person who loved him. The one person reaching out to these silos to help. All because of his own guilt and self-loathing for loving her back. "Here's a rundown of the events," he said, forgetting what he was looking for.

"Get to the point," Darcy said. "What's this all about? My shift is up in two hours, and it'll be daylight soon. I'll need both of you under lock and key before then."

"I'm getting there." Donald wiped his eyes and composed himself, waved his hand at a corner of the table. "All of these silos went dark a long time ago. A dozen or so of them. It started with Forty. They must've had some kind of silent revolution. A bloodless one, because we never got any reports. They never acted strange. A lot like what's going on in Eighteen right now—"

"Was," Charlotte said. "I heard from them. They've been shut down."

Donald nodded. "Thurman told me. I meant to say 'was'. Thurman also hinted that they were originally going to build fewer silos but kept adding more for redundancy. There are a few reports I found that suggested this as well. You know what I think? I think they added too many. They couldn't monitor them all closely enough. It's like having a camera on every street corner, but you don't have enough people watching the feeds. And so this one slipped under the rails."

"What do you mean when you say these silos went dark?" Darcy asked. He sidled closer to the table and studied the layout under the glass.

"All the camera feeds went out at the same time. They wouldn't answer our calls. The Order mandated that we shut them down in case they'd gone rogue, so we gassed the place. Popped the doors. And then another silo went dark. And another. The heads on shift here figured that in addition to the camera feeds, they'd sorted out the gas lines as well. So they sent the collapse codes to all of these silos—"

"Collapse codes?"

Donald nodded and drowned a cough with a gulp of water. He wiped his mouth with the back of his sleeve. It was comforting to see all the notes out on the table. The pieces were fitting together.

"The silos were built to fail, and all but one of them will. There's no gravity to take them down, so they had us build them—they had me design them—with great slabs of concrete between the levels." He shook his head. "It never made sense at the time. It made the dig deeper, increased costs, it's an insane amount of concrete. I was told it had something to do with bunker busters or radiation leaks. But it was worse than that. It was so they'd have something to take down. The walls aren't going anywhere—they're tied to the earth." He took another sip of water. "That's why the concrete. And it was because of the gas that they didn't want lifts. Never understood why they had us take them out. Said they wanted the design more 'open.' It's harder to gas a place if you can block off the levels."

He coughed into the crook of his arm, then drew a finger around a portion of the conference table. "These silos were like a cancer. Forty must've communicated with its neighbors, or they just took them offline as well, hacked them remotely. The heads on shift here in our silo started waking people up to deal with it. The collapse codes weren't working, nothing was. Anna figured they'd discovered the blast charges in Forty and had blocked the frequency—something like that."

He paused and remembered the sound of static from her radio, the jargon she'd used that gave him headaches but made her seem so smart and confident. His gaze fell to the corner of the room where a cot once lay, where she used to sneak over in the middle of the night and slip into his arms. Donald finished his water and wished he had something stronger.

"She finally managed to hack the detonators and bring the silos down," he said. "It was this or they were going to risk sending drones up or boots over, which is last-page Order stuff. Back of the book."

"Which is what we've been doing," Charlotte said.

Donald nodded. "I did even more of it before I woke you, back when this level was crawling with pilots."

"So that's what happened to these silos? They were collapsed?"

"That's what Anna said. Everything looked good. The people

in charge over here were relying on her, taking her word. We were all put back to sleep. I figured it was my last snooze, that I'd never wake up again. Deep Freeze. But then I was brought out for another shift, and people were calling me by a different name. I woke up as someone else."

"Thurman," Darcy said. "The Shepherd."

"Yeah, except I was the sheep in that story."

"You were the one who nearly got over the hill?"

Donald saw the way Charlotte stiffened. He returned his attention to the folders and didn't answer.

"This woman you're talking about," Darcy said. "Was she the same one who messed up the database?"

"Yeah. They gave her full access to fix this problem they were having; it was that severe. And her curiosity got her looking in other places. She found this note about what her father and others had planned, realized these collapse codes and gas systems weren't just for emergencies. We were all one big ticking time bomb, every single silo. She realized that she was going to be put in cryo and never wake up again. And even though she could change anything she wanted, she couldn't change her gender. Couldn't make it so that anyone would wake her up, and so she tried to get me to help. She put me in her father's place."

Donald paused and fought back the tears. Charlotte rested her hand on his back. The room was quiet for a long moment.

"But I didn't understand what she wanted me to do. I started digging on my own. And meanwhile, Silo Forty isn't gone at all. The place is still standing. I realize this when another silo goes dark." Donald paused. "I was acting head at the time, wasn't thinking straight, and I signed off on a bombing. Whatever it took to make it all go away. I didn't care about the tremors, being spotted, just ordered it done. We cratered anything over there that was still standing. Drones and bombs started thinning them out."

"I remember," Darcy said. "That was about when I got on shift. There were pilots up in the cafeteria all the time. They worked a lot in the middle of the night."

"And they worked down here. When they were done and went back under, I woke up my sister. I was just waiting for them to leave. I didn't want to drop bombs. I wanted to see what was out there."

Darcy checked the clock on the wall. "And now we've all seen it."

"There's another two hundred years or so before all the silos go down," Donald said. "You ever think about why this silo only has lifts, doesn't have any stairs? You want to know why they call it the express but the damn thing still takes forever to get anywhere?"

"We're rigged to blow," Darcy said. "There's that same mass of concrete between every level."

Donald nodded. This kid was fast. "If they let us walk up a flight of stairs, we'd see. We'd know. And enough people here would know what that was for, what this meant. They might as well put the countdown clock on every desk. People would go insane."

"Two hundred years," Darcy said.

"That might feel like a lot of time to others, but that's a couple naps for us. But see, that's the whole point. They need us dead so no one remembers. This whole thing—" Donald waved at the conference table with the depiction of the silos. "It's as much a time machine as a ticking clock. It's a way of wiping the earth clean and propelling some group of people, some tribe chosen practically at random, into a future where they inherit the world."

"More like sending them back into the past," Charlotte said. "Back into some primitive state."

"Exactly. When I first learned about the nanos, it was something Iran was working on. The idea was to target an ethnic group. We already had machines that could work on a cellular level. This was just the next step. Going after a species is even easier than targeting a race. It was child's play. Erskine, the man who came up with this, said it was inevitable, that someone would eventually do it, create a silent bomb that wipes out all of humanity. I think he was right."

"So what're you looking for in these folders?" Darcy asked.

"Thurman wanted to know if Anna ever left the armory. I'm pretty sure she did. Things would show up down here that I couldn't find on the shelves. And he said something about gas lines—"

"We've got an hour and a half before I need to get you back," Darcy said.

"Yeah, okay. So Thurman found something here in this silo, I think. Something his daughter did, something she snuck out and did. I think she left another surprise. When they gassed Eighteen, Thurman mentioned that they did it right this time. That they undid someone's mess. I thought he was talking about my mess, my fighting to save the place, but it was Anna who had changed things. I think she moved some valves around, or if it's all computerized, just changed some code. There are two types of machines, both of which are in my blood right now. There are those that keep us together, like in the cryopods. And then there are the machines outside around the silos, those we pump inside them to break people down. It's the ultimate haves versus the have-nots. I think Anna tried to flip this around, tried to rig it up so the next silo we shut down would get a dose of what we get. She was playing Robin Hood on a cellular level."

He finally found the report. It was well-worn. It had been looked through hundreds of times.

"Silo Seventeen," he said. "I wasn't around when it was put down, but I looked into this. There was a guy there who answered a call after the place was gassed. But I don't think it was gassed. Not correctly. I think Anna took what we get in our pods to stitch us up and sent that instead."

"Why?" Charlotte asked.

Donald looked up. "To stop the world from ending. To not murder anyone. To show people some compassion."

"So everyone at Seventeen is okay?"

Donald flipped through the pages of the report. "No," he said. "For whatever reason, she couldn't stop the airlock from popping. That's part of the procedure. And with the amount of gas outside, they didn't stand a chance."

"I spoke to someone at Seventeen," Charlotte said. "Your friend . . . that mayor is over there. There are people there. She said they tunneled their way over."

Donald smiled. He nodded. "Of course. Of course. She wanted me to think she was coming after us."

"Well, I think she's coming after us now."

"We need to get in touch with her."

"What we need to do," Darcy said, "is start thinking about the end of this shift. There's going to be a helluva beating in about an hour."

Donald and Charlotte turned to him. He was standing by the door, right near where Donald had been kicked over and over.

"I mean my boss," Darcy said. "He's gonna be pissed when he wakes up and discovers a prisoner escaped during my shift."

Silo 17

53

JULIETTE AND RAPH stopped at the lower deputy station to look for another radio or a spare battery. They found neither. The charging rack was still on the wall, but it hadn't been wired into the makeshift power lines trailing through the stairwell. Juliette weighed whether or not it was worth staying there and getting some juice in the portable or if she should just wait until they got to the Mids station or IT—

"Hey," Raph whispered. "Do you hear something?"

Juliette shined her flashlight deep into the offices. She thought she heard someone crying. "C'mon," she said.

She left the charger alone and headed back toward the holding cells. There was a dark form sitting in the very last cell, sobbing. Juliette thought it was Hank at first, that he had wandered up to the nearest thing like a home to him, only to realize what state this world was in. But the man wore robes. It was Father Wendel who peered up at them from behind the bars. The tears in his eyes caught in the glare of the flashlight. A small candle burned on the bench beside him, wax dripping to the ground.

The door to the holding cell wasn't shut all the way. Juliette pulled it open and stepped inside. "Father?"

The old man looked awful. He had the tattered remains of an ancient book in his hands. Not a book, but a stack of loose pages. There were pages scattered all over the bench and on the floor. As Juliette cast her light down, she could see that she was standing on a carpet of fine print. There was a pattern of black bars across all the pages, sentences and words made unreadable. Juliette had seen pages like this once in a book kept inside a cage, a book where only one sentence in five could be read.

"Leave me," Father Wendel said.

She was tempted to, but she didn't. "Father, it's me, Juliette. What're you doing here?"

Wendel sniffled and sorted through the pages as though he were looking for something. "Isaiah," he said. "Isaiah, where are you? Everything's out of order."

"Where's your congregation?" Juliette asked.

"Not mine anymore." He wiped his nose, and Juliette felt Raph tug on her elbow to leave the man be.

"You can't stay here," she said. "Do you have any food or water?"

"I have nothing. Go."

"C'mon," Raph hissed.

Juliette adjusted the heavy load on her back, those sticks of dynamite. Father Wendel laid out more pages around his boots, checking the front and back of each as he did so.

"There's a group down below planning another dig," she told him. "I'm going to find them a better place, and they're going to get our people out of here. Maybe you could come to one of the farms with us and see about getting some food, see if you can help. The people down below could use you."

"Use me for what?" Wendel asked. He slapped a page down on the bench, and several other pages scattered. "Hellfire or hope," he said. "Take your pick. One or the other. Damnation or salvation. Every page. Take your pick. Take your pick." He looked up at them, beseeching them.

Juliette shook her canteen, cracked the lid, and held it out to Wendel. The candle on the bench sputtered and smoked, shadows growing and shrinking. Wendel accepted the canteen and took a sip. He handed it back.

"Had to see it with my own eyes," he whispered. "I went into the dark to see the devil. I did. Walked and walked, and here it is. Another world. I led my flock to damnation." He twisted up his face, studied one of the pages for a moment. "Or salvation. Take your pick."

Plucking the candle from the bench, he held a page close to it in order to see it better. "Ah, Isaiah, there you are." And with the baritone of a Sunday, he read: *"In the time of my favor I will answer you, and in the day of salvation I will help you; I will keep you and will make you to be a covenant for the people, to restore the land and to reassign its desolate inheritances."* Wendel touched a corner of the page to the flame and roared again: "Its desolate inheritances!"

The page burned until he had to release it. It moved through the air like an orange, shrinking bird.

"Let's go," Raph hissed, more insistently this time.

Juliette held up a hand. She approached Father Wendel and crouched down in front of him, rested a hand on his knee. The anger she had felt toward him over Marcus was gone. The anger she had felt as he instilled outrage in his people toward her and her digging was gone. Replacing that anger was guilt—guilt from knowing that all of their fears and mistrust had been warranted.

"Father," she said. "Our people will be damned if they stay in this place. I can't help them. I won't be here. They are going to need your guidance if they're to make it to the other side."

"They don't need me," he said.

"Yes, they do. Women in the depths of this silo weep for their babies. Men weep for their homes. They need you." And she knew this was true. It was in the hard times that they needed him the most.

"You will see them through," Father Wendel said. "You will see them through."

"No, I won't. You are their salvation. I am off to damn those who did this. I'm going to send them straight to hell."

Wendel looked up from his lap. Hot wax flowed over his fingers, but he didn't seem to notice. The smell of burnt paper filled the room, and he rested a hand on Juliette's head.

"In that case, my child, I bless your journey."

The trip up the stairwell was heavier with that blessing. Or maybe it was the weight of the explosives on her back, which Juliette knew would've been useful for the tunneling below. They could be used for salvation, but she was using them for damnation. They were like the pages of Wendel's book in that they offered plenty of both. As she approached the farms, she reminded herself that Erik had insisted she take the dynamite. There were others eager to see her pull this off.

She and Raph arrived at the lower farms, and she knew something was wrong the moment they stepped inside. Cracking the door released a surge of heat, a blast of angry air. Her first thought was a fire, and she knew from living in that silo that there were no longer any water hoses that worked. But the bloom of bright lights down the hall and along the outer grow plots hinted at something else.

There was a man lying on the ground by the security gates, his body sideways across the hall. Stripped down to his shorts and undershirt, Juliette didn't recognize Deputy Hank until she was nearly upon him. She was relieved when he moved. He shielded his eyes and tightened his grip on the pistol resting on his chest; sweat soaked his clothes.

"Hank?" Juliette asked. "Are you okay?" She was already feeling sticky herself, and poor Raph seemed liable to wilt.

The deputy sat up and rubbed the back of his neck. He pointed to the security gates. "You get a little shade if you crowd up against them."

Juliette looked down the hall at the lights. They were drawing a ton of power. Every plot appeared to be lit at once. She could *smell* the heat. She could smell the plants roasting in it. She wondered how long the skimpy wiring job in the stairwell could withstand such a draw of current.

"Are the timers stuck? What's going on?"

Hank nodded down the hallway. "People've been staking plots. A fight broke out yesterday. You know Gene Sample?"

"I know Gene," Raph said. "From Sanitation."

Hank frowned. "Gene's dead. Happened when the lights went out. And then they fought over who had rights to bury him, treated poor Gene like fertilizer. Some folks banded together and hired me to restore order. I told them to keep the lights on until things got settled." He wiped the back of his neck. "Before you lay into me, I know it ain't good for the crops, but they were already ravaged. My hope is to sweat these people out, make enough of them move on to give everyone some breathing space. I give it another day."

"In another day, you'll have a fire somewhere. Hank, the wiring outside runs hot enough already with the lights cycling. I'm shocked they can power all of this. When a breaker goes out up on the thirties, you're gonna have nothing but dark for a very long time down here."

Hank peered down the hall. Juliette saw rinds and cores and scraps of food on the other side of the gates. "How're they paying you? In food?"

He nodded. "The food's all gonna go bad. They plucked everything. People were just actin' crazy when they got here. I think a few headed up, but there are all these rumors that the door to this silo is open and if you go up much further, you die. And if you go down, you die. Lots of rumors."

"Well, you need to dispel those rumors," Juliette said. "I'm sure it's better up or down than it is here. Have you seen Solo and the kids, the ones who used to live here? I heard they came up this way."

"Yup. A few of those kids were staking a plot right down the hall before I rigged the lights. But they left a few hours ago." Hank eyed Juliette's wrist. "What time is it, anyway?"

Juliette glanced at her watch. "It's a quarter past two." She saw he was about to ask another question. "In the afternoon," she said.

"Thank you."

"We're going to try and catch up with them," Juliette said. "Can I leave you to handle these lights? You can't draw this much power. And get more people to move up from here. The farms in the Mids are doing much better, or they were when I was here. And if you have people looking for work, they can use hands in Mechanical."

Hank nodded and struggled to his feet. Raph was already heading to the exit, his coveralls spotted with sweat. Juliette clasped Hank on the shoulder before heading off as well.

"Hey," Hank called out. "You said what time it was. But what day is it?"

Juliette hesitated at the door. She turned and saw Hank gazing at her, his hand shielding his eyes. "Does it matter?" she asked. And when Hank didn't respond, she supposed it didn't. All the days were the same now, and every one numbered.

54

JIMMY DECIDED TO search for Elise on two more levels before turning back. He had begun to suspect that he'd missed her, that she'd run inside a level after her animal or to use the bathroom and he'd gone right by. Most likely, she was back at the farms with everyone else while he was stomping up and down the silo alone.

At the next landing, he checked inside the main door, saw nothing but darkness and silence, called out for Elise, and debated going even one level further. Turning back to the stairwell, a flash of brown caught his eye above. He shielded his old eyes and peered up through the green gloom to see a boy peering over the rails at him. The kid waved. Jimmy did not wave back.

He headed for the stairs with a mind of returning to the lower farms, but he soon heard the patter of light footsteps spiraling down toward him. Another kid to look after, he thought. He didn't wait for the boy, but continued along. It took a turn and a half before the child caught up to him.

Jimmy turned to berate the kid for bugging him, but he recognized the boy up close. The brown coveralls and the wiry mop of corn-colored hair. It was the kid who had chased Elise through the bazaar.

"Hey," the boy hissed, breathing hard. "You're that guy."

"I'm that guy," Jimmy agreed. "I suppose you're looking for food. Well, I don't have a thing—"

"No." The kid shook his head. He had to be nine or ten. About the same age as Miles. "I need you to come with me. I need your help."

Everyone needed Jimmy's help. "I'm a bit busy," he said. He turned to go.

"It's Elise," the boy said. "I followed her here. Through the mines. Some people up there won't let her go." He glanced up the stairwell, his voice a whisper.

"You've seen Elise?" Jimmy asked.

The boy nodded.

"What do you mean, people?"

"It's a bunch of them from that church. My dad goes to their Sundays."

"And you say they have Elise?"

"Yeah. And I found her dog. Her dog was trapped behind a busted door a few levels down from here. I penned it up so it couldn't get loose. And then I found where they're keeping Elise. I tried to get to her, but some guy told me to scram."

"Where was this?" Jimmy asked.

The boy pointed up. "Two levels," he said.

"What's your name?"

"Shaw."

"Good work, Shaw." Jimmy hurried to the stairwell and started down.

"I said *up* from here," the boy said.

"I need to grab something," Jimmy told him. "It's not far."

Shaw hurried after him. "Okay. And look, mister, I want you to know how hungry I was. But that I wasn't going to eat the dog."

Jimmy paused and allowed the boy to catch up. "I didn't think you would," he said.

Shaw nodded. "Just so Elise knows," he said. "I want to make sure she knows I would never do that."

"I'll make sure she knows," Jimmy said. "Now c'mon. Let's hurry."

Two levels down, Jimmy peeked inside a dark hallway; he played his flashlight across the walls, then turned guiltily to Shaw, who crowded behind him. "Went too far," Jimmy admitted.

He turned and began climbing back up a level, frustrated with himself. So hard to remember where he put everything. Such a long time ago. He used to have mnemonics for recalling his stashes. He had hidden a rifle way up on level fifty-one. He remembered that because it took a hand to hold the rifle and another finger to pull the trigger. Five and one. That rifle was wrapped in a quilt and buried in the bottom of an old trunk. But he'd left one down here as well. He had carried it down to Supply a lifetime ago; it would've been the trip when he found Shadow. Hadn't carried it all the way back up—not enough hands. One-eighteen. That was it. Not one-nineteen. He hurried up to the landing, his legs getting sore, and went inside the hallway he and Shaw had passed moments prior.

This was it. Apartments. He had left things in lots of them. Poop, mostly. He didn't know you could go in the farms, right in the dirt. The kids taught him that late in life. Elise taught him. Jimmy thought of people doing something bad to Elise, and he remembered what he'd done to people when he was a boy. He'd been young when he'd taught himself to fire a rifle. He remembered the noise it made. He remembered what it did to empty soup cans and people. It made things jump and fall still. Third apartment down on the left.

"Hold this," he told Shaw, stepping inside the apartment. He handed his flashlight to the boy, who kept it trained in the center of the room. Jimmy grabbed the metal dresser shoved against one wall and pulled it out a ways. Just like yesterday. Except for the thick dust on the top of the dresser. His old bootprints were gone. He climbed up to the top and pushed the ceiling panel up and to the side, asked for the flashlight. A rat squeaked and scattered as he shined the light in there. The black rifle was waiting on him. Jimmy took it down and blew the dust off.

Elise didn't like her new clothes. They had taken her coveralls from her, saying the color was all wrong, and had wrapped her in a blanket that was sewn up the front and scratchy. She'd asked to leave several times, but Mr. Rash said she had to stay. There were rooms up and down the halls with old beds, and everything smelled awful, but there were people trying to clean it up and make it better. But Elise just wanted Puppy and Hannah and Solo. She was shown a room and was told it would be her new home, but Elise lived beyond the Wilds and never wanted to live anyplace else.

They took her back to the big room where she'd signed her name and had her sit on the bench some more. If she tried to go, Mr. Rash squeezed her wrist. When she cried, he squeezed even harder. They made her sit on a bench they called something else while a man read from a book. The man with the white robes and the bald patch had left, and a new man had taken his place to read from a book. There was a woman off to the side with two other men, and she didn't look happy. A lot of people on the benches spent time watching this woman instead of the man reading.

Elise was both sleepy and restless. What she wanted to do was get away and nap somewhere else. And then the man was done reading, and he lifted the book up into the air, and everyone around her said the same thing, which was really strange, as if they all knew they were going to say it beforehand, and their voices were funny and hollow like they knew the words but didn't know what they meant.

The man with the book waved the men and the woman up, and it seemed almost like they carried her. There were two tables pushed together back near the colored window with the light shining through it. The woman made a noise as they lifted her to the tables. She had a blanket on like Elise's but bigger, making it easy for the men to expose her bare leg. The people on the benches strained to see better. Elise felt less sleepy than she had before. She whispered to Mr. Rash to find out what they were doing, and he told her to be quiet, not to talk.

The man with the book brought a knife out of his robes. It was long and flashed like a bright fish.

"Be ye fruitful and multiply," he said. He faced the audience, and the woman moved about on the tables, but she couldn't go anywhere. Elise wanted to tell them not to hold her wrists so tight.

"Behold," the man said, reading from the book, "I establish my covenant with you, and with your seed after you." And Elise wondered if they were going to plant something. And he went on and said, "Neither shall all flesh be cut off anymore. And it shall come to pass, when I bring a cloud over the earth, that the blade shall be seen in the cloud."

He held the knife even higher, and the people on the benches mumbled something. Even a boy younger than Elise knew the words. His lips moved like the others'.

The man took the knife to the woman, but he didn't give it to her. There was a man holding her feet and another her wrists, and she tried to be still. And then Elise knew what they were doing. It was the same as her mom and Hannah's mom. And a fearsome scream came from the woman as the knife went in, and Elise couldn't stop watching, and blood came out and down her leg, and Elise could feel it on her own leg, and tried to squirm free, but then it was her wrist being held, and she knew one day this would be her, and the screaming went and went, and the man dug around with the knife and his fingers, a shine of sweat on the top of his head, saying something to the men, who were having trouble with the woman, and there were whispers along the benches, and Elise felt hot, and more blood until the man with the knife erupted with a shout and stood facing the benches with something between his fingers, blood running down his arm to his elbow, his blanket drooping open, a smile on his face as the screams died down.

"Behold!" he shouted.

And the people were clapping. The men bandaged the woman on the table, then brought her down, though she could barely stand. Elise saw that there was another woman by the stage. They were lining up. And the clapping gained a rhythm like when she and the twins would march up the stairs watching each other's feet, *clap, clap* at the same time. The clapping grew louder and louder. Until there was a giant clap that made them all go quiet. A clap that made her heart leap up in her chest.

Heads turned to the back of the room. Elise's ears hurt from the loud bang. Someone shouted and pointed, and Elise turned and saw Solo in the doorway. White powder rained down from the ceiling, and he had something long and black in his hands. Beside him stood Shaw, the boy in the brown coveralls from the bizarre. Elise wondered how he was there.

"Excuse me," Solo said. He scanned the benches until he saw Elise, and his teeth shined through his beard. "I'll be taking that young lady with me."

There were shouts. Men got up from their seats and yelled and pointed, and Mr. Rash shouted something about his wife and property and how dare he interrupt. And the man with the blood and the knife was outraged and stormed down the aisle, which made Solo lift the black thing to his shoulder.

Another clap like it was God doing it with his biggest palms, a bang so loud it made Elise's insides hurt. There was a noise after it, a shattering of glass, and she turned and saw the pretty colored window was even more broke than before.

The people stopped shouting and moving toward Solo, which Elise thought was a very good thing.

"Come along," Solo said to Elise. "Hurry now."

Elise got up from the bench and started toward the aisle, but Mr. Rash grabbed her by the wrist. "She is my wife!" Mr. Rash shouted, and Elise realized this was a bad thing to be. It meant she couldn't leave.

"You do marriages quick," Solo said to the quiet crowd. He waved the black thing at them all, and this seemed to make them nervous. "What about funerals?"

The black thing pointed at Mr. Rash. Elise felt his grip on her loosen. She made it to the aisle and ran past the man with the dripping blood, ran to Solo and Shaw and down the hall.

55

Juliette was drowning again. She could feel the water in her throat, the sting in her eyes, the burn in her chest. As she climbed the stairwell, she could sense the old flood around her, but that wasn't what made her feel as though she couldn't breathe. It was the voices ranging up and down the stairwell shaft, the evidence already of vandalism and theft, the long stretches of wire and pipe gone missing, the scattering of stalk and leaf and soil from those hurrying away with stolen plants.

She hoped to rise above the injustices strewn about her, to escape this last spasm of civility before chaos reigned. It was coming, she knew. But as high as she and Raph climbed, there were people throwing open doors to explore and loot, to claim territory, to yell down from landings some finding or shout up some question. In the depths of Mechanical, she had lamented how few had survived. And now it seemed like so many.

Stopping to fight any of this would be a waste of time. Juliette worried about Solo and the kids. She worried about the razed farms. But the weight of the explosives in her pack gave her purpose, and the calamity surrounding her gave her resolve. She was out to see that this never happened again.

"I feel like a porter," Raph said, wheezing between words.

"If you fall behind, we're heading for thirty-four. Both of the

Mid farms should have food. You can get water from the hydro pumps."

"I can keep up with you," Raph insisted. "Just saying it's unbecoming."

Juliette laughed at the proud miner. She wanted to point out the number of times she'd made this run, always with Solo lagging behind and waving her on, promising he'd catch up. Her mind flashed back to those days, and suddenly her silo was still alive and thriving, churning with civilization, so far away and moving forward without her—but still there and alive.

No more.

But there were other silos, dozens of them, teeming with life and lives. Somewhere, a parent was lecturing a child. A teenager was stealing a kiss. A warm meal was being served. Paper was being recycled into pulp and back into paper; oil was gurgling up and being burned; exhaust was being vented into the great and forbidden outside. All of those worlds were humming forward, each of them ignorant of the others. Somewhere, a person who dared to dream was being sent out to clean. Someone was being buried, another born.

Juliette thought of the children of Silo 17, born into violence, never knowing anything else. That would happen again. It would happen right here. And her annoyance with the Planning Committee and Father Wendel's congregation was misplaced, she thought. Had her mechanics not lashed out? Was she not lashing out right then? What was any group but a bunch of people? And what were people but animals as prone to fear as rats at the sound of boots?

"—catch up with you later, then," Raph called out, his voice distant, and Juliette realized she was pulling away. She slowed and waited for him. Now was not a time for being alone, for climbing without company. And in that silo of solitude, where she had fallen for Lukas because he was there for her in voice

and spirit, she missed him more terribly than she ever had.
Hope had been stripped away, foolish hope. There was no getting back to him, no seeing him ever again, even as she was
deathly sure that she would join him soon enough.

A foray into the second Mids farm won some food, though it
was deeper than Juliette remembered. Raph's flashlight revealed signs of recent activity: boot prints in mud that had not
yet dried, a watering pipe broken for a drink that continued to
drip but had not yet emptied, a stepped-on tomato that was not
yet covered in ants. Juliette and Raph took what they could
carry—green peppers, cucumbers, blackberries, a precious orange, a dozen underripe tomatoes—enough for a few meals. Juliette ate as many blackberries as she could, for they travelled
poorly. She normally shied away from them, hated how they left
her fingers stained. But what once was nuisance now seemed a
blessing. This was how the last of the supplies went in a hurry,
each of a few hundred people taking more than they needed,
even the things they didn't truly want.

It wasn't far to thirty-four from the farm. For Juliette, it almost felt like a return home. There would be ample power
there, her tools and her cot, a radio, some place to work during
this last tremble of a dying people, some place to think, to regret, to build one last suit. The weariness in her legs and back
spoke to her, and Juliette realized she was climbing once again
in order to escape. It was more than vengeance she was after.
This was a flight from the sight of her friends, whom she had
failed. It was a hole she was after. But unlike Solo, who had lived
in a hole beneath the servers, she was hoping to make a crater
on the heads of others.

"Jules?"

She paused halfway across the landing of thirty-four, the
doors to IT just ahead. Raph had stopped at the top step. He

knelt down and ran his finger across the tread, lifted it to show
her something red. Touched his finger to his tongue.

"Tomato," he said.

Someone was already there. The day Juliette had wasted
curled up and crying in the belly of the digger haunted her now.

"We'll be fine," she told him. The day she had chased Solo
came back to her. She had thundered down these steps, had
found the doors barred, had snapped a broom in half getting inside. This time, the doors opened easily. The lights inside were
full bright. No sign of anyone.

"Let's go," she said. She hurried quietly and quickly. It
wouldn't do to be spotted by people she didn't know, wouldn't
want them following her. She wondered if Solo had at least
been cautious enough to close up the server room and the grate.
But no, at the end of the hall she saw the server room door was
open. There were voices somewhere. The stench of smoke. A
haze in the air. Or was she losing her mind and imagining Lukas and the gas coming for him? Is that why she was here? Not
for the radio, to find a home for her friends, nor to build a suit,
but because here was a mirrored place, identical to her own,
and maybe Lukas was below, waiting for her, alive in this dead
world—

She pushed her way into the server room, and the smoke
was real. It gathered at the ceiling. Juliette hurried through
the familiar servers. The smoke tasted different than the burnt
grease of an overheating pump, the tang of an electrical fire, the
scorched rubber of an impeller running dry, the bitterness of
motor exhaust. It was a clean burning. She covered her mouth
with the crook of her arm, remembered Lukas complaining of
fumes, and hurried into the haze.

It was coming from the hatch behind the comm server, a rising column of smoke. There was a fire in Solo's hovel, his bedding, perhaps. Juliette thought of the radio down there, the

food. She unzipped her coveralls and pulled her sweat-soaked undershirt up over her face, heard Raph yelling at her not to go as she reached down and lowered herself onto the ladder, practically slid down it until her boots slammed into the grating below.

Staying low, she could just barely see through the haze. She could hear the crackle of flame, a strange and crisp sound. Food and radio and computer and precious schematics on the walls. The one treasure not on her mind as she rushed forward was the books. And it was the books that were burning.

A pile of books, a pile of empty metal tins, a young man in a white robe throwing more books onto the pile, the smell of fuel. He had his back turned, a bald patch on the back of his head glimmering with sweat, but he seemed unconcerned by the blaze. He was feeding it. He returned to the shelves for more to burn.

Juliette ran behind him to Solo's bed and grabbed a blanket, a rat scurrying out of its folds as she lifted it. She hurried toward the fire, eyes stinging, throat burning, and tossed the blanket across the pile of books. The blaze was momentarily swallowed, but it leaked at the seams. The blanket began to smoke. Juliette coughed into her shirt and ran back for the mattress, needed to smother the fire, thought of the empty reservoir of water in the next room, all that was being lost.

The man in the robe spotted her as she lifted the mattress. He howled and threw himself at her. They tumbled into the mattress and the nest of bedding. A boot flashed toward her face, and Juliette jerked her head back. The young man screamed. He was like a white flapping bird loose in the bazaar and swooping at heads. Juliette yelled for him to get away. The blaze leapt higher. She tugged at the mattress, him on top of it, and the man spilled off the other side. Only moments to get the fire under control before all was lost. Only moments. She grabbed Solo's other blanket and beat at the flames. Couldn't fight them and the man both. No time. She coughed and yelled for Raph, and the man in the robes came at her again, his eyes wild, arms flailing. Juliette lowered her shoulder into his stomach, ducked beneath his arms, and the man spilled over her back. He fell to the ground and encircled her legs, dragging her down with him.

Juliette tried to wriggle free, but he was clawing his way from her ankles to her waist. Flames rose behind him. The blanket had caught. The man screamed unholy rage, had lost his mind. Juliette pushed against his shoulders and squirmed on her ass to pull free. She could barely breathe, could barely see. The man on top of her screamed with renewed fervor, and it was his robes on fire. The flames marched up his back and over them both, and Juliette was back in that airlock, a blanket over her head, burning alive.

A boot flew across her face and struck the young priest, and she felt the strength leave the arms clinging to her. Someone pulled her from behind. Juliette kicked free, the smoke too thick now to see. She tried to get her bearings, was coughing uncontrollably, wondered where the radio was, knew it was gone. And someone was tugging her down a narrow hall, Raph's pale face making him little more than a ghost in smoke, urging her up the ladder ahead of him.

The server room was filling with smoke. The fire down below would spread until it ate up all that burned, leaving just charred metal and melted wires behind. Juliette helped Raph out of the ladderway and grabbed the hatch. She threw it on top and saw that it was useless for keeping out the smoke, was a blasted grate.

Raph disappeared behind one of the servers. "Quick!" he yelled. Juliette crawled on her hands and knees and found him pressed against the back of the comm hub, one foot against the server beside it, shoving with all of his might.

Juliette helped him. Aching muscles bulged and burned. They rocked against the unmoving metal, Juliette dimly aware of screws holding the base to the floor, but the weight of the tower helped. Metal groaned. With a heave, screws tore loose and the tall black tower tilted, trembled, and then crashed atop the hole in the ground, covering it.

Juliette and Raph collapsed, coughing, heaving for air. The room was hazy with smoke, but no more was leaking inside. And the screams far below them eventually died out.

Silo 1

56

THERE WERE VOICES outside the drone lift. Boots. Men walking back and forth, searching for them.

Donald and Charlotte clung to one another in the darkness of that low-ceilinged space. Charlotte had looked for some way to secure the door, but it was a featureless wall of metal with just a tiny release for the latch. Donald held back a cough, could feel a tickle in his throat grow until it covered every square inch of his flesh. He kept both hands clasped over his mouth and listened to the muted shouts of "clear" and "all clear".

Charlotte stopped fumbling with the door, and they simply huddled together and tried not to move, for the floor made popping noises any time they shifted their weight. They had spent all day in the small lift, waiting for the search party to come back to their level. Darcy had left to be on shift when everyone woke up. It had been a long day of fitful non-sleep for Donald and his sister, a day when he knew the search party would expand and grow desperate. Now they had a killer on the loose and an escaped prisoner from Deep Freeze, too. He could imagine the consternation this was causing Thurman. He could imagine the beating he would get when they were discovered. He just prayed these boots would go away. But they didn't. They grew nearer.

There was a bang on the metal hangar door, the pounding of an angry fist. Donald could feel Charlotte tense her arm across his back, crushing his cracked ribs. The door moved. Donald tried to push against it to hold it in place, but there was no leverage. The steel squeaked against his sweaty palms. This was it. Charlotte tried to help, but someone was cracking open their hiding spot. A flashlight blinded them both—it shined right in their eyes.

"Clear!" came the yell, close enough that Donald could smell the coffee on Darcy's breath. The door was slammed shut, a palm slapping it twice. Charlotte collapsed. Donald dared to clear his throat.

It was after dinner by the time they finally emerged, tired and starving. It was quiet and dark in the armory. Darcy had said he would try to come back when his shift started, but he had been worried the night shift wouldn't be as quiet as usual, not so suited to slinking away.

Donald and Charlotte hurried down the barracks hall and into separate bathrooms. Donald could hear the pipes rattle as his sister flushed. He ran the sink and coughed up blood, spat and watched the crimson threads spiral down the drain, drank from the tap, spat again, and finally used the bathroom himself.

Charlotte already had the radio uncovered and powered up by the time he got to the end of the hall. She hailed anyone who might hear. Donald stood behind her and watched her switch from channel eighteen to seventeen, repeating the call. No one answered. She left it on seventeen and listened to static.

"How did you raise them the last time?" Donald asked.

"Just like this." She stared at the radio for a moment before turning in her seat to face him, her brow furrowed with worry. Donald expected a thousand questions: How long before they were taken? What were they going to do next? How could they get someplace safe? A thousand questions, but not the one she asked, her voice a sad whisper: "When did you go outside?"

Donald took a step back. He wasn't sure how to answer. "What do you mean?" he asked, but he knew what she meant.

"I heard what Darcy said about you nearly getting over a hill. When was this? Are you still going out? Is that where you go when you leave me? Is that why you're sick?"

Donald slumped against one of the drone control stations. "No," he said. He watched the radio, hoping for some voice to break through the static and save him. But his sister waited. "I only went once. I went . . . thinking I'd never come back."

"You went out there to die."

He nodded. And she didn't get angry with him. She didn't yell or scream like he feared she might, which was why he had never told her before. She simply stood and rushed to him and wrapped her arms around his waist. And Donald cried.

"Why are they doing this to us?" Charlotte asked.

"I don't know. I want to make it stop."

"But not like that." His sister stepped back and wiped her eyes. "Donny, you have to promise me. Not like that."

He didn't reply. His ribs ached from where she'd embraced him. "I wanted to see Helen," he finally said. "I wanted to see where she'd lived and died. It was . . . a bad time. With Anna. Trapped down here." He remembered how he had felt about Anna then, how he felt about her now. So many mistakes. He had made mistakes at every turn. It made it difficult to make anymore decisions, to act.

"There has to be something we can do," Charlotte said. Her eyes lit up. "We could lighten a drone enough to carry us from here. The bunker busters must weigh sixty kilos. If we lighten another drone up, it could carry you."

"And fly it how?"

"I'll stay here and fly it." She saw the look on his face and frowned. "Better that one of us gets out," she said. "You know I'm right. We could launch before daylight, just send you as far as you can go. At least live a day away from this place."

Donald tried to imagine a flight on the back of one of those birds, the wind pelting his helmet, tumbling off in a rough landing, lying in the grass and staring up at the stars. He pulled his rag out and filled it with blood, shook his head as he put it away. "I'm dying," he told her. "Thurman said I have another day or two. He told me that a day or two ago."

Charlotte was silent.

"Maybe we could wake another pilot," he suggested. "I could hold a gun to his head. We could get you and Darcy both out of here."

"I'm not leaving you," his sister said.

"But you would have me go out there alone?"

She shrugged. "I'm a hypocrite."

Donald laughed. "Must be why they recruited you."

They listened to the radio.

"What do you think is going on in all those other silos right now?" Charlotte asked. "You dealt with them. Is it as bad there as it is here?"

Donald considered this. "I don't know. Some of them are happy enough, I suppose. They get married and have kids. They have jobs. They don't know anything beyond their walls, so I guess they don't have some of the stress about what's out there that you and I feel. But I think they have something else that we don't have, this deep feeling that something is wrong with how they're living. Buried, you know. And we understand that, and it chokes us, but they just have this chronic anxiety, I think. I don't know." He shrugged. "I've seen men happy enough here to get through their shifts. I've watched others go mad. I used to . . . I used to play solitaire for hours on my computer upstairs, and that's when my brain was truly off and I wasn't miserable. But then, I wasn't really alive, either."

Charlotte reached out and squeezed his hand.

"I think some of the silos that went dark have it best—"

"Don't say that," Charlotte whispered.

Donald looked up at her. "No, not that. I don't think they're dead, not all of them. I think some of them withdrew and are living how they want quietly enough that no one will come after them. They just want to be left alone, not controlled, free to choose how they live and die. I think it's what Anna wanted them to have. Living down here on this level for a year, trying to find some life without being able to go outside, I think it changed how she viewed all this."

"Or maybe it was being out of that box for a little while," Charlotte said. "Maybe she didn't like what it felt like to be put away."

"Or that," Donald agreed. Again, he thought how things would've been different had he woken her with some trust, had heard her out. If Anna was there to help, everything would be better. It pained him, but he missed her as much as he missed Helen. Anna had saved him, had tried to save others, and Donald had misunderstood and had hated her for both actions.

Charlotte let go of his hand to adjust the radio. She tried hailing someone on both channels, ran her fingers through her hair and listened to static.

"There was a while there when I thought this was a good thing," Donald said. "What they did, trying to save the world. They had me convinced that a mass extinction was inevitable, that a war was about to break out and claim everyone. But you know what I think? I think they knew that if a war broke out between all these invisible machines, that some pockets of people would survive here and there. So they built this. They made sure the destruction was complete so they could control it."

"They wanted to make sure the only pockets of people who survived were in *their* pockets," Charlotte said.

"Exactly. They weren't trying to save the world—they were trying to save themselves. Even if we'd gone extinct, the world would've gone right on along without us. Nature finds a way."

"People find a way," Charlotte said. "Look at the two of us." She laughed. "We're like weeds, aren't we, the two of us? Nature sneaking out along the edge. We're like those silos that wouldn't behave. How did they think they would ever contain all this? That something like this wouldn't happen?"

"I don't know," Donald said. "Maybe the kinds of people who try to shape the world feel like they're smarter than chaos itself."

Charlotte switched the channels back and forth in case someone was answering on one or the other. She seemed exasperated. "They should just let us be," she said. "Just stop and let us grow however we must."

Donald lurched out of his chair and stood up straight.

"What is it?" Charlotte asked. She reached for the radio. "Did you hear something?"

"That's it," Donald told her. "Leave us be." He fumbled for his rag and coughed. Charlotte stopped playing with the radio. "C'mon," he said. He waved at the desk. "Bring your tools."

"For the drone?" she asked.

"No. We need to put together another suit."

"Another suit?"

"For going outside. And you said those bunker busters weigh sixty kilos. Exactly how much is a kilo?"

57

"This is not a good plan," Charlotte said. She tightened the breathing apparatus attached to the helmet and grabbed one of the large bottles of air, began fastening the hose to it. "What're we going to do out there?"

"Die," Donald told her. And he saw the look she gave him. "But maybe a week from now. And not here." He had an array of supplies laid out. Satisfied, he began stuffing them into one of the small military backpacks. MREs, water, a first-aid kit, a flashlight, a pistol and two clips, extra ammo, a flint, and a knife.

"How long do you think this air will last?" Charlotte asked.

"Those bottles are for sending troops overground to other silos, so they must have enough to reach the furthest one. We just need to go a little further than that, and we won't be as loaded down." He cinched up the pack and placed it next to the other one.

"It's like we're lightening up a drone."

"Exactly." Picking up a roll of tape, he pulled a folded map out of his pocket and began affixing it to the sleeve of one of the suits.

"Isn't that my suit?"

Donald nodded. "You're a better navigator. I'm going to follow you."

There was a ding on the other side of the shelves from the direction of the lifts. Donald dropped what he was doing and hissed for Charlotte to hurry. They made for the drone lift, but Darcy called out to let them know it was just him. He emerged from the tall shelves with a load in his arms, fresh coveralls and a tray heaped with food.

"Sorry," he said, seeing the panic he'd caused. "It's not like I can warn you." He held out the trays apologetically. "Leftovers from dinner."

He set the trays down, and Charlotte gave him a hug. Donald saw how quickly connections were made in desperate times. Here was a prisoner embracing a guard for not beating her, for showing an ounce of compassion. Donald was glad for the second suit. It was a good plan.

Darcy peered down at the scattering of tools and supplies. "What're you doing?" he asked.

Charlotte checked with her brother. Donald shook his head.

"Look," Darcy said, "I'm sympathetic to your situation. I am. I don't like what's going on around here, either. And the more that comes back—the more I remember about who I was—the more I think I'd be fighting this alongside you. But I'm not all-in with you guys. And this—" He pointed to the suits. "This doesn't look good to me. This doesn't look smart."

Charlotte passed a plate and a fork to Donald. She sat on one of the plastic storage bins and dug into what looked like a canned roast, beets, and potatoes. Donald sat beside her and slid his fork through the slick roast, chopping it up into bites. "Do you remember what you did before all this?" Donald asked. "Is it coming back to you?"

Darcy nodded. "Some. I've stopped taking my meds—"

Donald laughed.

"What? Why's that funny?"

"I'm sorry." Donald apologized and waved his hand. "It's just that . . . it's nothing. It's a good thing. Were you in the army?"

"Yeah, but not for long. I think I was in the Secret Service." Darcy watched them eat for a moment. "What about you two?"

"Air Force," Charlotte said. She jabbed her fork at Donald, whose mouth was full. "Congressman."

"No shit?"

Donald nodded. "More of an architect, really." He gestured at the room around them. "This is what I went to school for."

"Building stuff like this?" Darcy asked.

"Building this," Donald said. He took another bite.

"No shit."

Donald nodded and took a swig of water.

"Who did this to us, then? The Chinese?"

Donald and Charlotte turned to one another.

"What?" Darcy asked.

"We did this," Donald said. "This place wasn't built for a just-in-case. This is what it was designed for."

Darcy looked from one of them to the other, his mouth open.

"I thought you knew. It's all in my notes." *Once you know what to look for,* Donald thought. Otherwise, it was too obvious and audacious to see.

"No. I thought this was like that mountain bunker, where the government goes to survive—"

"It is," Charlotte said. "But this way they get the timing down just right."

Darcy stared down at his boots while Donald and his sister ate. For a last meal, it wasn't all that bad. Donald looked down at the sleeve of the coveralls he'd borrowed from Charlotte and saw the bullet hole in them for the first time. Maybe that was why she had acted as if he was crazy for putting them on. Across from him, Darcy began to slowly nod his head. "Yeah," he said.

"God, yeah. They did this." He looked up at Donald. "I put a guy in Deep Freeze a couple shifts ago. He was yelling all this crazy stuff. A guy from accounting."

Donald set his tray aside. He finished his water.

"He wasn't crazy, was he?" Darcy asked. "That was a good man."

"Probably," Donald said. "He was getting better, at least."

Darcy ran his fingers over his short hair. His attention went back to the scattering of supplies. "The suits," he said. "You're thinking of leaving? Because you know I can't help you do that."

Donald ignored the question. He went to the end of the aisle and retrieved the hand truck. He and Charlotte had already loaded the bunker buster on it. There was a plastic tag dangling from the nose cone that she said he would need to pull before it was armed. She had already removed the altimeter controls and safety overrides. She had called it a "dumb bomb" when she was done. Donald pushed the cart toward the lift.

"Hey," Darcy said. He got up from his bin and blocked the aisle. Charlotte cleared her throat, and Darcy turned to see that she was holding a gun on him.

"I'm sorry," Charlotte said.

Darcy's hand hovered over a bulging pocket. Donald pushed the handcart toward him, and Darcy stepped back.

"We need to discuss this," Darcy said.

"We already have," Donald told him. "Don't move." He stopped the handcart beside Darcy and reached into the young guard's pocket. He withdrew the pistol and stuck it into his own pocket, then asked for Darcy's ID. The young man handed it to him. Donald pocketed this, and then leaned the cart back on its wheels and continued toward the lift.

Darcy followed him at a distance. "Just slow down," he said. "You're thinking of setting that off? C'mon, man. Take it easy. Let's talk. This is a big decision."

"Not arrived at lightly, I promise. The reactor below us powers the servers. The servers control everyone's lives. We're going to set these people free. Let them live and die how they choose."

Darcy laughed nervously. "Servers control their lives? What're you talking about?"

"They pick the lottery numbers," Donald said. "They decide who is worthy to pass themselves along. They cull and shape. They play mock wars to pick a winner. But not for long."

"Okay, but there's just three of us. This is too big for just us to decide. Seriously, man—"

Donald stopped the cart right outside of the lift. He turned to Darcy, saw that his sister had gotten to her feet to stay close to him.

"You want me to name all the times in history that one person led to the death of millions?" Donald asked. "Something like five or a dozen people made this happen. You might be able to trace it back to three. And who knows if one of those men was influencing the other two? Well, if one man can build this, it shouldn't take more than that to bring it all down. Gravity is a bitch until she's on your side." Donald pointed down the aisle. "Now come sit down."

When Darcy didn't move, Donald drew not the guard's gun, but the one from his other pocket that he knew was locked and loaded. The disappointment and hurt on the young man's face before he turned and complied was a physical blow. Donald watched him march back down the aisle, past Charlotte. He caught his sister's arm before she followed, gave her a squeeze and a kiss on the cheek. "Go ahead and get your suit on," he told her.

She nodded, followed Darcy, sat back down on the bin and began to work herself into her suit.

"This isn't happening," Darcy said. He eyed the pistol Charlotte had set aside while she squirmed into her suit.

"Don't even think about it," Donald said. "In fact, you should get busy getting dressed."

The guard and his sister both turned to peer at him quizzically. Charlotte was just getting her legs into her suit. "What're you talking about?" she asked.

Donald picked up the hammer sitting among the tools and showed it to her. "I'm not risking that it doesn't go off," he said.

She tried to stand up, but her feet weren't all the way through the suit legs. "You said you had a way of setting it off remotely!"

"I do. Remotely from you." He aimed the gun at Darcy. "Get dressed. You've got five minutes to get inside that lift—"

Darcy lunged for the gun sitting beside Charlotte. Charlotte was faster and snatched it off the bin. Donald took a step back, and then realized his sister was aiming the gun at him. "*You* get dressed," she told her brother. Her voice was shaky, her eyes shining. "This isn't what we discussed. You promised."

"I'm a liar," Donald said. He coughed into the crook of his arm and smiled. "You're a hypocrite and I'm a liar." He began to back toward the lift, his gun trained on Darcy. "You're not going to shoot me," he told his sister.

"Give me the gun," Darcy told Charlotte. "He'll listen if I'm holding it."

Donald laughed. "You aren't going to shoot me either. That gun's not loaded. Now get dressed. You two get out of here. I'm giving you half an hour. The drone lift takes twenty minutes to get to the top. The best thing to use for jamming the door is an empty bin. I left one over there."

Charlotte was crying and tugging at the legs of her suit, trying to get her feet all the way through. Donald had known she'd never go without him unless he made her, that she'd do something stupid. She would run and embrace him and beg him to come, insist that she would stay there and die with him. The only chance of getting her out had been to leave Darcy with her.

He was a hero. He would save himself and her both. Donald jabbed the call button on the non-express.

"Half an hour," he repeated. He saw that Darcy was already unzipping his suit to get in. His sister was yelling at him and try-ing to stand up, nearly tripped and fell. She started to kick the suit off rather than put it on the rest of the way. The lift dinged and opened. Donald leaned the cart back and pulled it inside. Tears welled up in his eyes to see the pain he was causing Char-lotte. She was halfway down the aisle toward him as the doors began to close.

"I love you," he said. He wasn't sure if she heard him. The doors squeezed shut on the sight of her. He scanned his ID, pressed a button, and the lift began to move.

Silo 17

58

THE COMM HUB COOLED, even as the fire raged below. Wisps of smoke curled out from underneath it. Juliette studied the interior of the great black machine and saw a ruin of broken circuit boards. The long row of headset jacks had shattered, and several of the wires at the base of the machine had stretched and snapped when it tipped over.

"Will it burn out?" Raph asked, eyeing the wisps of smoke.

Juliette coughed. She could still feel the smoke in her throat, could taste those burning pages. "I don't know," she admitted. She watched the lights overhead for any sign of faltering. "What power this silo has runs beneath the grates down there."

"So this silo could go dark as the mines at any time?" Raph scrambled to his feet. "I'm gonna get our bags, have our flashlights handy. And you need to drink some more water."

Juliette watched him trot off. She could feel those books burning beneath her. She could feel the wires inside the radio melting. She didn't think the power would go—hoped it wouldn't go—but so much else was being lost. The large schematics that had helped her find the digger might be ash already. The schematics to help her choose which silo to reach out to, which silo to dig for, gone.

Tall black machines hummed and whirred all around her,

those square-shouldered and unmoved giants. Unmoved save
for one. Juliette rose to her feet and studied the fallen server,
and the link between those machines and the silos became
even more obvious. Here was one collapsed like her home. Like
Solo's home. She studied the arrangement of the servers and remembered that their layout was identical to the layout of the silos. Raph returned with both of their bags. He handed Juliette
her canteen of water. She took a sip, lost in thought.

"I've got your flashli—"

"Wait," Juliette said. She twisted the cap back onto her canteen and walked between the servers. She went to the back of
one and studied the silver plate above the nest of wires. There
was a silo symbol there with its three downward-pointing tri-
angles. The number "29" was etched in the center.

"What're you looking for?" Raph asked.

Juliette tapped the plate. "Lukas used to say he needed to
work on server six or server thirty or whatever. I remember
him showing me how these things were laid out like the silos.
We have a schematic right here."

She set off in the direction of servers seventeen and eighteen.
Raph followed along. "Should we worry about the power?" he
asked.

"There's nothing we can do about that. The decking and
walls down there shouldn't get hot enough to catch. When it
burns out, we'll go see—" Something caught Juliette's eye as
she traced a route between the servers. The wires underneath
the floor grates darted in and out of their chutes, running to the
bases of the machines. It was a series of red wires amid all the
black ones that stopped her.

"What now?" Raph asked. He was watching her as though
he were worried. "Hey, are you feeling okay? Because I've seen
miners get a rock to their crowns and act loopy for a day—"

"I'm fine," Juliette said. She pointed to the run of wires,

turned and imagined those wires leading from one server to another. "A map," she said.

"Yes," Raph agreed. "A map." He took her by the arm. "Why don't you come sit down? You breathed a lot of smoke—"

"Listen to me. The girl on the radio, the one from Silo One, she said there was a map with these red lines on it. It came up after I told her about the digger. She seemed really excited, said she understood why all the lines went off and converged. This was before the radio stopped working."

"Okay."

"These are the silos," Juliette said. She held out her hands to the tall servers. "C'mere. Look." She hurried around the next row, studied the plates as she searched. Fourteen. Sixteen. Seventeen. "Here we are. And this is where we tunneled. And that's our old silo." She pointed to the next server.

"So you're saying we can choose which of these to call on the radio by seeing who's close? Because we have a map just like this down below. Erik's got one."

"No, I'm saying those red lines on her map are like these wires. See? Tunneling deep underground down there. The diggers weren't meant to go from one silo to the next. Bobby was the one who told me how difficult that thing was to turn. It was aimed somewhere."

"Where?"

"I don't know. I would need that map to tell. Unless—" She turned to Raph, whose pale face she saw was smudged with smoke and soot. "You were on the dig team. How much fuel did that tank in the digger hold?"

He shrugged. "We never measured in gallons. Just topped it up. Court had the tank dipped a few times to see how much we were burning. I remember her saying we would never use up what was in there."

"That's because it was designed to go farther. Much farther.

We need to dip the tank again to get an idea. And Erik's map should show which way that digger was pointing to begin with. If only—" She snapped her fingers. "We've got the other digger."

"I'm not following. Why would we need two diggers? We've only got one generator that works."

Juliette squeezed his arm, could feel herself beaming, her mind racing. "We don't need the other one to dig. We just need to see where it's pointing. If we trace that line on a map and project out where our own digger should've gone, those two lines should cross. And if the fuel supply matches that distance, that's like a confirmation. We can see where and how far this place is that she was telling me about. This seed place. She made it sound like another silo, but one out where the air was—"

There were voices at the other end of the room, someone entering from the hall. Juliette pulled Raph against one of the servers and threw her finger over her mouth. But someone could be heard coming straight for them, a quiet clicking, like fingers tapping on metal. Juliette fought the urge to run, and then a brown shape emerged at her feet, and there was a hiss as a leg was lifted, a stream of urine spattering her boot.

"Puppy!" she heard Elise scream.

Juliette hugged the kids and Solo. She hadn't seen them since her silo fell. They reminded her why she was doing this, what she was fighting for, what was *worth* fighting for. A rage had built up inside of her, a single-minded pursuit of digging through the earth down below and digging for answers outside. And she had lost sight of this, these things worth saving. She had been too concerned with those who deserved to be damned.

This anger melted as Elise clung to her neck and Solo's beard scratched her face. Here was what was left, what they still had, and protecting it was more important than vengeance. That's what Father Wendel had discovered. He had been reading the wrong passages in his book, passages of hate rather than hope. And Juliette had been just as blind. She had been prepared to rush off and leave everyone behind.

Raph joined her and the kids, and they huddled together around one of the servers and discussed what they'd seen of the violence below. Solo had a rifle with him and kept saying they needed to secure the door, needed to hunker down.

"We should hide in here and wait for them to kill each other," he said, a wild look in his eyes.

"Is that how you survived all the years over here?" Raph asked.

Solo nodded. "My father put me away. It was a long time before I left. It was safer that way."

"Your father knew what was going to happen," Juliette said. "He locked you away from it all. It's the same reason we're down here, all of us, living like this. Someone did the same thing a long time ago. They put us away to save us."

"So we should hide again," Rickson said. He looked to the others. "Right?"

"How much food do you have left in the pantry?" Juliette asked Solo. "Assuming the fire didn't get to it."

He pulled on his beard. "Three years' worth. Maybe four. But just for me."

Juliette did the math. "Let's say two hundred people made it over, though I don't think it was that many. What's that? Maybe five days?" She whistled. A new appreciation for all the various farms of her old home dawned on her. To provide for thousands of people for hundreds of years, the balance was meticulous. "We need to stop hiding altogether," she said. "What we need . . ." She studied the faces of these few who trusted her completely. "We need a Town Hall."

Raph laughed, thinking she was joking.

"A what?" Solo asked.

"We need a meeting. With everyone. Everyone left. We need to decide if we're gonna stay hidden or get out of here."

"I thought we were going to dig to another silo," Raph said. "Or dig to this other place."

"I don't think we have time for digging. It would take weeks, and the farms are ravaged. Besides, I've got a better idea. A quicker way."

"What about those sticks of dynamite you've been hauling? I thought we were going after the people who did this."

"That's still an option. Look, we need to do this anyway. We need to get out of here. Otherwise, Jimmy's right. We'll just kill each other. So we need to round everyone up."

"We'll have to do it back down in the generator room," Raph said. "Someplace big enough. Or maybe the farms."

"No." Juliette turned and surveyed the room around her. She saw past the tall servers to the far walls, saw how wide the space was. "We'll do it here. We'll show them this place."

"Here?" Solo asked. "Two hundred people? Here?" He seemed visibly shaken, began tugging on his beard with both hands.

"Where will everyone sit?" Hannah asked.

"How will they see?" Elise wanted to know.

Juliette studied the wide hall with the tall, black machines. Many of them clicked and whirred. Wires trailed from the tops and wove their way through the ceiling. She knew from tracing the camera feeds in her old home that they were all interconnected. She knew how the power fed into the bases, how the side panels came off. She ran her hand across one of the machines Solo had marked with the days of his youth. They had added up to years.

"Go to the Suit Lab and grab my tool bag," she told Solo.

"A Project?" he asked.

She nodded, and Solo disappeared amid the tall machines. Raph and the kids studied her. Juliette smiled. "You kids are going to enjoy this."

With the wires cut from the top and the bolts removed from the base, all it took was a good shove. It went over much easier than the comm hub. Juliette watched with satisfaction as the machine tipped, trembled, and then crashed down with a bang felt through her boots. Miles and Rickson slapped hands and whooped in the manner of boys destroying things. Hannah and Shaw had already moved on to the next server. Elise scampered up on top with a boost from Juliette, wire cutters in her hand, Puppy barking at her to be safe.

"Like cutting hair," Juliette said, watching Elise work.

"We could do Solo's beard next," Elise suggested.

"I doubt he'd like that," Raph said.

Juliette turned to see that the miner had returned from his errand. "I dropped over a hundred notes," he told her. "Couldn't write more than that. My hand was cramping. I sprinkled them around so some will be sure to get to the bottom."

"Good. And you wrote that there was food up here? Enough for everyone?"

He nodded.

"Then we should get that machine off the hatch and make sure we can deliver. Otherwise, we're going to have to raid the farms above us."

Raph followed her to the comm hub. They made sure the smoke wasn't curling up, and Juliette ran her hand along the base, feeling for heat. Solo's hovel was metal on all sides, so her hope was that the fire didn't spread past the pile of books. But there was no telling. The fallen hub made a horrible screech as it was shoved to the side. A cloud of dark smoke billowed out.

Juliette waved her hand over her face and coughed. Raph ran to the other side of the server and made as if to shove it back. "Wait," Juliette said, ducking out of the cloud. "It's clearing."

The server room grew hazy, but there was no great outpouring of smoke. Just a leak from what had been trapped down there. Raph started to lower himself into the hole, but Juliette insisted on going first. She clicked her flashlight on and descended into the dissipating smoke.

She crouched at the bottom and breathed through her undershirt. The beam of her flashlight stood out like a solid thing, as if she could strike someone with it if they came at her. But no one was coming. There was a form in the middle of the hall, still smoldering. The smell was awful. The smoke cleared further, and Juliette yelled up to Raph that it was okay to descend.

He clanged down noisily while Juliette stepped over the body and surveyed the damage in the room. The air was warm and muggy, and it was difficult to breathe. She imagined for a moment what Lukas had gone through, down there and choking. More than smoke brought tears to her eyes.

"Those were books."

Raph joined her and stared at the black patch in the center of the room. He must've seen that they were books when he rescued her, because there was no sign of them left. Those pages were in the air now. They were in their lungs. Juliette choked on memories of the past.

She went to the wall and studied the radio. The metal cage was still bent back from where she'd busted it off the wall so long ago. She flipped the power switch, but nothing happened. The plastic knob was tacky and warm. The insides of the thing were probably a single blob of rubber and copper.

"Where's this food?" Raph asked.

"Through there," Juliette said. "Use a rag on the door."

He went off to explore the apartment and pantry while Juliette studied the remains of an old desk, a misshapen computer monitor sitting in the center, the panel shattered from the heat. There was no sign of Solo's bedding, just a pile of metal boxes that once held books, some of them sagging from the extreme heat. Juliette saw black footprints trailing behind her and realized the rubber on the soles of her boots was melting from the heat. She heard Raph yelling excitedly from the next room. Juliette passed through the door and found him clutching an armload of cans, his chin pressed to the ones on top of the pile, a goofy grin on his face.

"There's shelves of this," he said.

Juliette went to the pantry door and shined her light inside. It was a vast cavern with an odd can here or there. But some of the shelves in the back appeared fuller. "If everyone shows up, it'll last us a few days, no more," she said.

"Maybe we shouldn't have called for everyone."

"No," Juliette said. "We're doing the right thing." She turned to the wall by the small eating table. The fire hadn't made it through the door. The tall schematics the size of blankets hung there, perfectly intact. Juliette flipped through them, looking for the ones she needed. She found them and ripped them free. Folding them up, she heard a muted thud far above them, the sound of another server falling.

59

THEY ARRIVED IN a trickle, and then in clumps, and then in crowds. They marveled at the steady lights in the hallways and explored the offices. None of these people had ever seen the inside of IT. Few of them had spent much time in the Up Top, except on pilgrimages after a cleaning. Families wandered from room to room; kids clutched reams of paper; many came to Juliette or the others with the notes Raph had folded and dropped, asking about the food. In just a few days, they looked different. Coveralls were stained and torn, faces stubbled and gaunt, eyes ringed with dark circles. In just a few days. Juliette saw that they had only a few days more before things grew desperate. Everyone saw that.

Those who arrived early helped prepare the food and push over the last of the servers. The smells of warm vegetables and soup filled the room. Two of the hottest servers, numbers 40 and 38, had been lowered to the ground with their power intact. Open cans were arranged atop their hot sides, the contents of each can simmering. There wasn't enough silverware, so many stood drinking the soups and vegetable juice straight from warm cans.

Hannah helped Juliette set up for the Town Hall while Rickson tended to the baby. One of the schematics was already pinned to the wall, and Hannah was working on the other. Lines were carefully traced with thread, Hannah double-checking Juliette's work. A charcoal was used to mark the route. Juliette watched another group file in. It occurred to her that this was her second Town Hall and that the first hadn't gone so well. It occurred to her that this would most likely be her last.

Most of those gathered were from the farms, but then a few mechanics and miners began to show. Tom Higgins and the Planning Committee arrived from the Mids deputy station. Juliette saw one of them standing on a fallen server with a charcoal and paper, jabbing his finger as he attempted to count heads, cursing the milling crowd for making it difficult. She laughed, and then realized it was important, what he was doing. They would need to know. A cleaning suit lay empty at her feet, one of her props for the Town Hall. They would need to know how many suits and how many people.

Courtnee arrived and squeezed through the crowd, which came as a shock. Juliette beamed and embraced her friend.

"You smell like smoke," Courtnee said.

Juliette laughed. "I didn't think you'd come."

"The note said it was life or death."

"It did?" She looked to Raph.

He shrugged. "Some of them might've said that," he said.

"So what is this?" Courtnee said. "A long climb for some soup? What's going on?"

"I'll tell everyone at once." To Raph: "Can you see about getting everyone in here? And maybe send Miles and Shaw or one of the porters to the stairwell to see if any others are on their way."

While he left, Juliette noticed that everyone was already sitting on the servers, backs to each other, slurping from cans while more were opened and arranged from the great stacks behind Solo. He had taken over popping the cans with some electric contraption that plugged into a floor outlet. Many of those seated were eyeing the pile of food hauled up from the pantry. Many more were eyeing her. The whispers were like an escape of steam.

Juliette fretted and paced as the numbers in the room swelled. Shaw and Miles returned to say the stairway was pretty quiet, maybe a few more heading up. It felt as though an entire day had passed since Juliette and Raph had fought the fire below; she didn't want to glance at her watch and know the truth of the hour. She felt tired. Especially as everyone sat there, tipping their cans to their lips and tapping the bottoms, wiping their faces with their sleeves, watching her. Waiting.

The food had them quiet and momentarily content. The cans had their hands and mouths busy. It had won her some reprieve. Juliette knew it was now or never.

"I know you're wondering what this is all about," she began. "Why we're here." She raised her voice, and the conversations across the fallen servers fell quiet. "And I don't mean here, in this room. I mean this silo. Why did we run? There are a lot of rumors swirling, but I am here to tell you the truth. I have brought you into this most secretive of rooms to tell you the truth. Our silo was destroyed. It was poisoned. Those who did not make it over with us are gone."

There was a hiss of whispers. "Poisoned by who?" someone shouted.

"The same people who put us underground hundreds of years ago. I need you to listen. Please listen."

The crowd quietened.

"Our ancestors were put underground so that we might survive while the world got better. As many of you know, I went outside before our home was taken from us. I sampled the air out there, and I think the farther we get from this place, the better the conditions are. Not only do I suspect this from what we measured, I have heard from another silo that there are blue skies beyond the—"

"Ratshit!" someone yelled. "I heard that was a lie, something they did to your brain before you went to clean."

Juliette found the person who'd said that. It was an older porter, one whose profession was the locus not just of rumors but also of secrets too dangerous to sell. While people whispered again, she saw a new arrival shuffle through the thick metal door at the far end of the room. It was Father Wendel, his arms crossed over his chest, hands stuffed into his sleeves. Bobby bellowed for everyone to shut up, and they gradually did. Juliette waved a greeting to Father Wendel, and heads turned.

"I need you to take some of what I'm about to say on faith," Juliette said. "Some of what I say I know for certain. I know this: We could stay here and make a life, but I don't know for how long. And we would live in fear. Not just fear of each other, but fear that disaster can visit us at any time. They can open our doors without asking, can poison our air without telling, and they can take our lives without warning. And I don't know what kind of life that would be."

The room was as still as death.

"The alternative is to go. But if we do, there's no coming back—"

"Go where?" someone yelled. "Another silo? What if it's worse than this one?"

"Not another silo," Juliette said. She moved to the side so they could see the schematic on the wall. "Here they are. The fifty silos. This one was our home." She pointed, and there was a rustle as everyone strained to see. Juliette felt her throat tighten with emotion at the overwhelming joy and sadness of telling the truth to her people. She slid her finger to the adjacent silo. "This is where we are now."

"So many," she heard someone whisper.

"How far are they?" another asked.

"I drew a line to show how we got here." She pointed. "It may be hard to see from the back. And this line here, this is where our digging machine was pointing." She traced it with her finger so they could see where it led. Her finger went sideways off the map and to the wall. Waving to Elise, Juliette had her come up and press her finger to a spot she'd already marked.

"This schematic is for the silo we're currently in." She moved to the next sheet of paper. "It shows another digging machine at the base—"

"We don't want your digging—"

Juliette turned to the audience. "I don't want to dig either. Honestly, I don't think we have enough fuel left, because we've been burning it since we got here and because we worked the machine hard to get her to turn. And I don't think we have food for more than a week or two, not for everyone. We're not digging. But our schematic matched the size and location of the machine we found back home. It matched it perfectly to scale and even the direction it was pointing. I have a schematic here of this silo and this digger." She ran her hand over the other sheet of paper, then went back to the large map. "When I plot this, look how the line goes between all the other silos, not touching any of them." She walked and slid her finger across the line until she touched Elise's finger. Elise beamed up at her.

"We have a good guess of the fuel we used to get to this silo, and how much remains. We know how much fuel we started with and how fast it burns. And what we determined is that the digger was loaded up with just enough fuel—with maybe ten percent extra—to have taken us directly to this spot." She again touched Elise's finger. "And the diggers are aimed slightly up. We think they were placed here to take us to this point—to get us out of here." She paused. "I don't know when they were go-ing to tell us—if they were ever going to tell us—but I say we don't wait to be asked. I say we go."

"Just go?"

Juliette scanned the audience and saw that it was one of the men from the Planning Committee.

"I think it might be safer out there for us than if we stay. I know what will happen if we stay. I want to see if it's better if we leave."

"You *hope* it's safer," someone said.

Juliette didn't search for the voice. She let her gaze drift across the crowd. Everyone was thinking the same thing, her-self included.

"That's right. I hope. I have the word of a stranger. I have whispers from someone I've never met. I have a feeling in my gut, in my heart. I have these lines that cross on a map. And if you think that's not enough, then I agree with you. I've lived my entire life only believing what I can see. I need proof. I need to see results. And even then I need to see them a second and a third time before I get a glimpse of how things truly are. But this is a case where what I know for certain—the life that awaits us here—is not worth living. And there's a chance that a better one can be found elsewhere. I'm willing to go see, but only if enough of you are with me."

"I'm with you," Raph said.

Juliette nodded. The room blurred a little. "I know you are," she said.

Solo raised his hand. With his other, he tugged on his beard. Juliette felt Elise take her hand. Shaw held a squirming puppy, but still managed to raise his.

"How will we get there if we don't aim to dig?" one of the miners hollered.

Juliette bent at the waist to grab something at her feet. While her head was down, she wiped at her eyes. She stood and lifted one of the cleaning suits, held it in one hand, a helmet in the other.

"We're going outside," she said.

60

THE FOOD DWINDLED while they worked. It was a grim countdown, these disappearing cans and what had been rounded up from the farms. Not everyone in the silo participated; many never came to the Town Hall; many more simply wandered off, realizing they could grab more grow plots if they hurried. Several mechanics asked for permission to head back down to Mechanical and round up those who had refused to make the climb, to try and convince them to come, to see if Walker could be stirred. Juliette was overjoyed with the prospect of gathering more people to go. She also felt the pressure mount as everyone worked.

The server room became a massive workshop, something like you'd see down the halls of Supply. Nearly a hundred and fifty cleaning suits were laid out, all of them needing to be sized and adjusted. Juliette was sad to see that it was more than they needed, but also a little relieved. It would've been a problem the other way around.

She had shown a dozen mechanics how the valves went together like she and Nelson had used to breathe in the Suit Lab. There weren't enough of the valves in IT, so porters were given samples and sent down to Supply, where Juliette was sure there would be more of these parts otherwise useless for survival. Gaskets, heat tape, and seals were needed. They were also told to secure and haul up the welding kits in both Supply and Mechanical. She showed them the difference between the acetylene bottles and the oxygen and said they wouldn't need the acetylene.

Erik calculated the distance using the chart hanging on the wall and reckoned they could put a dozen people to a bottle. Juliette said to make it ten to be safe. With fifty or so people working on the suits—the fallen servers acting as workbenches as they knelt or sat on the floor—she took a small group up to the cafeteria for what she knew would be a grim job. Just her father, Raph, Dawson, and two of the older porters who she figured had handled bodies before. On the way up, they stopped below the farms and went to the coroner's office past the pump rooms. Juliette found a supply of folded black bags and pulled out five dozen. From there they climbed in silence.

There was no airlock attached to Silo 17, not anymore. The outer door remained cracked open from the fall of the silo decades before. Juliette remembered squeezing through that door twice before, her helmet getting stuck the first time. The only barriers between them and the outside air were the inner airlock door and the door to the sheriff's office. Bare membranes between a dead world and a dying one.

Juliette helped the others remove a tangle of chairs and tables from around the office door. There was a narrow path between them where she had come and gone over a month ago, but they needed more room to work. She warned the others about the bodies inside, but they knew from collecting the bags what they were in for. A handful of flashlights converged on the door as Juliette prepared to open it. They all wore masks and rubber gloves at her father's insistence. Juliette wondered if they should've donned cleaning suits instead.

The bodies inside were just as she remembered them: a tangle of gray and lifeless limbs. The stench of something both foul and metallic filled her mask, and Juliette had a memory of dumping fetid soup on herself to drown the outside air. This was the stench of death and something besides.

They hauled the bodies out one by one and placed them in the funeral bags. It was grisly work. Limp flesh sloughed off bones like a slow roast. "The joints," Juliette cautioned, her voice hot and muffled by her mask. "Armpits and knees."

The bodies held together barely and enough, the tendons and bone doing most of the work. Black zippers were pulled shut with relief. Coughing and gagging filled the air.

Most of the bodies inside the sheriff's office had piled up by the door as if they'd crawled over one another in an attempt to get back inside, back into the cafeteria. Other bodies were in a state of more serene rest. A man slouched over on the tattered remnants of a cot in the open holding cell, just the rusted frame, the mattress long gone. A woman lay in the corner with her arms crossed over her chest as if sleeping. Juliette moved the last of the bodies with her father, and she saw how wide her father's eyes were, how they were fixed on her. She glanced over his shoulder as she shuffled backwards out of the sheriff's office, staring at the airlock door that awaited them all, its yellow skin flaking off in chips of paint.

"This isn't right," her father said, his voice muffled and his mask bobbing up and down with the movement of his jaw. They tucked the body into an open bag and zipped it up.

"We'll give them a proper burial," she assured him, assuming he meant it wasn't right how the bodies were being handled—stacked like bags of dirty laundry.

He removed his gloves and his mask, rested back on his heels, and wiped his brow with the back of his hand. "No. It's these people. I thought you said this place was practically empty when you got here."

"It was. Just Solo and the kids. These people have been dead a long time."

"That's not possible," her father said. "They're too well preserved." His eyes drifted across the bags, wrinkles of concern or confusion in his brow. "I'd say they've been dead for three weeks. Four or five at the most."

"Dad, they were here when I arrived. I crawled over them. I asked Solo about them once, and he said he discovered them years ago."

"That simply can't be—"

"It's probably because they weren't buried. Or the gas outside kept the bugs away. It doesn't matter, does it?"

"It matters plenty when something isn't right like this. There's something not right about this entire silo, I'm telling you." He stood and headed toward the stairwell where Raph was ladling hauled water into scrounged cups and cans. Her father took one for himself and passed one to Juliette. He was lost in thought, she could tell. "Did you know Elise had a twin sister?" her father asked.

Juliette nodded. "Hannah told me. Died in childbirth. The mother passed as well. They don't talk about it much, especially not with her."

"And those two boys. Marcus and Miles. Another set of twins. The eldest boy Rickson says he thought he had a brother, but his father wouldn't talk about it and he never knew his mother to ask her." Her father took a sip of water and peered into the can. Juliette tried to drown the metallic taste on her tongue while Dawson helped with one of the bags. Dawson coughed and looked as though he were about to gag.

"It's a lot of dying," Juliette agreed, worried where her father's thoughts were going. She thought of the brother she never knew. She looked for any sign on her father's face, any indication that this reminded him of his wife and lost son. But he was piecing together some other puzzle.

"No, it's a lot of *living*. Don't you see? Three sets of twins in six births? And those kids are as fit as fiddles with no care. Your friend Jimmy doesn't have a hole in his teeth and can't remember the last time he was sick. None of them can. How do you explain that? How do you explain these bodies piled up like they fell over a few weeks ago?"

Juliette caught herself staring at her arm. She gulped the last of her water, handed the tin to her father, and began rolling up her sleeve. "Dad, do you remember me asking you about scars, about whether or not they go away?"

He nodded.

"A few of my scars have disappeared." She showed him the crook of her arm as if he would know what was no longer there. "I didn't believe Lukas when he told me. But I used to have a mark here. And another here. And you said it was a miracle I survived my burns, didn't you?"

"You received good attention straight away—"

"And Fitz didn't believe me when I told him about the dive I made to fix the pump. He said he's worked flooded mineshafts and has seen men twice my size get sick from breathing air just ten meters deep, much less thirty or forty. He says I would've died if I'd done what I did."

"I don't know the first thing about mining," her father said.

"Fitz does, and he thinks I should be dead. And you think these people should be rotted—"

"They should be bones. I'm telling you."

Juliette turned and gazed at the blank wallscreen. She wondered if it was all a dream. This was what happened to the dying soul; it scrambled for some perch, some stairway to cling to, some way not to fall. She had cleaned and died on that hill outside her silo. She had never loved Lukas at all. Never gotten to know him properly. This was a land of ghosts and fiction, events held together with all the vacant solidarity of dreams, all the nonsense of a drunken mind. She was long dead and only just now realizing it—

"Maybe something in the water," her father said.

Juliette turned away from the blank wall. She reached out to him, held his arms in her hands, then stepped closer. He wrapped his arms around her and she wrapped hers around him. His stubble scratched her cheek, and she fought hard not to cry.

"It's okay," her father said. "It's okay."

She wasn't dead. But things weren't right.

"Not in the water," she said, though she'd swallowed her fair share in that silo. She released her father and watched the first of the bags head to the stairwell. Someone was rigging up spliced electrical cables for rope and running it over the rail to lower a body. Porters be damned, she saw. Even the porters were saying *porters be damned*.

"Maybe it's in the air," she said. "Maybe this is what happens when you don't gas a place. I don't know. But I think you're right that there's something wrong with this silo. And I think it's high time we get out of here."

Her father took a last swig of water. "How long before we leave?" he asked. "And are you sure this is a good idea?"

Juliette nodded. "I'd rather we died out there trying than in here killing each other." And she realized she sounded like all those who had been sent to clean, all the dangerous dreamers and mad fools, those she had mocked and never understood. She sounded like a person who trusted a machine to work without peeking inside, without first tearing it completely apart.

Silo 1

61

CHARLOTTE SLAPPED THE lift door with her palm. She had jabbed the call button right as her brother disappeared, but it was too late. She hopped on one foot to keep her balance, her suit only half on. Down the aisle behind her, Darcy was struggling into his suit. "Will he do it?" Darcy called out.

Charlotte nodded. He would. He had pulled the other suit out for Darcy. This was his plan all along. Charlotte slapped the door again and cursed her brother.

"You need to get dressed," Darcy said.

She turned and sank to the ground, hugged her shins. She didn't want to move. She watched Darcy wriggle into his suit and get the collar over his head. He stood and tried to reach around for the zipper, finally gave up. "Was I supposed to put this backpack on first?" He grabbed one of the bundles her brother had packed and opened it up. He pulled out a can, put it back. Brought out a gun, kept it out. He worked his head and arms back out of the suit. "Charlotte, we've got half an hour. How're we getting out of here?"

Charlotte wiped her cheeks and struggled to her feet. Darcy didn't have the first clue about how to get suited up. She worked her legs into her suit and left the sleeves and collar off, hurried down the aisle toward him. There was a ding behind her.

She stopped and turned, thinking Donald had come back, had changed his mind, forgetting that she had pressed the call button.

Two men in light blue coveralls gaped at her from inside the express lift. One of them peered at the buttons in confusion, looked back to Charlotte—this woman with a silver suit half on and half off—and then the doors slowly closed.

"Shit," Darcy said. "We really need to go."

A panic stirred in Charlotte, an internal countdown. She thought of the way her brother had looked at her from inside the lift, the way he had kissed her goodbye. Her chest felt as though it might implode, but she hurried to Darcy and helped him get his arms out and his pack on. Once he was in fully, she zipped up the back. He helped her do the same, then followed her to the end of the aisle. Charlotte pointed to the low hangar and handed him both helmets. The bin her brother had left was right where he'd said it would be. "Open that door up and jam the bin half-way inside. I'll go start the lift."

She threw open the barracks door and ran down the hall in an awkward waddle, the thick suit crowding her knees. Through the next door. The radio was still on and hissing. She thought of the waste that thing had been, all the time putting it together, collecting the parts, and now she was abandoning it. At the lift control station, she ripped the plastic off and flipped the main controls into the up position. She felt sure she'd given Darcy plenty of time to get it jammed. Another awkward waddle down the hall, past the barracks that'd been her home for these ago-nizing weeks, out into her armory hell, the last of her birds sulk-ing beneath their tarps, a single chirp ringing out from some-where. From the lift. The sound of boots storming their way, Darcy yelling at her to get inside the drone lift.

· · ·

Donald rode the lift toward the sixty-second floor. When he passed sixty-one, he hit the emergency stop button. The lift jerked to a stop and began buzzing. He steadied the bomb and pulled out the hammer, went ahead and removed the tag. He wasn't sure how much damage it would cause if he detonated it inside the lift, but he would if anyone came for him. He wanted to give his sister enough time, but he was willing to risk everything to put an end to that place. He watched the clock on the lift panel and waited. It gave him plenty of time to think. Fifteen minutes passed without him needing to cough or clear his throat once. He laughed at this and wondered if he was getting better. Then he remembered how his grandfather and his aunt had both gotten better the day before they died. It was probably something like that.

The hammer grew heavy. It was incredible to stand beside something so destructive as that bomb, to lay a hand on a device that could kill so many, change so much. Another five minutes went by. He should go. It was too long. It would take him some time to get to the reactor. He waited another minute, some rational part of his brain aware of what the rest of him was about to do, some buried part that screamed for him to think about this, to be reasonable.

Donald slammed the hold switch before he lost his nerve. The lift lurched. He hoped his sister and Darcy were well on their way.

Charlotte threw herself into the drone lift, her helmet banging on the ceiling, the bottle of air on her back causing her to tip over onto her side. Darcy threw his helmet inside the lift and began crawling in after her. Someone shouted from the armory. Charlotte began to shove at the plastic bin, which was the only thing keeping the lift from closing and heading up. Darcy pushed as well, but it was pinned tight. Another shout from beyond. Darcy fumbled for the pistol he'd taken from the pack. He turned on his side and fired out of the lift, deafening roars from inside that metal can. Charlotte saw men in silver coveralls duck and take cover behind the drones. Another shot rang out, a loud *thwack* inside the lift, the men out there returning fire. Charlotte turned to kick the bin with her feet, but the lid had buckled down where the door had pinched it. It had formed a wedge, wanted to come in with her, not go out. She tried to pull, but there was nothing to cling to.

Darcy yelled for her to stay put. He crawled on his elbows out the door, his gun firing *pop pop pop*, men taking cover, Charlotte cringing. He left the lift and began pushing the bin in from the other side. Charlotte yelled for him to stop, to get back inside. The door would slam shut with him out there. Another shot rang out, the zing of a miss. Darcy kicked the bin with his boot, and it moved several inches.

"Wait!" Charlotte yelled. She scampered to the door, didn't want to go on by herself. "Wait!"

Darcy kicked the bin again. The lift lurched. It was almost free, just a few more inches. Another shot from beyond the drones and no sound of a miss. Just a grunt from Darcy, who fell to his knees, turned and fired wildly behind himself.

Charlotte reached out and tugged on his arm. "Come on!" she yelled.

Darcy reached down and pushed her hands inside the lift. He leaned his shoulder against the bin and smiled at her. And before he shoved the bin inside, he said, "It's okay. I remember who I am, now."

The lift slowed on the reactor level, the doors opened, and Donald pressed a boot to the hand truck and tilted it back. He steered the bomb toward the security gates. The guard there watched him approach, eyebrows up with mild curiosity. Here was everything wrong with everything, Donald thought. Here was a guard not recognizing a murderer because he toted a bomb. Here was a man swiping an ID with Darcy's name on it, a green light, and the ennui of an interminable job as he was waved through the gates. Here was everyone seeing what was coming and ushering hell right along anyway.

"Thank you," Donald said, daring the man to recognize him.

"Good luck with that."

Donald had never seen the reactors before. They were closed off behind large doors and spanned three levels. On any one shift, there were nearly as many men in red as half the others combined. Here was the heart of a soulless machine, which made it the only organ of consequence.

He followed a curving hall lined with thick pipes and heavy cables. He passed two others in reactor red, neither of them noting the holes in the shoulder of his coveralls, or that the bloodstains had begun to brown. Just nods and quick glances at his burden, even quicker glances away lest they be asked to help. One of the hand truck's tires squeaked as if complaining about Donald's plan, unhappy with that terrible load.

Donald stopped outside of the main reactor room. Far enough. He reached into his pocket and pulled out the hammer. He weighed this thing he was about to do. He thought of Helen, who had died the way people were supposed to die. This was how it worked. You lived. You did your best. You got out of the way. You let those who come after you choose. You let them decide for themselves, live their own lives. This was the way.

He raised the hammer with both hands, and a shot rang out. A shot, and a fire in his chest. Donald spun in a lazy circle, the hammer clattering to the ground, and then his legs went out.

He clutched for the bomb, hoping to take it with him, to pull it down. His fingers found the cone, slipped off, caught the hand truck's handle, and they both tumbled. Donald ended up on his back, the bomb slamming flat to the ground with a powerful clang felt through his back, and then rolling lazily and harmlessly toward the wall, out of reach.

The drone lift opened automatically at the end of its long and dark climb. Charlotte hesitated. She looked for some way to lower the lift, to go back down. But the controls were a mile beneath her. The large tank of air on her back knocked against the roof of the lift as she crawled out. Darcy was gone. Her brother was gone. This was not what she wanted.

Overhead, black clouds swirled. She crawled up a sloping ramp, all of it familiar. She had been here before, if not in person. It was the view from her drones, the sight she'd been rewarded with on four flights. With the push of a throttle, she would be up there in those clouds, banking hard and flying free.

But this time, it was with weary muscles that she crawled up the ramp. She reached the top and had to lower herself down to a concrete ledge below. A grounded bird, a flightless traveler, she shinnied down this ledge and dropped to the dirt, a chick plummeting from its nest.

She wasn't sure at first which way to go. And she was thirsty, but her food and water were in a pack and trapped with her inside her suit. She turned and fought for her bearings, checked the map her brother had taped to her arm, and was angry at him for that. Angry and thankful. This was his plan all along.

She studied the map, was used to a digital display, a higher vantage, a flight plan, but the ramp leading down into the earth helped her establish north. Red lines on the map pointed the way. She plodded toward the hills and a better view.

And she remembered this place, remembered being here after a rain when the grass was slick and twin tracks of mud made a brown lacework of that gradual rise. Charlotte remembered being late from the airport. She had topped that very hill, and her brother had raced out to meet her. It was a time when the world was whole. You might look up and see vapor trails from passenger jets inching across the sky. You could drive to fast food. Call a loved one. A settled world existed here.

She passed through the spot where she'd hugged her brother, and any plan of escape wilted. She had little desire to carry on. Her brother was gone. The world was gone. Even if she lived to see green grass and eat one more MRE, cut her lip on one more can of water . . . why?

She trudged up the hill, taking a step only because her other foot had taken a step, tears streaming down her face, wondering why.

Donald's chest was on fire. Warm blood pooled around his neck. He lifted his head and saw Thurman at the end of the hall, marching toward him. Two men from Security were on either side, guns drawn. Donald fumbled in his pocket for his pistol, but it was too late. Too late. Tears welled up, and they were for the people who would live under this system, the hundreds of thousands who would come and go and suffer. He managed to free the pistol but could only raise it a few inches off the ground. These men were coming for him. They would hunt down Charlotte and Darcy out there on the surface. They would swoop down on his sister with their drones. They would take down silo after silo until only one was left, this capricious judgment of souls, of lives run by pitiless servers and soulless code.

Their guns were trained on him, waiting for him to make a move, ready to end his life. Donald put every ounce of his strength into lifting that pistol. He watched Thurman come at him, this man he had shot and killed once before, and he lifted his gun, struggled to raise it, could lift it no more than six inches off the ground.

But it was enough.

Donald steered his arm wide, aimed at the cone of that great bomb designed to bring down monsters such as these, and pulled the trigger. He heard a bang, but he could not tell what from.

The earth lurched and Charlotte fell forward on her hands and knees. There was a *thwump* like a grenade tossed into a deep lake. The hillside shuddered.

Charlotte turned on her side and glanced down the hill. A crack opened along the flat earth. Another. The concrete tower at the center listed to one side, and then the earth yawned open. A crater formed, and then the center of the scooped-out earth between those hills sank and tugged at the land further out, clawed and grabbed at the soil and pulled it down as if it were a giant sinkhole, plumes of white powdered concrete jetting up through the cracks.

The hill rumbled. Sand and tiny rocks slid downward, racing each other toward the bottom as the land became something that *moved*. Charlotte scrambled backwards, up the hill and away from the widening pit, her heart racing and her mind awed.

She turned and rose to her feet and climbed as fast as she could, a hand on the earth in front of her, crouched over, the land slowly becoming solid again. She climbed until she reached the crest, her sobs swallowed by the shock of witnessing this scene of such powerful destruction, the wind strong against her, the suit cold and bulky.

At the top of the hill, she collapsed. "Donny," she whispered.

Charlotte turned and gazed down at the hole in the world her
brother had left. She lay on her back while the dust peppered
her suit and the wind screamed against her visor, her view of
the world growing more and more blurred, the dust clouding
all.

Fulton County, Georgia

62

JULIETTE REMEMBERED A day meant for dying. She had been sent to clean, had been stuffed in a suit similar to this one, and had watched through a narrow visor as a world of green and blue was taken from her, color fading to gray as she crested a hill and saw the true world.

And now, laboring through the wind, the hiss of sand against her visor, the roar of her pulse and heavy breathing trapped in that dome, she watched as brown and gray relented and drained away.

The change was gradual at first. Hints of pale blue. Hard to be sure that's even what it was. She was in the lead group with Raph and her father and the other seven suited figures tethered to the shared bottle of air they lugged between them. A gradual change, and then it became sudden, like stepping through a wall. The haze lifted; a light was thrown; the wind buffeting her from all sides halted as stabs of color erupted, shards of green and blue and pure white, and Juliette was in a world that was almost too vivid, too vibrant, to be believed. Brown grasses like withered rows of corn brushed against her boots, but these were the only dead things in sight. Further away, green grasses stirred and writhed. White clouds roamed the sky. And Juliette saw now that the bright picture books of her youth were in fact faded, the pages muted compared to this.

There was a hand on her back, and Juliette turned to see her father staring wide-eyed at the vista. Raph shielded his eyes against the bright sun, his exhalations fogging his helmet. Hannah smiled down her collar at the bulge cradled to her chest, the empty arms of her suit twisting in the breeze as she held her child. Rickson wrapped his arm around her shoulder and stared at the sky while Elise and Shaw threw their hands up as if they could gather the clouds. Bobby and Fitz set the oxygen bottle down for a moment and simply gaped.

Behind her group, another emerged from the wall of dust. Bodies pierced a veil—and labored and weary faces lit up with wonder and new energy. One figure was being helped along, practically carried, but the sight of color seemed to lend them new legs.

Looking up behind her, Juliette saw a wall of dust reaching into the sky. All along the base, the life that dared approach this choking barrier crumbled, grass turning to powder, occasional flowers becoming brown stalks. A bird turned circles in the open sky, seemed to study these bright intruders in their silvery suits, and then banked away, avoiding danger and gliding through the blue.

Juliette felt a similar tug pulling her toward those grasses and away from the dead land they had crawled out of. She waved to her group, mouthed for them to come on, and helped Bobby with the bottle. Together they lumbered down the slope. After them came others. Each group paused in much the way Juliette had heard cleaners were prone to staggering about. One of the groups carried a body, a limp suit, the looks on their faces sharing grim news. Everywhere else was euphoria, though. Juliette felt it in her fizzing brain, which had planned to die that day; she felt it across her skin, her scars forgotten; she felt it in her tired legs and feet, which now could march to the horizon and beyond.

She waved the other groups down the slope. When she saw a man fiddling with his helmet latches, Juliette motioned for those in his group to stop him, and word spread by hand signal from group to group. Juliette could still hear the hiss from the air bottle in her own helmet, but a new urgency seized her. This was more than hope at their feet, more than blind hope. This was a promise. The woman on the radio had been telling the truth. Donald had truly been trying to help them. Hope and faith and trust had won her people some reprieve, however short. She pulled the map out of a numbered pocket meant for cleaning and consulted the lines. She urged everyone along.

There was another rise ahead, a large and gentle hill. Juliette aimed for this. Elise ranged ahead of her, tugging at the limits of her air hose and kicking up startled insects from the tall grass that came up past her knees. Shaw chased after her, their hoses near to tangling. Juliette heard herself laugh and wondered when she'd last made such a noise.

They struggled up the hill, and the land to either side seemed to grow and widen with the altitude. It wasn't just a hill, she saw as she reached the crest, but rather one more ring of mounded earth. Beyond the summit, the land swooped down into a bowl. Turning to take in the entire view around her, Juliette saw that this single depression was separate from the fifty. Back the way she had come, across a valley of verdant green, rose a wall of dark clouds. Not just a wall, she saw, but a giant dome, the silos at its center. And in the other direction, beyond the ringed hill, a forest like those from the Legacy books, a distant groundcover of giant broccoli heads whose scale was impossible to fathom.

Juliette turned to the others and tapped her helmet with her palm. She pointed to the black birds gliding on the air. Her father lifted a hand and asked her to wait. He understood what she was about to do. He reached for the latches of his own helmet instead.

Juliette felt the same fear he must've felt at the thought of a loved one going first, but agreed to let him. Raph helped with her father's latches, which were nearly impossible to work with the thick gloves. Finally, the dome clicked free. Her father's eyes widened as he took an exploratory breath. He smiled, took another, deeper one, his chest swelling, his hand relaxing, the helmet falling from his fingers and tumbling into the grass.

A frenzy broke, people groping at one another's collars. Juliette set her heavy pack down in the grass and helped Raph, who helped her in turn. When her helmet clicked free, it was the sounds she noticed first. It was the laughter from her father and Bobby, the happy squeals from the children. The smells came next, the odor of the farms and the hydroponic gardens, the scent of healthy soil turned up to claim its seed. And the light, as bright and warm as the grow lights but at a diffused distance, wrapping all around them, an emptiness above her that stretched out into forever, nothing above their heads but far clouds.

Suit collars clanged together with hugs. The groups behind were scurrying faster now, people falling and being helped up, flashes of teeth through domes, wet eyes and trails of tears down cheeks, forgotten bottles of oxygen dragging at the end of taut hoses, one body being carried.

Gloves and suits were torn at, and Juliette realized they'd never hoped for any of this. There were no knives strapped to their chests to cut away at their suits. No plan of ever leaving those silver tombs. They had left the silo in cleaning suits as all cleaners do, because a life cooped up becomes intolerable, and to stagger over a hill, even to death, becomes a great longing.

Bobby managed to tear his glove with his teeth and get a hand free. Fitz did the same. Everyone was laughing and sweating as they managed to work zippers and velcro at each other's backs, shake arms loose, work heads out of ringed collars, tug strenuously at boots. Barefoot and in a colorful array of grimy undersuits, the children squirmed free and tumbled in the grass after one another. Elise set down her dog—which she'd kept pinned to her chest like her own child—and squealed as the animal disappeared in the tall green fronds. She scooped him up again. Shaw laughed and dug her book out of his suit.

Juliette reached down and ran her hands through the grass. It was like weeds from the farms, but bunched together in a solid carpet. She thought of the fruits and vegetables some had packed away inside their suits. It would be important to save the seeds. Already, she was thinking they might last more than the day. More than the week. Her soul soared at the prospect.

Raph grabbed her once he was free of his suit and kissed her on the cheek.

"What the hell?" Bobby roared, spinning in circles with his great arms out and palms up. "What the hell!"

Her father stepped beside her and pointed down the slope, into the basin. "Do you see that?" he asked.

Juliette shielded her eyes and peered into the middle of the depression. There was a mound of green. No, not a mound; a tower. A tower with no antennas but rather some silvery flat roof jutting up and half covered in vines. Tall grass obscured much of the concrete.

The ridge grew crowded with people and laughter, and the grass was soon covered with boots and silver skins. Juliette studied this concrete tower, knowing what they would find inside. Here was the seed of a new beginning. She lifted her bag, heavy with dynamite. She weighed their salvation.

63

"No more than what we need," Juliette cautioned. She saw how the ground outside the concrete tower would soon be littered with more than they could carry. There was clothing and tools, canned food, vacuum-sealed plastic bags of labeled seeds—many of them from plants she'd never heard of. Elise had consulted her book and had pages for only a few of them. Scattered among the supplies were blocks of concrete and rubble from blowing the door open, a door that was designed to be opened from within.

Away from the tower, Solo and Walker wrestled with some kind of fabric enclosure and a set of poles, sorting out how it was supposed to prop itself up. They scratched their beards and debated. Juliette was amazed at how much better Walker was doing. He hadn't wanted out of his suit at first, had stayed in until the oxygen bottle went dry. And then he'd come out in a gasping hurry.

Elise was near them, screaming and chasing through the grass after her animal. Or maybe it was Shaw chasing Elise—it was hard to tell. Hannah sat on a large plastic bin with Rickson, nursing her child and gazing up at the clouds.

The smell of heating food wafted around the tower as Fitz managed to coax a fire from one of the oxygen bottles, a most dangerous method of cooking, Juliette thought. She turned to go back inside and sort through more of the gear, when Courtnee emerged from the bunker with her flashlight in hand and a smile on her face. Before Juliette could ask what she'd found, she saw that the power inside the tower was now on, the lights burning bright.

"What did you do?" Juliette asked. They had explored the bunker down to the bottom—it was only twenty levels deep, and the levels were so crazily packed together that it was more like seven levels tall. At the bottom they had found not a mechanical space but rather a large and empty cavern where twin stairwells bottomed out onto bare rock. It was a landing spot for a digger, someone had guessed. A place to welcome new arrivals. No generator, though. No power. Even though the stairwell and levels were rigged with lights.

"I traced the feed," Courtnee said. "It goes up to those silver sheets of metal on the roof. I'm going to have the boys clear them off, see how they work."

Before long, a moving platform sitting in the middle of the stairwell was made operational. It slid up and down by a series of cables and counterweights and a small motor. Those from Mechanical marveled at the device, and the kids wouldn't get off the thing. They insisted on riding it just one more time. Moving supplies outside and into the grass became far less tiring, though Juliette kept thinking they should leave plenty for the next to arrive, if anyone ever did.

There were those who wanted to live right there, who were reticent to venture any further. They had seeds and more soil than reckoning, and the storerooms could be turned into apartments. It would be a good home. Juliette listened to them debate this.

It was Elise who settled the matter. She opened her book to a map, pointed to the sun and showed them which way was north, and said they should move toward water. She claimed to know how to gather wild fish, said there were worms in the ground and Solo knew how to put them on hooks. Pointing to a page in her memory book, she said they should walk to the sea.

Adults pored over these maps and this decision. There was another round of debates among those who thought they should shelter right there, but Juliette shook her head. "This isn't a home," she said. "It's just a warehouse. Do we want to live in the shadow of that?" She nodded to the dark cloud on the horizon, that dome of dust.

"And what about when others show up?" someone pointed out.

"More reason not to be here," Rickson offered.

More debate. There were just over a hundred of them. They could stay there and farm, get a crop up before the canned goods ran out. Or they could carry what they needed and see if the legends of unlimited fish and of water that stretched to the horizon were true. Juliette nearly pointed out that they could do both, that there were no rules, that there was plenty of land and space, that all the fighting came when things were running low and resources were scarce.

"What's it going to be, Mayor?" Raph asked. "We bedding down here or moving on?"

"Look!"

Someone pointed up the hill, and a dozen heads turned to see. There, over the rise, a figure in a silver suit stumbled down the slope, the grass at their feet already trampled and slick. Someone from their silo who had changed their mind.

Juliette raced through the grass, feeling not fear but curiosity and concern. Someone they'd left behind, someone who had followed them. It could be anyone.

Before she could close the distance, the figure in the suit collapsed. Gloved hands groped to release the helmet, fumbled with the collar. Juliette ran. There was a large bottle strapped to the person's back. She worried they were out of air, wondered what they had rigged up and how.

"Easy," she yelled, dropping behind the struggling figure. She pressed her thumbs into the clasps. They clicked. She pulled the helmet free and heard someone gasping and coughing. They bent forward, wheezing, a spill of sweat-soaked hair, a woman. Juliette rested a hand on this woman's shoulder, did not recognize her at all—thought it was perhaps someone from the congregation or the Mids.

"Breathe easy," she said. She looked up as others arrived. They pulled up short at the sight of this stranger.

The woman wiped her mouth and nodded. Her chest heaved with a deep breath. Another. She brushed the hair off her face. "Thank you," she gasped. She peered up at the sky and the clouds in something other than wonder. In relief. Her eyes focused on and tracked an object, and Juliette turned and gazed up to see another of the birds wheeling lazily in the sky. The crowd around her kept their distance. Someone asked who this was.

"You aren't from our silo, are you?" Juliette asked. Her first thought was that this was a cleaner from a nearby silo who had witnessed their march, had followed them. Her second thought was impossible. It was also correct.

"No," the woman said, "I'm not from your silo. I'm from . . . somewhere quite different. My name is Charlotte."

A glove was offered, a glove and a weary smile. The warmth of that smile disarmed Juliette. To her surprise, she realized that she held no anger or resentment toward this woman, who had told her the truth of this place. Here, perhaps, was a kindred spirit. And more importantly, a fresh start. She regained her composure, smiled back, and shook the woman's hand. "Juliette," she said. "Let me help you out of that."

"You're her," Charlotte said, smiling. She turned her attention to the crowd, to the tower and the piles of supplies. "What is this place?"

"A second chance," Juliette said. "But we aren't staying here. We're heading to the water. You'll come with us, I hope. But I have to warn you, it's a long way."

Charlotte rested her hand on Juliette's shoulder. "That's okay," she said. "I've already come a long way."

EPILOGUE

RAPH SEEMED UNSURE. He held a branch in his hand, weighed it purposefully, his pale face a dance of orange and gold from the flickering fire.

"Just throw the damn thing in," Bobby yelled.

There was laughter, but Raph frowned in consternation. "It's *wood*," he said, weighing the branch.

"Look around you," Bobby roared. He waved at the dark limbs hanging overhead, the wide trunks. "It's more than we'll ever need."

"Do it, lad." Erik kicked one of the logs, and a burst of sparks buzzed in the air as if startled from their slumber. Finally, Raph threw the branch in with the rest, and the wood began to crackle and spark.

Juliette watched from her bedroll. Somewhere in the woods, an animal made a sound, a sound unlike any she'd ever heard. It was like a crying child, but sonorous and mournful.

"What was that?" someone asked.

In the darkness, they exchanged guesses. They conjured animals from children's books. They listened to Solo recount the many breeds from olden times that he had read about in the Legacy. They gathered around Elise with flashlights and pored through the stitched pages of her book. Everything was a mystery and a wonder.

Juliette lay back and listened to the crackle from the fire, the occasional loud pop from a log, enjoying the heat on her skin, the smell of meat cooking, the peculiar odor of grass and so much soil. And through the canopy overhead, stars twinkled. The bright clouds from before—the ones that had hidden the sun as it set behind the hills—were parted by the breeze. They revealed above her a hundred glittering pricks of light. A thousand. More of them everywhere the longer she looked. They glittered in her tear-filled eyes as she thought of Lukas and the love he had aroused in her. And something hardened in her chest, something that made her jaw clench tight to keep from crying, a renewed purpose in her life, a desire to reach the water on Elise's map, to plant these seeds, to build a home above the ground and live there.

"Jewel? You asleep?"

Elise stood above her, blocking the stars. Puppy's cold nose pressed into Juliette's cheek.

"C'mere," Juliette said. She scooted over and patted her bedroll, and Elise sat down and nestled against her.

"What're you doing?" Elise asked.

Juliette pointed up through the canopy. "I'm looking at the stars," she said. "Each of those is like our sun, but they're a long way away."

"I know the stars," Elise said. "Some of them have names."

"They do?"

"Yeah." Elise rested her head back against Juliette's shoulder and gazed up with her a moment. The unknown thing in the woods howled. "See those?" Elise asked. "Don't those look like a puppy to you?"

Juliette squinted and searched the sky. "Could be," she said. "Yeah, maybe they do."

"We can call those ones Puppy."

"That's a good name," Juliette agreed. She laughed and wiped at her eyes.

"And that one's like a man." Elise pointed at a wide spread of stars, tracing the features. "There's his arms and legs. There's his head."

"I see him," Juliette said.

"You can name him," Elise told her, giving her permission. Deep in the woods, the hidden animal let out another howl, and Elise's puppy made a similar sound. Juliette felt tears roll down her cheeks.

"Not that one," she said quietly. "He already has a name."

The fires settled down as the night wore on. Clouds swallowed stars and tents gobbled children. Juliette watched shadows move in one of the tents, other adults too jittery to sleep. Somewhere, someone was still cooking strips of meat from the animal Solo had shot with his rifle—the long-limbed deer. Juliette had marveled at Solo's transformation these last three days. A man who grew up alone was now a leader of men, more prepared for surviving in this world than any of them. Juliette would ask for another vote soon. Her friend Solo would make an excellent mayor.

In the distance, a silhouette stood over a fire and prodded it with a stick, coaxing more heat from dying embers. Clouds and fire—these two things her people had only ever feared. Fire was death in the silo, and clouds consumed those who dared to leave. And yet, as the clouds closed in overhead and flames were agitated higher, there was comfort in both. The clouds were a roof of sorts, the fire warmth. There was less here to fear. And when a bright star revealed itself through a sudden gap, Juliette's thoughts returned as ever to Lukas.

He had told her once, with his star chart spread across that bed in which they made love, that each of those stars could possibly hold worlds of their own, and Juliette remembered being unable to grasp the thought. It was audacious. Impossible. Even having seen another silo, even having seen dozens of depressions in the earth that stretched to the horizon, she could not imagine entire other worlds existing. And yet, she had returned from her cleaning and had expected others to believe her claims, equally bold—

A stick cracked behind her, a rustle of leaves, and Juliette expected to find Elise returning to complain that she couldn't sleep. Or perhaps it was Charlotte, who had joined her by the fire earlier that night, had remained largely quiet while seeming to have much she wanted to say. But Juliette turned and found Courtnee there, white smoke steaming from something in her hand.

"Mind if I sit?" Courtnee asked.

Juliette made room, and her old friend joined her on the bedroll. She handed Juliette a hot mug of something that smelled vaguely of tea . . . but more pungent.

"Can't sleep?" Courtnee asked.

Juliette shook her head. "Just sitting here thinking about Luke."

Courtnee draped an arm across Juliette's back. "I'm sorry," she said.

"It's okay. Whenever I see the stars up there, it helps put things into perspective."

"Yeah? Help me, then."

Juliette thought how best to do that and realized she hardly had the language. She only had a sense of this vastness—of an infinite possible worlds—that somehow filled her with hope and not despair. Turning that into words wasn't easy.

"All the land we've seen these past days," she said, trying to grasp what she was feeling. "All that space. We don't have a fraction of the time and people to fill it all."

"That's a good thing, right?" Courtnee asked.

"I think so, yeah. And I'm starting to think that those we sent out to clean, they were the good ones. I think there were a lot of good people like them who just kept quiet, who were scared to act. And I doubt there was ever a mayor who didn't want to make more room for her people, didn't want to figure out what was wrong with the outside world, didn't want to suspend the damn lottery. But what could they do, even those mayors? They weren't in charge. Not really. The ones in charge kept a lid on our ambitions. Except for Luke. He didn't stand in the way of me. He supported what I was doing, even when he knew it was dangerous. And so here we are."

Courtnee squeezed her shoulder and took a noisy sip of tea, and Juliette lifted her mug to do the same. As soon as the warm water hit her lips, there was an explosion of flavor, a richness like the smell of the flower stalls in the bazaar and also the up-turned loam of a productive grow plot. It was a first kiss. It was lemon and rose. There were sparks in her vision from the heady rush. Juliette's mind shuddered.

"What is this?" she asked, gasping for air. "This is from the supplies we pulled?"

Courtnee laughed and leaned against Juliette. "It's good, right?"

"It's great. It's . . . amazing."

"Maybe we should go back for another load," Courtnee said.

"If we do that, I might not carry anything else."

The two women laughed quietly. They sat together, gazing up at the clouds and the occasional star for a while. The fire nearest them crackled and spat sparks, and a handful of quiet conversations drifted deep into the trees where bugs sang a chorus and some unseen beast howled.

"Do you think we'll make it?" Courtnee asked after a long pause.

Juliette took another sip of the miraculous drink. She imagined the world they might build with time and resources, with no rules but what's best and no one to pin down their dreams.

"I think we'll make it," she finally said. "I think we can make any damn thing we like."

A NOTE TO THE READER

In July of 2011, I wrote and published a short story that brought me into contact with thousands of readers, took me around the world on book tours, and changed my life. I couldn't have dreamed that any of this was about to happen the day I published *Wool*. I thank you for making that journey possible and for accompanying me along the way.

This is not the end, of course. Every story we read, every film we watch, continues on in our imaginations if we allow it. Characters live another day. They grow old and die. New ones are born. Challenges crop up and are dealt with. There is sadness, joy, triumph, and failure. Where a story ends is nothing more than a snapshot in time, a brief flash of emotion, a pause. How and if it continues is up to us.

My only wish is that we leave room for hope. There is good and bad in all things. We find what we expect to find. We see what we expect to see. I have learned that if I tilt my head just right and squint, the world outside is beautiful. The future is bright. There are good things to come.

What do you see?

www.hughhowey.com